The Lady Needs a Rogue

A Rogue of Her Own Series
Book 2

TARA KINGSTON

DRAGONBLADE PUBLISHING, INC.

ARE YOU SIGNED UP FOR DRAGONBLADE'S BLOG?

You'll get the latest news and information on exclusive giveaways, exclusive excerpts, coming releases, sales, free books, cover reveals and more.

Check out our complete list of authors, too!

No spam, no junk. That's a promise!

Sign Up Here

www.dragonbladepublishing.com

Dearest Reader;

Thank you for your support of a small press. At Dragonblade Publishing, we strive to bring you the highest quality Historical Romance from some of the best authors in the business. Without your support, there is no 'us', so we sincerely hope you adore these stories and find some new favorite authors along the way.

Happy Reading!

CEO, Dragonblade Publishing

**Additional Dragonblade books by
Author Tara Kingston**

A Rogue of Her Own Series
A Rogue to Watch Over Me (Book 1)
The Lady Needs a Rogue (Book 2)

Chapter One

London, 1894

*H*EIRESS HUNTERS ARE *a maddeningly persistent lot, my dear Macie. You must lead them on a merry chase. Leave them with empty hands. And empty coffers.*

Smiling as her grandmother's words played in her thoughts, Mary Catherine Mason surveyed the veritable parade of London's posh elites gathered in Lady Lucretia Drayton's opulent ballroom. Debutantes decked out in their finery pranced about, the vibrant hues of their flowing silk gowns displaying their beauty to perfection, all the better to be seen by a potential husband or two. Dapper gentlemen strutted like peacocks, flaunting their wealth— or in its absence, the status bestowed by their noble birth. At times, Macie felt a twinge of pity for the penniless lords driven to barter a title for a fortune. Perhaps they felt as trapped as she had all those years ago, before her beloved Grandmama had shared the secrets few wanted her to know.

But now, as she stood in a shadowed corner of the ballroom, away from the crush, was not one of those times. Even while lingering in the shadows, Macie sensed an heiress hunter's eagle-eyed gaze hone in. Quite a nuisance, really. She allowed herself a little sigh. She'd hoped to enjoy the notes of the orchestra in peace and relative solitude. Were the fortune seekers conditioned from their first breath to find brides whose fathers possessed an abundance of funds?

Boldly, she met the man's intent gaze. His piercing eyes flashed with recognition, followed by a glimmer of opportunity that brightened his otherwise sallow features. Evidently, this one had yet to learn the word about town—Macie Mason did not intend to be caught. Much less by a greedy snob who hungered not for a taste of her lips, but for a smidgen of her father's fortune. He would not be the first to learn that lesson. And sadly, he would not be the last.

When would the entitled Lord Nobs realize it was a losing battle?

Seven years earlier, moments before Macie's debut at another crowded, equally lavish ballroom, Grandmama had clasped Macie's hands in hers and offered words of hard-won wisdom. Since that evening, which now seemed a lifetime ago, Macie had cherished the memory of her grandmother's heartfelt observation. Outsmarting the fops and ne'er-do-wells had become something of a game. Truth be told, she rather enjoyed devising schemes and scandals that would set fortune hunters running. Let them set their sights on more docile prey. She did not intend to be ensnared. Much less by the likes of them.

Looking past the beady-eyed baron—or was the fortune hunter a marquess?—she spotted her brother. *Drat the luck.* Jon was cutting a direct path toward her. Was he actually scowling? Why, he wasn't even trying to hide his exasperation. One would think he would be accustomed to her efforts to deter the most recent crop of money-hungry lords. Still, his look of horror as he took in her ensemble was more than a wee bit amusing.

"Good God, Macie." Still frowning, Jon met her gaze. "Tell me my eyes are deceiving me."

She feigned a look of bemusement. "Why would you want me to say something silly? We both know your eyes are functioning precisely as they should, even without your spectacles." She bit back a grin. "Is something wrong?"

A deep line formed between his brows, punctuating his exasperation. "Why in blazes are you wearing that . . . that *thing*?"

"The word is *dress,* dear brother." She pursed her lips in mock concern. "Have you suffered a recent blow to the head?"

"I might ask you the same question. You seem to have forgotten we are attending a ball tonight." He swept his hand toward the dancers gliding oh-so-gracefully across the ballroom floor. "Not a lecture by some rationally dressed suffragette. Where is the gown Madame Lorette designed for you?"

"Her name is Madame Delphine," Macie corrected, if only to stall for time.

"Whatever that pretentious woman is calling herself now is of no importance to me. We both know she's about as French as tea and crumpets." His scowl deepened. "She was paid to design a gown for you. Not this . . . atrocity."

Macie took a small step back, retreating into the shadows along the periphery of the ballroom. "To be quite honest, she did sketch a gown that might have earned your approval. But I asked her to make a few changes."

"A few changes?" Jon sounded as if he'd knotted his tie too snugly about his neck.

"She'd planned to use emerald-green silk. But that particular shade did not suit my coloring."

The crinkle between her brother's brows deepened to a crater. "I see. So you opted for the color of the mud caked on my boots after a heavy rain?"

"Really, Jon, you are going to worry yourself into wrinkles, and well before your time."

"We both know who I will have to thank."

Macie struggled to hold back a smile. Her older brother had always been so very responsible. So very dedicated to upholding the family name. And now, with their father putting it into Jon's head that the family's fine reputation rested on his ability to keep her out of trouble, he had grown far too serious. Far too staid.

Just like Papa.

"My, I had no idea my brother had become an expert on women's couture. When I asked Madame Delphine to design a more demure gown, she assured me this color was all the rage in Paris."

He rubbed the back of his neck as if it ached. "Do you expect me to believe that?"

"Not really." She smiled, if only to vex him. "But I can't say as I care."

Jon slowly shook his head. "You do know how to sabotage the best laid plans."

"I don't know what you're talking about, dear brother. This dress is perfectly suitable." Macie tried her best to appear innocent, but her facade wasn't working. She hadn't believed it possible, but Jon's scowl deepened. Much more of this, and he'd be fearsome enough to give the gargoyles atop the stairs outside their hosts' palatial home a fright.

"Suitable, perhaps, for one of your excursions to those blasted houses where you chase ghosts." His eyes narrowed as he slowly shook his head. "You look more like some blue-blooded matron's companion than an . . ."

"Than *what*, Jon?"

"Than an heiress." He bit off the word she so despised between his teeth, as if it was as distasteful to him as it was to her.

"Regardless of what Papa—and you, perhaps—may think, I am not a commodity to be bartered for the one and only thing Papa has not been able to buy. I am not one of those dollar princesses from across the pond. A title means nothing to me."

"It's not like that, Macie." Her brother's expression softened. "I do understand, more than you think. Father has it in his head that you'll be a countess. Or a duchess. But that doesn't mean you won't find a man with whom you can make a good life, title or not."

"In that case, I fail to see the problem with my gown. Or any of my other choices, for that matter."

Glancing down at her drab skirt, she smoothed out a small wrinkle. The peculiar blend of olive and brown and gray would not have been flattering under any circumstance. In nature, only a female bird employing camouflage would prefer feathers of such an abysmal shade. But wasn't that precisely what she was doing?

Camouflage seemed the most appropriate strategy to endure this infernal soiree.

"Whether I am cloaked in vibrant hues or in this . . . admittedly unusual shade, I am still *me*. A man well suited to a match will see that."

"Ah, Macie. You are an original."

"Quite the understatement." To her left, she spied a petite blonde garbed in a stunning teal gown, rather like the one she'd left hanging in the wardrobe of her Mayfair townhouse. "I do believe Miss Nolan has eyes for you, Jon. Your time would be better spent squiring her about the dance floor than lurking here with me."

Glancing toward the beauty who'd set her sights on him, Jon's eyes brightened. "You may have a point."

"I'm right, and you know it." Her gaze settled on the narrow strip of white silk he'd fastened a bit haphazardly about his throat. "All that worry about my gown, while you're standing here looking all topsy-turvy. Hold still." Reaching up, she quickly straightened his crooked bow tie. "Now go and enjoy yourself. At least one of us should have a good time tonight."

"Very well." His forehead furrowed again. "But promise me you'll make an effort to . . . mingle."

"Even looking so very hideous?" Macie teased.

"That word could never describe you, Macie. Even when you've pinned your hair back so tightly, the strands look to be in actual pain."

"I will have you know this style is rather fashionable." Macie touched her fingertips to her severe chignon. "I even selected a pearl-tipped hairpin especially for the occasion."

"That belongs to Mum. I must say, it is a good choice."

"At least something I've done meets your approval."

"You're every bit as pretty as our mother." An emotion Jon seldom revealed flickered in his eyes. "But you do possess a talent for making yourself as drab as a peahen."

She fashioned a look of mock confusion. "Modesty is a virtue, is it not?"

Her brother's gaze drifted back to the blonde, whose display of cleavage paid no tribute to that particular virtue. "I'd say that's open for debate."

"Jon, I know what I'm doing."

Turning his attention back to her, he cocked a brow. "Do you now?"

"Of course."

He sighed beneath his breath. "At times, I have my doubts. But for now, I will leave you to your peahen charade."

Peahen. The word, kinder than most she'd heard used to describe her, echoed in Macie's thoughts as her brother made a beeline toward the elegant blonde before her dance card filled.

Spinster. Wallflower. Bluestocking.

On the shelf.

The busybody gossips were right. But they did not realize that Macie had not been placed there by fate's cruel hand. At the rather ancient age of twenty-five, Mary Catherine Mason was there by choice.

A scandal here. A scandal there. Since her debut—an inauspicious event during which she'd *accidentally* toppled an entire glass of red wine onto the trousers of an overly amorous lord—she'd quickly learned that was all it took to send the Lord Rocks-for-brains of London on their merry way.

Over time, the conveniently spilled goblet of whatever beverage best suited the occasion had become a reliable strategy to deter the most persistent dolts. Of course, she didn't want to become predictable, now did she? Once, she'd employed a prop sword—a brilliant accessory for costume balls—to discourage the attentions of a particularly obnoxious earl. The memory of the boor's shocked expression as she'd jolted him in his noble bum still brought a smile to her lips. On another occasion, she'd experienced a delightfully convenient costume malfunction while garbed in a gown inspired by a Grecian goddess. And there was the time she'd arrived at a fancy ball while riding her bicycle.

She'd been perfectly respectable—in her eyes, at least—with the bloomers beneath her gown protecting her modesty. Of course, her poor, beleaguered brother had not seen it that way. And neither had the baron-to-be who'd reportedly sought to woo her and her dowry that night.

Over the years, she'd inspired most of the nobles her father saw as means to a title to politely tiptoe into the sunset. Come to think of it, one or two might actually have been running. A few others—weighted down by debt, and therefore less easily deterred—had worked up the courage to ask for her hand in marriage. Sadly for their cause, Macie knew how to utter the word "No" in a half-dozen languages.

When each heiress hunter scurried away before Macie's shenanigans could taint his most valuable asset—his *good name*—she'd breathe a sigh of relief and climb up upon a perch that seemed to grow higher and higher, ever more comfortable in a fate many viewed with a sense of quiet horror.

Sadly, her reprieve never lasted quite long enough.

For every debt-ridden duke or money-hungry marquess she chased off, another materialized. If her father had his way, she would settle for one of the bemused barons or vacuous viscounts who eyed her as greedily as a starving man might look upon a sumptuous feast.

No, that would not be her fate.

If Papa was disappointed in her, then so be it.

Macie had seen the quiet dread in the eyes of American dollar princesses and London heiresses alike whose futures had been bartered in exchange for a meaningless title. Why, her childhood friend had openly wept as she'd made her way down the aisle to speak her vows. *Tears of joy.* Or so the best man had whispered to the groom, a petrified young lord who looked as though he himself awaited the executioner's blade. He knew better. And so did Macie. For a brief moment before the ceremony, Cecily had appeared to give thought to Macie's urging to bolt before she spoke her vows. But in the end, she'd done her duty. Cecily had resigned herself to a fate that, while not worse than death, might have seemed like a premature burial.

Macie would not go quietly to such an existence. And so, she'd honed the art of chasing off heirs.

A chirpy, high-pitched voice, rather like a bird warbling in a cage, startled her from her thoughts. *Drat. Drat. And double drat.* She'd thought she might enjoy another moment's peace here in the shadows. But ambitious mothers of down-on-their luck nobles were even more skilled at sniffing out an heiress than their sons.

"Goodness, Miss Mason, there you are. I had begun to fear you were not going to join us tonight." Lady Drayton, the snowy-haired countess—or was it viscountess?—of something-or-other strolled toward her, her eyes narrowed with an assessing focus. The matron was best known for two things: her impeccable skill as a hostess and her unshakable hope of finding her only son a match that would replenish the family's dwindling coffers.

Ah, yes, if Macie squinted a wee bit and allowed her imagination to run unfettered, she could see the money bags dancing in Lady Drayton's cool blue eyes. Still, it wouldn't do to offend the woman. She'd have to at least pretend to enjoy the woman's hospitality. If only through clenched teeth.

Macie managed a smile. "So nice to see you, Lady Drayton."

"I am delighted you could attend. Arthur has looked forward to making your acquaintance."

Arthur. Lord Drayton. Yet another man with a title Macie's father would see as a trophy, even if Macie would be the one to gain it.

Pity she'd no inclination to share a bed with a title, noble or otherwise.

"It will be my pleasure." Macie forced out the words, one syllable at a time.

Following at Lady Drayton's side, Macie strolled by the couples on the dance floor. Spotting her brother engaged in a rather mechanical waltz, she repressed an urge to pull a face. Lucky dolt.

Jon felt no pressure to make an advantageous match.

In truth, neither should she. She planned to make the most of her time in the city. The prospect of setting up her camera in a gloomy old house was ever so exciting. The more cobwebs and mysterious creaks, the better. London boasted countless places said to be roamed by restless spirits and the occasional ghoul or two. The lure of one particular mansion had drawn her back to the city—her grandfather's home. Bennington Manor was now hers.

Hers to bring back to its former glory. Hers to cherish. Hers to portray in all its eccentric charm through the lens of her camera.

Preparing for the restoration and her next photographic exhibit would fill most of her days and nights. In what little remained, she would humor her father.

But in the end, he would be disappointed. Of that, she was quite certain.

"I must warn you, Arthur is a bit . . . studious," Lady Drayton went on, speaking the words as if she'd uttered a confession. "It's a rare night when he sets aside his telescope and his computations to socialize. Recently, he has devoted his evenings to observing some comet or other." Lady Drayton's thin mouth stretched into something resembling a smile. "He fancies himself to be a man of science. But soon, he will find a good woman who will interest him in more . . . conventional pursuits."

"I am sure he will." Macie said, resisting the urge to mention that *good woman* would *not* be her. After all, she was far more passionate about capturing an intriguing image with her camera than overseeing a stuffy dinner party with precisely the right delicacies and elegant china to impress her husband's guests. If she had her way—and she certainly intended to—she'd tote her camera everywhere from the Tower of London to the Pyramids of Giza. She would capture the images of her journey and develop her craft. Definitely *not* the stuff of a conventional marriage.

A sudden, angry shriek that might have shattered glass rang out. The mumbled words of an apology followed, though Macie had no desire to listen for the details. A willowy blonde stood in their path, fury flashing in her eyes. She fixed a dagger-filled look on the fair-haired, ruddy-faced man who stood within arm's length of her, his expression one of dire mortification.

"Oh dear, Lady Sylvie is in quite a stir," Lady Drayton said in Macie's ear. "Again."

The blonde continued to skewer the red-cheeked man with her gaze. "Now you've done it."

"Sylvie, you must know—"

"What I know is this, you clod—you've ruined my gown." Flicking her long, unbound hair over her shoulder, she turned on her heel and stomped to the door. The hapless man rushed after her, a not-quite-empty wine glass bobbing between his fingers.

"Nothing like a little lovers' tiff to liven up the evening." A sparkle brightened Lady Drayton's eyes as her attention lit on a lanky man who appeared to be avoiding the crowd. "Ah, there's Arthur," she said. "I simply must introduce—"

As Macie followed her hostess's brisk pace, she took a step, and then another. Suddenly, her right foot no longer touched the floor. Blast these flimsy, oh-so-pretty shoes. Slippers, indeed! A soft "Oh dear" escaped Lady Drayton's lips as Macie struggled to fend off gravity.

Farewell, dignity. The words flitted through Macie's thoughts, as if to taunt her.

Suddenly, powerful hands caught her from behind. Stopped her descent. Long fingers gripped the underside of her arms. She dangled in her unseen hero's hold, her bottom precariously close to the marble floor.

Gazing up, she met the eyes of the man who was at that moment the only thing between her and a rather ugly sprawl. If this were a gothic novel, she would gaze adoringly at her hero.

But this was *not* a novel. And this man most definitely was *not* her hero.

This is not happening. But it was. At the moment she'd kicked her foot up into the air like the world's dowdiest can-can dancer, she'd believed the night could not get any worse.

She had been mistaken. Quite so.

She knew those oh-so-familiar amber eyes. She knew the strands of caramel in his brown hair. Once, she had even brushed back the appealing lock that rebelled against his attempts to rein it into place. And above all, she knew that oh-so-arrogant smile.

Phineas Caldwell.

Of all the men in the ballroom who might have broken her fall, why did it have to be Finn? *Dash the infernal luck!*

Chapter Two

"M iss Mason, I presume."

Finn Caldwell stared down at the chestnut-haired woman he'd caught mid-tumble. The beauty who had draped her curves in a muck-colored travesty of a gown was indeed Mary Catherine Mason. He had not seen his friend's sister in nearly a decade, but there was no mistaking those big green eyes of hers. In those days, she'd been a reed-thin girl with a seemingly ever-present book in her hand. Now, she'd grown into her long legs and willowy neck. Macie was a true diamond of the first water. No dress, no matter how hideous, could disguise *that*.

Recognition flared on her face. So, she did remember him.

After what seemed a lifetime.

"Yes, I am. Now that we've settled that, would you be so kind as to assist me in regaining my footing?" she requested coolly, then added through gritted teeth. "Please."

"As ye wish." With that, he hoisted her none too gently to her feet and steadied her as she regained her balance. Had he gone mad, or was the frown on her plump lips appealing? Though he knew better, he could not resist teasing her. "Perhaps ye should go lighter on the punch."

Her eyes flashed, propelling an invisible dagger his way. "I have not imbibed a single drop this evening." She glanced at the wine puddled on the marble. "Evidently, the spill did not end up solely on Lady Sylvie's gown." Her frown softened. "I suppose I must thank you despite your horrid insinuation."

"I'd agree a bit of gratitude would be in order," Finn replied smoothly. "As for my insinuation, ye would not be the first to indulge a bit too much when away from her father's watchful eye."

"Mr. Caldwell, I must thank you for your assistance. It's quite fortunate that you were here," Lady Drayton spoke up, the taut set of her features contradicting her words.

"Think nothing of it. As a gentleman, I certainly would not allow a lady to take a nasty tumble."

"Of course. That goes without saying," Lady Drayton agreed coolly, even as her lifted brows betrayed her as he'd uttered the word *gentleman*. "I must confess, I had not expected you to join us tonight."

"Neither had I."

Not until he'd learned his old friend Jon Mason would be in attendance with his wedding-ring-averse sister in tow. Talk of the minor scandals Macie had cooked up to deter suitors—mild as they were, at least to his ears—had infiltrated even his club. He simply had to see for himself. So he'd invited himself to their dragon lady of a hostess's ball.

Lady Drayton's attention darted from him to a buxom red-head who was at that moment cutting a path through the crowd toward them. Lady Chastity Delacroix. Her doting husband was nowhere in sight. Had the old coot fallen asleep over his vermouth—again?

Lady Chastity's eyes glimmered with excitement as she met his gaze. Politely, she nodded to their hostess. "Lady Drayton."

"Good evening, Lady Chastity. It has been far too long," Lady Drayton precisely enunciated her name even as the frost in her tone contradicted her words.

"It is my pleasure." Lady Chastity's attention darted back to Finn. "One never knows who will appear on your guest list."

Lady Drayton did not even feign a smile. "Sometimes, even I don't know who has received an invitation."

"Good evening, Mr. Caldwell," Lady Chastity said, her ample assets threatening to spill over the low-cut bodice of her elegant blue gown.

"Where might I find your husband tonight? Now's as good a time as any to settle our recent wager." Finn kept his expression cool. He had no interest in providing the earl's wife a distraction from the boor she'd wed.

"He is spending the evening at his club. I'm afraid he was not in the mood for anything more . . . vigorous." Lady Chastity aimed a pointed smile his way.

"Have you made Miss Mason's acquaintance?" Lady Drayton spoke up to offer the usual introductions, if only to cut through the sudden, awkward silence.

Lady Chastity cocked her head toward Macie, regarding her as if she were a curiosity to be observed. "*The* Mary Catherine Mason?"

"Is there another?" Macie quipped.

"I suppose not. I've heard about you . . . and your photographs. How very scandalous! I love it."

Macie smiled, warm and genuine. "A woman with a camera creates quite the stir in our society. I must admit, I rather enjoy the notoriety."

"How very original!" Lady Chastity sounded genuinely impressed. "I've heard tales about town . . . they're saying you will soon set your camera aside to join the title hunt. Tell me it's not true."

The title hunt. So bloody pointless. The very words nearly set Finn's back teeth on edge. For her part, Macie appeared decidedly unenthused about the prospect of a well-connected marriage. *Good for her.*

"Pity there's no way to hunt the title without taking the man attached to it as well," Macie said with a slight smile. "The chase would be ever so much more fun."

"The fun comes later," Lady Chastity said with a wink. "My Archibald spends many an hour at his club. I only need to endure his presence when he wishes to be seen with an ornament on his arm."

"My, you should not be so bold," Lady Drayton admonished.

"It's quite fine," Macie replied. "I find this all rather fascinating. Lady Chastity, perhaps you would allow me to make your portrait while I am in London."

"While doing something naughty, I hope," Lady Chastity said with a sly smile.

"I am thinking of images in a gothic mansion," Macie said, her tone more vibrant now. "Beauty and the Beast, with the house cast as the beast."

"How very exciting! I would enjoy that. Truly," Lady Chastity said. "But I would not want to keep you from your . . . other pursuits."

Macie's brows knit together. Her face was as expressive as her voice, especially those emerald eyes of hers.

"Other pursuits?" she asked.

"The title hunt—if you are indeed in pursuit, you will definitely have some competition," Lady Chastity said. "I've heard Lord Darington is the catch of the season."

"I cannot say I'm at all concerned." Macie accented her reply with a bland shrug.

Finn bit back a chuckle. Lady Chastity had spoken as if she'd shared vital intelligence, but Macie had shown no blasted interest. By thunder, the tales of Mary Catherine Mason's aversion to noble arses and pompous dolts were true.

"I do understand," Lady Chastity went on. "Sometimes, it is best to play hard to get. After all, your father does own that wonderful store on Jermyn Street, doesn't he?"

"He does." A little frown played on Macie's mouth. "While we're at it, Papa also has stores in Cardiff, Liverpool, and Scotland."

Lady Chastity flashed a knowing smile. "Well then, that should be sufficient to get your hands on an earl, at the least."

As the buxom countess continued to dispense her pearls of

title-hunting wisdom, their hostess appeared to struggle against her rising irritation. Lady Drayton's complexion had paled to a marble-white while her mouth had thinned to a tight slash. As her pinched gaze lingered over the younger woman, she looked to be battling an urge to press a hand over Lady Chastity's ever-moving mouth.

Even Finn—a man with no experience in the subtleties of matchmaking or scheming, for that matter—could see the society matron had her eye on Macie's family fortune. Was it his imagination, or was Lady Chastity thoroughly enjoying the chance to frustrate the haughty crone's efforts to pair her scarecrow of a son with Macie?

The matron wobbled slightly, and she gave her head a little shake. If much more blood drained from Lady Drayton's face, she would require his services to hold her upright, even without a puddle of wine to slip on. "Miss Mason and her brother have to come to London to restore the old mansion on the hill," she said, her tone steadier than her expression as she deliberately changed the subject.

Watching Lady Chastity sabotage their host, wittingly or not, had been amusing, but Finn's interest perked up at the mention of the stately house that had long fascinated him. "Jon has inherited Bennington Manor?"

"No." Macie smiled. "Our grandfather's home now belongs to me."

Lady Drayton regarded Macie as though she had grown another head. "Andrew Bennington bequeathed his home to . . . a woman?"

"And why wouldn't he?" Macie pinned her with those captivating, dagger-throwing green eyes. "I am his granddaughter. He knew how I love that old house."

"It is a rather unusual circumstance, you must admit," Lady Drayton countered.

Macie's shrug was more casual than her tone. "Surely you must know my grandfather was an *unusual* man. Quite ahead of his time, really. Perhaps that's why my mother is unusual. As am I." Her voice brimmed with pride. *Good for her.*

"I study the place each time I pass by," Finn said. "The architecture intrigues me."

"In that case, you simply must come by. Jon has spoken of your expertise."

Lady Chastity leaned closer to Macie, as if to confide a secret. "You know it's haunted, don't you?"

Macie grinned. "I'm counting on it."

"How very . . . unusual. And daring." Lady Chastity flashed a slight smile. Turning back to Finn, she draped her gloved fingers over his forearm. "I must confess, Mr. Caldwell, I am also feeling a bit daring tonight. I've taken the liberty of adding you to my dance card."

He slowly shook his head. "Forgive me, but I did not come here to dance."

Lady Drayton's eyes narrowed, her expression making it clear she would welcome his departure. To the dance floor. To anywhere, in fact, where he was not impeding the introduction of the Drayton lord-in-waiting to the heiress. "Might I ask why you *are* here, Mr. Caldwell?"

"Curiosity." He cocked his head toward Macie. "Rumor had it ye'd invited a certain lady who is considerably more adept at scaling apple trees than at strolling across a ballroom floor. I wanted to see for myself."

A smile curved Macie's mouth despite the surprise in her eyes. "It has been a very long time since I've done any climbing."

"The two of you are acquainted?" Lady Drayton's brows hiked, as if Finn had revealed a vile secret.

"It has been a very long time. But I possess an excellent memory," Finn said rather blandly. "Do ye still run pedestrians off the road with that bicycle of yers, Miss Mason?"

Lady Drayton's jaw dropped, if only for a moment, even as Macie's smile reached her eyes. "I'll have you know I've replaced my bicycle with a more modern machine," Macie said. "It's easier to maneuver and ever so much faster. And before you ask, Mr. Caldwell, my father still abhors my bloomers."

If Lady Drayton's chin plummeted any lower, it might actually touch her chest. "How lovely that you've been afforded the chance for an impromptu reunion."

"How lovely, indeed," Lady Chastity spoke up. "I am still waiting for my dance, Mr. Caldwell."

He gave a disinterested shrug. "I doubt my toes would withstand the trauma."

Pressing her lips together into a pout she evidently intended to be beguiling, Lady Chastity motioned to the dance floor. "One waltz, Mr. Caldwell."

"Surely you would not refuse a lady," Lady Drayton urged, the color miraculously returning to her cheeks.

"I would not be so certain." He saw no point in encouraging Lady Chastity. Especially not now, when he'd much rather be looking into another woman's emerald eyes.

"Phineas Caldwell, I had not believed you to be a stick in the mud," Lady Chastity said, not quite teasing.

"A stick in the mud, is it?" Finn turned to Macie. "Might I inquire as to yer thoughts on the matter?"

She squared her shoulders and regarded him with a thoughtful tilt of her chin. "I am no authority on the matter, but this is a ballroom, after all. Dancing is to be expected, is it not?"

"I cannot counter yer logic, Miss Mason." He crooked an arm in offering. "Shall we dance?"

Chapter Three

*W*HY, THE GALL *of the man!*

Spotting the cocky glimmer in Finn's eyes, Macie bit back an unladylike reply. The man had no more desire to twirl about the dance floor than she did. Rather, he'd transformed Lady Chastity's unsubtle attempt to ease the tedium of her marriage to a man old enough to be her father into a means to sabotage Lady Drayton's scheme. If Finn possessed so much as a single gentlemanly inclination, she might have believed his invitation had been intended to offer her a reprieve, however brief, from their hostess's matchmaking.

But Phineas Caldwell was no gentleman.

His motives had nothing to do with chivalry, nor was he intent on looking out for her best interests. If anything, he was making the most of this opportunity to vex both Lady Drayton and Lady Chastity, if only to watch the younger woman pout.

The cocky curve of his smile seemed to challenge her. Macie resisted the urge to glare at him. He'd put her on quite the spot, hadn't he? Heaven knew she had no inclination to wade into the crowd of peacocks, much less while garbed as a mud hen.

Drat the man's arrogance.

Surely Finn knew better than to ply his charm on her.

Regardless of his intentions, she could wiggle out of this. A simple "No" would do the trick. But as Macie felt their hostess's gaze bore into her, as if willing her to utter the word that might free them from his presence, a fresh sense of rebellion reared its head. Lady Drayton regarded Macie as a fortune in skirts. The prospect of Macie—and her father's money—waltzing away in the arms of a very handsome rogue no doubt horrified the silver-haired paragon of society.

So much the better.

One dance. Whatever could be the harm in it? Perhaps, if she stepped just so, she might actually tread on this arrogant man's toes. That might be just the thing to wipe the brash smile from his face.

Or then again, probably not. He was not likely to give her the satisfaction of seeing him grimace. But it might be amusing to try.

"You're a brave one, aren't you? Have you considered I might take another tumble?" she teased, if only to watch Lady Chastity's mouth sag into a frown and Lady Drayton's thin to a razor's edge.

He hiked a brow. "If you fall, I shall catch ye."

"I suppose you will. After all, you have already demonstrated that ability."

"I consider it an unheralded talent."

Offering him the slightest of smiles, Macie accepted his arm and accompanied him to the ballroom floor. "Lady Drayton is not fond of you. Be thankful the daggers in her eyes are not real."

He flashed a grin as they made their way onto the polished dance floor. "I take it she's scowling at me again."

Macie glanced toward their hostess. "Oh, I'd say it has surpassed a scowl. If the woman possessed the ability to turn a man into a stone, you would be in a bit of trouble just about now."

"Medusa had nothing on that silk-clad bag of bones."

She laughed softly as they moved in time to the music. "I would say that's an understatement. Did you truly think you could charm your way into her good graces with that wicked smile of yours?"

"Not for a moment. I would have better luck riding an ill-tempered lioness. Bareback."

"Indeed." Macie suppressed a giggle. "Whatever did you do

to the woman?"

Finn hesitated for an incriminating second, then another. "It wasn't what I did to *her*."

"Ah, I see." Understanding dawned on Macie. "Or do I? Her niece made a match recently. To a baron, as I recall."

"A match? More of a negotiation, really." A sudden reflectiveness fell over his features. "Deandra was a pawn to her mother's queen."

"You cared for her?"

"Yes." His hesitation accented the word. "But we were not lovers, if that's what ye're thinking."

"Then why does Lady Drayton regard you as the devil's spawn?"

"'Tis a long story. Suffice it to say that Lady Drayton was set on overseeing her niece's path toward wedded bliss with a *respectable* man. As ye can imagine, she viewed me as an entirely unsuitable distraction."

"I see."

"Enough of that, Miss Mary Catherine Mason." The tinge of reflectiveness in his eyes evaporated, replaced by a hint of a smile that rendered his emotions unreadable. "I'd rather talk about ye. I'm told ye've scandalized the elites of London."

"Of London," she agreed with a smile. "Of Cardiff. And possibly, of Edinburgh."

"Ye always had the devil in yer eyes." Finally, his smile was genuine.

"You're a fine one to talk." She returned his smile as they moved easily to the beat of the waltz. "Rumor has it you've been raising Cain on two continents."

"Exaggeration." He looked pleased with himself. "For the most part. And ye?"

"I'm not nearly so wild as the gossips would have it. For the most part."

Macie lifted her gaze to meet his. She'd remembered him from the first moment she'd dangled inelegantly within his strong hands. Finn Caldwell was undeniably handsome, with a touch of devilish humor in his expression. Just as he'd been all those years before. But now, from a distinctly better vantage point—standing upright and firmly on her feet—she took a better look.

Nearly a decade had passed since that summer when Finn had visited their family's country home in Bristol for the last time. In those days, her brother's friend had worn his hair longer. Back then, the light brown strands had seemed a bit wild and untamed. Like him. His face had been fuller and ruddy cheeked. But the keen intelligence and brash confidence in his expression had not dimmed. Not one whit.

They'd been so young in those days, the three-year difference in their ages might as well have been a century. During that time, he'd regarded her—a slender, long-limbed girl of sixteen—with no more interest than if she'd been part of the furniture. But that hadn't stopped her from noticing the mischief in his gaze and the way tiny lines crinkled around his eyes when he smiled. Why, even their mother, prim and proper as she'd been, had not been able to resist smiling at his good-humored laugh. Finn Caldwell could charm any female in the room. With the current exception of Lady Drayton, that is. Given the hint of arrogance in his gaze, he was still well aware of that fact.

In those days, she'd thought Finn Caldwell appealing. Now, taking in his carved features and the sensuous curve of his mouth, she swallowed hard against an unfamiliar rush of heat. Ah, appealing was far too tame a word to describe the man Finn had become. The sensuous set of his full mouth and the rugged cut of his jaw drew her gaze with a nearly magnetic pull. As did the breadth of his shoulders, betraying a natural masculine power no amount of strategic padding could replicate. If she allowed her thoughts to wander, she could well imagine the sleek muscle beneath his unadorned white shirt and gray waistcoat. How would it feel to skim her fingertips over his skin, to learn the texture of the hair on his chest?

Oh, my. She blinked to clear her head. Could he have hazarded a guess as to the direction of her thoughts? If he had, he'd thankfully possessed the good sense to hide that awareness.

"I see ye've finally grown into yer legs," he said, his voice low and husky, nearly seductive. Other than the highly unexpected nature of his commentary.

She lifted her chin to meet his eyes. "I beg your pardon."

One corner of his mouth hitched, not quite a smile. "I remember a girl who had legs like a young colt, too blasted long for the rest of her."

"I cannot imagine you were ever privy to the sight of my legs, too long or otherwise."

"Surely ye haven't forgotten the scandal ye stirred?"

"Scandal?" She bit back a smile. "Surely you have me confused with another."

"Impossible. Ye're one of a kind, Macie."

She gave a deliberate little shrug. "One might say the same of you. I don't believe I've ever seen a young man practice his arrogant stare to perfection as you did."

"I'll have ye know I had no need to practice. Some things come naturally," he said with a gleam in his eyes. "But I'd never confuse ye with another lass on horseback. Those riding breeches ye wore while gallivanting about the countryside on that gelding of yers spurred every old biddy in the county to talk."

"Ah, I loved that horse." Wistful recollection swept her away. "Adonis was a gentle beast."

"As I recall, yer father turned a rather alarming shade of red— or was it purple?—when ye trotted past those lords he was out to impress, all gathered at yer fine country house."

"Red," Macie said. "Papa does tend to become agitated far more frequently than is healthy."

"Am I to surmise ye're the cause?"

"At times." She glanced at Lady Drayton, catching sight of the woman's frosty gaze as Finn led her in time to the waltz.

Finn chuckled. "If he were here, he'd be that shade right about now, wouldn't he?"

"Most likely. If he had his way, I'd be finding my way off the shelf."

Finn's brows hiked. "Wed to some lofty lord or another?"

"Papa has decided the one thing our family has yet to acquire is a title."

"And the Viscount Drayton could offer that."

Macie shrugged. "Among others. Papa would prefer the lord in question to have his own fortune, but he's willing to . . . negotiate."

Finn nodded his understanding. "But ye're not?"

She allowed herself a brief smile. "So far, I've made it my life's purpose to foil his plan."

"As I hear it, ye've enjoyed smashing success. If I had a glass of champagne, I would raise a toast."

"Somehow, I cannot envision you drinking champagne."

He gave a lazy shrug. "It's not my drink of choice. But I would make the sacrifice." His smile faded, his expression suddenly contemplative. "Ye know yer strategy won't work forever, Macie. Sooner or later, ye'll run into a man who isn't afraid of a scandal or two."

She studied Finn's carved features for a long moment, taking in the face that had inspired more than one girlish fantasy of heroes and other such romantic rot. Until the night he'd quite thoroughly shattered her naïve dreams. At the time, she'd hoped never again to look into those wicked amber eyes.

But now, she was older. Wiser. Well beyond the illusions that had made her young heart so very vulnerable. A spark of inspiration kindled into the tiniest of flames. Perhaps, just perhaps, Finn Caldwell's unexpected appearance might well serve a purpose in her life.

Yes, that was it. What she needed was a scandal.

And not just any scandal. Shaking off the heiress hunters on her trail had not proven easy all these years. No, she would create a scene certain to hike the eyebrows of London's oh-so-dignified elite and make even a woman like Lady Chastity blush. She'd cook up a scandal that would banish the notion of a wedding from the minds of money-hunting men and their scheming mothers once and for all.

A scandal like that required a man. And not just any man.

She needed a rogue.

Since her arrival in London, Macie had heard talk of Finn's exploits. If even a fraction of the rumors were true, charming, clever Finn Caldwell had become a rogue, through and through. Why, he could give her rake of a brother a run for his money.

As luck would have it, the man who might play a vital part in her plan was, at that very moment, whisking her around the ballroom.

This is madness. Reason and logic battled the wild notion.

And then, she felt Lady Drayton's diamond-hard gaze drilling into her. Assessing her worth as *marriage material.*

At times, a brief madness is just the thing.

"You're quite right. I suppose it is a matter of time before one of them catches up to me," she said with a steady tone that belied the surging of her pulse. "Unless I tarnish my heiress halo so thoroughly even Papa's money won't be able to polish it away."

He regarded her curiously. "An ambitious plan, even for you, Macie."

"Ambitious." She veiled her gaze with her lashes and pulled in a calming breath. "That's one way of putting it. But to achieve the desired outcome, I need a man." She lifted her gaze to lock with Finn's. "A rake, to be precise."

His casual smile faded. Slowly, he shook his head. "And what makes ye think the *rake* in question would not welcome marriage to an heiress?"

She met his questioning eyes. "He would have to be someone I could trust. That goes without saying."

"A trustworthy rake?" He coughed for effect. "A contradiction, indeed."

"Not necessarily. If the man in question had certain ties to my family."

Furrows etched between his dark brows. "Ye're suggesting we start a scandal?"

"It may just prove amusing." She forced a little smile.

"Staring down the wrong end of a pistol in yer father's hand?" Finn slowly shook his head. "Or worse yet, being dragged before a vicar?" He pretended to shudder. "I see no humor in either case."

She hiked her chin, shoring up her confidence. "I am not considering anything so dramatic."

The tiny lines on his forehead deepened. "I will not be responsible . . ." He seemed to struggle for the words, uncharacteristically at a loss. "For compromising ye."

She plastered on a deliberately vapid stare. "Might I ask why you believe I have not yet been *compromised*?"

"Have ye, then?" His tone was as bland as if he'd requested a glass of water from the elegantly clad server who strolled by with a tray of goblets.

Heat rushed to her cheeks. "A gentleman would not ask such a question."

"A moment ago, ye wanted a rogue. Now ye want a gentleman."

"What I want truly does not matter. Not to Papa. Not to Jon. And especially not to vultures like Lady Drayton. For now, I am on the shelf. And I'd prefer to stay there."

"I consider yer brother a friend. I will not betray him. Or ye, for that matter."

"We would not even have to *do* anything. The appearance of impropriety, the mere suggestion that I've been compromised would serve my purpose."

"What ye're suggesting will get the two of us dragged to utter vows." He frowned. "Count me out."

"Well, this *is* a disappointment. Given the reputation that precedes you, I was expecting you to be far more bold."

He scrubbed his hand over his jaw. "There is a fine line between boldness and idiocy."

"Do tell," she challenged.

"Creating a stir with an heiress whose father is extremely skilled at hitting his target is a risk I am not willing to take."

"Don't be so dramatic" She pulled in a low breath. "A little scandal never hurt anyone. Surely you, the consummate rogue, are well acquainted with the concept."

Once again, he shook his head. "The price would be too high."

"My brother will understand," she said, still confident she could bring him around to the notion. "I will explain it is nothing but a ruse."

"Even so, the cost will be far too high . . . not for me, Macie. For ye." He gazed down at her as the notes of the waltz faded, and the musicians fell silent. "My answer is 'no.'"

The couples who had filled the dance floor strolled to the perimeter of the ballroom. His expression unreadable, Finn escorted her from the floor.

Dash the luck. She'd happened upon a rogue with a conscience. *How very unexpected. And more than a bit disappointing.*

"A bit of scandal might be entertaining," she said for his ears alone, if only to lighten the mood.

Turning to her, he spoke in a low, husky rasp. "If ye're intent on tarnishing your pretty crown, ye'll do it without me."

"There is no changing your mind?"

"Not a chance." He plowed a hand through his hair. "Ye *will* get in over yer head."

She forced a lightness she did not feel into her voice. "And you will not be there to save me?"

As Lady Drayton's gaze honed in on her, Macie squared her shoulders and cocked her chin. Her all-too-brief reprieve was coming to an end. Moving closer to Finn than was proper, she struggled to read the contradictions in his eyes. Just as she had all those years before, when she'd been drawn to him with a sixteen-year-old girl's infatuated heart. Back then, she'd found his quick wit as endearing as his amber-brown gaze. Until the cool, moonlit night when Finn had shown his true colors. The night he'd put her firmly in her place.

Spinster-in-training.

The words he'd uttered that starry midnight suddenly echoed in her thoughts. Now, they were adults. And he'd done it again.

Of all the men in that ballroom who might have caught me, why did it have to be Finn Caldwell?

For a heartbeat, perhaps two, she toyed with brushing a kiss against his cheek, if only to shock their hostess. But she leaned in close to him and spoke the truth.

"Years ago, you were wrong about me, Finn Caldwell. And you still haven't figured me out." As she turned on her heel to walk away, she threw a forced smile over her shoulder. "I suspect you never will."

Chapter Four

THE MORNING AFTER Macie had endured both Lady Drayton's attempts at matchmaking and an encounter with a vexingly noble rogue, she faced the day with a clear determination to put the tiresome night behind her. She could think of no better place—in London, at least—to lift her spirits than Bennington Manor. Smiling to herself as she strolled through the main hall, she drank in the beauty and flaws and eccentricities of her grandfather's once-grand house. No, she corrected herself. *Her house.* Finally, she felt at home. Bennington Manor was where she belonged.

Pity the same could not be said of her friend. Macie couldn't recall a time when Nell Blake had seemed so skittish. Why, if the willowy blonde's eyes went any wider, she would look as if she had seen a ghost. And not the friendly kind Grandpapa had spoken of with such great fondness.

"Bennington Manor *is* haunted. Isn't it?" Nell gazed up at a portrait of one of Macie's ancestors, an imposing man whose staid expression, full mane of silver hair, and black eye patch lent him the look of a fierce buccaneer—a buccaneer who'd been reformed by the love of a proper woman. At least, that was the tale Grandpapa had recounted with great pride about his own grandfather.

"Grandpapa was convinced his ancestors roamed these halls."

"You sound quite pleased at the thought. I certainly cannot

say the same. This place gives me a chill." Nell clasped her arms over her chest as if warding off a shiver.

"Surely you are not frightened by a harmless wee ghost." Macie shot her friend a glance as they proceeded along the corridor toward the parlor.

"A *wee* ghost? No." Nell paused again, this time to sweep her gaze over a fig-leaf-clad marble Adonis who peered down upon them from his solid perch. "But who's to say that's the only spectral creature roaming through this place?"

"I encountered my first spirit here when I was a girl still in braids," Macie said. "As you can see, it did no harm."

Nell reached up to brush a cobweb from the Adonis's meticulously chiseled buttocks, then slanted her a skeptical look. "Perhaps it liked you because it sensed a kinship. Unlike you, I've no desire to bandy words with a phantom. When I'm alone in the dark, I much prefer to dream about some dashing scoundrel or two."

"How very outrageous!" Macie said, pressing her hands to her cheeks in a look of feigned shock.

"Oh, don't even try to pretend you have not invited a rake into your boudoir, even if the gent is imaginary. I can only hazard a guess as to how many times you've read and reread *Pride and Prejudice*. And I suspect it's not merely to enjoy Lizzie Bennet's wit."

Macie pursed her lips. "And I suppose you have never swooned over a romantic hero."

Nell waved away the thought. "I make no such claim. Why, only last night I dreamt of Mr. Darcy. He was preparing for a hot bath after a vigorous bout of bare-knuckle boxing."

"Oh, dear. You certainly do know how to paint a vivid picture with words." Macie playfully fanned herself. "Pity Fitzwilliam Darcy is not a true scoundrel."

Nell lifted a brow. "Unlike the rogue who gallantly saved you from a nasty tumble?"

"Good heavens, word does travel quickly."

Nell looked to be biting back a little grin. "Mr. Caldwell's quick reflexes are a valid subject of conversation, I would say."

"I'd imagine my decided lack of grace was of more interest."

"From what I've heard, more than one woman in attendance regretted she had not thought to take a conveniently timed spill," Nell teased. "I'd say it was a rather brilliant stroke of luck. After all, a dashing scoundrel is precisely what you needed to send Lord Drayton and his harpy of a mother scurrying off."

An image of a man who fit the bill rather nicely invaded Macie's thoughts, and she fought the urge to frown. Scoundrels weren't supposed to care about her honor. Rakes did not give two half-pennies about compromising a woman. Rogues would not spare a thought to preserving a woman's good name.

But Finn had done just that.

Drat the luck

"Sadly, Lady Drayton was not so easily deterred," Macie said, motioning to Nell to follow her to the parlor. "Though I must say her son had little interest in his mother's scheme. He'd much rather have been peering through his telescope than making inconsequential banter with me."

"If you truly wish to scare off Lord Drayton, simply inform him you wish to take up residence here." Nell paused as they passed a marble bust of some long-dead king and blew a bit of dust off the bloke's prominent nose. "That should do the trick."

"The ghost of MacBeth himself could not deter Lady Drayton."

Entering the parlor, she pondered the rays of sunlight creeping in through the glazed windows. For now, she'd leave the off-white sheets in place on the settee and chairs, optimizing the mood. So much the better to create a scene that brought specters to mind.

"Good heavens, Macie! What is that?" Nell's usually melodic voice had gone up an octave or so.

"That?" Macie struggled to discern what precisely had set her friend into a stir.

"That . . . lurking there." Nell pointed to the draperies by the parlor window. Had her shudder at the simple rustling of curtains been genuine or a demonstration of her decided flair for the dramatic?

The fabric swayed, and one small black paw poked out from the shadows. "Oh, Cleo, you naughty minx," Macie said, coaxing her cat from her hiding place.

"That little beast is going to give me heart palpitations." Nell glared at the feline, then smiled as she crouched to pet her. A ray of sunlight glimmered off its collar. "You are a sneaky little girl, aren't you?" She glanced up at Macie. "I'm tempted to believe you taught her to give me a fright."

Macie grinned. "If only that were possible. Cleo is far too independent to be trained."

"A bit like you, my friend." Scooping up the cat, Nell studied its sparkly, adorned collar. "Crystals? For a cat? This must've cost a pretty penny."

"An exquisitely pretty penny. And then some."

"Does your father know how much you spent?"

Macie shrugged. "Not yet. But once his man of business attends to my shopping accounts, I imagine Papa will include a few choice words in his next letter."

"Even so, my father is not nearly so generous."

"Generous?" Macie hiked a brow. "I'm not quite sure that's the right word. Papa has a plan. And fortunately for me, that plan requires funds. Gowns to tempt Lord High-and-Mighty don't come cheap, you know."

"Like that atrocity you wore last night?"

Macie grinned. "I'll have you know that gown was an original. Madame Lorette said she'd never created anything like it."

"Original?" Nell scoffed. "I admire your way with language. I can only imagine the dressmaker has never before had such a request. I do wish I'd seen the impression you made with my own eyes."

"You will have your chance soon enough. Madame Lorette is

putting the finishing touches on another creation as we speak."

Nell's eyes went wide again. "Tell me it's not the same style as the last one."

"Not even close."

"I suppose Jon will be relieved."

"Perhaps." She shrugged. "But does it really matter?"

A frown pulled at her friend's mouth. "Macie, what have you done now? I wouldn't be entirely shocked if you arrived at a ball dressed in a grain sack."

"Now that would be quite brilliant." Macie mulled the notion in her head. "Perhaps that will be my next commission."

"Oh, dear, I've inspired you, haven't I?"

"And for that, I must thank you," Macie said with a grin. "The gown Madame Lorette's seamstress is creating was inspired by the tales of Robin Hood."

"Maid Marian?" Nell looked hopeful.

Macie gave a little shake of her head. "Friar Tuck."

Nell's brows hiked in unison. "If you keep this up, your brother's hair will gray in no time."

"You are rather concerned about him," Macie observed. "Please don't tell me you've gone sweet on that stick in the mud."

"Of course not. Jon has always been . . . like a brother to me." The rosy hue in Nell's cheeks contradicted her words.

"In case you haven't noticed yet, he's still very much available."

Her flush deepened. "I am quite content with the way things are. There's so much of the world I want to see before I'm settled by the hearth with a husband and babe in arms."

"Indeed." Macie agreed. "We shall both enjoy this time."

"Absolutely." A thin smile crossed Nell's face. "While we have it. We both know it cannot go on forever."

Macie studied her friend's pensive expression. Nell had relished this time in London, especially those rare moments when she considered casting her ever-practical nature to the wind. Over the years, Macie had grown to view Nell as her calm, rational sister-of-the-heart. Her even, level-headed nature had been the primary reason Macie's father had agreed to Nell's unofficial role as Macie's companion. She could be counted on to rein in Macie's impulsive ways far more effectively than some hired biddy. Or so Papa thought.

What Papa didn't know wouldn't hurt him. Or her, for that matter.

"My, what a gloomy Sue," Macie said, even as she heard the truth in Nell's voice. Sooner or later, their wings would be clipped. But dash it all, she intended to delay that moment as long as possible.

The squawk of the entry door opening and closing yanked Macie from her thoughts. The rhythmic beat of boot heels upon the floorboards in the entry hall confirmed they were no longer alone.

"Someone's here." Nell whispered. My, she seemed unduly susceptible to alarm. Perhaps the strings of cobwebs by the fireplace and the gloomy shadows in the corners of the room had rattled her nerves more than Macie had expected.

Oddly enough, Macie felt quite at home.

"It's Jon, most likely. He was due this afternoon to assess the needed renovations and prioritize the improvements. I had not expected him so soon." She sighed. *Drat the luck.* She'd hoped for more time to plan her photography exhibit without disruption.

Two familiar male voices confirmed her assumption. Her brother had stopped in the corridor beyond the parlor, looking over the massive wooden staircase that led from the entry hall to the second floor. Finn Caldwell stood at his side, tapping his walking stick against his palm as he examined the intricate carvings on the banister.

Oh, dear.

She certainly had not expected to face him so soon after their impromptu discussion the night before. Truth be told, she'd hoped to avoid seeing him again throughout her stay in London. It wasn't as if he frequented society soirees. His appearance at Lady Drayton's ball had been unexpected, even to their hostess.

What fresh manner of torment is this?

"He's not alone," Nell observed for effect rather than out of necessity. "Perhaps Mr. Caldwell wished to see you again."

"Dash it all, Nell." She threw her friend a scowl. "You know better than that."

"I understand the two of you made quite a pair, whirling about Lady Drayton's ballroom," Nell said in a teasing whisper.

"Our *whirling* had more to do with deterring Lady Drayton's schemes than in any interest beyond that one waltz."

Nell smiled. "I would not be so sure."

Turning toward Macie, Finn looked to be biting back a smile. Had he overheard their hushed comments? Should she now add *eavesdropping* to the list of his most vexing qualities? Heaven knew the newly gained sense of propriety he had wielded to throw water on the sparks of her plan was a poor fit for the rogue, no matter how well-tailored his gentleman's clothing. At the very least, her scheme to create a stir of gossip would have proven amusing, even if she had failed to thwart her father's hopes.

She would *not* give him the satisfaction of displaying her annoyance at his unexpected visit to her cobweb-draped sanctuary. Macie forced a smile. "What brings you here today, Mr. Caldwell?"

"I seek another place on yer dance card, my lady." He sketched a half-hearted bow.

She resisted the urge to scowl. He'd enjoy her pique far too much.

"Dance card?" She softly shook her head. "I cannot say I've ever required one. And I doubt I ever shall."

"I would not be so sure. I suspect yer attention will be in demand in ballrooms throughout London. Unless, of course, Lord Drayton made a considerable impression on ye."

"He wanted nothing more than to have the evening over and done with. Just as I did. In that regard, we were quite compatible."

Finn's gaze swept over her, none too discreetly. "I see ye

decided against wearing that shroud again."

Macie toyed with the cuffs of her crisp white mutton-sleeved blouse. "I'll have you know I reserve my shrouds for special occasions."

Finn cocked a brow as Nell looked to be suppressing a giggle. "Ah, so that's yer strategy."

"So far, I'd say it has been a grand success."

"Have ye made it yer life's work to give yer brother a case of dyspepsia?"

It was Macie's turn to hike her brows. "Everyone is overly concerned with Jon's wellbeing, as if my conduct is of paramount importance to his happiness."

"If his hair turns gray before his time, don't say I didn't warn you," Nell quipped as her gaze lit on Finn's walking stick. "Mr. Caldwell, that's quite a clever design. I'm rather accustomed to seeing silver wolves or lions. But a gargoyle? How very intriguing."

"A Welsh silversmith crafted it," he replied.

Macie studied the intricate detail. "When my brother was a lad, he would tease me with tales of the creatures perched high atop old buildings, ready to swoop down upon a willful child. Like me."

"I see ye managed to dodge the beasts." Mischief flashed in Finn's amber eyes. "Well done."

"Does it conceal a blade?" Nell asked, moving closer to examine the walking stick. "For purposes of defense, of course."

He shook his head. "I've no need for a sword stick. Wielded with purpose, this serves as a powerful deterrent."

"Indeed," Nell agreed. Her features lit up as Macie's brother strolled up behind Finn.

Seemingly oblivious to what had gone between Macie and Finn the night before, Jon regarded her with an expression usually reserved for funerals. Judging from the furrows in his forehead, he'd been assessing the necessary repairs to the mansion.

"Honestly, Macie, we would be well-advised to salvage the

more valuable fixtures and tear the place down," Jon said, ever practical as always. He was like that, the sensible heir always striving to prove his worth in their father's eyes. Jon was a scholar at heart, not a cutthroat tycoon. In Papa's view, that was a definite disadvantage.

"How can you say such a thing?" She shot him a fierce look. "This house holds so many fond memories."

"And ghosts," Nell chimed in.

"Memories will not pay the bills." Jon's frown deepened. "Unless the ghosts lurking about are skilled carpenters, it would make better sense to put this place out of its misery."

"I won't hear of it." Macie kept her voice steady, reining in her emotion. "Grandfather left this house to me. He knew I would preserve it. There's a great deal of history within these walls."

"I have to agree with Miss Mason." Finn spoke up. Returning to the entry hall beyond the parlor, he tugged on the handrail of the main staircase. "Solid, as you can see. The house looks worse than it is. The place has good bones."

Macie regarded him for a long moment, nearly shocked into speechlessness. If he had uttered artificially poetic compliments of her beauty, her attire, or her ability to waltz without treading upon his toes, his words would have been meaningless to her. But he had actually agreed with her. And contrary to her brother's view, no less. That was truly something.

Jon scowled at his old friend. "Remind me why I even thought to let you know we were in London."

Finn regarded him with a patient expression. "Perhaps ye recall that between bouts of gambling and raising Cain while we were at university, I did learn a bit about architecture."

Her brother regarded him with a dubious slant of his brows. "On those rare occasions when you actually showed your face in the lecture hall."

"As I recall, the university actually provided me with a piece of parchment bearing my name in a fancy script. I suppose that means something." As he turned back to Macie, the faintest of smiles curve his mouth. "I take it ye will put some faith in my opinion."

Faith? It was a bit too soon for that, wasn't it? But she wasn't about to admit that. Not in front of Jon, at least.

"As long as we can persuade my tight-fisted brother not to abandon this house, I suppose I must."

"Humbug," Jon muttered, though he looked a bit too cheerful to have made a convincing Scrooge.

She folded her arms at the waist and glared at him. "Such a pity our parents did not think to name you Ebenezer."

"Surely you're not forgetting what it's going to take to convince the old man to advance the funds to restore this place? You and I both know that Father won't spend a dime unless he views it as an investment."

Jonathan hadn't intended his words to cut. But they did. *Investment.* Such as this time in London. Macie knew full well why her father had agreed to finance this visit to the city. And she also knew the payment he expected to extract from her in the form of a fancy title.

"I am aware of that." She pulled in a low breath. "Don't worry, Jon. Papa will get what he wants. He always does."

Chapter Five

SEATED AT HIS usual corner table in the Rogue's Lair, Finn leaned back in his chair, stretched out his legs, and took in the sights and brashly cheerful sounds of the tavern. Relaxing for the first time in hours, he idly swirled the rich amber whisky in his glass. Lifting his gaze, he studied Jon's expression. Seeing the expression on his friend's face, he realized his own respite would be short-lived.

Jon reached for his drink and downed a gulp of scotch. The whisky seemed to ease the set of his jaw, but there was no disguising the rigid tension in his body. His once-jovial nature had evaporated, the strain of living up to his father's expectations etched in the lines on Jon's face.

Finn had first noticed the transformation upon his friend's return to London, but tonight, Jon seemed especially on edge. When he'd requested that they find a place to talk—specifically, a place away from Macie's ears—his tone had been terse, sharply clipped.

What in blazes was going on? And what did Macie have to do with it?

Had Jon's father settled on a whey-faced but suitably titled nitwit for Macie? *Bloody hell.* The very thought of it set Finn's back teeth on edge. Macie didn't deserve to be bartered for a puffed-up title that might allow her father to drown out the talk of *new money* he so detested.

"Well, well, look what the cat dragged in." Logan MacLain strolled up to the table. Newly married to a beauty who'd tamed the man once rumored to be an outlaw, the tavern's owner bore the unmistakable look of a man thoroughly contented with his life. *Lucky bastard.* At least Logan had the good sense to know how bloody fortunate he was.

"Is that any way to greet yer favorite cousin?" Finn replied with a chuckle.

"Favorite?" Logan cocked a brow. "Given how prolific my father's siblings have been at reproduction, I've more than a dozen kin who could fit that description."

"Ah, ye wound me," Finn said dryly, slipping into the brogue that came easily when he was in the company of his Highland kin. "If I had not spoken certain words of wisdom, an ocean might now separate ye from the lass ye took as yer bride."

"I would have come to my senses soon enough." A smile played on Logan's mouth. "With or without your *wisdom.* If I'd had to swim across the blasted Atlantic, I would've gone after Amelia."

Finn shrugged. "I'd like to think my advice saved ye the trouble. Not to mention keeping ye from becoming food for the sharks."

A grin touched Logan's mouth. "If ye're looking to get a round on the house, consider it done." He turned to Jon. "It's good to see ye in London again. Ye're here on business?"

Jon offered a small nod. "In a matter of speaking."

"A matter of speaking, eh?" Logan replied. "I understand yer sister has accompanied you. Mary Catherine, if memory serves."

Jon nodded again. "Macie is looking to photograph historic buildings in the city. She might be interested in setting up her camera here."

"The lass will be welcome any time. Amelia's planning to invite her to tea at our home. She's hopeful Macie might be interested in photographing her library."

"She'll be delighted at the opportunity." Jon smiled for the first time that night. "Tell me, MacLaine, have you heard tales of ghosts in the place?"

Logan's brow furrowed. "Ghosts, ye say?"

"My sister is fascinated by the possibility of spectral activity."

Logan nodded thoughtfully. "I do not doubt there's a spirit or two rumbling around Amelia's library. The building certainly has a history."

"Interesting," Jon said. "Please, do have your wife reach out to her."

"Ye can count on it." Logan glanced over his shoulder at the bar. A loudmouth's harsh tones carried back to their table. "If you'll excuse me, I need to have a little talk with this gent. In the meantime, I'll send another round. On the house. I wouldn't want our mothers to think me a skinflint where my *favorite* cousin is concerned."

Jon watched as Logan cut a direct path to the bar. "He seems happy enough with his lot in life."

"I've never seen a man more content," Finn said without hesitation. "His new bride is as fetching as she is kind, the tavern is thriving, and Mrs. Langford has found herself a beau, so she's not hell-bent on taking out Logan's brougham at all hours of the night."

"Mrs. Langford?" Questions brimmed in Jon's eyes. "She drives his carriage?"

"The woman is family to him, though not by blood." Finn reached for his glass and downed a healthy draught of whisky. "It's a long story. Too long to get into now. Someday, I'll fill in the details."

"Fair enough. Changing the subject, might I ask what the devil you were thinking at the old house? Good bones, eh?"

"I spoke the truth," Finn said coolly. "Renovating the house will not prove as daunting a task as ye've imagined."

Jon swished the liquor in his glass. "If I didn't know better, I'd think Macie had convinced you to stand on her side."

"So, ye're on to us. Yer sister and I have hatched a plot, a sinister scheme to browbeat ye into restoring your grandfather's home."

Jon plowed a hand through his hair. "She is so bloody fond of that dusty old tomb. I've never seen her so blasted sentimental about anything, let alone an old building." A muscle clenched and unclenched in his jaw. "Our grandfather knew she'd move heaven and earth to preserve his house."

Even as lads, Finn had been able to read his friend's expression. He set his glass down on the table with a *clink*. "What's on yer mind, Jon? Ye look like a man condemned to the Tower."

"A stay in the Tower might be bloody preferable." Jonathan leaned back against the leather-upholstered chair. "Time on the rack might be easier to abide than trying to rein Macie in."

"Ye'd have an easier time taming the ocean." Finn balked at the notion. For some reason he couldn't quite explain, even to himself, the idea of *reining Macie in* irritated him like a pebble in his shoe.

"Now that, my friend, is an understatement." Jon's expression was weary.

An all-too-intriguing image of Macie's impish smile the night before waltzed into his thoughts. Delighted with her own cheek, she'd mingled with London's elite while wearing a gown that might have passed for a shroud. In the process, she had proven one irrefutable truth: it simply wasn't possible to dull her beauty.

Finn resisted the urge to grin at the very recent memory. "She has a good bit of yer mum in her."

"Another understatement." Jon rubbed his temples with his fingers. "Macie and our mother are the only people on the planet who can render Father speechless. He and Mum are complete opposites. By all rights, she should've driven him mad years ago. But he's still wild for her."

"And that is as it should be," Finn said. "I take it she is well."

"Quite so. Better than our father, in fact." The furrows in Jon's brow deepened. "Since Father pushed Macie into this infernal husband hunt, Mum has cultivated a layer of frost toward him as thick as an iceberg."

"That does not surprise me. I cannot imagine yer mother would place any value on a title."

"Precisely the opposite. She married Father when his prospects were far from illustrious. He was a second son, brash and brave—as Mum has said, a bold young man with scarcely a shilling to his name. But that did not stop her from spurning some high-and-mighty earl to become his bride. And much to her own father's discontent, I might add."

"Yer father is a lucky man."

Jon waved away the thought. "These days, he's turned into a character straight out of Dickens."

"He is contemplating his legacy. That's plain to see."

Jon regarded him for a long moment. "Caldwell, when did you become a philosopher?"

"I am a man of many talents." Finn took another drink. "And ye, my friend, should pay little heed to yer father's insistence on a title yer sister does not want."

Jon took another drink. "Someday, this quest will be done, and I won't have to witness the scenes she concocts to scare off the heiress hunters, as she calls them. From one day to another, I don't know what she's going to do next."

Finn bit back a smile. "Heiress hunters, eh?" He'd have described the shameless money-hungry blokes in far cruder terms.

"Prince Bloody Charming himself could court her, and she'd have no interest. Not that I can fault her." Jon shoved a hand through his hair. "Beyond that, she doesn't care one whit about propriety. She won't even wear a blasted bustle. No, Macie insists on *sensible* dress. God above, that travesty she wore last night—a gown commissioned from the most esteemed dressmaker in the city—was enough to stir the biddies to talk."

"It . . . it wasn't so bad." Finn struggled for a charitable description.

"She could've garbed herself in one of the sheets draping the furniture at the old house for far less money." Jon scowled into his glass. "That might have been an improvement."

"Ye must admit, the gown was modest."

"If you had not been there to keep her from taking that spill last night, I can only imagine the scene. She would've strolled out of there, drenched in a fine vintage from Lady Drayton's wine cellar." Jon drummed his fingers against the table in an agitated rhythm. "Just one blasted week without Macie conjuring some disaster or other to set the gossips into a frenzy, whether contrived or purely by chance. That's all I want."

"Ye're not her keeper."

"That would be easier to believe if my sister's nickname was not *Calamity*."

"I must say it does fit, especially given her grace and poise," Finn said with an ill-advised smile.

Jon shot him a glare. "You're enjoying my pain too bloody much."

"It's one of my few pleasures these days. I tell ye, being a reformed rogue is not easy."

"And now, a situation has arisen." Jon stared down at his whisky. "I've been called away from London."

"That's not unusual."

Jon lifted his glass and took a drink. "But this time, Macie is here. In the city. And she has no desire to leave."

"That's not to be unexpected. Yer sister is a woman, capable of making her own way for a time. And she's not alone. I presume Miss Blake will remain in the city as her companion while ye're away."

"Companion?" Jon pinched the bridge of his nose. "Partner in crime might be a more accurate description. Nell Blake is nearly as a much of a free spirit as Macie."

"They can share their misadventures," Finn said, employing an optimist's tone. "If ye have concerns, have yer father call her home."

"I've already sent a telegram." Jon slowly shook his head. "He insists she stay."

"No doubt to continue the husband hunt."

Jon nodded. "He intends to use Bennington Manor to moti-vate her to make a suitable match. He'll fund the restoration of the house. But in return, he expects to see a wedding ring on her finger by the end of the year. If she returns home now—or if she creates a scandal his money cannot overcome—he's not inclined to 'toss good coin after bad.'"

Bloody hell. The thought of Macie's father using the house she cherished as leverage set Finn's back teeth on edge. "Ye're serious?"

"He only wants what's best for Macie."

"And ye believe that?"

"What I believe does not signify. Not at the moment, at least." Jon downed the whisky in his glass to the last drop. "As I will not be here to keep a watchful eye on her, I'm quite sure I can count on my most trusted ally—that would be you, Phineas Caldwell."

Bollocks. Any time anyone used his given name, trouble fol-lowed. Finn had learned that lesson as a boy. "What in blazes are ye saying?"

For a moment, Jon regarded him with an unreadable expres-sion. A cryptic smile crept over his features. "Allow me to make a prediction—before this week is done, you will feel a touch of the *joy* that comes part and parcel with watching over Macie."

Finn cocked his head. *Watching over Macie.* Surely he'd mis-heard.

"Come again?"

"My friend, you will experience the challenge of keeping my dear sister's name off the lips of every gossipmonger in town."

Finn tapped a fingertip against Jon's glass. "Precisely how much of this stuff did ye imbibe before we walked through the door?"

"Not so much as a drop."

"Absinthe?"

Jon shook his head. "Never touch the stuff."

"An opium den?"

"Never."

Finn studied his friend. "Perhaps ye wandered too close and inhaled the smoke?"

"Not a chance." For the second time that night, Jon smiled. "You came to London to secure a contract for your family's distillery," Jon finally said. "Did you not?"

"That was part of it," Finn said. "What are ye getting at?"

"As you know, we are planning to offer a gentleman's smoking room within our department stores," Jon went on.

Finn nodded his agreement with the idea. "Offering men a respite while their wives peruse the merchandise is a stroke of brilliance."

"True." Jon offered a bland nod. "And if the blokes have a tumbler of whisky in their bellies, they will likely open their wallets even wider. My father is a shrewd one, I'll give him that. But—"

Finn studied his friend's face. "Ye have doubts?"

"No," Jon answered quickly. "But the business of managing the venture has grown more complicated. Keeping all the parts of the plan moving in the right direction is a blasted pain in my arse. And now, there's another complication."

"Such is the plight of the astute man of business," Finn said with a chuckle, only to be met with an intent frown.

"I've been called away to Scotland. A complication has arisen at the Inverness property. *Minor catastrophe,* my assistant stated in his wire, whatever the bloody hell that means. I expect to be gone for a fortnight. And that, my old friend, is where you come in. If you agree to this arrangement, your family will supply the liquor served in our smoking rooms for years to come."

"Arrangement?" The tension in Finn's gut warned he would not like whatever the hell Jon had in mind. "*Blackmail* might be more to the point."

"Call it what you will. It's actually a rather simple task." The tightness in Jon's tone contradicted his words. He cleared his throat. "I need you to watch over Macie."

Finn felt his own brows hike. *Ye'd have more luck taming the ocean.* His own words had come back to haunt him. "Ye do realize I am a *man*—a man whose reputation precedes him? The bloody gossips' suspicions will flame out of control."

"I—of all people—am aware of your reputation. But desperate times call for desperate measures. With any luck, Miss Blake's presence will hold the biddies at bay."

"Surely there is someone else . . . someone better suited to playing chaperone to a headstrong lass." *A woman. Or a man so ancient, he would long for a comfortable chair far more than for a beauty like Macie.*

"She does not require a chaperone. My sister needs a bodyguard."

"A bodyguard? She will never agree to such a thing."

"Macie's agreement—or lack of it—is not pertinent to my decision." Jon leaned back against his chair. "She dashes about this city with little more than her parasol for defense. Macie is not foolish. Not in the least. She understands that being the daughter of a wealthy man makes her a target. But that knowledge has not held her back from gallivanting about London with her blasted camera and Miss Blake in tow. I don't need someone merely to guard her good name. I need someone who can defend her."

Blast it to hell, but Jon was making sense. Despite Macie's determined will and independent nature, she was not as worldly as she believed. A woman of her means had been shielded from the darkness permeating the city. If she found herself in the sights of a man with ill intentions—whether a street tough or an entitled noble—she would be vulnerable. *Defenseless.*

The thought of Macie falling victim to some gutter-dweller plowed into Finn's gut like a fist. By hellfire, he was entering a trap. And he knew it.

But there wasn't a blasted thing he could tell himself that might convince him to walk away.

"Tell me this, Jon. Why me?"

"You already know the answer, Finn. You know how to use your fists when you need to. You've never shied away from a fight." Jon met his gaze. "I need to know Macie is protected. Above all, I need someone I can trust."

Trust. How bloody unexpected.

"It goes without saying that discretion will be required," Jon went on. "I am counting on you to keep her safe. And out of trouble."

Finn dragged a hand through his hair. Bloody hell, what was he getting himself into? "Protecting her is one thing. Keeping her out of trouble is quite another."

"How well I know," Jon agreed. "It is imperative that she does not create another scene that sets tongues wagging."

Jon's tone was so staid, it was hard to reconcile this man with the rowdy rogue who'd once ridden a horse *into* a tavern for the sake of an ill-considered wager. When had his friend cast aside his amusement over his sister's harmless scandals? He threw him a speaking glance.

"No, we wouldn't want her to do that, would we? By the way, did ye ever put Thunder out to stud?"

"There's no need to remind me of my misspent youth. God only knows Father takes great pleasure in that pursuit." Jon frowned. "You seem to admire Macie's talent for wreaking havoc."

"Some might consider it an art form." Finn didn't bother to hold back his smile. "Is it true she dumped a cup of cold punch over some unlucky baron's head?"

"Something like that." Jon looked as if he'd gritted his teeth at the memory. "As I recall, he was a viscount."

"I'd wager the bastard deserved it."

"He did." Jon glanced at the gold timepiece he wore on a chain tethered to his waistcoat. "Surely you can understand my reasons for asking you to watch over her. Keep her safe. And out of trouble. If she can land a noble by the time I return, so much the better."

Finn considered his words for a long moment. "I cannot imagine Macie wishes to call herself *Lady Birdwit*. Are ye telling me ye're willing to sacrifice her freedom for a title she neither needs nor wants?"

"I don't give a damn about hitching Macie to some high-browed fop. Our families could buy and sell most of these so-called lords any day of the week. But Father has gotten it into his head that Macie should pursue a title, that she deserves to be a lady."

His friend's words dug into his stomach like a fist. "Jon, she already *is* a lady."

"You think I don't know that?" Jon drummed his fingers in an irritatingly precise rhythm. "I do care about Macie. She deserves a chance to shine. If she ruins her chances simply to sabotage our father's whims, that will be a blasted shame."

Finn kept his peace for a long moment, considering Jon's words. "And if I agree to this arrangement?"

"The contracts will be yours. No further negotiation required." Jon's fingers stilled, thankfully silencing the nervous beat. "But there is one thing . . . one thing I must say before we make this agreement." His eyes narrowed strategically. "You *will* bear in mind that she is *my* sister . . . at all times."

"That goes without saying. Ye do realize that Macie regards me as fondly as she might look upon a burr in her shoe?"

"I am not a green lad. Frost can be melted. My mother and father are proof of that. But I am trusting you will not be the one to chisel away the ice Macie uses as a shield."

"Ye've no worries on that matter." Finn resisted the urge to down another gulp of whisky as Macie's scandalous proposition echoed through his thoughts, contradicting his own words.

"I'm counting on you to watch over her. Even if it means protecting my sister from her own schemes."

Bloody hell, was he up to that challenge? "What makes you think she'll go along with this?"

"Macie will see the logic in this arrangement." Jon sounded like he was trying to shore up his confidence. "You'll see."

Chapter Six

"BODYGUARD? REALLY, JON?" Macie stared at her brother, fury replacing her confusion as she realized his absurd proposal was not a pitifully unfunny attempt at humor. When he'd requested that she join him in his study, she had expected him to quiz her about her plans for the upcoming gala. Given his decidedly perturbed state upon seeing the gown she'd worn to Lady Drayton's soiree, she would not have been surprised if he'd wanted to see what she had in mind for the next event. But this— this was beyond the pale.

Her gaze roamed over the man who stood by his side. Finn Caldwell met her eyes, his expression unreadable. *Drat the luck.* After the night before, she'd rather hoped that another ten years or so would pass before she had to look into those amber-brown eyes again. The notion that Finn, of all the men in London—on the planet, for that matter—would act as her protector was utter madness.

Jon leaned against his desk and stretched out his long legs. "He is our best choice."

"Best choice?" She could scarcely believe her own ears. Her gaze darted between her brother and Finn. "Have you both gone daft?"

"Daft?" Her brother gave his head a rueful shake. "All those years of tutelage by the most refined governesses. Father's money was indeed well spent."

"I assure you, these are my censored thoughts. Even the most *refined* of my governesses could not have exercised greater restraint in this circumstance." She pulled in a low breath, as if that might calm her. "You would not like to hear my true opinion of the suggestion that Finn should squire me about town. Why, the very idea is beyond outlandish."

Jon regarded her with a look of practiced calm. Years of dealing with their father had taught him to mask emotion. Cool and unflappable, no matter what he faced.

Or in this case, what he expected Macie to face.

"It is not a suggestion. It is the plan," he said with a tone of finality.

"*Your* plan. Not mine." She hiked her chin defiantly. "I will have no part of it."

"Be reasonable, Macie." Jon's tone had softened, if only just a bit.

She shifted her attention to Finn. The scoundrel with a new-found moral compass—the rake who wouldn't even consider compromising her, not so much as to stir a biddy or two to gossip—was to serve as her escort about town in Jon's absence. The very notion was absurd.

"As for you, Mr. Caldwell, what leverage does he have over you? Whatever could have inspired you to go along with this nonsensical scheme?"

Finn folded his arms over his chest like a shield. A wry grin played on his full mouth. *Damn the man and his tempting smile.*

His amber eyes gleamed. "You doubt my penchant for chivalry?"

She shot him a scowl. "I'd sooner believe you've a wish to tame some wild beast in the circus."

"A lioness, perhaps." His wry tone left no doubt to his meaning. Good thing for him, she didn't have her parasol at the ready. She might well have given him a taste of it, right in the breadbasket.

For his part, Jon frowned. A developing-a-whopper-of-aheadache type of frown. *Good enough.* Her brother deserved a touch of misery, given what he proposed to inflict upon her.

"If you claimed to be jesting, I would believe you," she said to her brother. "We'd have a chuckle over it, and then we could put the matter to rest."

"I am entirely serious, Macie. I must leave for Scotland. But you do have a choice."

"Good." She studied him, her flicker of optimism doused as she took in his gloomy expression. "Why didn't you mention that earlier?"

"Because you're not going to like the other option." Jon was more blunt than usual. "It's quite simple, really. You can tote your camera about London, accept a sufficient number of invitations from Lady Drayton and her ilk to humor Father, and accept that Finn will watch over you. For your safety as well as Nell's, I might add. Or you both shall pack your things and board a train for Bristol before I depart."

"Simple? How easy for you to say!" Macie fought to keep her tone measured and controlled. "You endure no such constraints. No asinine requirement to tolerate a nanny." She shot Finn a glare. "A nanny who could use a good shave, no less."

It was Finn's turn to send a scowl her way. "I cannot imagine yer parents ever managed to keep a nanny on staff. Even when ye were a wee lass, I'd wager ye ran about, getting yerself into every fix ye could conjure up."

"I was a studious child," she countered. "I spent many an hour with my face in a book."

Finn's eyes flashed. "And just as many driving yer governess-es to drink."

"In that case, I hope you possess an ample supply of liquor to see you through the next fortnight."

"My account at the Rogue's Lair is in good standing. I expect that will suffice."

Oh, what a frustrating man!

"I do not appreciate having my wings clipped." She punctuated her words with another glare. "Nor do I intend to be put up for inspection, night after night, an heiress up for bidding."

"Believe me, I have no intention of clipping yer blasted wings," Finn said, heat penetrating his tone. "Personally, I could not give a rat's arse about the balls ye attend or whether ye're spotted at the right party. As for yer photographic endeavors, I have no reason to stand in yer way. I will escort ye about the city as needed, standing at the ready should ye require my assistance."

She planted her hands on her hips. "I do not foresee a need for any *assistance* you might render."

"I had not taken ye for a naive lass. Surely ye can envision Lord Roaming Hands seeking to take advantage while Jon is not around. If ye need protection, I will be there."

"I have my own methods to deter *Lord Roaming Hands,* or any other stoat-faced bloke who grows too bold. I am quite adept at using my own weapons."

"Weapons, my dear Miss Mason?" Finn regarded her with a lazy half-smile. "And what might those be?"

"A well-placed knee works wonders," she replied, as Jon nodded his agreement. So, he recalled the rather infamous incident with the Earl of Addlepate, or whatever the sot's blasted name was.

"She's right," Jon said, adding a small wince for emphasis. "You taught the man a lesson he won't soon forget."

"A fan snapped against the knuckles sends a powerful message. As does a parasol to the midsection or across the bridge of the nose," Macie went on, proud of her repurposing of classic instruments of feminine wiles.

His expression glum, Jon raked a hand through his hair. "Again, she's right."

"And it goes without saying that a lady will be forgiven for not-so-accidentally tipping her sherry onto a persistent suitor if he becomes overly vexing."

Finn's gaze met hers. "So, ye've got it all figured out, do ye?"

"I believe I do."

His expression shifted to something less inviting. Nearly grim. "Ye're prepared for civilized men in environments which rein them in. But there are men out there, Macie—and women—who view others as prey. Are ye prepared for that?"

"Well," she said, gathering her thoughts. "I do not associate with those sorts."

"Yes, ye do." Finn's tone had gone hard, raw at the edges. "The predators are there, hiding in plain sight. Yer bony knee and trusty fan will not deter them from taking what they want."

She met his eyes, hoping to spot a trace of humor. But there was none to be found. "It isn't like you to be so dramatic."

Slowly, he shook his head. "Ye've never been on your own, Macie. Never been in the city without yer brother or someone else who might shield ye from its ugly underbelly."

"It's not as if I intend to roam the likes of Whitechapel," she scoffed.

"Come now, Macie. Surely ye realize a gentleman garbed in finery may pose a greater threat than a cutpurse roaming the rookeries. Not even yer parasol will protect ye if a predator sees ye are without an adequate defense."

"And that's where you come in?"

"I blend in with the dandies in the ballroom. But I'm not one of them." Finn's gaze hardened. "They know it. They won't try anything with me around."

"My, my, Mr. Caldwell. I'd no idea you had such a dangerous side. Is there something shocking in your past?"

He chuckled, an unhappy sound. "More than ye would want to know."

Something about Finn's expression intrigued her, even as a knot twisted deep within her. *Dash it all.* She did not want to admit it. But he was right. Even with Nell by her side, she was vulnerable. Especially if an unscrupulous man saw a ruthless path to her dowry.

Staring down at the intricate pattern on the Aubusson carpet, she mulled her options. The very thought of returning home so soon landed in her belly like a lead weight. She had only begun to capture the images for her exhibition. She certainly wasn't about to stop now. Besides, if they were forced to make a premature departure, Nell would be devastated. Her friend had so eagerly looked forward to this time. But remaining in London alone was not entirely practical, especially if Macie planned to be out and about, capturing the history and beauty of the city with her lens.

Dash it all. The rogue-turned-saint was her best hope. She had wanted to enlist him in tarnishing her blasted *good name.* But now, Finn was to be her protector.

How bloody ironic.

She'd simply have to make the best of it. Finn's presence might actually prove useful. She supposed she could endure a bodyguard. Especially one who could give Adonis a run for his money. She could go along with Jon's scheme.

But on *her* terms.

"As much as it pains me to say it, I agree with you."

As her brother appeared ready to sigh with relief, a look of surprise washed over Finn. "I can't recall ever hearing those words from yer lips," Finn said.

"I suspect you may never again." She glanced down at her hands as her teeth grazed her lower lip. "The situation calls for a semblance of protection. The defense you will provide is better than none."

"A whole-hearted endorsement if ever I've heard one," Finn said dryly.

"Trust me, I would not even describe it as half-hearted." She lifted her gaze, meeting his eyes. "As you well know, I'm in a bit of a fix. If you wish to play the chivalrous knight, then so be it."

"Good," Jon said. "Now that we've settled Finn's role—"

"His *role* is not settled," she said, steeling her voice. "I have some conditions."

"Oh, good God," Jon mumbled, plowing his hand through his hair yet again. At this rate, gray hair would be the least of his worries, as he was in danger of raking himself bald.

"I am not a girl fresh out of the schoolroom. This is not my first London expedition, and until I find myself wearing a wedding ring and a shiny new title, Papa's mandated husband hunt will continue. At least for another year or so, when he declares it—and me—a lost cause. So, it is to my advantage to buy time by keeping potential suitors at bay."

"You're scheming again, Macie." Jon began to pace. "I can see it in your eyes."

"Call it whatever you will, dear brother. But I sense an opportunity. And I have you to thank for it." Inspiration percolated in Macie's brain. "You've no need to concern yourself. I give you my word that I will not embarrass Papa or further tarnish the family's questionably good name. What I have in mind is between me," she said, her gaze shifting to Finn, "and my gallant protector."

Chapter Seven

F INN LEANED AN elbow against a massive bookshelf in Jon's study and glanced toward the door. If he had any sense, he'd run while he still could. His friend's plan might have been uncomplicated and logical, but if life had taught him anything, it was that the end result of any scenario involving his sister would be anything but simple.

Macie studied him with those keenly intelligent emerald eyes of hers. *I sense an opportunity.* If ever a man had a reason to run for the hills, her pronouncement summed it up beyond all argument. Especially since the opportunity involved him.

Blast it all, it would be easier to turn away if his own cursed curiosity hadn't taken control. For some reason he couldn't even explain to himself, her expression intrigued him, even more than her words. Of course, the fact that her emerald-green walking suit hugged her curves in all the right places didn't help matters. She'd appealed to him even in the bloody abysmal gown she'd worn at Lady Drayton's soiree, but today, in the light of day and wearing hues that did not resemble the muck in a stable, he could take in her natural beauty without distraction. In his gut, he knew he would not like what she was about to propose. But like a moth nearing the heat of a flame, he did not veer away before it was too late.

Finn met her gaze. "What manner of scandal are ye devising now?"

A hint of a smile curved her full mouth. "Scandal?" she scoffed unconvincingly. "Why, I wouldn't think of it. After all, I promised that I will not tarnish the family name."

By thunder, the woman was maddening. And so blasted fascinating, he could not look away. Let alone leave.

"Then what is it ye want of me?"

The corners of her mouth pulled higher. "A distraction, if you will."

"A distraction?" Jon echoed. His brow had furrowed like a washerwoman's board.

Her shoulders rose and fell in a little shrug. "I suppose *decoy* would be more to the point."

Decoy? "What in thunder are ye getting at?" Finn pinned her with his gaze, expecting the truth.

"I suppose that is the correct term. Rather like the replica of an owl on the barn at our country home—it keeps away undesired creatures."

Jon pinched the bridge of his nose. "Have you gone a bit mad, Macie?"

"No, she hasn't." Finn didn't like it one whit, but he took her meaning. "Ye think to use me to frighten off a man who shows an interest in ye."

Her slight smile transformed into a grin. "Precisely, Mr. Caldwell. My, you are a clever one." She cocked a brow. "Played right, this little game might actually prove entertaining."

"Count me out." Finn had had enough. He had come to London to arrange a deal between Mason's enterprises and his family's business. Being a blasted human scarecrow was not part of the bargain.

Macie pulled out a chair, swished her skirts out of the way, and took a seat. "Won't you join me, Mr. Caldwell?" she said, patting the chair at her side.

He sent her a look that made it clear he had no intention of accepting her invitation. Or was it a command? "I don't know where this *Mr. Caldwell* has come from. I've been *Finn* to ye since ye were a girl in braids."

She shrugged again. "But I am not a girl in braids any longer. And since propriety is a virtue, I thought a more *proper* form of address appropriate."

"In any case, suffice it to say I will play no part in chasing away yer suitors."

"Chase away?" She pursed her coral lips. "No, that won't be necessary. Your very presence will serve as a deterrent." Her gaze swept over him, from the tip of his boots to his head. "You are, after all, a rather imposing man, with your height and what I presume are genuine muscles under your suit."

Finn could not resist his own curiosity. "Genuine muscles?"

"It's rather a long story, I'm afraid, but there was one rather unfortunate marquis who thought to impress the ladies with his powerful physique. Unfortunately, at one point during a rather vigorous dance—the polka, as I recall, or was it the mazurka?— the padding beneath his jacket slipped. You can only imagine the poor man's mortification when his *broad shoulders* ended up somewhere they should not have been." She gave a little sigh. "I did feel badly for that one."

Jon nodded along. "That was a rather horrific sight. I suspect he'd also padded his thighs. After the excursion onto the ballroom floor, his knees appeared rather lumpy, didn't they?"

Macie nibbled her bottom lip, as though to stifle the giggle she could not entirely silence. "Oh, dear, I'd forgotten about that. For once, *I* was not the one who created the scene."

Jon plowed his hand through his hair. "That *was* quite a spectacle."

"Indeed." Macie smiled. "I'd wager my last shilling that will not be an issue for Finn."

"You should not be commenting on a gentleman's . . . build," Jon said, his expression weary.

"As he has pointed out, I've known him since I was a girl. In that time, I certainly was able to observe that he has acquired an athletic build from his sporting pursuits. I see no difference between that observation and noting that his eyes are brown."

Jon frowned. "You know what I mean, Macie."

"My *athletic build* is not relevant," Finn said, eyeing the door.

"To the contrary, it plays a part in the scenario I'm envisioning. I've heard rumors that you're quite good with your fists. Is it true you enjoy the sport of boxing?"

Bollocks. How much gossip had she heard about him since she returned to London? "It is true that I enter the ring from time to time."

"Well, I'm confident the scrawny milksops I've encountered in the city would not want to cross a man who is unafraid of violence."

He cocked a brow, flashed a purposeful scowl, and went to the door. "Protecting ye is one thing. Playing the role of walking and talking *lord repellent* is another. I will not create one scandal while trying to prevent another."

"Are you positive you want to leave now, Mr. Caldwell?" She cocked her chin. Her eyes were the color of a lush forest on a spring Highland morn. "I know my brother well enough to understand that he is not above applying a bit of leverage to work a situation to his advantage. Now, I don't know precisely what Jon has offered that would convince you to watch over me like an oversized governess—but are you certain you can simply leave it behind?"

Bloody hell. "Oversized governess? Shakespeare's shrew had nothing on ye, *Miss Mason.*"

Her eyes flashed. "Unlike Kate, I have no intention of being tamed."

"What man would possess the patience?" he asked coolly.

"Macie, what are you talking about?" Jon spoke up, his tone betraying his alarm.

"Come now, dear brother. Surely you don't think me so naïve as to believe Finn Caldwell's offer to serve as my unofficial bodyguard is motivated solely by a dedication to protect me from the villains who evidently lurk in every shadow of every corner in

London."

Her words cut, though Finn didn't entirely understand why he gave a damn. "I meant what I said, Macie. Ye put yerself in positions where ye're vulnerable. The *villains* might not be lurking in every shadow. But the curs are there, even in the ballrooms of the city's most affluent mavens."

Her features were set in an impassive expression, but she did not hide the scowl in her eyes. "And you, of all people, took it upon yourself to watch over me. How very noble."

Jon shot him a look of confusion, but Finn ignored it. At the moment, this was between him and Macie.

"It is nothing of the sort. We both know that. I can protect ye. It's not complicated." He felt the weight of the truth he'd omitted even as he spoke the words. He wanted the blasted contracts. The deal mattered to him. And to his family. But above that, he wanted to know Macie was safe while she was on her own in the city. He wanted to be there to watch over her. Somehow, that mattered even more than the bargain he'd made with her brother.

"You're right—it isn't complicated. The way I see it, your presence will create an illusion that will work to my advantage."

"What in blazes are ye getting at?"

"If you don't walk away . . . if you don't leave, I will tolerate your presence as bodyguard of sorts." She pulled in a breath, as though the words had been difficult for her to speak. "But in the process, you will assist me in creating an illusion."

"I'm still here," he said after a long moment. If he had any sense, he'd walk out of the door. Right then. Right there. But somehow, he couldn't leave her. "What is it ye have in mind?"

"When I'm out and about, you intend to be there, watching over my every move in the name of security. Do you not?"

"That would stand to reason."

"And if we were to give the impression that there is . . . something between us?"

"Macie, I don't like the sound of this," Jon protested.

"Is that supposed to matter to me?" Macie's gaze flared with defiance.

"Let her speak," Finn said. "It is her plan we're talking about, after all."

Jon scowled and folded his arms. "Go on, Macie."

"The way I see it, the best way to discourage an heiress hunter is to lead him to believe I am no longer on the market."

Jon began to pace. "You cannot be serious."

"Unfortunately, that strategy won't work," she said matter-of-factly. "If Father got word of anything that sounded like a betrothal without his approval—and you know he would—he might well suffer an apoplexy."

"Gads, ye would not want the man to think ye'd settle for the likes of me now, would ye?" Finn said with a deliberately bland tone.

"It's not like that," she said quickly, sounding a trifle sheepish, though Jon did not voice any disagreement with Finn's assessment.

He studied her face, seeing the touch of regret in her expression. Did she feel she'd wounded him? Somehow, that look of caring in her eyes seemed much more like that kind girl she'd once been than the enterprising woman who sought to use this situation for her benefit.

Not that she had hurt him. He possessed, above all else, a firm perspective on the realities of life in this city, with the nose-in-the-air old money types and the new-money industrialists who desperately wanted to be part of a club that did not want any part of them, other than their tin.

"What in thunder are ye planning?" he asked directly.

"As I said, I am thinking about creating an illusion. I'd like the fortune hunters to think of me as not-quite spoken for." She smiled. "After all, a man like you will stand as quite a boulder in their paths."

"Boulder, is it? So now ye're comparing me to a rock?" No wonder she suspected her father would keel over at the thought of his daughter becoming Finn's bride. He bit back the first words that sprang to mind. Definitely not suitable for a lady's ear. But then again, Macie was not the typical lady.

She gave a little shrug. "I thought it was a rather appropriate image."

"Ye still have not told me what ye intend for me to do."

"It's simple, really. You'll be there with me at the balls and soirees and gatherings I'm expected to attend. I can hear the chatter now. *The heiress and her rake.* That should be all it will take to buy a reprieve from their oh-so-dull efforts at courtship. At least until Jon returns."

"Rake? I think I preferred *boulder*."

"I'll try to remember that," she said lightly, glancing toward her brother. Jon's expression was a cross between a scowl and utter defeat. "Don't look so glum, Jon. I'm intending to have a bit of fun, that's all."

Jon slowly shook his head. "I know how your *fun* usually turns out."

"The way I look at it, the options are clear. I will be seen about town with a protective, somewhat besotted bodyguard whose presence will spur the noble nobs of London to set their sights on someone—anyone—other than me. And you, Mr. Caldwell, will get what Jon had promised you—not that I truly care to know the details of your bargain. Or I will devise a scandal that will make even rogues blush. In which case, I can only assume that you will walk away empty-handed from whatever deal you've hatched with my brother. So, which is it?" A smile played on her lips as she turned back to Finn. "Do we have an agreement?"

Chapter Eight

S CARCELY FORTY-EIGHT HOURS after he'd struck his deal with the devil in skirts, Finn lingered at the edge of some high-and-mighty aristocrat's marble ballroom, battling the urge to tug at his blasted-too-tight collar. Decked out in a jacket and trousers that had been expertly tailored to fit his frame but did not suit his soul in the least, he bided his time. Damned if he didn't feel like a fish flopping about on the bank of a river. Why in blazes had he allowed himself to become tangled in Jon's—and Macie's—schemes?

Soon after her return to London, Macie had received a coveted invitation to Lady Evansdale's moonlight gala. The former dollar princess's parties were the talk of London, and for once, Macie was eager to attend. With Finn in tow, no less. Macie saw the gathering as a crucial first test. What better opportunity to make their debut as heiress and bodyguard?

Macie's scheme was simple enough. While they were out and about at Lady Shoes-Too-Pinched's and Lady Nose-in-the-Air's parties, Finn would keep would-be suitors at arm's length. He'd offer the gossipy elites of London reason to speculate that her unofficial bodyguard was actually something more. Were they—or weren't they—enamored with one another? She wanted to keep the society types guessing. Macie would emerge both free of matrimony and with her good name intact if she could convince London's ballroom Lotharios that capturing her heart—and her fortune—was a lost cause.

Deuced shame Finn possessed no dramatic talent. The best he could do was follow her about and glare at the men who tried to impress her. If that wasn't good enough, then he'd happily escort her to the theater district to find an actual actor to fill the role of decoy.

At the moment, he was enjoying a reprieve from the act, of sorts. Macie had joined a few of the women in the ballroom for a spirited discussion. Looking on from a casual distance, he found himself reluctant to tear his attention from her. Blasted shame she had not worn another atrocity like the shroud she'd worn to Lady Drayton's affair. Tonight, she'd draped herself in pale, unadorned green silk, a flowing gown that displayed her gorgeous curves to perfection. Her natural beauty captured his gaze with a magnetic pull. Bloody hell, he didn't want to look away. At this rate, he'd convince the guests he was a lovestruck fool without even trying.

Discouraging the fortune hunters would be the easy part. He wouldn't even need to hide his contempt for the fops sniffing after Macie's money. But keeping Macie safe from her own escapades was another story.

She was a free spirit. Her keen wit made for energizing conversation while her sparkling eyes could draw a man in, seemingly without conscious effort on her part. Macie was beautiful, but she didn't seem to care. If anything, in her eyes, her loveliness was a liability. Her pretty face made her even more attractive to the *Lord Nobs* who lusted after her fortune, so she'd grown adept at dulling her natural radiance.

But tonight was different. On this night, she had not chosen a disguise. To the contrary, she had shined a beacon on herself. Half of the men in the place watched her like hungry wolves. The other half wished they could escape the knowing view of their wives and sweethearts, if only long enough to drink her in.

And he was no different. His jaw clenched at the thought.

By hellfire, he needed a distraction. Spotting one of Jon's business partners, he engaged him in an increasingly half-hearted conversation. Edmund Barlow might have possessed a genius for making money, but as the man droned on, Finn started looking for another diversion. How in blazes could Jon and his associate endure the trivial logistics of their latest venture? To Finn, it was a bloody mystery. He'd never given a damn about squeezing every penny of profit from an enterprise. Putting Scrooge to shame haggling over the cost of linens was not in his nature. Designing a new structure or planning the restoration of a past-its-prime building engaged both his intellect and his instincts.

He tugged at the tie encircling his throat. Bloody hell, the length of silk felt like a noose. He seldom bothered with such formalities, but tonight, he'd put in an effort to at least look the part of Macie's devoted escort. God knew he didn't belong here, surrounded by elites who turned up their noses at the likes of him.

He had money. More money than most of these highborn milksops. But in their world, that wasn't enough. Like Macie's father with his *new money* fortune, Finn's family had earned their wealth. In the eyes of pasty nobles and elite sots, the notion of actually working for a shilling was beneath them. But marrying into a fortune—that was different.

How bloody ironic.

Finn's father had toiled day and night to parlay their family distillery into a thriving enterprise that supplied whisky to the finest establishments in Scotland. For decades, his father had endeavored to secure the company's future. Now it was Finn's turn.

God only knew his father seldom looked upon him with pride. Not that he could blame his father. In the years after he'd graduated from university, he had not distinguished himself in the man's eyes. Unlike his older brother, the heir apparent and responsible model of business and propriety. This deal with the Mason empire was his chance to prove himself. To his father.

And to himself.

Considering the stakes of the fortnight to come, he pulled in a breath. The funds generated by the contracts with Mason Enterprises would ensure the company's financial stability for years to come. He had to close this deal.

It wasn't supposed to be complicated. Jon Mason was an old friend, a man he'd have trusted with his life. At one time, that is. Since they'd been rough-and-tumble lads, they had raised hell together. Jon had been there to celebrate triumphs and to offer a shoulder and a stiff drink in that horrible time when grief and guilt threatened to tear Finn's heart to pieces. But now, everything had changed. Who in blazes could ever have predicted that Jon would use the contracts Finn needed as leverage?

Bloody hell.

Truth be told, he understood Jon's motives. He needed to protect his sister, and he knew Finn would go along with his devil's bargain. If only for Macie's sake. Despite her rebellious streak, the lass had been sheltered. Macie had never seen the true ugliness of the world. Predators did not confine their deeds to deserted alleys. A carefully honed smile and expensive suit could provide a dangerous man an effective disguise.

Years ago, he had learned that hard, ugly lesson. He hadn't been able to protect his vivacious cousin from the brutal act of a so-called gentleman. An invisible fist dug into Finn's gut. After enduring the painful aftermath of Colleen's vile murder, he would not wish that misery on anyone. Not even an old friend who'd resorted to civilized blackmail.

He would protect Macie. Whether or not she liked it.

While other guests chatted amiably and aimlessly, Finn's attention drifted back to Macie. She stood by an elegantly appointed table laden with ridiculously small bits of cake, engaged in conversation with their hostess. By thunder, Macie's hands moved as animatedly as her mouth. Lady Evansdale, now the widow of an earl, had taken to the suffragette cause since her husband's untimely demise—a cause Macie appeared eager to join.

Intrigued by this woman he'd known since she was a girl, he

followed Macie's every gesture. Took in every smile. Drank in the way her almond-shaped green eyes gleamed with unabashed delight. She was a beauty. With her deep brown hair swept into an appealing style and her elegant gown, she could've had her pick of every unattached man in the place. But Macie had no interest in flirting or seduction. Rather, she relished the opportunity to engage in a clever, energetic discussion. Watching her, he realized that he truly didn't want to look away. *How blasted strange.*

Forcing himself to focus on something—anything—but Macie, he glanced around at the lavish decor. Ladies in silk conversed as light from the chandeliers reflected off their gems. Men clad in suits of the finest wool tugged at their tight collars when they thought their wives were not looking. A dark-haired jewel of the London stage strolled past, her hand resting on the arm of an obscenely wealthy industrialist. She flashed a coquettish smile, then turned a narrow-eyed gaze on the prune of a man who'd financed her West End play.

The beautiful soprano cast a lingering glance over her shoulder, but Finn's attention wandered. Not long before that night, he might have felt emboldened by the invitation in her gaze. He might have endeavored to charm his way into her bed. But now, the thought left him cold.

Tonight, he could scarcely take his eyes off Macie.

How bloody unexpected.

With considerable effort, he forced his attention to study the intricate mural on the ceiling. The artist had not rivaled Michelangelo. But the painter had achieved quite a feat with the complexity of the work.

Yet again, his gaze drifted to Macie, a magnet pulling to true north.

It was a bloody losing battle.

While conversing with Macie and their hostess, Nell slanted him a glance. A slight smile tipped up the corners of her mouth. Had she noticed the way his attention had riveted to Macie? She took a small sip from her glass, as if to disguise her amusement. Suddenly, Nell appeared to choke on her drink.

A man whose suit hung too loosely on his long-limbed frame approached the women. *Lord Drayton.* But Nell looked past him, appearing to search for someone.

Bollocks. Was the man's harpy of a mother close behind?

Finn moved closer, observing their hostess's cordial greeting to Lady Drayton's spawn and the conversation that followed. Though he couldn't make out their words, the women appeared quite engaged by the astronomer's remarks.

Continuing to stay at a distance, Finn watched as Macie snapped open her lace fan with a flick of her wrist, lightly fanning herself while a smile played on her mouth. Was it his imagination, or had she actually blushed? He had not believed it possible, but this gangly, falling-over-his-own-feet man appeared to be melting Macie's ice right before their eyes.

Bloody hell, had she cast aside her plan to dissuade the fortune hunters so soon? His job might be easier than he'd thought. Of all the titled snobs in London, Drayton might well be the least opportunistic. The man spent his nights staring out of a telescope and his days composing academic studies of his findings. He seemed good-natured. Harmless. Certainly not a rake who would motivate Finn to roll up his sleeves and teach him a lesson about the dangers of attempting to compromise a lady.

So why did the thought of tossing the overly solicitous lord straight through the door—and down the marble steps for good measure—appeal to him?

It was high time he saw what the man was up to. Finn edged toward the women as they continued their discussion with Drayton. He thought he might send the bloke a well-timed glare, but Nell stepped into Drayton's line of sight.

"I understand you're a fellow of the Royal Astronomical Society," she said. "I've heard you are tracking a comet."

He offered a nod. "You know of my work?"

Nell's smile lit her blue eyes as she and the astronomer animatedly discussed some giant ball of cosmic gas the man sought to discover.

"With any luck, I will have the good fortune to study under Sir George Darwin," Drayton went on, his tone surprisingly humble.

A rosy hue tinted Nell's cheeks. "How fascinating."

"A marvelous opportunity, indeed," Macie said blandly. Was she growing bored with the aristocrat so soon?

"But enough about me." Drayton regarded Macie with unfiltered interest. "I must confess, I am curious about your name. Macie is rather unique. Is there a story behind it?"

"As with most things regarding my dear friend, there *is* a story," Nell said with a chuckle.

"Indeed." Macie smiled. "When I was a little girl, my oh-so-proper name, Mary Catherine, seemed a bit much to pronounce. Mum began to call me Macie."

"I suspect she enjoyed the irony of naming you after your father's American rival," Finn said, making his presence known.

She flashed a fetching grin. "He has learned to live with it."

"Your name conveys a vibrant spirit. It suits you." Drayton drew yet another smile from Macie.

The man is certainly laying it on thick. Much more of this, and Macie would find herself betrothed before her brother returned. A stroke of luck, if ever Finn had heard of one.

Blasted shame Finn wasn't in a mood to appreciate his good fortune.

IN THE MOMENTS after Lady Evansdale had excused herself to continue her duties as hostess, Macie struggled to hide her disappointment. She had thoroughly enjoyed their conversation, hanging on the widow's every word as she'd recounted attending one of the American suffragist Susan B. Anthony's invigorating speeches. But now, as Lord Drayton blathered on—and on—Macie glanced at the ornate grandfather clock. Surely enough time had passed that she could gently make her exit.

Finn had already made his escape. Or so it seemed. He'd offered to fetch her another drink, but it appeared he had somehow become lost on his return. At the moment, Macie possessed neither a beverage nor patience. Perhaps she'd plead a sudden need for fresh air and venture to the garden. Alone, if need be.

And then, she spotted him. Bearing two crystal glasses, Finn deftly navigated the crush. She didn't want to admit it, but her so-called protector looked particularly dashing. His golden-brown hair brushed his collar, beckoning her touch. Never a dandy, he wore a dark coat and trousers that had been precisely tailored to his lean, muscular frame. His linen shirt was pristine, while the ivory tie at his throat stirred all manner of thoughts. First, she'd free the knot and glide the length of silk from his body. The pearly white buttons on his shirt would come next.

Oh dear. Macie hoped she had not flushed. Why, if anyone could read her mind, they would be utterly scandalized. She bit back a grin. Was it any wonder she was losing patience with the astronomer's detailed expositions regarding his newest acquisition, a state-of-the-art telescope for his personal observatory?

Offering a tight smile with the flute of champagne, Finn came to stand close—perhaps too close—by her side. "For ye, my dear Macie."

He regarded her with a look she supposed was meant to appear adoring. Unfortunately, his features looked pinched, and his overly solicitous tone didn't fit him at all. Was it so very difficult to pretend an interest in her?

"Thank you," she said, and he edged even nearer. Much more, and he might well tread on her skirt. She shot him a glare as she took a step to the side, just in time to avoid his shoe treading upon her hem. What in blazes was he up to? She'd observed his casual ease with women long enough to know him to be far from a clumsy oaf. Did he think this would discourage her from her plan?

Nell's brow furrowed, but she happily accepted the glass he offered. "You simply must tell Lord Drayton about our latest adventure," she said. "The ghost in the chapel. In Cardiff."

"Oh, *that*." Macie reflected on the memory. "It may have been a trick of the light."

"You must admit, the image you captured looks very much like a spirit," Nell replied. "A rather nasty-looking phantom who might've given Mr. Dickens a nightmare or two, at that."

"Whatever it was, I did not find it frightening. Not in the least."

"She is quite brave," Nell went on. "I fear I would have fainted dead away."

"It's a good thing I did not. Just lying there, I fear I would have resembled a sack of grain."

"The key is to swoon gracefully." Nell's carefully timed glance slid to Lord Drayton. "But only when a gentleman is there to catch you."

"I cannot say that I possess any experience with swooning." Macie smiled to herself. "Would taking a spill in a puddle of wine count?"'

Drayton appeared to resist the urge to chuckle. "Ah, the unfortunate ballroom incident."

"Oh, Macie, *that* was not a swoon," Nell declared. "A true swoon would be slower. More gentle. Rather graceful, I'd imagine."

"Rest assured, if I were lying unconscious on cold marble, I'd not give a fig about the art of the swoon. Graceful or otherwise," Macie countered.

"According to an article in an esteemed ladies' magazine, swooning is most effective when one is *not* truly unconscious," Nell went on, undeterred. "Of course, a lady should be within arm's reach of a gentleman." She slid Finn a pointed glance. "Or perhaps, a rogue."

Finn met the good-natured teasing with a touch of a smile. "Ye wound me, Miss Blake."

"There is a saying." Nell cocked a brow. "If the shoe fits."

He scrubbed a palm against his cheek. "I cannot say I've ever drawn a reference to Cinderella before."

Drayton cleared his throat. "Mother was relieved you were not injured," he said. "She prides herself on being the consummate hostess." Was that a touch of sarcasm in his tone?

"Please, do reassure your mother her reputation for graciousness remains untarnished," Macie replied. "She certainly could not have anticipated a puddle of wine beneath my slipper."

"Tell me, Miss Mason, what have you chosen as the subject of your latest work?" Drayton said, deftly changing the subject.

"Before we undertake the restoration of my grandfather's mansion, I plan to capture the nuances of its past, the beauty the years have not dimmed."

"Tell him the truth, Macie," Nell spoke up. "Your grandfather thought the house was haunted. You're hoping to find a ghost to capture with your lens. Just as we did in that old chapel."

Finn's brows hiked. "Ye believe ye encountered a phantom?"

"Indeed," Nell said with a nod. "The spirit in that gloomy place was not a trick of the light. I found it rather alarming. But Macie did not so much as flinch."

"It would take more than a ghost to send me into a dither," Macie said truthfully.

"Ye'd be wise to exercise caution in decrepit old buildings," Finn said. "If the staircase is unstable, a specter might be the least of yer worries."

"Words of caution from London's most daring rogue." Macie pinned him with her gaze. "Isn't it true you attempted to scale the Stirling Old Bridge while you were on holiday from university?"

"An exaggeration, though I won't deny my reckless youth," he replied. "But that does not change the fact that ye take too many chances."

"Surely you are not afraid I will get in over my head."

Challenge flashed in his eyes. "It would not be the first time."

"And likely not the last. I may now be London's answer to Calamity Jane following my unladylike tumble."

"We both know I was not referring to dangers to yer dignity," Finn said. "I'm more concerned with that pretty neck of yers."

She shot him a deliberately cheeky grin. "So, Mr. Caldwell, given your concern for my well-being, the question is—the next time I fall, will you be there to catch me?"

"Do ye have any doubt?" A look of mischief brewed in Finn's eyes. "Shall we test out Miss Blake's theory?"

Oh, dear.

"Theory?" Macie choked out the word.

"Of swooning," he said matter-of-factly.

Macie squared her shoulders, shoring her resolve. "As tempting as the idea may be, I have no desire to swoon tonight. Or any other night, for that matter."

An emotion she couldn't quite read filled his eyes. The teasing look had faded away, and a rather serious expression had taken its place. It was all part of the act. Wasn't it?

"Very well, Macie. But remember this: if you fall, I *will* be there to catch ye."

Chapter Nine

ANOTHER NIGHT. ANOTHER *ball. Another noble Nob to outwit.*
Macie sighed. Her life had fallen into an irksomely predictable pattern.

She'd imagined her romantic charade with Finn might prove amusing. But she hadn't anticipated that Finn was perhaps the worst actor in all of England. Other than the heartwarming pledge he'd uttered at Lady Evansdale's ball, he had been anything but convincing. Was it truly a Herculean task to appear smitten?

Memories of the night before taunted her. *Will you be there to catch me?* Her teasing query echoed in her thoughts. Again. And again.

Had she actually flirted with Finn? Most likely, he'd believed her words had been part of their act, intended to create the illusion she desired.

Or had he seen through her carefully crafted smile to the truth?

Typically quick with a witty retort, he'd paused for a breath or two as he appeared to search for a glib reply. But his response, when it came, had turned the tables.

"Do ye have any doubt?" His words had been spoken with a banter-like quality. Yet, she'd seen the intensity in Finn's gaze, a heat flickering there that even the sly grin playing on his mouth had not cooled.

Tempting, indeed. Far, far too tempting.

And now, she sat by a fountain at yet another party, her thoughts dulling the pleasant noises of an orchestra and oh-so-genteel guests.

Years before, at some posh gala whose hostess she could not name, Macie had been barely seventeen. The dances and balls and soirees were still rather exciting then, even though she preferred to remain on the periphery and watch the goings-on. She could still remember the sight of Finn as he'd entered the ballroom that evening. He'd been all of twenty. His features had been less chiseled than now, his chest and shoulders not quite as well-muscled. But he was undeniably handsome, and her breath caught as he met her gaze. But there was more—a bit of contradiction about her brother's roguish friend she'd found quite intriguing.

She hadn't been able to puzzle him out, as she could quite readily with most of Jon's associates. She'd seen how effortlessly Finn drew the female gaze with the slightest amused crook of his mouth. The ladies who preened with their prettiest smiles and corset-enhanced bosoms never looked past his witty charm. Yet, there had been a seriousness about him he could not entirely conceal, a sense of sadness only revealed when he let down his guard.

Even then, somehow, she'd known Finn was different from the heiress hunters who desired a taste of her father's fortune far more than they hungered for her kiss. Then—as now—he'd possessed the ability to leave her feeling thoroughly vexed. Yet, her every instinct had insisted she could trust him, though she couldn't put her reasons into words. Now, nearly a decade after she'd caught sight of him across some dignified lady's ballroom, she still put her faith in him.

And she was still drawn to him. To the humor in his eyes. To his brash confidence. And more than anything, to the thoughtful seriousness he'd shown to her, even when he'd hidden it from the world.

Now, Finn stood by a massive stone hearth in Lady Brookshire's palatial home, carrying on a spirited reminiscence with an old acquaintance with whom he'd presumably raised the devil during their days at university. On the other side of the room, Nell animatedly conversed with Lord Drayton. The astronomer now seemed to turn up at every function Nell attended.

Seeking to escape her own thoughts, Macie searched for a diversion. Scanning the crush, she spied a familiar face. Goodness, were her eyes deceiving her? She navigated through the crowd, hoping for a better look at the tall man with unruly sable brown hair who stood near the door to the main hall. His neatly tailored suit was the same shade as his dark hair, while his white necktie appeared slightly off-kilter, as though it had been looped around his throat in quite a hurry.

Surely that wasn't the newly minted university professor who'd assisted her grandfather in cataloging his collection. Was it? She hadn't laid eyes on Peter Aylesworth in at least two years. He'd been in Greece—exploring an ancient temple or something of that nature—at the time of her grandfather's funeral and had sent his regrets. In the past, he'd made it clear he disliked currying the favor and funds of the moneyed elites of London society. But as she made her way through the crush, she felt certain the man—who looked as ready to make his escape as she was—was indeed Mr. Aylesworth.

As they made eye contact, a spark of recognition brightened his expression. Suddenly, he no longer appeared bored. To the contrary, a smile pulled at his mouth.

He closed the distance between them. "Miss Mason, it is you, isn't it?"

"The one and only," she said, flashing a small smile. "I must say, this is a pleasant surprise."

"Indeed." His brown-eyed gaze swept over her. "It has been quite some time, hasn't it?"

"Too long," Macie said. "I understand you've been exploring ruins near the Mediterranean."

He nodded. "The site has yielded a trove of pottery, among other relics."

"It all sounds quite fascinating." Macie pictured the small figure of Athena on the bookshelf behind Grandpapa's desk. "My grandfather was intrigued by the art of that era."

"Indeed, he was."

Macie met his smile. My, she'd forgotten how young Aylesworth had been when he first began assisting and advising her grandfather. Only the crinkles around his eyes and the few sprinkles of silver at his temples betrayed the passing of the years. He was a bit older than her brother, perhaps in the midst of his thirties. He was handsome, especially when he wore those gold-rimmed spectacles. But somehow, she'd never taken the time to notice. Perhaps it was the way the youthful professor had been so very serious about his work. Or perhaps it was the faint air of intellectual superiority that he had not yet learned to suppress.

"Your knowledge was invaluable to him. My grandfather's intellectual curiosity never abated. Up to his last days, he learned as much as he could about the beautiful items he collected and donated."

"Mr. Bennington—your grandfather—was a brilliant man. I was deeply saddened to learn I would never again have the opportunity to discuss my latest explorations with him."

"He relished those conversations. At times, he could become a bit fixed in his opinions, but he so enjoyed an invigorating debate."

"My colleagues at the university could not have kept pace with him."

"Oh, I don't doubt that. Not one whit," Macie said. "How long will you be in London before adventure calls?"

"I expect to remain in the city for at least six months. I am working on a new field of study and will be involved in research before I return to Greece."

"Someday, I shall travel to Athens," she said. "I'd love to prepare an exhibit there."

"Don't put it off." His expression grew serious. "I've seen the mood you can invoke with your camera."

His words caught her by surprise. "You've attended one of my exhibits?"

"I cannot say as I have. But I shall seize the first opportunity." He smiled. "Your grandfather was very proud of your talent. He showed me some of your photographs. Very impressive, Miss Mason."

The thought of her grandfather proudly sharing her art warmed her heart. "Thank you."

Aylesworth's gaze trailed over her shoulder. His expression shifted. "It would appear we have company."

Finn strolled toward them, his strides long and relaxed. "Aylesworth, it's been a long time."

A cryptic smile tugged at the professor's mouth. "I'd heard you were squiring Miss Mason about town in Jon's absence."

Finn's gaze hardened. He moved closer to Macie. Possessively so. Her pulse raced, and she pulled in a low breath.

"That's not the only reason I'm here with her tonight." His voice was low, with a flinty edge.

Aylesworth shrugged. "I'm not surprised Jon enlisted you to watch over his sister. You do know how to make a man rue the moment he decided to raise his fists against you." His gaze hardened. "But then again, so do I."

"Raised fists?" Macie spoke up. "I don't much like the direction this conversation has taken."

"My apologies, Miss Mason." To her surprise, a brief grin played on Aylesworth's lips. "Caldwell and I are old acquaintances. We shared a mutual interest in pugilism."

"Good God, man. Ye make it sound so blasted civilized." The tension on Finn's face eased into a look of familiarity. "Neither of us played by gentlemen's rules."

Aylesworth pointed to the slight crook in the bridge of his nose. "At times, I can still feel the crack of your knuckles. You left your mark, my friend."

"Ye got yer payback. Cracked my rib, as I recall." Finn uttered the rather unpleasant reminiscence in a casual tone.

Macie marveled at the scene. Two intelligent, educated men, looking rather pleased over memories of pummeling one another. Would she ever understand the male of the species?

"Two of them, if memory serves," Aylesworth corrected.

"That's right." Finn's hand went to his side, indicating the site of the injuries. "But enough reminiscing. I would not want Macie to think me a brute." He gently placed his hand on her forearm, the gesture proper. Yet somehow, rather intimate.

Aylesworth quirked a brow. "Not a brute. But definitely a fighter."

"Which ye'd do well to remember," Finn said, his tone cocky.

Macie's breath caught. Throughout the evening, Finn had showed little interest in their charade. But now, he was playing his part a bit too well.

"Ah, there you are!" Nell's voice cut through the quiet tension. Thankful for the distraction, Macie turned on her heel to see that she was not alone. *Gads.* Lord Drayton walked by her side, looking as if his toes were rather pinched.

"Mr. Aylesworth, I had not expected to see you here," Nell sounded a bit too pleased at the unplanned reunion. Years earlier, she'd harbored a girlish crush on the professor. Judging from the excitement in her eyes, it would not take much to rekindle that flame.

Following an exchange of pleasantries, the professor took a rather deliberate look at his watch. "I'm afraid I must part company. I am scheduled to meet with one of the museum patrons. Our little chat is the primary reason I came tonight. I do hope you all understand."

"Of course we do," Nell said brightly. "Now that you've returned to London, I do hope we will have the pleasure of an invigorating conversation."

"Indeed," Aylesworth's gaze shifted from Nell to Macie. "You may count on it."

THE MORNING AFTER Lady Brookshire's party, as Macie set up her camera on the pavement steps beyond the red brick exterior of Bennington Manor, her tripod was frustratingly unstable. She attempted to properly position a support that was not quite level, but the device stubbornly resisted her efforts to right it. As she fiddled with the cantankerous metal legs, her thoughts were as off kilter as the camera stand.

Encountering Professor Aylesworth at the gathering had been a delightful surprise. Reminiscing about her grandfather with a man who'd actually seen his brilliant mind at work had been quite enjoyable. Until Finn strode up and the conversation shifted to long-ago bouts of fisticuffs and such. At one point, Finn had actually seemed possessive of her, perhaps even a bit jealous. Had he been merely playing his part in their scheme? Or had the steely tension in his eyes been real?

"Might I assist with your equipment?" Nell's question pulled Macie back to the moment and, thankfully, back to the task at hand. There was little time to waste. The low haze in the sky created an atmosphere that was perfect for the concept Macie wanted to create. Best to capture the image before the clouds shifted and the sky became too foreboding and gray.

"Thank you, but not yet." Macie tugged on one leg of the tripod, adjusting it with the other supports. The cobbles in the pavement were not ideal for leveling her camera, but she wasn't about to let a bit of inconvenience stymie her. She would portray the beauty of the magnificent old home for others to appreciate. Just as she did.

Her grandfather's house—somehow, it still felt like his home—wore the passage of time like an embellishment. Some might call the subtle marks in the brick facade blemishes. To Macie, they were signs of character, remnants of its storied history, of the decades long past when her ancestors had lived and died within those walls.

"Nell, I believe I left my lens case in the parlor," she said, fiddling with the uncooperative tripod. "Would you get it, please?"

"Of course." Nell hurried up the front steps and into the house.

Macie made another adjustment, setting the camera level atop the tripod. "Finally." She studied the building, contemplating the image she wished to capture.

A sudden coolness washed over her. A sensation like icy fingers trailed over her nape. *How very odd.* There was no hint of breeze. Not so much as a wisp of wind that might have chilled her. An innate warning murmured in her thoughts.

Was someone watching her?

Turning toward the street, she faced the house across the road. A tall, lean man stood an arm's length from the townhouse's massive front porch. His bushy gray brows lifted slightly as his pale eyes met her gaze. His focus seemed to intensify, as if he was studying her.

The chill along her hairline trailed down her spine, and she broke eye contact. *Don't be a goose.* The gent was old enough to be her father, after all. Quite possibly his vision was not precise and he'd confused her for someone else. There was no cause for alarm.

Pity her body's instincts did not agree.

She glanced back at him. Was he in need of assistance? Perhaps she should cross over and speak to him, if only to be sure.

Slowly, the elderly man shook his head. *How very peculiar.* Had he anticipated her intention to come to him? He turned away then, ambling at a steady pace down the street. Away from the house. Away from Bennington Manor.

"Macie, is something wrong?" Nell hurried down the front stairs, case in hand.

"Not at the moment."

Macie pulled in a long breath, attempting to calm her slightly accelerated pulse. Try as she might, she could not entirely cast off her reaction to the man who'd seemed to be watching her.

Nell's gaze swept over her features. "You're quite sure?"

"Of course." Macie wished she believed her own words.

Nell turned to catch sight of the elderly gent making his way along the cobblestones. "I saw the way that man was staring at you. Do you know who he is?"

"I don't recall ever laying eyes on him before today."

"Perhaps he knew your grandfather."

"That could well be the case," Macie agreed. Nell's suggestion was reasonable. Utterly rational. But deep within, she sensed the explanation was not quite so simple.

She reached for her lenses. "Let's get to work, shall we? The light is perfect."

Nell threw another glance behind her. "Macie, there is one thing that seemed a bit odd to me."

Macie quirked a brow. "Just one thing?"

"This was not the first time I've seen that gentleman."

A slight jolt of alarm coursed through Macie. "Here?"

Nell nodded. "I noticed him one day last week. If memory serves, you were inside, fiddling with your camera. I'd come out onto the porch for a breath of cool air when I saw a posh carriage roll up." She toyed with the lacy scarf at her throat. "The man descended from the coach, took a brief look about the area, then looked away as soon as he saw me. Moments later, he entered the carriage, and it rattled off as suddenly as it had arrived."

"You're certain it was the same man?"

"I am not absolutely sure." Nell's brows knit together in a frown. "But I do believe the man we saw today was in that carriage. I cannot help but wonder why someone—even if he was indeed an acquaintance of your grandfather—would come here on two separate occasions, only to turn and leave without ever saying a word."

Chapter Ten

PUNCTUALITY WAS A virtue Macie had never aspired to possess. Since she was a girl, her family had teased that *Macie-time* could not be accurately measured by the hands on a clock. It wasn't that she did not want to follow a schedule or did not attempt to arrive at appointments at the arranged time. Rather, it was a matter of her keen interest in the pursuits that captured her attention. From the days in her childhood when she sat in the garden, painting flowers with her watercolors, to these enjoyable moments expressing her creativity through the lens of her camera, she'd immersed herself in the creative challenges she found fascinating. And in the process, her awareness of time faded into the background. So, when Nell's pointed tones cut through the pleasant tranquility she'd found behind the camera that afternoon, Macie was not surprised she'd lost track of time.

"Macie, I don't want to be *that person* who goes about reminding others about the virtues of punctuality." Nell made a point of tapping the small watch she wore pinned to her lapel.

"But we really must be running along if we are going to make it to Lady Yarbury's soiree." Macie flashed a little smile. "I suspect your concern has less to do with punctuality than with the expected presence of that dashing viscount who recently returned from an expedition. Lord . . . Lord Highbrow. Something like that."

"As you well know, his name is Daniel Craigston." Interest

flashed in Nell's eyes as she uttered the Egyptologist's name. "I understand he is quite esteemed in his field."

Macie could not help but grin at the enthusiasm in her friend's voice. "I hear he is very much available."

"He is. For now," Nell said with a conspiratorial tone. "If we hurry, I'll have time to slip into something a bit *less* sensible."

Macie quirked a brow. "A bit more decadent, perhaps?"

"Oh, dear. Have you developed the ability to read my mind?" Nell teased.

"I know you very well. Neither of us possesses a talent for disguising our thoughts and feelings."

"How very true." Nell smiled. "Perhaps one of Professor Craigston's colleagues will be in attendance this evening. Wouldn't it be something if you fell for an explorer? The mere thought of riding off on an expedition through the desert heats my blood."

"Does it now?"

"Ah, yes." Nell's voice was ever so slightly breathless. "I can imagine how dashing he might be, atop an Arabian stallion, riding off into the sunset."

Macie's brows lifted higher. "With you, of course?"

Nell's cheeks flushed. "Of course. Heading off to some vibrant oasis."

"Goodness, what sorts of sensation novels have you been reading lately?"

"The best kind," Nell replied coyly. "Don't worry. I'm sure he'll have an equally dashing friend for you."

"Explorers come in pairs, do they?" Macie said dryly.

"I would imagine so," Nell said with a hopeful tone. "No one in his right mind would go into one of those dusty old tombs on his own. Can you imagine being swept up into an expedition with a rugged archaeologist?"

"Oh, I can see it now. My skirts flapping in the wind as I struggle to balance on some cantankerous camel's hump. Perhaps my daring explorer will catch me before I fall face-first into the sand."

"You never know. A daring explorer might be precisely the one for you."

"Only if he has a lofty title. That's the only thing that will make my father happy."

Nell's smile faded. "But does that really matter?"

"I suppose not. I'm not willing to tie myself to some highborn dolt simply to satisfy Papa's wishes." Macie pictured her beautiful, vivacious mother. So lively. So filled with joy. And so very happy with the man she had vowed to love until her last breath. "If Mum had cared about titles and all that nonsense, she would never have given my father a kiss, let alone two children. Papa had scarcely a shilling to his name when he proposed. And she's never regretted saying 'yes.'"

"They do seem quite content with one another."

"Content?" Macie smiled to herself. "My mother would never have settled for mere contentment. I've seen how she looks at Papa. Even now. At times, his stubborn ways drive her mad, but he can melt away her irritation with a smile."

"I must confess, I've never seen that side of her."

"Oh, I know she can seem a bit airy. But Mum possesses a fire that she rarely shows to anyone other than Papa."

"How very unexpected," Nell said. "Whoever would have imagined?"

"Mother defied her family to marry Papa. Her father threatened to disown her. But her belief in our father was fierce. Utterly unshakable. Behind a pensive smile that might have inspired da Vinci, she has a will of iron."

"Like her daughter."

Nell had spoken the words as a compliment, but Macie could not bring herself to agree. Her mother had defied Macie's grandfather and had never looked back. And yet, Macie could not bring herself to do so. Not outright. Instead, she played these rebellious games so she didn't have to tell Papa the truth. She would never substitute an existence with a titled bloke for the kind of love Mum had savored throughout many rewarding years of marriage.

Someday, Papa would give up on his dream of Macie forging a socially advantageous marriage. Sooner. Or later. With any luck.

GRIPPING THE EDGE of the seat as the coach rattled over the pavement, Macie peered into the waning daylight. Thank heavens the route to the Mayfair townhouse she shared with Nell was neither long nor arduous. The bumps in the road gave her a new appreciation for the padding afforded by her bulky skirts.

Dash it all! She pictured her sketchbook in her mind's eye. She'd placed it on the desk in her grandfather's study. Surely she had not forgotten it. She would not have been so absent-minded. Hope flickered in her thoughts. She tapped Nell on the hand to pull her out of a daydream.

"By any chance, did you think to take my book of drawings on your way out of the house?"

Nell shook her head. "I take it you left it behind?"

Drat her forgetfulness. Preoccupied with talk of dashing Egyptologists and bouncing along on camels to some sheik's oasis, she'd neglected to gather it with her equipment. She needed that book. She had planned to pass most of the night sketching scenes of the grand ballroom of the Yarburys' magnificent home with images of Finn sprinkled in for good measure. If the nosy belles helped themselves to a look, they'd come to their own convenient conclusions about her choice of subject matter.

She sat up tall in her seat. "I must retrieve it."

Nell frowned in puzzlement. "You need the notebook this evening?"

"Indeed, I do." Macie pulled a cord to alert the driver of the hansom.

"Shall we turn back, Miss Mason?" the man called from his bench.

"No need," she replied. "From here, I can walk quickly and take another cab to the house. I shall only be a bit behind schedule."

"Walk?" Nell regarded her as if she'd proposed a journey on foot to the Highlands. "Don't be silly. We'll have to go back."

"I shall enjoy the exercise and the fresh air," Macie countered.

"You won't have time to prepare for Lady Yarbury's party."

"Nell, you'll want time to ready yourself to enjoy the gathering. But you know I could not give a fig about styling my hair just so. I won't need more than a few minutes to prepare."

Her friend's brow furrowed. "Is retrieving that sketchbook truly so urgent?"

"I'll see you within the hour." Making her way out of the carriage, she smiled over her shoulder. "'Till we meet again.'"

Macie hurried away before Nell could say another word. Truth be told, she was rather looking forward to a few moments of relative peace and quiet while she made the short trek back to the mansion.

Bustling up the steps, she retrieved her key from her reticule. As she reached for the door, she stopped. With a light touch against the latch, the sturdy oak door swung inward. She'd had no need for the key in her hand. The door had not been fully closed.

How very peculiar. Pulling in a low breath, she shook off her doubts. Surely there was a simple explanation. Busy as Nell's thoughts had been with preparations for the elegant soiree—with an eligible and adventurous lord in attendance—she'd likely forgotten to secure the door. The newly stirring breeze had done the rest.

Still, a whisper of warning nagged at her. Taking one of her grandfather's canes from the stand in the entry hall, she curved her fingers around the handle. It certainly would not hurt to carry some sort of protection, just in case. Proceeding with brisk steps up the stairs to her grandfather's study, she spotted nothing out of place. As she entered the room her grandfather had considered a sanctuary, she spotted her sketchbook lying open on a marble-topped table. Rather curious, that. She was quite certain she'd left it on his desk. How had it ended up turned to a page where she'd jotted images of an old church?

Had Nell glanced over her notes? Perhaps that was it. After all, the simplest explanation tended to be the most logical.

A sudden draft from the window by the fireplace prickled her skin. Her fingers tensed around the handle of the cane. *Oh, don't be a goose.* She was letting her imagination get the better of her.

An unexpected noise cut through the echoes in the nearly silent house. A heavy *thump*. And then, another *thud*. More pronounced than footsteps, rather like the sound of something—books, perhaps—striking the floor. What in blazes was going on?

A sensation like icy raindrops trickled over her nape. Her gaze darted to the double doors connecting the study with her grandfather's library. The doors had been closed when she'd left with Nell. Now, one of the chestnut panels was ajar.

Someone was in her grandfather's library.

Someone was tossing his books to the floor.

Dear Lord. Her pulse raced. She had to leave. She could not stay in the house a moment longer. Dragging in a calming breath, she gripped the cane firmly, readying herself to use it.

Suddenly, a cry drifted to her ears. A man's voice. Weak. Quavering.

"Please . . . please, help me."

"Who's there?" Macie's heart hammered in her chest. Fear murmured in her thoughts. *Run!* But something held her back. The voice beyond the door sounded frail. Powerless. Desperate.

She reached for the glass knob. Without warning, the heavy panel shifted, tugging the knob out of her grasp. Stunned, she gazed up at a man who clutched a hefty tome against his body.

Good heavens.

She'd seen those pale eyes hours earlier while he'd stood across the street, silently watching her. This close, he seemed taller. More imposing. With his pallid skin and silver-gray hair pulled back in a queue, the elderly man might have passed for a specter from a century long past.

His lips were stretched taut, misery etching his angular features. Pressing a hand to a shelf to hold his unsteady frame upright, he held tight to the book.

"Help . . . me." The words sounded choked from his throat.

"Who are you?" Her voice sounded remarkably calm to her own ears.

Slowly, he shook his head. Was the man refusing to answer? Or was he simply too weak?

"You've been injured," she said. "Let me help you to a chair. Then I will summon a physician."

Again, he shook his head. "No." The word was a near-whisper, yet unmistakably firm.

"Tell me who you are."

He struggled to speak. His voice was a low rasp. "Murder."

Dear God. Macie's blood ran cold.

He took a lumbering step forward. Then another. Macie backed away, careful not to trap herself against the wall.

His eyes were glassy with pain. "Murder," he repeated in a low murmur.

She edged along the hallway, keeping her gaze on him. "You need help."

"Leave." His eyes implored her. "Before he comes . . . for you."

He staggered forward. Reached for her. Instinct taking over, she darted away from his grasp.

His gaze fixed on her, a wild desperation in his eyes moments before his legs buckled. Like a puppet unmoored from its strings, he collapsed. Unmoving. Still.

Too still.

Macie heard a scream. Vaguely realizing the sound had come from herself, she raced away. Down the hall. Through the entry door. Cool air on her face reassured her she was out of the house.

Away from the intruder who'd seemed a walking phantom.

Her cumbersome skirts nearly tripping her, she rushed down the steps and continued to run. Until the moment she careened into a man. Into his broad chest, to be specific.

Gasping for breath, she gazed up into familiar amber eyes.

"We must stop meeting like this." Finn's mouth had crooked at the corners, but as he stared down at her, the amusement faded from his eyes. "Ye look as if ye've seen one of yer ghosts."

"Not a ghost," she managed between breaths. "An old man. In the study."

Finn's gaze hardened. "If he hurt ye—"

"He didn't," Macie murmured. "He did not hurt me. I think . . . dear God, I think he's dead."

Chapter Eleven

STAYING CLOSE TO Finn, Macie led him to her grandfather's library. Before entering the house, he'd instructed the elderly driver he trusted at the reins of his ebony enameled carriage to summon a constable and a physician. As they entered the room, Macie spotted the slight rise and fall of the stranger's chest. A small sigh of relief escaped her. The man was alive. *Thank heaven.*

Motioning for her to stay back, Finn went to the unconscious intruder and crouched by his side. He pressed two fingers to the man's throat. "His pulse is weak." His tone was grim as he opened the man's jacket, baring his white shirt for inspection.

Macie crouched down. Her gaze traveled over the man's chest. No blood. No torn fabric. Not so much as a missing button.

Finn met her eyes. "Was he in this condition when ye first encountered him?"

"He was on his feet, though he was quite unsteady." Her hands trembled as fear shuddered through her. "Nell and I had left for the day, but I came back. And then, I found him here."

Finn proceeded to look the man over, searching for an injury. "I can't be sure, but I see no sign of a wound. He may have suffered a seizure of the heart."

"How very awful." A bitter taste filled Macie's mouth. "But why would he come here? Why wouldn't he seek out a physician?"

"It doesn't make any blasted sense." He shrugged off his

jacket, folded it, and placed it as a cushion beneath the stranger's head. "Do ye have any idea who he is?"

"I have no idea." She swallowed against a lump in her throat. "Finn, he was pleading for help."

Finn's gaze swept over the books scattered on the floor. More than a dozen volumes had been strewn haphazardly over the wooden planks. If she had not heard the tomes landing on the floor, she might've believed there had been a struggle. His jaw hardened as he turned to her.

"Ye said he didn't hurt you."

She shook her head as the old man's murmurs played in her thoughts. *Leave. Before he comes . . . for you.* "I suspect he was trying to warn me. Though I've no idea about what."

"While he was ransacking the library?"

"I don't think he intended any harm. He looked like he'd been searching for something."

"Did he know yer identity?"

"I cannot be sure," Macie said. "He never addressed me by name."

Finn rose to face her. His brow furrowed. "What in blazes did he say to ye?"

Murder. The very thought of the man's low, desperate whisper unfurled a chill along the length of her spine. Would Finn become too protective if she told him the content of the stranger's warning? Would he try to keep her away from the mansion?

"He was out of his head with pain. And perhaps fear. It's possible he was suffering from a delusion and believed me to be someone else."

"Tell me what he told ye," Finn pressed.

"First, he called for help. He sounded quite desperate. And then, he rambled on about a murder."

Finn plowed a hand through his hair. "Bloody hell."

A stocky gent boasting bushy gray mutton-chop whiskers marched through the door. His physician's satchel swung in his hand as he headed directly to the unconscious man. A patrolman followed close on the doctor's heels.

"What's all this about, Caldwell?" The patrolman punctuated his question with a scowl.

"And a good day to ye, Constable Lewis," Finn said, appearing unfazed by the man's expression. "Miss Mason encountered an intruder."

"Ye had nothing to do with the man's current state, I presume." The constable didn't hide the note of skepticism in his voice.

"I arrived after the man had fallen unconscious."

Tempering his scowl, the constable turned to Macie. "Miss, I need ye to tell me what happened."

"First things first," the physician interrupted. "This man needs immediate transport to the hospital."

Constable Lewis went to the door, calling over his shoulder. "I shall summon an ambulance."

"Do it now." The physician's tone was grim. "With any delay, he may not survive."

As he escorted Macie through Metropolitan police headquarters, Finn spotted a detective approaching them. He resisted the impulse to utter an epithet. *Inspector Bradley.* The by-the-book clod's terse words of introduction confirmed he had been tasked with investigating the now-unconscious intruder in Bennington Manor.

Bollocks.

Inspector George Bradley was a stuffed shirt whose skill at deduction had yet to be demonstrated. Why, the horse pulling Finn's carriage might have possessed more instinct for bringing criminals to justice.

The detective's redundant questioning dragged on until well past sundown. When the dull bloke finally indicated that Macie was free to leave, they returned to Finn's waiting coach.

His driver, Reggie, peered down at them from bench. Concern filled his eyes. "Have they deduced a reason for that bloke to be in the lady's house?"

"Not yet." Finn kept his tone bland. He didn't have much faith they would get an answer to that pressing question that night, if at all.

Reggie adjusted his flat brimmed hat on his gray-haired head. "Good thing ye arrived when ye did."

"Indeed," Macie agreed, flashing a soft smile. Once inside the carriage, she took a seat on the upholstered bench and peeled back the curtain, appearing to settle her gaze on the crescent moon. "I had not expected Inspector Bradley to go on and on as he did. I suspect the man does enjoy the sound of his voice." A little sigh escaped her. "Thank goodness we were able to dispatch a messenger to Nell. She does tend to worry."

Finn settled in across from her. "Does she now?"

"At times." A look of amusement played on her lips. "She's a bit on edge when we're traipsing about old houses. All those gothic novels she's so fond of have her jumping at every *creak* of the floorboards."

"That's understandable. After all, ye never know what ye'll find."

"That's the point, isn't it?" Macie posed the question with a little grin.

By thunder, she was pretty when her eyes sparkled with mischief. "I'm starting to see why Jon is going gray," he said, if only to disguise the direction of his thoughts.

"My brother rather exaggerates the toll my supposed antics have taken upon him," she said lightly. "I do hope Nell is enjoying the soiree. She was so looking forward to the evening with Lady Yarbury and her guests. The countess is a gracious hostess. She'd generously offered her personal carriage to transport us to her home." Once again, she glanced up at the moon. "I suppose we are well past the point of arriving fashionably late."

"I am a poor judge of such matters," he admitted. "Tonight, I'm more concerned with keeping ye safe."

"Inspector Bradley seemed quite sure I was not in danger." She turned to him. "Certainly that poor man in Grandfather's library poses no threat."

"I do not share his confidence." Now was not the time to mince words. Not when Macie's safety was at stake.

Her eyes narrowed in surprise. "You disagree with his conclusion?"

"The man pays more attention to the starch in his collar than to any evidence of danger."

"Inspector Bradley sent patrolmen to search the house. I understand they found no one there," she countered logically. "No evidence of theft, nor of some other sort of criminal scheme."

"I would not rely upon Bradley to solve the taking of sweets from a chocolate shop, let alone trust him to resolve a case where your safety is at stake."

Folding her arms before her, she hiked her chin. At that angle, the light from the streetlamp cast a glow over her features, in particular the luscious little dimple on her left cheek.

"The detective believes there is no further threat. It does seem the most reasonable conclusion."

"It is also the most convenient. The *esteemed inspector* arrived at his deduction in less time than it takes for paint to dry. I have little reason to have faith in his instincts."

God knew the detective had exerted neither his brain nor his brawn in searching for the bastard who'd left his kind-eyed young cousin lying dead in a dismal alley.

"My, I had not taken you for a cynic." The lightness in her voice was not echoed by her eyes.

"It's too soon to know if Bradley has it right this time."

"This time?" Her brows rose. "You have a previous acquaintance with the inspector?"

"Not an acquaintance." Finn measured his words. "Bradley was the lead detective on a case of personal interest to me."

Her expression softened with compassion. "Your cousin?"

Finn nodded, steadying himself against the bitter memories. "Colleen's murder was never solved."

Macie's mouth thinned. Sadness filled her warm green eyes as she placed her hand gently upon his. "I was heartbroken to learn of her death."

"We all were. If I had been on my guard, I might've intervened," Finn said. "Before it was too late."

"Jon told me what happened." She softly squeezed his hand. "It was not your fault." Her gentle touch and words warmed his heart.

"That may be true. But I will carry regret in my heart to my dying day. In any case, I have no faith in the detective's abilities. Nor in his judgment."

"Nothing is going to happen to me," she said, her tone resolute. "It's quite likely the intruder was himself a victim. It is not far-fetched to believe he was attacked by street criminals."

"In that posh part of London?"

"It is entirely possible," Macie went on, seeming to reassure herself. "When the old man spoke to me, he seemed quite desperate."

"Need I point out that no one knows the man's identity? We cannot be certain he was alone in the house before ye came upon him."

Her chin hiked a fraction higher. "You will not frighten me into living like a caged bird, Mr. Caldwell."

He smiled despite himself. "Please, for the love of Zeus, stop calling me Mr. Caldwell. I've known ye since ye were a girl in braids and ribbons."

"And we're all grown up now, aren't we, *Mr. Caldwell?*" She put deliberate emphasis on his name.

"We most definitely are, *Miss Mason.*" Two could play her game. "As a man who honors his word, I intend to see that ye remain in one piece until yer brother returns. After Jon steps off the train, ye will once again be his—"

"Problem." She completed his sentence, her eyes sparkling like the most precious of emeralds. Damnation, when she looked at him like that—so blasted beautiful, so tempting and yet so very off-limits—his more primal instincts reared their head.

A knowing little half-smile played on her mouth. Did the minx know precisely the effect she'd had on him?

Not that it mattered. He had meant every word he'd said to her when she'd proposed her bold scheme to send the fortune hunters in search of other prey. He would watch over her. He would protect her, and he would do his damnedest to chase off the vultures. But if she decided to tear her good name to shreds with a foolish act that could not be undone, he would not be a party to it.

Even if the mere thought of kissing her heated his blood. Even if the temptation to close the curtain, draw her into his arms, and explore her sweetly curved body urged him to cast aside all reason.

Even if he no longer gave a bloody damn about her brother's blasted devil's bargain.

"Tell me, Phineas Caldwell, why *are* you here?" Her voice had gone low and velvety, though her eyes had cooled.

"Ye've forgotten so soon?" he said, meeting her questioning gaze.

"You know what I mean." She pressed the matter. "Why are you playing a role that doesn't suit you at all?"

Something in her expression gave him pause. Was she starting to sense the truth? Did she realize that he would watch over her—contracts be damned—simply because he couldn't bear the thought of some bastard hurting her?

He plastered on an expression that betrayed none of his thoughts. "Is it not enough to believe that I intend to protect ye while yer brother is not here to watch out for ye?"

"If Jon were truly worried about my safety, he might have

hired an actual bodyguard. A big, burly fellow with a fierce scowl, if you will."

"I had not realized a scowl was a requirement for protecting ye. I'll have to remember that," he countered.

She gave a little shrug. "I doubt that it would matter. When you scowl, it's not at all frightening. In fact, it's rather—"

"Rather *what*?"

She hesitated for a long moment. Her cheeks had turned a bit pink, while a look of amusement danced in her eyes. "The word that comes to mind is *brooding*. Rather like a moody poet."

Bollocks. In his life, he'd been called a rogue and a rake and a rotter. But never had he ever imagined being dubbed a blasted poet, moody or otherwise.

"A villain would not find me menacing?"

She nibbled her lower lip, seeming to consider his question a bit more seriously than he'd expected. "Perhaps if you were in your fisticuffs—or is it brawling?—stance. That might give a villain pause."

"I will have to keep that in mind. Perhaps I'll add a well-timed snarl."

She bit back the grin that sparkled in her eyes. "That might do the trick. In any case, I do wonder what Jon could possibly have offered to convince you to take on the monumental task of keeping *me* out of trouble."

"I thought ye did not care to know the details."

The amusement drained from her eyes, replaced with a more pensive expression. "I suppose I am curious, that's all."

For a heartbeat, he considered revealing the bargain he'd made, the simple trade-off of protecting Macie and her all-important family name in exchange for a lucrative contract that would ensure the prosperity of his family's business. After all, she was not some starry-eyed schoolgirl who didn't understand how the world worked. She was the daughter of a tycoon. An heiress. She would understand.

Perhaps he should tell her the truth. But what was the truth?

Was the bargain the whole story?

Or was it that he couldn't bear the thought of someone—anyone—dimming the bright light that was Macie? Even if a man like him could never fully drink in the warmth of that light.

"It's not complicated, Macie." He caught her hand within his fingers, seeing the surprise on her features. "This city can be a brutal place. And I will do whatever it takes to keep you safe."

Chapter Twelve

I WILL DO *whatever it takes . . .*

At the touch of Finn's hand to hers, Macie's heartbeat nearly skipped a beat. His voice had gone low, the husky rasp stirring an instinctive awareness within her. Gone was the lightly teasing banter in his tone, the humor in his words when he contemplated adding a snarl to appear more forbidding. The man whose gaze studied her face in that moment had uttered the words as a vow.

How very unexpected. She'd looked upon Finn as a man who'd lived his life on his own terms. Seeking unfettered experience, he had not burdened himself with bonds of the heart. Yet his words rang true. He was set on protecting her.

Drawing in a low breath, Macie steadied her emotions, and with them, the beat of her heart. The heat of Finn's hand against hers had been quite delicious. There was no denying her body's response to his nearly chaste touch.

The expression in his eyes was entirely unfamiliar. The young man she'd known all those years ago had been light-hearted, a brash rogue whose ready smile afforded him the ability to charm his way out of any fix. Why, he could even elicit a chuckle from her notoriously gruff father. A rare feat, indeed.

Now Finn had grown so very serious. Truth be told, his determination to protect her touched something deep within her. She trusted him, a rare thing, indeed.

If only he did not appear so suddenly dour. Shepherding her about town while pretending an infatuation should not seem a Herculean task. At the moment, she rather missed the charming man who'd shown up to a ball simply to see if she'd grown into the legs which had once seemed a bit too long for her body.

She let out a little sigh. "All this talk of danger . . . I don't know what has come over you, but I do not much care for it."

Raking long fingers through his hair, he studied her. "We both know what a woman on her own may face. I gave my word that I would watch over ye."

Watch over. The words chafed like too-tight shoes. Good heavens, she was a woman, not a giddy schoolgirl. The very notion cut against the grain. If Finn thought to use the elderly intruder as justification to cage her like some blasted parakeet, he would soon find he was very much mistaken.

"I'm sure you're aware my brother is far more worried about our not-quite-spotless name—at least protecting it from further tarnish—than protecting me from a ghoul or two lurking about after dark."

"It's not the blasted ghouls that concern me." He sounded gruff and grouchy and all–too appealing. "In any case, we should see to getting some food in our bellies. I know of a quiet café— not nearly as posh as a countess's drawing room, but the cook knows what he's about and the company is good."

"That would be lovely."

"Ye're certain?" His forehead furrowed. "If ye're disappointed about the countess's gathering, we can make an appearance. Unfashionably late or not."

"Disappointed?" She eyed him skeptically. "Surely you know that is not the case."

"I suspected as much." A smile played on his mouth. "But ye found my effort gentlemanly, did ye not?"

"Even Sir Lancelot could not have appeared more gallant."

"Ah, so I'm in good company," he said, then called up to Reggie, alerting the driver to their change of destination—the Rogue's Respite.

"A café for rogues?" Macie arched a brow.

"Seems appropriate, does it not?" The slightest of grins quirked one corner of his mouth.

"Quite so," she agreed.

He leaned back against the upholstery, appearing relaxed for the first time that night. "Ye'll like it, lass. Besides, there's someone I'd like ye to meet."

"I simply must seek out a chat with Lady Yarbury. I've heard she is quite fascinating. Each month, on the night of the full moon, she invites a medium to conduct a seance. I'd relish the opportunity to set up my camera and capture the scene."

"Full moon, eh?" His brows hiked. "Does the medium intend to summon a wulver?"

"A Scottish wolf-man?" Macie could not help but smile. "I suppose he might be wearing a kilt."

"All the better to accommodate his tail," he said in mock seriousness. Amusement gleamed in his eyes. Now that was the Finn she knew.

"If such a creature would put in an appearance, I would like to make its portrait. Sadly, I doubt it would cooperate long enough to pose."

"Ah, that's where ye're wrong." A grin played on his mouth. "Any self-respecting Scot would savor the opportunity to spend his night with a lovely woman."

"Including you?" she teased as the carriage slowed.

"Ye already know the answer, lass." His eyes flashed with the same cockiness that flavored his husky voice. Why did she find his brash confidence so very appealing?

The driver brought the coach to a stop before a quaint café on a pleasantly quiet street. A light fog had descended upon the city. As Finn escorted her from the coach, gaslight filtered through the haze, casting golden light over his chiseled features.

My, the man could certainly conjure a delicious dream or two. Decidedly improper dreams, to be sure. Her eyes drank in his strong chin. His full mouth. *Oh, his kiss would be so very, very tempting.*

One kiss would never be enough.

Macie let out the breath she hadn't realized she'd been holding. Putting on an act was one thing. But dreaming of his caress—while fully awake, no less—was a recipe for disaster. She would be in over her head before she knew it. The peculiar longing in the region of her heart was all the proof she needed. Giving in to temptation would be far too dangerous. Definitely a chance she could not take.

Or would the surrender be worth every moment of risk?

SAVORING A FINE Scotch, Finn drank in the quiet of Logan MacLain's latest venture, a café MacLain had aptly dubbed the Rogue's Respite. Gaslight cast a subtle ambiance on the deep-brown woods and leather décor while a lone pianist played with a light touch, enhancing the relaxed atmosphere. Seated across from him, Macie nibbled on finger-sized watercress sandwiches. Meeting his gaze, Macie's mouth curved into a subtle smile. Serene, for all to see.

But Finn knew better.

Despite the years and distance that had separated them, he could still read the subtle hints of tension. The slight narrowing of her eyes. The thinning of her lips. The light tap of her finger against the tabletop. Deep inside, Macie was anything but calm. Anything but at ease. Had the discovery of an intruder at the old house shaken her more than she wished to let on?

He leaned back against the plush upholstered chair, catching sight of Logan and his wife as they strolled into the café. Logan nodded a silent greeting before heading to the immense oak bar, while Amelia MacLain hurried to their table. Her warmth shone bright in her eyes. Logan was a lucky man. Bloody lucky, indeed.

She beamed with a genuine smile. "It's good to see you, Finn."

"Ye're radiant, as always," he said, speaking the truth.

A slight blush spread over her cheeks. "You are too kind." Her smile widened as she turned to Macie. "This must be Miss Mason. I've heard so much about you."

"Please, call me Macie. It's my pleasure to meet you."

"I'm afraid I've been a bit remiss in sending an invitation to our home," Amelia said. "In the last few weeks, I've been preoccupied with preparing the nursery. I suppose I will be able to relax once Logan and I have settled on a name for our babe. Suffice it to say, we do not see eye to eye on the subject."

"Ye'll work it out," Finn said. "Ye always do."

"Quite so," Amelia beamed. "You had faith in us from the very beginning, didn't you?"

"I had no doubt. From the very first, I could see the way he looked at you."

Logan turned from the bar. As he headed to their table, his wife's gaze warmed. "Ah, the king surveying his kingdom," she said, flashing a cheeky grin.

"King, eh?" Logan cocked a brow at his wife. "Remember that when we are at home tonight, my love."

"*This* is your kingdom," she countered. "Our home is not."

Logan wrapped a possessive arm around her. "Is it any wonder I love this woman?"

"'Tis not a mystery," Finn said. His cousin had found happiness with a woman he would treasure until his last breath.

"I do hope you'll join us?" Macie said with a broad smile.

"We would be delighted," Amelia replied.

After the MacLains settled in at the table, a robust conversation followed, continuing through their meal. Finn had savored his last bite of beef stew before their discussion turned to the intruder at Bennington Manor.

"I understand the man has not yet regained consciousness," Logan said, direct as ever.

"Word has traveled at the Rogue's Lair, I take it," Finn replied.

"The local constable is a talkative gent. Do the detectives

have any clue as to the stranger's identity?"

"I don't believe so," Macie spoke up. "He carried no identification."

"Such an unfortunate situation," Amelia said.

"I suspect the man was harmless," Macie went on. "Though my heart was in my throat when I discovered him rummaging through my grandfather's books."

"How frightening." Amelia's brow furrowed with concern. "And you have no idea of his reasons?"

"He may have been seeking help," Macie replied. "Inspector Bradley is of the opinion the man poses no threat."

"Bradley, eh?" Logan's tone betrayed he shared Finn's disdain for the man.

"The bloke came to that conclusion with remarkable haste. He presumes the intruder's presence was merely a random turn of events," Finn explained. "Blasted convenient, if ye ask me."

Logan turned to Finn. "Ye've secured the house?"

Finn felt a muscle in his jaw tighten. "For now. I'll do more in the morning."

"The inspector is confident there is no danger," Macie said. "I see no reason to worry."

"Worry serves no point," Finn agreed. "But we will not let down our guard until we know how a stranger found his way into the place."

"I will assist ye in thoroughly inspecting the premises in the morning," Logan said.

"Excellent." Macie's mood seemed to brighten. "In that case, we shall put our concerns to rest. I'm more concerned with the lighting tomorrow afternoon. With any luck, conditions will be perfect to set up my camera."

"Ye should not be alone," Finn countered. "The Tower would be bloody safer than working in that house."

Macie frowned, scrunching her pert nose. "Sadly, that might be a bit of a challenge to arrange. A haunted mansion or two will have to suffice."

The little dimple in her cheek pulled his gaze like a magnet. Blast it all, he could be a much more effective bodyguard if her every expression did not draw him in. He cleared his throat, if only to buy time to refocus his thoughts.

"After what happened today, ye will *not* stay alone at that house."

"Oh, won't I?" Her coral lips pursed. "I intend to establish my photography studio within Bennington Manor. Besides, I am planning an exhibition with a gothic aesthetic. What better place to start than my own personal haunted house?"

Gothic aesthetic. Haunted houses. Bloody hell, what had he gotten himself into? Chasing off money-hungry lords was one thing. But this . . . this was something else entirely. By thunder, the woman was impossible to predict. He doubted he could ever fully anticipate—let alone prepare for—what she'd come up with next. Blasted shame that intrigued him so much.

"You believe your grandfather's house is home to spirits?" Amelia's eyes lit with interest.

"Oh, most definitely," Macie said with a gleam in her eyes. "I've felt a chill on more than one occasion."

"Not surprising in that drafty old house," Finn said with a chuckle.

She flashed a little scowl. "In any case, I would like to believe the tales my grandfather told—at least some of them—are true. I'll have you know I've seen things that cannot be explained."

"One of them is lying in the hospital," Finn said. "Until the bloke recovers enough to be questioned, there's no telling why he was there."

"The detective believes the poor man had suffered a violent threat. His heart could not endure the strain," Macie countered.

"Bradley is wrong," Finn disagreed. "Street toughs did not attack that man. I'd wager my last shilling on that."

"Phineas Caldwell, I had never taken you for a worrier," she said with a lightness that did not reach her eyes.

Worrier. The casually spoken word felt like a pebble beneath his heel. No one could have described him in those terms. But in all fairness, he had never before taken on the task of protecting anyone. Much less a woman.

A woman like Macie.

In his gut, he knew the inspector was wrong. The elderly intruder had been on the verge of death. And yet, he'd used the last of his strength to tear through the books on the shelves. He'd been searching for something. But what?

"The man in yer grandfather's library was not there by chance. In yer bones, ye know that as well as I do," Finn said. "Until the old gent wakes up, there's no bloody way of telling what he was after. Or who else may be coming after it."

"Ye suspect the man was not working alone?" Logan said.

"That may be the case."

Macie propped her chin on her folded hand. "Surely you don't believe there's another stranger lurking about, ready to pounce?"

Finn met her gaze. "We cannot rule it out. Not yet."

"He's right," Amelia said in a low voice. "I do not wish to frighten you, Macie, but you must exercise caution. Some time ago, I experienced a rather similar occurrence."

Macie's eyes widened. "Good heavens, I had no idea. Will you tell me more?"

Amelia's features pulled taut with tension. "Before Logan and I married, I'd established a small library, not far from here. One evening, I encountered a violent intruder ransacking the shelves. Logan was there to stop him, and for a time, I wanted to believe the moments of danger were over and done. But I was mistaken."

"Oh, dear," Macie said softly. "What happened?"

"Someday, I shall tell you the entire story, but for now, suffice it to say the intruder was not the only vile threat we faced." Amelia's mouth thinned at the memory, but the tense set of her features eased as her gaze fell on her husband. "The only bright side to all the unpleasantness was that it brought us together."

"Indeed," Logan said, sending his wife a warm glance. "As for the present situation, until we can be certain the man ye encountered did not have an accomplice, ye must not let down your guard."

"I do understand." Macie's expression was pensive. "Well, this does complicate our arrangement, doesn't it?"

"Ye could say that," Finn agreed. "Jon trusted me to keep ye safe. And I intend to do just that."

"While I do see the need for caution, I cannot bear the thought of being confined to a luxurious prison." Her eyes glimmered with determination. "Are we to assume that Phineas Caldwell, my ever-vigilant protector, will stand at the ready against any threat, including the occasional villain?"

Why did he have the sudden feeling he was about to walk into quicksand? "If need be."

Her plump mouth curved into a defiant, too blasted tempting smile. "I plan to spend my days at Bennington Manor. And wherever else the muse may lead. I trust you do not harbor a fear of ghosts."

He scrubbed his hand against his jaw, as if that might ease the tension coursing through his bones. Macie had no right to be so blasted appealing, especially when she was determined to make his life a blasted challenge.

"The dead do not concern me. The creatures I'm watching for still live and breathe."

Her eyes widened. Appearing to mull over his words, she grazed her teeth over her plump lower lip.

"I thought as much." She regarded him rather intently. "In that case, I will count on you to chase off whatever loathsome creatures are lurking in the dark. I suspect most will be of the four-legged variety, but I do hope the rumors of your rough-and-ready exploits are true."

He resisted the urge to scowl. *Blast it.* Had Jon regaled Macie with puffed-up tales? Boxing was a means of using his fists to ease the tension in his mind. He confined his bouts to the gymnasium, with notable exceptions. More than one arrogant bloke had underestimated Finn's drive to win. But no one would ever have confused him with Gentleman Jim Corbett.

"Rough-and-ready exploits. Do tell," Amelia said.

"I'd wager Miss Mason's brother has exaggerated my success in the ring." Finn kept his tone cool.

"And I'd bet a bottle of good Scotch he was not talking about yer civilized bouts," Logan said with a knowing smile. "Jon chose you to protect his sister because you possess certain skills. We both know that at times, it takes a brawler to defend a lady."

Chapter Thirteen

*I*T TAKES A *brawler to defend a lady.*

Logan's words swirled in Macie's thoughts. For reasons she could not begin to explain, even to herself, she found the notion utterly delicious. An image of the man in what could only be described as a primal masculine state began to take shape in her mind. *How very unexpected.*

If anyone could have read her thoughts, my, how scandalized they would be.

Heaven knew her own reaction caught her off guard. It wasn't as though she had never thought about Finn taking on opponents with both his fists and his wits. With a little shake of her head she hoped no one had noticed, she cleared her thoughts. Goodness, what had come over her?

Finn had left his seat to head to the bar with Logan. Pulling in a low breath, she allowed her gaze to trail his long, sure strides. Even fully clothed in gentleman's attire, Finn could not conceal the powerful build of his chest and the sleek, lean strength of his legs. With that clever, quick-witted mind of his, she had no doubt the man could bring down a larger, heavier opponent by employing strategy and calculation in his blows.

Lowering her gaze, she pretended an interest in the lemony dessert that sat before her. As an educated woman of an independent mind, the notion of Finn perpetuating violence in the name of sport should be entirely repellant to her. But her response was quite the contrary.

Finn Caldwell fascinated her.

Tall, infuriating, and more handsome than a man had a right to be, he intrigued her beyond all reason. Utterly so.

How very ironic that the man who filled her waking dreams was standing before her. Yet he was off limits.

Heaven knew her father would not approve of such a match.

Finn was not a duke. Nor an earl, viscount, or baron, for that matter. Beyond that, his reputation as an unrepentant rogue preceded him. On more than one occasion, she'd overheard her brother regaling his friends about their exploits.

No, Finn Caldwell was not suitable. Not at all.

But that didn't stop her from drinking him in. Feeling a bit bold, Macie savored the sheer masculine appeal of the man. In her mind's eye, she sketched a picture of him facing off against an opponent. His trousers hugging his lean muscled legs. The muscles of his bare chest flexing, a light sheen from exertion enhancing the contour of his biceps and pectorals. The set of his jaw as he eyed his combatant with utter focus. His wheat-brown hair, slightly dampened with perspiration. The seductive half-smile playing on his full mouth.

Her imaginary Finn turned to her and threw a wink, cheeky as ever.

Her mouth went dry. *How very intriguing.*

Had her cheeks actually heated?

Macie banished the delicious, far-from-chaste image from her mind. Her thoughts of the man tasked with playing bodyguard were more heated—and more risky—than any scandal she'd ever concocted. She could no longer look upon him as a means to deter the heiress hunters.

No. Finn was more than that.

Could she play out the romantic charade she'd planned without getting carried away?

"Rumor has it you're exceedingly proficient at well-timed moments of, shall we say, a deliberate lack of grace." Amelia's question offered a welcome distraction. Leaning closer, she dropped her voice to a conspiratorial tone. "Is there any truth to the stories?"

"Perhaps." Macie reached for her glass of white wine. "Though I suspect some of the tales might be a bit tall, so to speak."

"I suspected as much. Heaven knows I would never take what the gossips say at face value. Why, some of the bored biddies believed my husband to be an outlaw. In the American west, no less. Of course, he does look the part, doesn't he?" Amelia's coy half-smile revealed more than her words. "And he did spend time in America. I suppose he was a bit of a rogue in those days."

"My brother spoke of Logan's travels. I do believe Jon would have loved to have joined him, but he's spread rather thin with his various enterprises."

"I've made his acquaintance. He seems to be a most responsible man."

"Responsible," Macie repeated as more apt descriptions ran through her thoughts. *Staid. Stodgy. Oh-so-dedicated to Papa's businesses.* "That is one way of putting it. He's so very sensible. I do wish he would loosen up and enjoy life a bit."

"Perhaps that time will come." A reflective look fell over Amelia's features. "Not long ago, I would have described myself in like terms. Sensible, but a bit too independent to be prim and proper. Above all, I wanted a quiet, serene life. Until the day when Logan marched into my library, clad in black from head to toe. The very thought of him still makes a bit warm all over." Amelia's mouth curved in a little grin. "Trust me when I tell you that marriage to a reformed rogue can be quite delicious."

"I do hold out hope. Perhaps, someday, I'll be swept off my feet."

"As I said, I put little stock in the rumor mill. But the tales of your shenanigans putting bores in their place are delightful."

"Putting bores in their place," Macie repeated. "I do like the sound of that."

"I simply must know what really happened at the Midsummer's Night masquerade." Amelia's eyes brightened. "I'm told the incident involved a fairy wand, of all things."

"Ah, the summer party. I cannot say precisely how I accomplished that feat, though I'm certain a bit of luck was involved." Macie smiled at the memory. "My costume was quite a bit of fun, with lovely ruffles, sea-blue wings, and a large, pointy wand. The villainous viscount should consider himself fortunate he walked away unscathed."

"The villainous viscount?" Amelia chuckled. "What a marvelous title for a penny dreadful."

"Ah, the man was an utter cad. I had no intention of causing a scene that night. The ballroom was rather crowded, and I was enjoying the lovely evening. Until the viscount invited to me to dance. I saw no harm in it, but when we attempted to waltz—despite the dolt's utter lack of rhythm—he dared an overly bold maneuver. As I slipped away from his reach, the tip of the wand struck him soundly across his face."

Amelia looked to be fighting laughter. "Good heavens."

"Oh, it gets worse. The fop's monocle flew off his face and landed in the midst of a lady's ample cleavage." Macie grinned. "I can still picture her look of utter shock."

"Oh, dear," Amelia said. "I can well imagine the scene. You must tell me this . . . did the cad retrieve his eyepiece?"

"He did," Macie said with a little giggle. Before she could elaborate, Finn and Logan returned to the table. Their expressions were somber. Perhaps even grim.

She set her wine glass to the side as a slight prickle of alarm trickled over her nape. A visitor had arrived at the café a few minutes earlier, a wiry young man clearly known to both Finn and Logan. He had joined them at the bar for a few moments before making a hasty exit.

"Logan, why was your assistant here?" Amelia did not hide her concern. "Is something wrong?"

"One of the regulars at the Rogue's Lair has a connection to the detective bureau. He tends to ramble, but the bloke usually knows what he's talking about." Logan kept his voice low. "Tim figured we'd want to know what the man revealed about the intruder. The old man has not regained consciousness. But the physicians believe they know why he collapsed."

Macie leaned closer. "Did his heart give out?"

Finn shook his head. "Nothing of the sort. What happened . . . was not due to natural causes."

An invisible weight sunk into the pit of Macie's stomach. "Not natural?"

Finn plowed a hand through his hair. "The physicians observed certain signs of poison."

"Poison?" Macie repeated dully.

Logan replied with a grim nod. "They suspect a toxin that accelerated his heart."

"Will he . . . will he recover?" Amelia inquired gently.

"At this point, there's no way to know," Finn said. "They still have not identified him."

"We'll pay a visit to Inspector Bradley in the morning" Logan rested his hand on his wife's shoulder, appearing to comfort her. "For tonight, Amelia and I would welcome ye as our guests."

"An excellent idea," she agreed readily, casting her husband a smiling glance. "We have ample room. I do hope you will join us tonight."

"Oh, I wouldn't think of imposing, much less at this late hour," Macie said. "My friend Nell and I will be safe at home, locked behind stout doors."

Amelia smiled graciously. "It would be no imposition."

"Ye're both welcome to stay with us. As is Finn," Logan added.

Macie mulled their offer. "I truly appreciate your hospitality, but I cannot leave my housekeeper on her own tonight. Mrs. Tuttle will be worried as it is. If she has managed to fall asleep, I simply could not expect her to be awakened to travel to another residence, let alone at this time of night."

"Mrs. Tuttle," Finn repeated the name as if it were distasteful. He'd met her stern housekeeper years earlier, when he'd joined Jon for a holiday visit at her family's country house. The perpetually cross woman was perhaps the only soul that Finn could not charm.

"You remember her, do you?" Macie said, if only to confirm what she already knew.

"How could anyone forget such a feisty old bag of bones. The woman possessed the ability to make a feather duster seem as threatening as a medieval mace."

Macie shot him a small smile as he frowned. "She is a bit grouchy, I'll give you that. But surely you understand my reluctance to leave her to fend for herself . . . or to rouse her from her bed at this hour of the night."

"I must confess, this situation does make me a bit anxious. There are many questions left to be answered. You simply must be cautious." Amelia's concern showed on her taut features. "After the first incident in my library, I wanted to believe the threat was over after the attacker was jailed. But it wasn't. The cur was not acting alone. Macie, that might be the case here. The threat may be quite real."

"I do realize that," Macie said. "Which is another reason why I cannot take refuge in your home. I cannot chance bringing danger to your doorstep. Much less with you expecting a child."

"I do understand," Amelia said while her husband lightly massaged her shoulders. "If something happens . . . if you experience a change of heart, our door will open to you and Nell any time of the day or night. Any friend of Finn's is a dear friend of ours."

Finn reached for his glass and took a drink. Macie could not recall ever seeing such a serious expression on his features. "I agree with ye, Macie. I would not think to expose Amelia to any risk, much less at this time. Until we can be certain ye will be safe, ye'll be safe in my home. Even the old bag of bones."

Good heavens, what was the man thinking? Finn had spoken with great confidence, uttering the words as though she would treat them as a command. Spend the night? At his residence? Even by her standards, that would be a scandal too far.

"Well, then," Macie said, folding her hands together to form a little perch for her chin and met his eyes. "Have you perhaps experienced a temporary lapse in reason?"

The firm set of his jaw told her he was entirely serious. "I will not leave ye undefended, much less while you sleep."

"It's simply out of the question," she said with a shake of her head. "Even if I had no concerns for myself, I cannot put Nell's good name at risk."

"Macie, I do understand your concerns. I believe I have a solution." Amelia spoke up, gentle yet direct. She turned to Finn. "Unfortunately, I suspect you are not going to like it."

As THEY MADE their way up the steps to the townhouse she shared with Nell, Macie bit back a giggle. Judging from Finn's scowl, he was not looking forward to the night ahead. He'd pulled a knitted wool cap low to cover his hair and his forehead. With any luck, nosy neighbors burning the midnight oil would think her brother had returned early from his trip.

As Macie turned the key in the lock and opened the door, her housekeeper emerged from the darkened corridor leading to the foyer. Puzzlement was etched on Mrs. Tuttle's careworn face. Her brows knit together as her gaze fell upon Finn.

"Who's that you've brought with you?" She squinted hard. "My eyes must be playing tricks on me." She shot Macie a frown. "Phineas Caldwell? Under this roof?"

He shrugged. "Would ye believe me if I said I was on assignment for the Crown?"

"Should I?" She batted the question back to him.

At that, he grinned. The old woman was a spry one, wasn't she? "Not a chance."

Mrs. Tuttle's eyes twinkled. "I must say, that's a relief. I'd hate to think the fate of Her Majesty depends on the lot of you." She turned to Macie, pinning her with her gaze. "I saw you coming up the steps. If ye're thinking to pass him off as your brother, you'll have to work harder than that."

"It was not a well-thought plan," Macie said. "But I can explain."

"Might I suggest that the next time you feel the need to smuggle in a man, you borrow my departed husband's cloak. I'd imagine it would be a better fit." Mrs. Tuttle studied him. "The tweed would do justice to those broad shoulders."

Finn stared at the polished oak planks, looking as if he longed to disappear into the woodwork.

Macie bit back a grin. "Why, Mrs. Tuttle, are my ears deceiving me? If I didn't know better, I'd think you're trying to flatter my bodyguard."

"Bodyguard?" Mrs. Tuttle's cough was strategically timed. "Somehow, I don't think this is what your brother intended."

Macie shrugged. "Jon is not here to offer his opinion on the matter."

Mrs. Tuttle folded her arms and offered a sage nod. "After what happened to you at that gloomy old house, I suppose it would not be a bad thing to have a man about the place."

"Indeed. Mr. Caldwell insisted on staying on to watch over us. He is chivalrous to the bone, a knight in not-so-shiny armor."

Mrs. Tuttle chuckled under her breath. "Chivalry? So that's what they're calling it now."

Finn summoned his most disarming smile. He'd melted the icy shields around many a lass's heart with that subtle curve of his mouth. Unfortunately, Mildred Tuttle was not one of those women. As the housekeeper met his gaze, the glimmer of amusement in her eyes disappeared, replaced by an Arctic-thick frost.

"Surely ye do not doubt my intentions. Jon Mason is an old friend. I would not betray his trust. Ye do know that, don't ye now, Mrs. Tuttle?"

"If Macie trusts that guarding against villains is all you have on your mind tonight, who am I to be doubting you?" Mrs. Tuttle's eyes narrowed, strategic as her little cough. "But keep this in mind—I am a light sleeper. And let me assure you, Finn Caldwell, you will not be getting anything polished tonight." A slow smile lifted the corners of her thin mouth. "Not even your armor."

FINN SHIFTED RESTLESSLY on the too-blasted-short settee that had served as his bed through the night. Drifting in that realm between sleep and awareness, he tugged the knitted blanket around him, still not quite ready to drag himself from slumber despite the ache in his bones. In his thoughts, he drifted on what seemed a calm wave, while a low, rhythmic sound that brought to mind the one his grandfather had made when he dozed off before the fireplace filled his ears.

But why in blazes was the noise so close? And why did he feel a gentle, even breath brush the tip of his ear? Bollocks, what was that touching the nape of his neck?

Opening his eyes scarcely enough to let in light, he craned his neck. *Bloody hell.* A midnight-black cat lay on the back of the sofa, blinking its amber gold eyes as it stirred from rest. One paw dangled over the upholstery, just low enough to touch Finn's neck, while the rest of the cat's plump body balanced on the wood trim at the back of the settee. Was it his imagination, or did the creature look annoyed that Finn had moved just enough to disturb her? The cat regarded him for a long moment, then yawned.

So this was Cleo, fishy breath and all. Jon had warned him

about the feline curmudgeon who possessed a penchant for sharpening its claws on expensive rugs, ornate upholstery, and the occasional trouser leg. Macie had toted the cat with her across the continent, and if Jon's claims were true, the cat was the bane of Mrs. Tuttle's existence. That alone was enough to make Finn like the wee beast. Jon had speculated that his sister had trained the cat to drive off unwanted callers. Was it possible to perform such a feat? If it were, Finn didn't doubt that Macie would've figured out a way to do it.

Regarding Finn with lazy interest, Cleo stretched out a paw, lightly brushing it against his shoulder. No claws. No hisses. Simply a look of intense curiosity about the human who'd taken over her sleeping spot in the parlor.

With what looked to be an expression of feline disdain, Cleo shifted her attention to something or someone behind him. Blinking against the morning light that streamed in between the gap in the curtains, Finn turned to face Macie's housekeeper. Mrs. Tuttle stood in the doorway, her mouth pinched in a look of annoyance.

Behind him, the cat yawned again, stretching her body over the back of the settee. Mrs. Tuttle's eyes narrowed, nearly as pinched as her mouth. "There you are, you willful minx."

Minx? He'd been called a lot of things in his twenty-nine years of life, but this was a first. Fortunately, his drowsy mind stirred to alertness and he realized she was speaking to the cat before he could embarrass himself with a reply.

"She isn't supposed to be on the furniture," the housekeeper said, as if he'd somehow been complicit in the cat's disobedience.

Finn sat up straight, tugging his shirt tails down as his bare feet landed on the braided rug. He threw the cat a glance over his shoulder. Was it his imagination, or did the cat appear amused by Mrs. Tuttle's reaction?

"Doesn't anyone sleep in this house?" he asked while lazily stretching his arms over his head.

"There is work to be done, Mr. Caldwell." She walked over to the windows and opened the curtains. Bright rays of morning sun streamed in. "The morning meal will not cook itself. I presume you have a hearty appetite."

"So I've been told," he said.

Planting her hands on her hips, she pinned him with her weary gray gaze. "I know why you're here. I trust Mr. Jon would not have called upon you to watch over her if he did not trust you. But I cannot say that I share that faith."

"I won't let anyone harm her, Mrs. Tuttle. Ye can count on that."

She regarded him silently for a long moment, seeming to consider his words. "Miss Macie is a good girl, she is. Despite the worldly act she puts on." Mrs. Tuttle met his gaze. "You will respect that."

Despite the distrust in her eyes, Finn saw the protectiveness underlying the old woman's hard veneer. The emotion in her voice touched him. More than he'd imagined possible.

"I will treat Miss Mason like the lady she is." He spoke the truth. "Ye have my word."

"I'll hold you to it." Mrs. Tuttle's stern expression eased, the thin line of her mouth relaxing. "You're not like the others, Mr. Caldwell. Not like those dukes and barons and whatever they like to call themselves, with their noses high in the air, sniffing around for every pence they might get out of Miss Macie's father. She knows how to send those rotters scurrying away. But you . . . I'm not so sure she knows how to protect herself from the likes of you."

Chapter Fourteen

AN INVITATION TO the Countess of Fenwick's costume ball was a sure sign they had made a mark in London society. Or so Nell insisted, even as Macie massaged her temples against a sudden megrim.

"I do wish I shared your enthusiasm," Macie said, gently pressing her fingertips to the spots that seemed to throb with her friend's every word.

"You'll have a grand time," Nell assured her. "I have a fitting for my costume this afternoon. I trust you will come along to put the final touches on your ensemble."

Macie shook her head. "I am taking my camera to the manor today."

Nell looked shocked. "But your costume?"

"Madame Lorette sent word that the seamstress has completed her work. I expect she will deliver it within a day or so."

"I suppose there's not much to be done to a gown modeled after a medieval tunic."

Macie grinned at the thought of arriving at the countess's elite ball garbed as a female incarnation of Friar Tuck. Wouldn't that have made the biddies' tongues cluck? Pity she'd had a rather practical change of heart. "I've rethought my ensemble."

Standing suddenly still by the parlor table, Mrs. Tuttle looked up as her feather duster stopped its energetic sweeps of a lamp's stained glass shade. Macie bit back a smile. The housekeeper had certainly become adept at timing her tasks to coincide with a conversation she wished to hear.

The door chimes sounded, announcing a visitor. A soft mumble of annoyance escaped Mrs. Tuttle, followed by an unsubtle comment. "He's back so soon?"

"Until you answer the door, we won't be certain," Macie said lightly. "If Mr. Caldwell has returned, please show him in."

"Your brother should've employed a real bodyguard," Mrs. Tuttle grumbled as the chimes rang out again. "Not that rogue."

"I am quite sure Mr. Caldwell's defensive skills will suffice."

"It's not the man's *defensive skills* that worry me." With that, Mrs. Tuttle hurried out of the room.

Nell's gaze trailed the housekeeper's path, then leaned closer and lowered her voice. "Has she always been so cross?"

"Mrs. Tuttle has a heart of gold, but she detests any disruption to her routine."

"I don't think that's the problem, Macie. Not in this case."

"You may be right," she said as Finn's voice drifted down the corridor. "She tends to be rather protective of me."

"And with good cause." Nell took another sip from the delicate cup. "So, what have you settled on for your costume? Please tell me you are not dressing as Robin Hood."

"Nothing of the sort. I've decided to be a bit more, shall we say, conventional."

"Thank heaven." Nell appeared to let out a sigh of actual relief. "The very idea of you carrying a quiver of arrows—even if they aren't real—gives me pause."

Macie's attention was drawn to the doorway as Mrs. Tuttle returned. The older woman's expression brightened. "I must say, that's a relief."

"And what might that be?" Macie said, allowing a bit of teasing into her tone.

"You know what I'm talking about," Mrs. Tuttle said. "After the incident with your sword last year, I shudder to think what nature of trouble you'd stir up with a bow and arrow within reach."

"Sword?" Finn's eyes crinkled with amusement as he strolled into the parlor. "Arrows? Good God, the very thought of those in your hands is enough to send a man running."

Macie shrugged. "Isn't that the idea?"

His brows rose. "Should I take cover?"

"Not yet." She smiled. "I assure you, you will know if it's necessary."

Finn went to the burgundy velvet couch and leaned against its wooden-framed back. Casually attired in dark trousers, charcoal waistcoat, and an unadorned pale gray shirt open at the collar, his hair curled at the ends, still damp from what was obviously a recent bath. A light growth of new beard covered his jaw, intensifying the contours of his features.

My, he is a tempting one, isn't he? And I suspect he knows it.

"Do ye intend to leave me in suspense?" He stretched his long legs out, crossed his ankles, and regarded her with a look of what seemed to be genuine curiosity. "The words *incident* and *sword* are not ones I would readily connect with a lady."

Nell's expression brightened. "Oh, Macie, can I tell him about Lord Rocks-for-brains?"

Macie shot her a look. "You would enjoy that, wouldn't you?"

Setting her teacup on a doily, Nell perched on the edge of her seat. "I always relish an opportunity to regale a listener with tales of your adventures. Especially an adventure involving Henry VIII."

"Good heavens," Mrs. Tuttle said with a weary shake of her head. "The tales that bring you amusement."

"Henry VIII?" Finn folded his arms as furrows marked his forehead. "He'd be a bit long in the tooth now, wouldn't he?"

"We were attending a masquerade." A smile pulled at Nell's mouth. "But I suppose you already knew that."

Finn's eyes crinkled at the corners. "I had my suspicions."

Macie pictured the outlandishly costumed noble in her mind. "I suspect Henry VIII might've been more pleasant than the so-called gentleman in question."

"The man was wearing a codpiece, of all the ridiculous things," Nell added matter-of-factly. "The sot deserved what happened to him that night."

"Because he was wearing a codpiece?" Finn asked dryly.

"Goodness. Would the two of you stop saying that word?" Mrs. Tuttle sank into a chair, still clutching her feather duster. "It does not seem proper."

"You must admit, there are few opportunities to use the word in this day and age," Nell said as Finn chuckled his agreement.

"My, you are a cheeky miss," Mrs. Tuttle said, massaging her temples.

"In any case, Lord Rocks-for-brains had come in costume as Henry VIII that night. It appeared he had imbibed a bit too much."

Finn nodded his understanding. "And he wanted Macie to become wife number seven?"

"That about sums it up," Nell replied. "But Macie taught him she is not one to be trifled with. The cad should count himself fortunate the sword at her hip was made of wood and not steel."

Finn's gaze settled on Macie. "Ye attended a fancy costume ball . . . clutching a sword?"

Macie flashed a grin. "What better accessory for Joan of Arc?"

"Good God," Finn said. "The bloke evidently relished a challenge."

"One might say that," Nell said. "Fortunately for him, Lord Rocks-for-brains had padded his middle."

"Definitely a stroke of luck there," Finn observed.

"The man was not easily discouraged. I suspect he thought I was playing hard to get," Macie said.

Nell nodded her agreement. "Until you rather conveniently managed to spill an entire goblet of wine onto his tunic."

"The clod had the audacity to pursue me into the reception hall. I did not mean to collide with that elderly duke's drink." Macie's words were not convincing, even to herself. She smiled to herself at the memory. "I can still picture the expressions on the guests' faces as he stomped away. Covered in red wine as he was, he looked as if I had taken a real blade to him."

"Impressive," Finn said with a tone of surprising sincerity.

"I do believe you would've enjoyed that night." Macie met Finn's gaze. "I wasn't expecting you until this evening. You have news?"

"I spoke with Inspector Bradley. The intruder has shown signs that he may regain consciousness. It may take hours. Or days. But it looks as though the old man's fighting to stay alive."

"That would certainly be good news." Macie sent Mrs. Tuttle a speaking glance. "Once we hear from his own mouth that he meant no harm, the worrywarts can cease their fussing over me."

"I will not stop worrying over you while you're still gallivant-ing about London with that camera of yours," Mrs. Tuttle said.

"Such a mother hen," Macie said affectionately. "Speaking of my camera, the conditions for putting it to good use should be quite satisfactory this afternoon. Nell, I'll have the cab deliver you to your fitting before I proceed to the house."

Nell's brow furrowed. "You think it wise to go on your own?"

"She will not be alone." Finn said, a smile in his eyes as his gaze locked with Macie's. "I will accompany ye."

"That won't be necessary," Macie countered.

"I'd like to take a better look around the house. If I'm to offer an assessment of what needs to be done about the place, I'll need more than a brief tour of the premises."

His words were logical and sounded quite sincere. But the look in his eyes told Macie his motives had more to do with watching over her than with renovating the old house. "You're quite certain you wish to take up your day in a stuffy old house?"

"There's nowhere else I'd rather be." A smile tugged at the corners of his mouth.

Macie resisted the urge to chuckle at his blatant falsehood. "Has anyone ever told you you're a poor liar?"

"Ah, ye've got me there. Honest to a fault, I am."

Mrs. Tuttle's cough seemed rather strategic. "A true choir boy if ever I've seen one."

"Sadly, I cannot sing a note," Finn replied smoothly. "I do possess an ulterior motive."

Macie hiked a brow. "And what might that be?"

He regarded her with a solemn expression she suspected was an act. "The place is haunted, is it not?"

"Rumor has it that my ancestor roams the halls."

"So I've heard." Finn plowed his long fingers through his hair. "With any luck, we'll come upon one of the legendary ghosts of Bennington Manor. But if a man who still lives and breathes is lurking in those halls, he will regret it."

IN HIS NEARLY thirty years of life, Finn believed he knew what beauty was. A pretty face with a come-hither expression in her eyes, a lush figure strategically enhanced with a corset to draw attention to all the right places, and a glimpse of a shapely ankle were undeniably attractive. Undeniably appealing. That was, until he stood at the base of the staircase in the entry hall of Bennington Manor, leaning casually against a carved oak post, unwilling to look away as he watched Macie with her camera.

He'd seen his fair share—if not more—of lovely women. Lasses in taverns from Inverness to Glasgow had drawn him in with their pretty faces and comely figures, while the *diamonds* of London's ballrooms draped themselves in finery of silk and velvet. Lush waves of hair framed perfect faces, the corsets cinching their waists accentuated their assets, and eyes flashing with desire would lure his gaze. He was, after all, merely a man. With a man's hungers. A man's desires. A man's appreciation of an inviting smile.

But until that moment, he had never encountered the true beauty of a woman engaged not in drawing his gaze, but in an intense pursuit of her creative passion.

He'd seen through the plain facade Macie had often employed to camouflage her beauty. She simply could not hide it. No matter how severely she wore her hair or how unattractive her dress, she could not conceal her natural loveliness.

On this afternoon, Macie wore a plain white blouse and dark wool skirt, her hair piled in casual curls upon her head. Sunlight streaming in through a high window danced over her reddish-brown hair and her cheekbones. As he concentrated on the task at hand, she pursed her lips. The intelligence and keen focus on her features intrigued him. His gaze pulled to her, and he did not want to look away.

As Finn leaned casually against the polished banister, he observed Macie's skilled, confident motions as she set up her camera and prepared to capture the character of this old house. Watching her, he felt something unfamiliar. Something quite new. He couldn't quite name it. Interest. Perhaps even fascination. And something more. Something magnetic.

As if he'd spotted his true north.

Macie glanced up from adjusting the tripod. "Is anything wrong?"

Bloody hell. Had he been so obvious that he'd given away the path of his thoughts?

He shook his head, a quick, perfunctory gesture, adding the first reasonably rational string of words that came to mind. "Will the light be sufficient?"

"Quite so." She met his gaze with a smile. "The shadows are rather perfect, really."

"If ye do not require my assistance, I'll take a look around. I need to examine the staircases for signs they require reinforcement."

"Thank you," she said. "I'm hopeful Papa will approve of the repairs. Your recommendations will go a long way toward convincing him to move forward with the restoration."

"I'll see what I can do," he said with a lightness he did not feel. Bringing the grand old house back to its true glory would be a significant undertaking. And a costly one as well. He knew damned well that Macie's father had the money to do it. But could he be convinced to part with his hard-earned funds?

"Wait just a moment," she said, fiddling with her tripod again. "I'd like to show you something."

"One of the ghosts of Bennington Manor?"

"If only we were lucky enough to have one come out of hiding," she said in a tone that may or may not have been serious. "It's rather curious, really. I don't know how my mother or my grandfather could have been descended from anyone with the slightest case of shyness."

Macie joined him at the base of the stairs. "Come with me," she said, bustling up the steps. She stopped at the first landing, standing directly before an oil portrait of an imposing man, silver streaks marking his full head of dark hair and beard. Every inch the tycoon, he sat in a tapestried chair that resembled a throne, the beautiful, chestnut-haired woman at his side displaying an impish smile that seemed rather at odds with the regal atmosphere the painter had obviously attempted to create. At her feet, a large, sedate dog gazed adoringly up at the woman.

"She is your grandmother," he said, turning to Macie.

Macie nodded. "How did you know?"

"Ye're the very image of her," he said truthfully.

"Thank you," she said, nibbling her lower lip. "I do hope so. That is how I remember her. She always had a touch of mischief in her expression."

"As does yer mum."

"Ah, you've noticed." Macie seemed pleased. "My grandfather always said I was my grandmother's miniature."

"Ye inherited her smile."

And the lively spark in her eyes.

"I think so, too," she said. "My grandfather had seemed so very serious, the shrewd man of industry. He spent his youth making his fortune, just as my father did. Most regarded him as a fierce businessman, but I knew he had a soft heart. Especially for me."

"He was a lucky man."

"Sadly, my grandfather would not have agreed . . . not after he lost her." A note of lingering grief infused her words. "Grandmama took ill not long after the portrait was completed. He brought in the most knowledgeable physicians. But they could not save her." She let out a soft sigh. "Grandpapa was never the same."

Finn pressed a gentle hand to her shoulder. "Such a loss can crush a man."

"Indeed." She turned to him, seeming to study him. "I was just a girl when she died. If my mother had not been a devoted daughter, I don't know that Grandpapa would've made it through his sadness. Mum explained he was so very angry at the world. He'd worked so very hard for years to make a fortune. But it couldn't buy him what he truly wanted most." Macie blinked back a sheen of tears. "Eventually, he clawed through the pain. In those years, he channeled his energy into his passion for antiquities. He studied with professors of archaeology, becoming something of an expert in his own right."

"I understand he funded acquisitions destined for museums."

She nodded, the faintest of smiles curving her mouth. "Several collections throughout England and the British Isles benefitted from his donations. At first, he worried Mum would be concerned that he was giving away so much of his fortune—a fortune she was to inherit. But my mother's only concern was his happiness and his legacy."

"Yer mum is a special lady." Finn spoke the truth. She had always treated him with hospitality, kindness, and a radiant smile. When he'd been at his lowest point, her wise words helped lift him from the hole of his own grief.

"Well, enough of this. My grandfather would not want me to feel sadness while I was in this house. He knew I cherished what lies within these walls."

"It makes sense that he entrusted it to ye."

Her eyes beamed at his words. "I'm so glad you understand. And that is a rare thing."

"His rationale was perfectly sound. Who better to take care of the place?"

"Who better, indeed." She sighed. "I do wish Jon agreed."

"He'll come around," Finn said. With any luck, he was not being overly optimistic.

"I hope so." She flashed a faint smile. "Oh, I did want to show you something. Follow me."

Macie hurried up the stairs, nimbly navigating the steps despite her long skirts. He followed her, heading along the corridor to the elegant, shelf-lined room that had been her grandfather's study.

"I wanted you to see this."

She cut a direct path to an exceedingly small wing chair. Bloody hell, the piece looked to be a perfect child-sized replica of a Chippendale.

"Have ye a notion to pretend ye're Goldilocks and test it out?"

Her mouth curved into a playful frown. "You know better than that, Finn Caldwell. This chair fit me—quite nicely, as I recall—when Grandpapa had it made for me. I was about seven at the time. We'd come into this room, and he would tell me tales about those who had come before in our family. His grandfather, a wily old buccaneer, actually came to live in this house. He passed away long before I was born, but Grandpapa boasted he still roamed the halls day and night, watching over his kin."

Finn regarded her with a deliberately bland expression. "Why doesn't it surprise me that yer ancestor was a pirate?"

"It seems to fit, doesn't it?" She tapped her fingertip to her chin. "Perhaps I should embellish the story a bit. A fierce pirate watching over me might run off a baron or two."

"I don't know about a baron, or a duke, for that matter. But the notion of yer ghostly pirate ancestor pursuing me down the hall might send me bolting from this place."

"I thought you wanted to see the ghost of Bennington Manor for yourself."

"That was before I knew he was a bloodthirsty scalawag," Finn said.

"Oh really? The man was not bloodthirsty. At least, I don't think he was." She pursed her lips. By thunder, did she realize how tempting her mouth was when she looked at him like that? "Phineas Caldwell, surely you, of all the rogues in London, are not afraid of a phantom."

"I haven't decided yet." He shrugged. "It would depend on the ghost."

"You can't fool me. It would take more than a grouchy spirit to send you running."

"Don't be so sure. I've never had to fend off a ghost, let alone an ill-tempered one."

"You don't have to chase it off. You simply have to acknowledge it and go about your day. Or night, for that matter."

She flashed a little grin. The woman had no right to be so appealing. Much less when she knew there wasn't a damned thing he could do about it. Not if he wanted to see this infernal deal with the devil through to the end.

"So, ye're an authority on the matter, are ye?" Finn cocked a brow, attempting to distract himself from her lips with thoughts of her pirate ancestor.

"Perhaps," she said, her tone teasing.

"Ye've seen him roaming about, have ye?"

"I'm sure that I have. When I was a girl." Her teeth grazed her bottom lip, drawing his eye once again. "Though Jon believed I had an overly active imagination." She motioned him to the large mahogany desk near the fireplace. She handed him a silver-framed image that had been displayed by a neatly arranged pile of books. "My grandfather looked at this photograph every time he sat at this desk."

Finn gazed at the decades-old memory preserved by a camera's lens. The woman he recognized as Macie's grandmother had been rosy-cheeked and vibrant, dressed in a prim white gown trimmed in lace. Her smile gleamed in her eyes despite the softly curved set of her mouth. Macie's grandfather stood at her side, tall and lean, looking to be barely in his twenties. Decked out in what must have been his best suit of clothing, he looked rather nervous as he posed for the photograph. Perhaps that had something to do with the tall, imposing man who stood to the side of the young couple, his expression far less joyful than that of the lovely woman he'd wager had been Macie's great-grandmother. An equally tall and somber man, a generation older than the others but still boasting a full head of silver hair, stood near the groom.

"This portrait was made on the day of my grandparents' wedding. Grandpapa said he treasured it above all the others he'd commissioned over the years."

"Yer grandmother was a beauty," Finn said, taking in Macie's keen resemblance to the young bride. He pointed to the stone-faced man and the joyful redhead. "Those are yer great-grandparents?"

She nodded. "My grandmother's father was not pleased with the choice she'd made. His expression made that quite clear. But Grandmama was ahead of her time. Just as my mother did, she spurned a match to a man with a fortune to marry the man she loved. That may have been why Grandpapa was driven to make his own fortune, if only to justify her faith in him."

"She was strong willed. Like ye."

"I like to think so." She tapped her fingertip to the glass covering the photograph. "That's him," she said, pointing out the man with his gray mane. "My ancestor, the pirate. Quite a dignified fellow, as you can see."

"He looks like a man of grit and determination," Finn observed. "And not a hook or peg leg in sight."

"You do realize that all pirates did not resemble Blackbeard."

"I cannot say I've ever given it much thought."

"He did have a small scar from a dagger on his cheek. Or so I was told. You can scarcely make it out in the photograph."

Finn spotted the curved mark near the man's jaw. Reflexively, his hand went to his own face, touching the scar he'd borne for nearly two decades.

Macie's gaze followed his movement. Her eyes narrowed, her expression growing curious. "Were you and Jon up to some mischief when you were boys? It left its mark."

"Something like that," he said, the lie tasting bitter on his tongue.

Her brow furrowed. "I'm sorry. I did not mean to pry."

Blast it, the last thing he wanted to talk about was that small, fading mark on his skin. He had never given a damn about the flaw. But the memory of the night he'd received that scar cut deeper than the blade of the bastard who had inflicted it.

"No need to regret yer question. There's not much to say about it, is all," he said, softening his tone. "Now, tell me more about the fierce ghost of yer ancestor."

"Whether or not he was a pirate, he was a seafaring man, bold and brave. My grandfather remembered he was quite formidable in protecting what was his."

He placed the photograph back in its place. "If the man has come back as a spirit, I suspect he would watch over ye."

"Yes, I imagine he would." She flashed a grin. "So I suggest you continue to be a gentleman while you are in this house."

"A gentleman, eh?"

"Most definitely." She reached up, drawing the pad of her thumb over the contour of his jaw. Bloody hell, was she trying to drive him mad?

He pulled in a low breath. "That would be wise."

"Unfortunately, I must agree." Her plump mouth curved at the corners. "We would not want to shock the ghosts, now would we?"

"I'd wager they've seen their share of ungentlemanly scenes."

"I suspect you're right." She shrugged. "If they are so rude as to spy on us, perhaps we should give them something to talk about."

"Ye do enjoy a scandal, don't ye, lass?"

"At times. Pity you do not share my interest."

"I have no interest in stirring the gossips to talk, much less those who no longer walk among the living."

He met her vibrant eyes. Macie was playing with fire. Ah, he had an interest. But it didn't have a bloody thing to do with scandal or ghosts or staging a well-timed scene. No, it had everything to do with the woman who stood temptingly within reach. If he wasn't careful, a man could lose himself in her emerald gaze.

"I've found creating a minor stir to be rather amusing," she went on, her expression turning pensive. "Dabbing a bit of tarnish onto my *good name* has been a matter of self-preservation."

"Self-preservation, eh?"

Her teeth grazed her lower lip. "I do not expect you to understand."

For a long moment, he considered her words. "Macie, I know more than ye think."

"Do you?" She lowered her gaze, then met his eyes again. "Since my debut, I've been viewed as a prize to be taken. Valued not for myself. Not for my talent. Not for my wit. But only as a means to an end."

As a means to her father's fortune. The unspoken words hung in the air.

"So ye've chased the blighters away, using whatever tool is at yer disposal."

"Much to my father's consternation." She veiled her eyes with her lashes. "Well, then, enough of this. I didn't come here today to blather on about noble nobs and my oh-so-tragic plight. We both have far better things to do."

"Ye're not blathering, Macie." Gently, he brushed a rebellious curl behind her ear, his fingertip lingering over her silky cheek. "Ye're right to drive away the hare-brained dolts. They don't deserve a woman like ye."

She studied him for a long moment. "You do surprise me, Finn Caldwell. Every time I think I have puzzled you out, I realize I cannot."

"I am not an enigma, Macie." He shrugged. "I am just a man."

A man who can see the true beauty of the woman who is standing before him. A man who wants to hold her. To touch her. To kiss her senseless.

The faintest of smiles curved her mouth. Gazing down at her, he drank her in. She was so bloody tempting. As he watched her, she pulled in a breath, as if to steady herself. Had she sensed the hunger in him? Did it please her? Or did it threaten to tear the fragile bond they'd managed to forge?

Blast it. He was a fool to think he could stand so close to her and not want to kiss her. Not want to touch her. Not want to hear his name on her lips, breathless with need.

Releasing her from his light touch, he turned away and went to the window. None too gently, he shoved the curtains aside. "The light is fading. Ye'd best be finishing up whatever it was ye'd planned for today."

Macie followed him. "There's still time." She reached for him, brushing her fingers against the edge of his jaw. "You're not like the others. Somehow, I've always known that much is true."

Gently, he caught her hand in his, stilling her. He had given his word he would protect her. Even from himself. He bloody well had to remember that simple fact.

Fool that he was, he wanted to kiss her. Now, it was his turn to play with fire.

With one finger, he softly tipped up her chin. He drew the pad of his thumb over her mouth, over her plump lower lip. If she responded to his caress—if she wanted him—could he force himself to turn away?

Macie met his gaze, the slight curve of her smile betraying a hint of pleasure at his touch. Her forest green eyes searched his face for a truth he could not allow her to see.

Unexpectedly, the sound of the door chimes cut through the thick silence. She blinked, as if jarred out of a haze.

"That must be Nell," she said, taking a step back as his hands fell away. "Her fitting must not have taken as long as we'd expected." Was that a note of disappointment in her voice?"

"I'll let her in." Finn turned to the door, giving silent thanks for the interruption.

Macie's hand brushed his, stopping him in his tracks. "Before you do, I have one question."

He met her gaze, seeing an unfamiliar hesitation. "What is it, Macie?" His voice sounded gruff to his own ears.

"Is it so very hard to see, Finn?" Her voice was slightly husky and flavored with emotion. "The truth of who I am . . . the woman. Not the heiress."

"Ye are an original, Macie. One of a bloody kind. Any man who doesn't want ye for who ye are . . . he's a blasted fool."

Chapter Fifteen

S HIFTING RESTLESSLY ON the chaise in her study, Macie stared down at the novel she was reading. Actually, *attempting* to read. As her eyes took in the words on the page, Miss Austen's witty dialogue was all but drowned out by the echo of Finn's words in her thoughts.

Any man who doesn't want ye for who ye are . . . he's a blasted fool.

Nearly twenty-four hours after she'd posed the question that had long weighed on her, Finn's gruff voice played in her memory. Again. And again. His tone had been low and flavored with an emotion she could not quite puzzle out. *Quite intriguing, indeed.*

Setting the book aside, she closed her eyes. Truly, was it his surprising pronouncement that had put her in a stir? Or was it the possibilities of what might have gone between them if Nell had not returned home at that precise moment. Had he wanted to kiss her? Would she have savored the press of his lips to hers?

Good heavens, what had come over her? She knew better than to allow this man—of all the men in London—into her heart. Pretending that a romance had blossomed with Finn—no, not a romance, a mere infatuation, she corrected herself—had promised to be quite a clever charade. He had been the logical choice. But now, it was not nearly as simple as she'd thought it would be. She'd never imagined this man who'd been so very vexing would speak the words that soothed the doubts she'd harbored for so very long.

But she had to keep her head about her. Despite the moments when it seemed a true bond was being forged between them, Finn was a rogue. For a man like him, a kiss, a caress—even a tumble in her bed—would be little more than a fleeting moment of desire. He knew about passion. He could bring a woman pleasure. Of that, she had no doubt.

But love? Well, that was another story, wasn't it? She couldn't allow herself to be swept away by a delicious romantic fantasy. If she did, her heart might bear the scar long after their deal was done. Long after Finn had satisfied whatever bargain he'd worked out with her brother.

Drat. Drat. Double drat. Someday, she'd look back upon this moment and wonder at these fanciful longings.

It simply isn't meant to be.

But would a love affair *ever* be meant for her? For years, she'd driven away one entitled Lord Nob after another. Would she need to settle for a placid existence in which she would never feel the depth of passion her mother and father had shared over decades of love and laughter and the occasional heartache?

Allowing herself a sigh, she tucked a ribbon into place and closed the book. Perhaps later, with any luck, could focus on the witty characters on the pages.

She glanced at the grandfather clock. It wouldn't be long before sunset. The hazy light cast shadows on the wall, and she allowed her imagination to run wild for a few moments until the sound of brisk footsteps caught her attention.

Mrs. Tuttle marched into the room, chin up, looking as if her every nerve was as prickly as a porcupine's quill. "Miss Macie, he's here again." She did not try to hide her exasperation.

"He?" Macie replied blandly, though she already knew the answer.

"You know of whom I speak." As Mrs. Tuttle folded her arms at the waist, the tension in her mouth eased, if only a sliver. "Mr. Caldwell is in the parlor with Miss Nell. She's got it in her head that he must have a costume for the masquerade tomorrow night."

"Oh, dear. I suppose I should rescue him."

The housekeeper shrugged. "I wouldn't be in too much of a hurry to spare that man from Nell's notions. With any luck, she'll send him on his way without even realizing what she's doing."

"Not likely. He's got good reason to stick around," Macie said as she joined Mrs. Tuttle at the door.

"Does he now?"

"Soon, we will talk over tea," Macie replied. "By then, it won't matter."

"Won't matter, eh? I don't like the sound of that," Mrs. Tuttle said. "We both know how you like to scheme. I do hope you're not getting in over your head this time."

"I know better than to take a risk I cannot navigate. Much less with that man." Macie sounded more confident than she felt.

The older woman gave a little sigh. "Will he be in the residence *again* tonight?"

"Possibly," Macie said. "He's determined to be the noble protector while Jon is away."

"Phineas Caldwell? Noble?" Mrs. Tuttle scoffed. "I suppose I've heard everything now."

"Ah, don't be so grumpy," Macie said lightly. "I believe his reasons are sound."

A line of worry creased the older woman's brow. "The police still haven't found why the old man was in the old house, have they?"

Macie shook her head. "Not that I am aware. With any luck, they'll be able to rule out a connection with our family after the man revives."

"I'll prepare the spare room for Mr. Caldwell. Just in case." Mrs. Tuttle pulled back her shoulders, affecting an air of efficiency.

"An excellent idea." Macie smiled. "Thank you."

"There was no time last night."

"It was definitely an unforeseen development."

Mrs. Tuttle nodded. "What would your brother say about all of this?"

Macie gave a little shrug. "I'd like to think he would put our well-being ahead of false notions of propriety. But truth be told, what Jon doesn't know won't hurt him."

MACIE WAS NO stranger to unexpected scenes. After all, she'd become quite adept at creating them. But even she could not have expected to come upon Nell's determined attempt to convince Finn to be fitted for a medieval tunic, of all the things.

"I have it on good authority that she is dressing as Maid Marian," Nell said as Macie approached the doorway. "Her escort's attire should complement hers."

Finn stood by the fireplace in the parlor, his back to Macie. Though she could not see his face, she could readily picture the rise of his eyebrows as he spoke. "Have ye gone batty, lass?"

"Batty." Nell blinked, looking a bit taken aback. "That was most unnecessary."

"All right, then. Daft."

Nell sighed. "You wound me, Mr. Caldwell."

"Be thankful I consider ye a lady. Those are the mildest words I could come up with on short notice. Ye're mad if ye think I'm wearing a blasted tunic to a ball."

"Madame Lorette assured me she could devise a costume within a few hours. Once she has your measurements, of course."

Macie strategically cleared her throat. "You have it on good authority, do you, Nell?"

"Oh, dear," Nell said, with a touch too much dramatic flair. "Well, it's true, isn't it?"

"So, Madame Lorette revealed my secret?" Macie said, crossing into the room. "I was hoping my costume would be a surprise."

"She did not," Nell explained a bit sheepishly. "But one of the seamstresses mentioned that she'd had recently finished your gown. I was able to puzzle it out."

"That makes me a bit cross, but I must forgive her. Her needlework is perfection."

"Indeed," Nell said. "I was quite relieved to learn you'd changed your mind. Your original idea would have been rather . . . unconventional."

"Lady Godiva?" Finn sounded rather hopeful.

"An intriguing idea," Macie said. "Though I doubt I could control a horse inside the ballroom. Lady Fenwick would have every reason to be displeased."

"A man can dream," he said, a smile in his eyes.

"You are incorrigible," Macie said.

"One of my better traits." Finn scratched his chin. "So, what was this *unconventional* costume?"

"I'll leave you in suspense for the time being. I may choose to wear it to another ball."

Nell turned her attention back to Finn. "Now that we've confirmed Macie's costume, I'm even more convinced that Maid Marian needs her Robin Hood."

"There's a greater chance I will be knighted in the morning than that I will wear *blasted hose*." Finn looked as if the words were painful to utter. "And a hat with a feather, no less."

"I imagine you would look quite dashing. But I have confidence you will come up with something on your own. Something better suited." Macie bit back a giggle. "A villain, perhaps."

"Better than a blasted merry bloke in Sherwood Forest," he agreed with a nod.

"Well then, I suppose that's settled," Nell said with a little pout. "Though Robin and Marian would present such a romantic image." She folded her arms and pursed her lips, as she did when she was mulling a problem. "That is what you want, isn't it, Macie? An illusion of romance?"

"Quite so. But actions speak louder than costumes." She

turned to Finn. "Don't you agree?"

He shrugged. "Do I have a choice?"

"There is always a choice." Macie kept her tone light. "I've been thinking about the night of Lady Drayton's ball. As I'm sure you'll recall, we shared a dance."

"Even if I attempted to pry the memory from my mind, my toes would not allow me to forget," he said.

My, he was a cheeky one. "I did not tread on your toes that night." *Though I probably should have stomped one or two for good measure.*

"Are ye so certain, then, lass?"

"I saw the two of you on the ballroom floor," Nell said, her tone betraying a bit of hesitation. "Macie looked as though she'd rather have been waltzing with the devil himself."

Finn folded his arms casually and leaned against the back of a settee. "Lass, yer eyes did *not* deceive ye."

"As I recall, I was in no mood to dance. My shoes were pinching my feet." Macie attempted to explain away Nell's observation.

"So that was it, was it?" Finn said, his tone deliberately bland.

Macie studied him for a long moment. The coolness in his expression bore little resemblance to the way he'd looked at her at the old house. She pulled in a breath, attempting to dull her feelings. "To be quite honest, this charade has proven more challenging than I'd hoped."

"I say we toss this deceptive game upon the rubbish heap and enjoy the masquerade. Perhaps Maid Marian will find her Robin Hood after all."

"The *rubbish heap* is not an option. Heaven knows I have no desire to find my own personal Robin Hood. The very thought of some porridge-faced nob gallivanting about in a tunic and plumes makes my stomach a bit unsettled." She marched up to Finn, hiking her chin and looking into his eyes. "With that carved jaw of yours and that devil-may-care expression, I've no doubt you have charmed more than your fair share of women. Who's to say that I could not be one of them?"

Indeed. Perhaps he already has.

But that was a truth best kept close to the heart.

He shrugged again. "Anyone who knows us."

"At times, I do believe you are truly impossible." She sighed. "But you're my best hope. I feel confident we can put on a convincing performance."

"Convincing, eh?" He gazed down at her, his amber eyes gleaming with mischief. "So, am I to seduce ye right then and there, with all of yer host's high-born friends taking in the show?"

"You know better than that," she said. "Believe it or not, Finn Caldwell, I can read you better than you know. After all, I had a lot a practice when you and Jon were lads."

"Did ye now?"

She smiled, the memory of a younger, far less cynical Finn smiling in her thoughts. "You know I'm speaking the truth. Now, we'll need to practice a bit and get . . . comfortable with one another if this is going to work."

"Ye really believe that's possible?" The mischief had drained from his eyes, replaced by an emotion she couldn't quite read.

"We don't need to convince anyone that you're ready to drop down upon one knee and profess your undying love," Macie said, the vision her imagination conjured of him doing precisely that as fantastical as the notion of him dashing about Sherwood Forest, bow and arrows in hand.

His brows rose. "Well, that's a bloody good thing then, isn't it? Undying love is not my strong suit."

"Truer words have seldom been uttered," she agreed. "But if we are to discourage the noble snobs, a hint of infatuation will do."

A thin smile tugged at his mouth. "If one dares to touch ye, I'd offer a *hint* of bodily harm."

Macie tried not to smile at the image of Finn hauling up a whey-faced lord by his lapels, putting his lean strength on display for all to see. "In the interest of sparing my dear brother yet another gray hair, I would prefer a non-violent approach. Would it be so difficult to act as if you have a tender affection for me?"

"Macie, do ye even know what that would look like?" His forehead furrowed as he studied her. "All this time ye've done everything ye could to chase a man away, short of carrying a sword at yer hip."

"Actually, she has done that," Nell quipped with a little grin.

"Ah, that's right. Henry VIII and his infernal codpiece," Finn said. "How in blazes could I forget that tale?"

"In my defense, it was not an actual sword." Macie sent Nell a speaking glance. "You are enjoying this a bit too much, my cheeky friend. Whose side are you on? His? Or mine?"

"Both." Nell replied. "If your plan is going to succeed, you need to look as if you are smitten. But given the choice between embracing one another or hugging a porcupine, I'm not entirely sure you wouldn't opt to embrace the spiny little beast."

Macie sighed. "That is an exaggeration." *But perhaps only a bit.*

"The lass has a point," Finn said. "This scheme of yers will not work."

Macie narrowed her eyes at him. "Why, Finn Caldwell, I had not taken you for a man who runs from a challenge."

His eyes gleamed like amber as he met her gaze. "I've never run from anything in my life. Save for an ornery wildcat yer brother and I once stumbled upon in the Highlands."

"I thought as much," Macie said truthfully. "In that case, we can and we will prepare for this challenge."

"So what is it ye're looking for, lass?" Macie felt Finn's gaze on her. "Do ye even know?"

She glanced at the intricate design woven into the carpet, stalling for a better answer than the truth. Tracing the pattern with her gaze, she realized she was rather stuck. "Tender affection would suffice," she said finally.

He quirked a brow. "And what precisely does that look like?"

She pulled in a low breath. "I'd imagine the way Robin Hood would have looked upon Maid Marian."

"Robin Hood?" He raked his fingers through his hair. "How

does a man trying to keep his neck out of a noose have time for *tender affection?*"

"Oh, theirs was quite the love story," Nell said. "So very romantic. I do enjoy a tale of true love." She studied him for a moment. "Of course, I also find star-crossed love and a tormented hero rather appealing. Don't you agree, Macie?"

Macie bit back a smile. "I do fancy a ripping good gothic."

"Blast it, I'd figured as much." He plowed his fingers through his hair. "The both of ye would get along famously with my sister. She actually shed tears while reading a tale of some bloke who went mad longing for his *one true love,* as she put it. The heroine had conveniently died, so the madman did not need to listen to her prattle on for eternity. I suppose *that* was an advantage."

"Oh, I think I've read that story. I simply adore it." Nell shot him a little frown. "Of course, no one would confuse you with a true romantic."

He shrugged. "Perhaps I should carry a book of poetry at all times."

"An apt accessory, indeed," Macie said, cocking a brow. "As I understand it, flowery poetry is a tool for accomplished rogues."

"I am not an *accomplished* rogue," he said with a grin that was as infuriating as it was appealing. "I consider myself an amateur."

"Perhaps that is to all of our benefit," Macie replied. "After all, I can well imagine you reading a sonnet with a look of utter torment on your face."

"Speaking of torment, a bit of practice for the dances may be helpful," Nell suggested, her tone cheeky.

Macie glanced about the room with its abundance of furniture and artwork. She shook her head. "This space is far from ideal."

"It will work." Finn said quickly moved the furniture off the carpet, rolled up the rug, and motioned to the space he'd cleared. "Yer ballroom awaits, my lady."

Nell crossed the room to the baby grand piano. "We will

begin with a waltz."

For the briefest of moments, Finn looked as though he was heading for his own execution. But then, he took Macie by the hand. "Shall we dance?"

Chapter Sixteen

MACIE HAD NEVER considered herself graceful. Heaven knew she could manage to stumble over the tiniest lump in a carpet, slip upon the slightest of rain puddles on the pavement, or tumble over her own skirts. That questionable talent was the reason she'd ended up in Finn's strong hands in the first place. But somehow, it had never become a matter of concern.

Until now.

Familiar notes in three-four time filled their makeshift ballroom as Nell's fingers moved skillfully over the keys, but Macie struggled to follow the precise rhythm. Somehow, following the lead of her partner had never before seemed so difficult. Finn's every movement seemed mechanical. Awkward. His every step appeared to be an act of drudgery.

"I'm not quite sure how to put this," Nell observed without missing a note. "The waltz is romantic. Perhaps even seductive. And what I'm seeing now is definitely . . . not."

"Romantic, eh?" he repeated in a gruff voice. "Blasted nonsense, if ye ask me."

"If I might be so bold, I'd suggest that you relax a bit," Nell went on.

"What man could relax while waltzing with Calamity Macie?"

Forcing a little smile, Macie purposefully stepped on his foot. "At least now when you complain of smashed toes, you'll be speaking the truth."

"Oh, dear." Closing the lid over the piano keys, Nell stood, leaning her bustle against the piano as she folded her arms at the waist. "This act will not fool anyone, much less a determined suitor."

"We will figure this out," Macie countered, despite the nagging realization that Nell might be right.

Finn released Macie from his easy hold. "I agree with ye. This is an impossible task." A hint of a smile curled his mouth. "But in my life, I've heard that many times and proven the naysayers wrong."

Nell looked as though she wanted to be cross with him, but that impulse was no match for the charm in his eyes. "I would suggest behaving as if the two of you want to be in the same room."

"A monumental challenge if ever I've heard one." A touch of humor flavored his tone.

Nell's brow furrowed, as it tended to do when she mulled a problem. "Perhaps there's no need to worry over the dances. I don't imagine heiress hunters would be deterred by your nimble footsteps in the ballroom. But a little romance might send them running. Those fops do not want to tangle with a jealous man."

Finn shrugged. "A little romance, eh?"

Nell offered a sage nod. "What better way to nudge a pesky suitor to set his sights on a dollar princess who gives a fig about a title?"

"My fists would make more of an impression," he said, sounding as if he was not jesting.

"My, that would be a rather delicious scene, wouldn't it?" Nell clearly enjoyed the dramatic notion.

"Let's hope it does not come to that," Macie said. "Creating such a stir would not be prudent."

His brows hiked. "Since when has Calamity Macie been known for her prudent ways?"

"I am beginning to detest that nickname," she said with a deliberate little sigh.

His eyes flashed with amusement. "Hence, why I am using it."

"You must have been incorrigible as a lad," she replied.

"I still am, and ye know it."

Ah, the man had no right to be so appealing. And so infuriating.

In those moments at the old house—when they'd been alone and there'd been no need to put on an act—she'd seen an honesty in his eyes. When he'd brushed his thumb over her lip, his touch had been so very gentle. So very tender. Yet now, he displayed a glib nonchalance. Had she misread his expression and his actions? Which was the true reality?

For now, she had to focus on the present, exasperating as it was. "I'm beginning to feel this discussion is rather pointless." Macie resisted the urge to sigh. "After all, it should not be so very difficult to create an illusion, to do just enough to keep people guessing. It's not as if anyone is expecting to see you sweep me off my feet."

"Or carry ye over the threshold, lass?" His tone was not entirely flippant.

An image flashed through her thoughts. Powerful arms holding her tenderly. Finn's desire-filled gaze meeting hers. His masculine smile that promised a lifetime of wickedly sweet kisses. *Oh, dear.* She'd never been prone to flights of fancy. Until now.

She pulled in a low breath, banishing the thought. "Good heavens, no." She smiled to herself. "Besides, who would believe it?" Macie said blandly.

Nell's brow furrowed again. "Stranger things have happened," she said, quieter than she'd been.

"Not to me." Macie shored up her resolve. "It's not as though I shall be overcome with longing."

"Ye don't think I could make that happen?" His question sounded like a challenge.

"Don't take it personally, Finn." She hiked her chin, trying desperately to sound more confident than she felt. "I've never lost my rational sense over a man."

An emotion she could not quite read danced in his eyes. "I suspect ye've never had a man worthy of ye give it a go." His voice was low and edged with gravel.

His words took her by surprise, but she tried not to show it. She managed a bland shrug. "You will get no argument from me."

His sly smile reached his eyes. "Well, it's bloody high time we changed that."

For a long moment, perhaps a few swooshes of the pendulum on the clock on the mantle, Macie stood quite still. He'd issued what had seemed a challenge, but she saw the questions in his eyes.

Her pulse and her mind raced. Suitable replies tumbled and spun through her thoughts. His words had been bold. Perhaps even brazen. Yet, his tone had contained a note of what seemed a raw honesty.

She deliberately lifted a brow. "And you think you are the man who could make me cast all reason aside for the sake of his kiss?"

He grinned, cocky as a man could be. "'Tis a monumental task, but I'm up for the challenge."

"Are you now?" she countered, his touch of humor easing her nerves.

An unfamiliar heat flared in his eyes. "Better than ye know, Macie."

"You know they say I have a heart of ice, don't you?"

"As I told ye, they're bloody fools, Macie."

An unreadable emotion marked his features. His gaze was intently focused, his eyes crinkling at the corners as though he found her rather intriguing. When his mouth curved at the corners, the slightest of smiles, waves of warmth rippled through her.

"Yet again, we are in agreement." She pulled in a low breath, but it did little to quiet her pulse. "A rare thing, that."

Nell cleared her throat, a quiet, strategic little cough. Another sound—a louder, more pronounced *humph*—followed. Macie's attention jolted toward the doorway. Mrs. Tuttle stood silently, holding a neat, dress-sized box tied with a lovely blue satin ribbon. Her cheeks were drawn, her mouth pulled tight as if she'd held back from uttering the thoughts on the tip of her tongue. Her gaze was directed at Finn, a cross between daggers and worry gleaming in the woman's eyes.

"Miss Macie, you have a delivery," she said finally, her tone strained. As her gaze settled on Finn, her eyes flashed. "It seems to have arrived at the perfect time."

I SUSPECT YE'VE never had a man worthy of ye give it a go.

At the moment when Finn had spoken the words that had seemed both a challenge and a promise, Macie knew she was playing a dangerous game. For years, she'd erected a frosty shield around herself. She'd quite thoroughly convinced herself that she neither needed nor wanted a man's kiss. A man's passion. She was content simply outrunning and outsmarting them all.

Until she'd gotten caught up in a snare of her own making.

Finn had looked at her as if she was something unique. Something special. How could she pretend that the heat in his eyes had not begun to melt her protective, icy armor?

She suspected Finn had not walked away unaffected by those moments. In the evening, when he joined them for the supper Mrs. Tuttle had prepared, he'd kept his attempts at conversation uncharacteristically sparse. Afterwards, he'd headed to the Rogue's Lair. She'd heard him return well past midnight, entering through the back door with the key she'd insisted he take so as not to disturb the housekeeper at the wee hours. When Macie awoke not long after sunrise, he'd already awakened, dressed, and headed out to attend to his business interests. Or so the briskly penned note he'd left with Mrs. Tuttle indicated.

Now, she sat in her study, pretending that her world had not somehow tilted ever so slightly on its axis. She would spend a few productive hours with her camera before they began preparations for the countess's masquerade.

Sunlight streamed through the stained glass windows, casting a colorful reflection upon the wall behind Nell. "I take it Mr. Caldwell plans to go about his business this morning," she commented idly while fiddling with a ribbon around a shepherdess's staff.

Macie nodded. "I've much work to do to prepare for this exhibit, I'm rather relieved we will be on our own."

"He's become rather protective, hasn't he?"

"In his own way," Macie agreed.

Nell looked up as Cleo jumped upon the arm of the settee. "Don't even think about it," she said, snatching away the bright red ribbon as the cat made a bold grab for it. As Cleo replied with an irked *meow*, Nell sent the feline a playful scowl. "Perhaps I will dress you as a lamb. With the libations freely flowing, I doubt anyone would notice."

Cocking her tail at a jaunty angle, Cleo navigated her way off the settee onto the carpet. Rolling onto her back, she stretched out lazily, unfazed by Nell's threat.

Macie reached out, touching the crook that was longer than the woman who would carry it was tall. "Really, Nell, is that thing truly necessary?"

Nell's brows hiked. "You've carried swords and, if I'm not mistaken, a medieval mace to costume balls. I doubt this wooden stick can compare."

"You'll be pleased to see that my costume tonight requires no accessories of that sort."

"I am quietly thrilled at the thought. Though I am rather disappointed that you won't be wearing that bizarre little hat the seamstress made."

Macie shrugged. "Perhaps I'll wear it next time. Tonight, I wanted a more feminine appearance."

"If what I've heard about the guest list is true, the heiress hunters will be out in full force tonight. Mr. Caldwell will be busy chasing them off."

Macie reached down to pet Cleo. "I do wish some of the noble nobs would give up hope."

"Some will," Nell said. "But I suspect one or two may be more motivated to continue the chase. Perhaps Mr. Caldwell will see a need to put his pugilistic skills to use."

"You do relish the thought, don't you?"

Nell shrugged. "I can't quite put into words why the notion appeals to me. I only know that it does." She set the staff aside. "I feel confident that he would not hesitate to defend you in any manner necessary."

Macie patted Cleo's head, eliciting an enthusiastic purr. "He definitely would not shrink from a fight."

"He is quite protective of you. Perhaps more so than a hired bodyguard."

Why was Nell's expression so very serious? It wasn't like her. And Macie wasn't entirely sure she liked this new side of her friend.

"He has good reason to be. Jon is holding something over his head. It's to Finn's advantage that I make it through the next fortnight with both my name and my person untattered."

"I don't think that's all there is to it." Nell went to the window and glanced outside. She turned back to Macie. "I see how the man looks at you."

"Don't be silly." Macie dismissed the thought. "You're the one who encouraged *a little romance*, as you put it."

Nell slowly shook her head. "Macie, a West End thespian would not be so convincing."

"Really, Nell?" Macie reached for her cup and took a sip of tea. "You thought he was anything but romantic while we were dancing."

Nell stared down at the rug for a moment, seeming to collect her thoughts. "I saw the look in his eyes."

Steeling herself against a rush of emotion, Macie gulped a breath. "Finn is a known rogue. He relishes a challenge." She navigated around Cleo, who'd decided to stretch out over the carpet and groom her dark fur. "Don't worry that I'm going to be swept away by a man with an endearing brogue and a tender touch. I know better. Especially where Finn Caldwell is concerned."

Nell's mouth thinned. "This charade you've designed might not go the way you'd planned."

"Good heavens, Nell. I know what I'm doing." Macie nibbled her lip. *Let's hope so.*

"He's not like the others, Macie. I can sense it." Nell let out a brief sigh. "The two of you are playing a risky game. And this time, I'm not entirely sure you will be able to guard your heart."

Chapter Seventeen

Since she'd been a girl, Bennington Manor had seemed a haven to Macie. Now she was a woman, with an independent mind and pursuits, but the old house still represented a place where she could be entirely herself. Especially when she had her camera set up, experimenting with the light and lenses and shadows to capture the beauty of the grand old house. Finding a few hours in the day, Macie seized the opportunity to make her escape there.

Nell had made a dash to the library, intent on exploring Macie's grandfather's collections. While Macie set up her tripod, her friend strolled down the porch steps, toying with the miniature silver scepter her grandfather had kept on his desk. Good heavens, why had Nell decided to bring out the toy Macie had played with as a girl, of all things?

"It's lovely." Nell examined the tiny garnets gleaming against the silver. "How did your grandfather acquire it?"

"I believe he had it made especially for me." Fond memories of the toy filtered into Macie's thoughts. "Believe it or not, I pretended to be a princess when I was a little girl. Grandpapa had me convinced it was real and quite priceless."

Nell tapped the length of silver that was a bit longer than her hand against her palm. "It has a bit of weight to it." She threw Macie a speaking glance. "You should borrow this for Lady Fenwick's masquerade. There's a fair chance you'll encounter

Lord Hands-a-lot."

Macie pictured the pinch-faced boor with his swath of pale-yellow hair and meaningless title. During their last encounter at Lady Who-ever's soiree, she'd had to resist the impulse to toss her champagne, flute and all, at the viscount when he became a bit too free with his bony hands. She'd settled on *accidentally* treading upon his toes and making her escape. But this time, it would be different. In her mind's eye, she pictured Finn taking action if the weasel dared to touch her. Surely Finn would face the viscount down with a stare that would make the bleary-eyed lord quake in his shoes.

"I don't believe I will be needing that." Macie smiled to herself and turned her attention back to her camera. The shadows surrounding the house were becoming ideal for the image she wished to capture. But not quite yet.

Focus.

Nell twirled the scepter. "In that case, I suppose I should put it back. Are there any other treasures I might come upon?"

"Most likely. Grandfather had a love of antiquities and all sorts of curiosities. Did I show you his collection of puzzle boxes?"

"I don't believe so."

"There are several on the shelves in his study. I think you'll find them rather fascinating."

"May I attempt to solve one?"

"To your heart's content."

"You're quite sure?" Nell said with an eager grin.

"Very sure."

"Just call out if you need any help. I'll be in the study." Flashing an eager grin, Nell hurried up the steps and disappeared behind the massive doors of the house.

Finally. She could focus her thoughts. Taking a step back, Macie assessed the angle of the shot. Positioning the camera just so, she juxtaposed the image of the bustling street with the staid old house. The shadows had fallen perfectly, creating the moody atmosphere she'd envisioned.

Just then, a jaunty coach briskly made its way over the cobbles. The driver tipped his hat and continued past. As the carriage rumbled out of view, her attention pulled to a larger, more imposing conveyance. The *clop-clop* of the immense steed pulling a midnight-black brougham stood out among the sounds of the city. Slowing to a stop across the street, the driver scrambled from the bench to assist his passenger from the coach.

A man disembarked and turned to Macie. With a hawk-like focus, he fixed his gaze on her. The gent might have been her father's age, his bright-blue eyes creating a stark contrast with his silver-gray beard and hair. Boldly, he kept his attention on her and offered a nod, as if to confirm that he had indeed put her in his sights.

He approached with a brisk vigor that belied his years, his brass-tipped walking stick bobbing in his hand. As he neared, Macie noticed the unique handle of his cane.

As she tried to dismiss her instinctive wariness, the beady ruby eyes of the wolf's head seemed to watch her. Something about the metallic beast sent a chill through her which the man's overly broad smile could not warm away.

How very odd.

"I hope I did not frighten you, Miss Mason." As he neared her, his voice sounded robust and cheerful. "Hiram Neville, at your service."

Macie stepped away from her tripod. How did the man know her name? "I was a bit startled. Nothing more." She searched for a memory of him. Surely she would've remembered those vivid eyes. "Have we met? I can't say as I recall the occasion."

"I wouldn't expect you would remember me." His smile broadened. "You were a wee girl the last time I laid eyes on you, young enough to bounce upon your grandfather's knee."

His words should have reassured her, but they rang strangely hollow. The faint essence of liquor on his breath intensified her uneasiness, but she forced a bland smile. "What brings you to

London, Mr. Neville?"

His expression shifted, suddenly solemn. "Your grandfather, my dear."

An invisible weight plummeted into her stomach. "I'm sorry if you've come a long way. He passed away. It's been nearly a year."

"Andrew's death is why I've come. I only recently received the news, and I wished to pay my respects. I will miss my old friend."

Was her imagination running wild, or did the odd gleam in his eyes belie his words?

"Thank you," she said, even as her senses remained on edge. "Might I ask how you and my grandfather were acquainted?"

"Ah, we'd known each other since we were lads," he explained. "Some time ago, we parlayed our mutual interest in antiquities into a shared venture."

Macie met his eyes, searching for a reason to trust this man whose words posed as many questions as answers. Her grandfather had seldom passed up an opportunity to reminisce about his youthful exploits. Why, he'd relished those tales nearly as much as he'd enjoyed a rousing ghost story. Yet she could not recall a single mention of Hiram Neville.

"I am not familiar with the details of your enterprise," she said truthfully.

"Sadly, I cannot say I am surprised. The endeavor did not succeed. Andrew no doubt wished to put the experience behind him." He tapped the brass handle of his walking stick against his palm in a precise rhythm. "But that isn't why I've come here today, Miss Mason."

"Then . . . what might I do for you?"

He drew nearer, still toying with the cane. Each movement seemed to contain a nervous energy. His thin smile faded. "I understand you now hold the deed to Bennington Manor." This close, there was no mistaking the odor of spirits. "That is correct, is it not, Miss Mason?"

My, the conversation had taken a peculiar turn. Suddenly, Macie wanted nothing more than to be away from this stranger who claimed a vague connection with her grandfather. Pulling in a low breath, she offered a crisp response. "That is correct. Not that it should be of any of your concern."

The man's gaze sharpened. His words were cool as a winter morn. "Your grandfather was a free thinker. He prided himself on being ahead of his time. Indeed, few would toss tradition to the refuse bin and bypass the true heir."

The shift in his tone unsettled her as much as his words. "I presume you are referring to my brother."

"As I recall, your grandfather was exceedingly proud of your brother. He believed Jonathan has a fine head on his shoulders. And yet, he bequeathed his most precious asset to you. Rather unexpected, you must admit." He tapped his walking stick against the ground with restless energy. "I suppose he trusted you to care for this house. Just as he had."

"Indeed, he did." She kept her response bland, even as a tingle of warning ran along her spine.

"And what of his collections and his library?" Interest lit his pale gaze. "Have they remained with the house?"

"Several museums have benefitted from his bequests, as was his wish. Might I ask what concern this is of yours?"

"Your grandfather devoted years to the study of ancient cultures. The library he acquired reflected his dedication. If I may be so bold, his research should now be in the hands of those who could truly benefit from his work—not locked away behind the doors of this house."

"In time, my family and I intend to see to the proper disposition of his collection, including his library." The thought of it twisted like a fist in her belly.

"As I see it, *intend* is a rather unfortunate word." The old man's jovial attitude had been replaced by a diamond-hard look of scrutiny. "One can have the best of intentions, Miss Mason. But the wherewithal to follow through is what truly matters."

Biting back the words that came to mind, Macie met his frosty gaze. Her nerves seemed to stand on edge. Instinct urged her to promptly dismiss him. But she would, however, act the part of a proper lady, if only for her grandfather's sake.

"As I see it, Mr. Neville, my *wherewithal* is not of your concern." To her own ears, her voice sounded tightly controlled, the ice in her tone making clear he had crossed a line.

"I am very much interested in your grandfather's library." He tapped the silver wolf's head against his palm. "Especially the documentation of his field research."

His words caught Macie off guard. "You are referring to my grandfather's notebooks?"

"I am." He gave a crisp nod. "I have a keen interest in acquiring the collection. Especially Andrew's research."

"I'm sorry, but my grandfather's books and papers are quite precious to me. I could not possibly part with them."

"This . . . this is what matters to you." Mr. Neville pointed his cane toward her camera. "Not volumes of research that have no meaning to you. Of course, I would be willing to compensate you. The price I have in mind is most generous."

"I cannot put a monetary value on my grandfather's journals and papers."

"Your grandfather did not intend that his library would sit behind the walls of this house and collect dust. It belongs in the hands someone who can make use of it." Despite his otherwise bland expression, his eyes glimmered with a look of pure calculation. "I have delivered an offer to your solicitor. You shall find it most generous."

"Mr. Neville, I am afraid you've wasted your time."

He pinned her with his gaze. "Allow me to be blunt. I have my doubts that you possess the funds needed to fully restore this house. Without the compensation I am offering you, I cannot envision that you will manage to preserve it."

She squared her shoulders and met his steely gaze. "That is not a matter of your concern."

"You are mistaken, Miss Mason. What happens to this house is very much my concern. I presume you are aware of its history."

"Of course. Grandfather spoke in great detail about the generations of our family who'd lived within its walls."

"Lived." He tapped the walking stick against the lowest step. "And died."

Was that a note of warning?

Or a threat?

Macie's senses responded in instinctive awareness. Suddenly, she needed to flee his presence. She wanted to be far away from this man who'd offered a jovial expression but was not what—or likely whom—he'd claimed to be.

"I appreciate that you've come to pay your respects to my grandfather." She held her voice steady. "But I must be getting back to my work. Good day, sir."

"I shall be on my way." He met her dismissal with a glare. "But not yet."

"I would not like to be discourteous, but I must ask you to take your leave."

His fingers tightened around the head of his walking stick. "Andrew Bennington indulged the women in his life." His words sounded flat with an effort of restraint. "His wife. Your mother. And now, *you*."

Indulged. The word stung like a slap. Macie hiked her chin and met his icy stare. The man's civil mask had not slipped. It had fallen away, leaving behind a look of clear contempt.

"Mr. Neville, I must insist that you go."

"You would be wise to consider my offer." He tapped his cane in a distinct rhythm against the pavement. "Perhaps I'll simply bide my time. Talk about town has it that your father has no intention of pouring hard-earned funds into Bennington Manor. It won't be long until you can no longer maintain the house. Then I shall purchase this place for a pittance."

"How dare you?" Anger heated her cheeks, but she summoned the will to hold her voice steady. "I cannot fathom why my grandfather would have associated with the likes of you. I have grave doubts that you even knew him."

"I have no desire to deceive you, Miss Mason." He leaned heavily on the cane. "I'm too bloody old for games. I knew your grandfather. Quite well, indeed. Perhaps I shall buy the house and everything in it. I would be doing you and your family a favor."

"Leave, Mr. Neville." She bit the words between her teeth. "Now."

"When the time comes—and I assure you, it will—your solicitor will know how to reach me." He regarded her with an expression she couldn't quite read. "Believe me when I say you'd be better off far from this place."

As Macie's gaze trailed Hiram Neville's coach, the hair at her nape rose. Each *clomp* of his carriage horse pulling the conveyance away from Bennington Manor eased more tension from her body.

My, what an abrasive man. Why had her jovial, good-natured grandfather associated with such a flinty-eyed weasel?

She pulled in a calming breath. Then another. Turning back to her camera, she caught sight of Finn's approach. His brisk strides made short work of the distance between them.

As he neared her, his brow furrowed. "Who in blazes was that man?"

"He claims an acquaintance with my grandfather."

Finn's jaw set in a hard line. "Shall I have a talk with him?"

"That should not be necessary. I doubt I will encounter him again." She felt the tension creep back into her bones. If only she could be certain.

"What brought him here?" Finn pressed.

"The pinched old stoat expressed an interest in acquiring my grandfather's library and his research notebooks." She let out a low breath. "Among other things."

"Does the pinched old stoat possess a name?"

"Hiram Neville." She glanced down the street toward his posh carriage. "I cannot say I'd ever heard my grandfather speak of him."

"And yet he showed up here today."

Macie pulled in a calming breath, hoping to appear more confident than she felt. "I made it quite clear that I have no interest in dealing with him."

Finn plowed his fingers through his hair. "After I have a talk with him, we'll be sure of that."

"I don't believe that will be needed."

Finn shook his head. "The man needs to know ye have someone watching over ye."

"The dreadful toad would not be the first to try to intimidate me into selling my grandfather's possessions for a pittance. But we both know I'm not easy prey."

Macie toyed with her cuffs, pressing unpleasant memories back into their proper place in the back of her mind. Since she'd come of age, she'd fended off all manner of unscrupulous so-called gentlemen. Pauper lords and would-be tycoons. Men who might have seen only her father's fortune when they looked into her eyes.

Except for Finn.

Her gaze trailed over his familiar features, dancing over the carved lines of his jaw. The curves of his mouth. His clever wit, gleaming in his amber-brown eyes. Unbidden, a low heat coiled deep within, a yearning words could not fully describe.

"So, I'm to stand by and do nothing?" Finn's husky words drew Macie from her thoughts.

"For the time being, that would be best course of action."

"Not bloody likely," Finn muttered under his breath. He plowed his fingers through his hair, his slight scowl making it clear they did not see eye to eye. "I'll respect yer wishes. But if the stoat returns, I will be paying him a visit," he said as Nell appeared at the top of the stairs.

"Who was that fellow?" she asked as she navigated the steps to the pavement.

"He claims to have known my grandfather."

"I was in the library, standing by the front window," Nell

said. "I couldn't help but overhear that man say something about this house."

"He blustered a bit of nonsense about purchasing Bennington Manor. I suspect he was in his cups."

"Buy the house out from under ye?" Finn's brow furrowed. "Ye had not mentioned that."

"Given the liquor on his breath, I put no stock in his words." Macie pictured the man's contemptuous twist of his mouth as he'd taken his leave.

"If he dares to show his face here again, ye *will* let me know. Just because the bloke presents himself like someone's churlish uncle doesn't mean he is not dangerous." Finn's jaw set in a hard line.

Finn's protectiveness appealed to her on an instinctive level. But she certainly didn't need him to dash off and confront a man nearly twice his age.

Macie met his stern gaze. "Mr. Neville is a curmudgeon. Rather unpleasant, but I've no reason to fear him. After all, it's not as if he issued a threat."

In her mind, she heard his voice, the words he'd spoken in a cold, contemptuous tone.

You'd be better off far from this place.

A fresh ripple of apprehension set her nerves a bit ajar as an inner voice whispered in Macie's thoughts.

No, not a threat. But perhaps a warning.

Chapter Eighteen

A S A YOUNG man, Finn had learned to follow his gut. Despite Macie's protests to the contrary, he didn't trust the miserable bloke she'd encountered by the old mansion. Why in blazes did Hiram Neville have an interest in her grandfather's house—and with it, a library full of scholarly books?

His gut warned something was afoot. The trespasser Macie had found in the library had not searched for valuable antiquities. Instead, he'd rummaged through thick, dusty tomes. Could he be connected with Neville? *Bloody peculiar.* Damned if he wasn't going to find out what the cantankerous old goat was after.

As he sat at the reins of his carriage, transporting Macie and Nell to their townhouse, he could not help but overhear Nell's excited chatter about the upcoming ball. For the life of him, he could not understand her anticipation of an event that involved traipsing about in a blasted costume, hobnobbing with preening socialites and whey-faced lords. He had no bloody choice but to honor his agreement with Macie and suffer through the night.

Truth be told, he would've been there watching over her, blasted deal or not. Nothing and no one would keep him from her side. In the beginning, he'd expected to shield her from money-hungry jackals who might seek to coerce a beautiful heiress into a lucrative marriage. But now, he needed to protect her from a far greater menace than penniless lords seeking to marry into a fortune.

On the surface, Macie's response to her encounter with Hiram Neville had been calm and dismissive of any threat the old man might pose. But he'd seen a different response in her eyes. He'd detected a quiet alarm in their depths, an instinctive reaction she couldn't entirely hide.

The rumble of the carriage over the pavement helped him focus his thoughts away from Nell's eager expectations for the night ahead to his next course of action. By the time he arrived at the townhouse, he'd decided on his next steps.

"You're leaving now?" Macie's brows quirked after he escorted them inside and informed the ladies he'd be heading to the Rogue's Lair until later in the evening. "You'll regret missing Mrs. Tuttle's supper."

"It's a sacrifice I'm prepared to make." He kept his tone light. "I need to shore up my strength before tomorrow's ordeal."

"Lady Fenwick's parties are quite well done. You might be a grouch, but I fully intend to enjoy myself." She flashed a little frown. "You're looking for information about Mr. Neville from Logan's contacts, aren't you?"

"While I'm fortifying myself with a pint or two, I'll see what I can draw out of his regulars."

Her mouth curved at the corners. "You are dedicated to your duty, aren't you?"

"My duty?"

Her smile was soft and genuine. "You're quite the efficient bodyguard."

"Trust me when I say this, Macie—my interest in keeping you safe has nothing to do with any blasted duty."

IN FINN'S EXPERIENCE, a drinking hole was the best place to dig out the skeletons in the closets of so-called gentlemen, down-on-their luck gamblers, and buttoned-up pillars of the community with something to hide. In the years since Logan MacLain had offered his first round of whisky at the Rogue's Lair, the tavern had become a popular destination for moneyed blokes and down-on-their-luck lords, the best place in London for a man to put his ear to the ground for news that would never make it into the morning edition.

As Finn maneuvered around the patrons gathered around the billiard table, gaslight cast a glow over the polished wood tables at the Rogue's Lair. He headed straight to the spot where the barkeep stood, polishing a silver stein. Murray set down the stein, turned to him, and passed him a mug filled with his favorite ale.

"I saw you come in, Caldwell," he said. "You looking for Logan?"

"He's here tonight?"

Murray nodded. "In the back. Knowing him, he already aware you're here."

"He doesn't miss much," Finn agreed, offered thanks for the drink, and headed back to Logan's office.

Seated at a massive oak desk, Logan looked up from the paperwork he'd been reviewing. His brows quirked in surprise.

"I hadn't expected to see ye tonight. I thought ye'd be hard at work trying on the hose for the ball tomorrow night."

"Bloody hell, MacLain. I will not be wearing blasted tights, or any such nonsense. Where would ye get a notion like that?"

"Amelia informed me that there's a rumor ye're dressing as some medieval archer who shall remain nameless."

"Not a chance in Hades. Your dear wife has been misin-formed."

Logan motioned for him to take a seat. "In that case, have ye come seeking advice on your costume? Amelia dragged me to one of those torturous affairs last winter."

"Blasted shame I wasn't there to see that."

"She decided we should dress as a pirate and his wench. Oth-er than the bandana and the sword at my hip, I looked as I do every night at this place." He glanced down at his black trousers and shirt. "And I forced myself to mutter the words 'Avast ye mateys' a few times. But Amelia played the wench with the flair of a natural-born actress. Bloody hell, she was lovely." Logan grinned at the memory. "I suspect that was the night our babe—" With a shake of his head, he broke off the statement before he said too much.

"I doubt the ball will prove as memorable for me," Finn spoke the truth. "But for different reasons. With any luck, the night will prove a bore."

"I'd say that's unlikely given the company ye're keeping."

"I suspect ye're right. But I'm not here for advice. I need information," Finn said. "If ye've got it."

Logan's brow furrowed. "What do ye need?"

"This afternoon, a stranger approached Macie outside of Bennington Manor. He gave the name Hiram Neville and claimed to have known her grandfather."

"Hiram Neville? I've heard the name." Logan leaned back in his leather wing chair. "But not in this place."

Seated across from Logan, Finn reached for his mug and took a drink. "What do ye know about him?"

"Amelia was having a tea last week with some of her library patrons. One of the women is an active supporter of one of the museums. I recall hearing the name. An upstanding citizen, or so the lady said. Evidently, he's one of the museum's most generous donors. What business do ye have with him?"

"That doesn't sound like the same bloke who took it upon himself to threaten Macie this afternoon. But if it is, I'll be paying him a visit if he shows his face to her again."

Logan's brow furrowed. "What in blazes did the man do?"

"He wants to get his hands on her grandfather's library and possibly the house." Finn stretched out his legs, letting out a low breath. "He'll have to go through me first."

Logan took a drink, regarding him with a cryptic look. Finally, he said, "Ye're taking the role of protector seriously, aren't ye, my friend?"

"I gave Jon my word I'd watch over her."

"Ye'll honor yer word. Ye always do." Logan nodded his understanding. "Ye care about her, don't ye?"

"Ye could say that," Finn said coolly. "She's a lady and deserves to be treated like one."

"The lass is clever. Full of spirit." Logan regarded him for a long moment, as if he'd seen the truth behind Finn's bland words. "She could challenge a man like ye."

"A woman like Macie could challenge any man. She's a bloody original."

"She's a diamond. Ye know that, don't ye?"

Finn stared down at the ale in his stein, stalling for time. Logan's question had caught him off guard. "That she is. There's no denying it. And that's where I come in—it's my job to discourage the heiress hunters who treat her like a prize to be won."

"Ah, the noble nobs." Logan smiled. "Amelia was quite amused by Macie's description of the fortune hunters intent on courting her."

"She's held them off all this time." Finn stared down at his drink. "A man would have to be a blasted fool to fall for Macie Mason."

"Does that include ye, cousin?"

Finn shot him a scowl. "Ye've better odds of seeing the queen dance the can-can at Covent Garden than of seeing me lose my head over a woman. Not that it would make a blasted bit of difference if I did. The lass wants a diversion, nothing more. I'm a decoy she can use to run off the money-hungry blokes desperate enough to put up a chase."

Logan leaned back in his chair and scratched his chin, as he often did when he was pondering a matter. "Ye're sure of that?"

"Macie and I are like fire and ice. We're too bloody different."

"That's where ye're wrong." Logan slowly shook his head. "From what I've seen of Miss Mason, yer natures are very much alike."

"What in blazes do ye mean by that?"

Logan shrugged. "Ye'll see. In due time. But that's not why ye came here tonight. Ye want me find out what I can about Neville. I'll see what Amelia can gather from her friends while we keep alert for any talk of the man around the bar."

"I'd appreciate that," Finn said, toying with one of the chess pieces on Logan's desk. The knight. Fitting indeed, given the way he felt like he was clanking around in rusty armor, all too eager to play defender to his queen.

"There's something else," Logan said. "The gent from the detective bureau who likes the sound of his own voice was in here tonight. Murray steered his talk to the old man in the hospital. The detectives believe they've learned his identity."

"Bloody hell," Finn said under his breath. "Who is he?"

"The talker told Murray the intruder's name is Smythson. He's not a common thief. To the contrary, he's a scholar."

"What in blazes are ye telling me?"

"A woman came searching for a relative who'd gone missing. She confirmed the man lying in that hospital is her uncle. Evidently, the old gent stirred a bit at the sound of her voice."

"Bloody hell."

"The man was a professor at a university in Scotland, an expert in the same ancient statues and such that Miss Mason's grandfather sought for his collection."

"Her grandfather was an expert in his own right. They may have known each other."

"It's a distinct possibility. Until we find out what the professor was doing in that old house, I'd suggest ye not leave her unattended."

"She'll chafe at the very thought of being tethered to me."

Logan took a swig of his drink, as if fortifying himself for what he was going to say next. "I have an idea, but ye're not going to like it."

"Good God." Finn read his cousin's expression before he could utter the words. "Ye're thinking I should call on . . . the Dragon?"

Logan nodded. "Amelia's convinced the fire-breather in skirts would be a perfect companion for Miss Mason and her friend, especially as they travel about the city during the day."

"Bollocks," Finn said under his breath. "Ye do like to see yer cousin suffer, don't ye?"

"Ah, ye're a man of courage," Logan said with a chuckle. "Ye can take it."

"I'm not so blasted sure of that." Finn rubbed a sudden ache in his neck. The Dragon—better known as Logan's aunt, Mrs. Elsie Johnstone, was a force of nature. When they were lads, they'd compared her to the fiery, mythical creature. Not much in the woman's temperament had changed since then. But Mrs. Johnstone did possess a unique set of skills, and she was the most trustworthy soul he'd ever met.

"What do ye think?" Logan asked.

"This might just work. The key word being *might*. If we were to seek her assistance, how should we go about it?"

"Amelia takes tea with her at least once a week. She'd be happy to send her a message in the morning. Aunt Elsie is planning to attend the masquerade tomorrow night. It's all she's talked about for the last fortnight. She'll have no trouble breaking the ice with the ladies."

"That's what I'm afraid of," Finn said with a chuckle. "They'll form an alliance."

Amusement flashed over Logan's features. "So much the better for ye," he said. "Miss Mason possesses a natural boldness. Ye can't be there every minute to watch over her. But Aunt Elsie can teach her some ways to protect herself."

Once again, the back of Finn's neck tightened with tension. "More ways for Macie to send the heiress hunters running for cover?"

Logan slowly shook his head. "It's not the *heiress hunters* ye need to worry about." The amusement drained from his eyes. "It's the bastard who wanted the professor dead."

ON MORE THAN one night, during that time Finn looked back upon with a certain nostalgia as his *wild* youth, he had stealthily returned home at an hour that would've forced his mother to pretend she was shocked. He'd enjoyed the hours before his covert entrance—imbibing ale, learning how to throw and take a bare-knuckled punch, and if he wasn't too bruised and battered, charming a barmaid or two. The experience had been well worth the risk of incurring a stern lecture from his father that included the words *wastrel* and *vagabond*.

In the years since, Finn had never had to sneak into a home, save for one time when invited by a particularly fetching dollar princess who longed for a dalliance before her marriage to some tight-collard viscount. Until the night Macie and her friend had cloaked him in the ridiculous disguise and ushered him into their residence.

At least tonight, he had a bloody key to the house. And he had not needed to conceal his features. However, as always, there was a catch.

Mrs. Tuttle has prepared a room for you. Before he'd headed to the Rogue's Lair, Macie had told him with a little grin on her face that he would no longer have to endure sleeping upon the sparsely upholstered, half-a-foot-too-short object of torture she called a settee. But there was a caveat—Mrs. Tuttle had insisted— for the sake of decorum, of course—that he occupy one of the servants' quarters and return to the house through the servants' entrance.

At that moment, he'd thought nothing of it. A bed was a bed. He'd get sleep, and his back and legs would not feel hobbled in the morn.

But now, lying on a comfortable bed in a modest, neatly appointed room, he knew why he'd detected an air of mischief in Macie's smile. Surely she'd known what he'd be facing that night, alone in his quarters.

Mrs. Tuttle's chamber was directly beside his. He presumed the housekeeper was alone behind the door to her room. But she was chattering enough for two, at the very least.

The woman talked in her sleep. Bloody hell. But *talking* didn't quite describe the range of sounds emanating from the housekeeper's chamber. A few words he couldn't quite make out drifted through the wall between their chambers, followed by a shout. A few minutes after that, a cry jarred him while he was taking off his boots. One fell to the floor with a thud. Later, while he lay in bed, more chatter with a hearty laugh mixed in for good measure yanked him from the beginnings of slumber. Good God. Was this going to go on all night?

Suddenly, the sound of a soft snore—or was it a purr?—joined the erratic chorus coming from Mrs. Tuttle's chamber. But this was closer. Very close, indeed.

"Cleo, ye wee minx," he said, lighting a lamp. He spotted Macie's cat, curled up on a side chair, happily dozing.

He rolled over, pounded a pillow to smooth out a few lumps of feathers, and closed his eyes. The cat's contented snores permeated the confined space, a somehow fitting accompaniment to Mrs. Tuttle's unsettled murmurs. At least one of them was getting some rest that night.

Through it all, his mind wandered. It was going to be a bloody long night. Again and again, Logan's words echoed in his thoughts.

It's not the heiress hunters ye need to worry about. It's the bastard who wanted the professor dead.

Chapter Nineteen

OF ALL THE parties, balls, galas, and soirees Macie had attended in London, she counted Lady Fenwick's masquerade as the highlight. Mingling with the guests at the magnificent costume ball, Macie engaged in a lively discussion of Jane Austen's works with a strutting peacock, danced with a rather bashful tiger, and made the acquaintance of a vivacious American suffragette dressed as a fairy tale princess with shiny slippers designed to resemble glass. The orchestra's stirring notes filled the great hall of Fenwick House with smooth melodies, while the finger sandwiches and beverages were delectable. The guests were attired in all manner of ensembles, decked out as charming creatures, regal heroines, and the occasional dastardly villain. All in all, the countess's guests appeared to be thoroughly enjoying the grand affair.

Pity her grumpy bodyguard was perhaps the sole exception. Finn had spurned the notion of an elaborate costume—not that Macie could blame him, especially given Nell's rather insistent suggestion that he don tights and tunic to play Robin Hood to Macie's Maid Marian. Instead, he'd chosen to dress as a character who might've blended in with civilized men throughout the city; his version of Dr. Henry Jekyll was more dapper than she'd ever envisioned. His midnight black wool suit was precisely tailored to show off his broad shoulders, while his burgundy silk waistcoat and silvery-gray tie added an appealing vibrance to the ensemble.

Quite the handsome mad scientist, indeed. He'd caught the attention of many a female decked out in tiaras, feathers, and even the occasional set of fairy wings. Such a shame his face bore the pained expression of a man whose shoes were a bit too tight.

At the moment, he was engaged in discussion with a tycoon whose carved features were set in a look that appeared equally pinched. Trenton McAvoy was tall and lean, perhaps a bit older than Finn, given the few strands of silver marking his appealingly silky dark hair. Dressed as a younger, undeniably handsome imitation of Buffalo Bill, complete with a mustache that was most definitely not an imitation, the American industrialist cut a striking figure amongst London's elite dandies.

Observing them from across the room, Macie felt suddenly restless. Though she was enjoying the sights and sounds of the affair, the night was not going according to plan. Nearly two hours had passed, and Finn had made little effort to spend time with her, let alone provide the noble nobs any reason to think twice before seeking her attention. Why, already that evening, a boisterous baron in a toga that bared his bony knees had attempted to entice her into a stroll to the garden, supposedly to enjoy a pristine view of the night sky. Finn's well-timed approach and fierce glower had sent the long-legged fop scurrying in search of a more amenable heiress—preferably one who was not accompanied by a rather imposing escort whose scowl might send even a warrior running for cover.

Not long after the lanky lord had abandoned his efforts, another heiress hunter had made his move. The newly minted viscount had been far more persistent than Lord Drayton. And ever so much more unpleasant. Dressed as Shakespeare—or some other gent who wore a ruff about his neck—he appeared to be deep in his cups. Emboldened by the spirits, he had eyed Macie from head to toe, then uttered a bold declaration.

"It's high time you took yourself off the shelf."

The gall of the man! Macie's cheeks had burned at the smug lord's grating words.

She'd spotted Finn as he closed the distance between them, his scowl already in full force. "If I were ye, I'd think twice before saying another word." He stood within arm's reach of the viscount's reddened face.

"This does not concern you," the arrogant sot ground out.

Finn cocked a brow. "Ye think not?"

The viscount gulped a breath. "This may be a misunderstanding." He tugged agitatedly at his ruff as if suddenly the neckpiece was too tight.

"Indeed," Finn agreed. "Ye will not speak to the lady in that manner. If I hear another word from yer mouth, ye'll answer to me. Do I need to say more?"

The boor shook his head. "That won't be necessary."

"I thought as much," Finn said.

The viscount had slunk away, his eyes still radiating anger. With the situation under control, Finn offered a few stiff mumbles of conversation, spotted a man he recognized from his time at university, and politely left Macie to her own devices while Nell chatted with a gallant buccaneer.

Now, nearly an hour later, Macie spotted Finn carrying on a robust discussion with a man dressed as a cowboy. Her mood brightened as a server bearing a fully laden silver tray crossed her path and offered a flute of champagne. She happily accepted, then sipped generously from the crystal glass as she debated her next move.

Perhaps she should invite herself into Finn's conversation. At the very least, she might enjoy a bit of flirtation with the handsome cattleman. There'd be no harm in that, now would there?

Navigating the crush, Macie's progress halted when she bumped into the back of yet another guest attired as if he'd stepped out of the American frontier. A large hat added to his already considerable height. *Good heavens, another aficionado of Buffalo Bill.* Since William Cody had brought his Wild West show to London a few years earlier, the rough-and-ready showman had inspired guests at many a masquerade.

The man turned and tipped his cowboy hat. "Good evening, Miss Mason," Peter Aylesworth said with a smile.

"It's good to see you. I wasn't aware you were acquainted with Lady Fenwick."

Macie took a step back, gazing up at him. Something about the rugged costume brought out an air of masculinity in the man he usually kept tightly controlled.

"Her brother and I met while we studied in Italy. He is currently excavating ruins that predate Caesar."

"How exciting."

Aylesworth nodded. "I'm looking forward to my return. The research fascinates me."

"I can well imagine."

"I have some matters to attend to in London, but I will travel to Athens by the end of the year."

"What I would not give to bring my camera to such a site."

"That might be arranged. Our team could utilize your talents to document our discoveries."

"Oh, don't tease me so cruelly," she said lightly. "I cannot imagine that I might take part in such an expedition."

"Miss Mason, I am quite serious." A thin smile played on his mouth. "A photographer of your ability would be vital to chronicle the excavation." His brow furrowed. "Of course, you would need a traveling companion."

"I imagine Nell would be excited to take part in the journey."

Glancing over at her friend—who had moved on from her buccaneer to flirt with Finn's American acquaintance—he shook his head. "I am thinking of someone in their maturity, an older woman with experience in the field."

"Of course. I do understand." Macie said. "I must say, the very thought of documenting an antiquities exploration is quite exciting. Perhaps I shall pursue a journey."

"I hope you will consider it."

"You've definitely given me something to think about."

Glancing over Mr. Aylesworth's shoulder, she spotted Finn as he made his way through the crush.

"You would be a true asset," Aylesworth said, slanting Finn a glance.

She flashed a brief smile. "It would be the adventure of a lifetime."

Finn acknowledged Professor Aylesworth with a curt nod. "I hadn't expected to see the likes of ye here."

"I might say the same, Caldwell. Who twisted your arm to suffer through a masquerade?"

Finn's gaze lit on Macie. "Only Miss Mason would be capable of such a feat."

"But at least my pride is intact." He shot Aylesworth an assessing glance. "Buffalo Bill, eh?"

"Something like that." Aylesworth tipped his overly large hat. "I borrowed this gargantuan thing from a colleague. I've no idea why he would have such a garment, but it was preferable to my first idea."

"And what was that? An intrepid explorer?" Macie asked.

He shook his head. "Tossing a blasted sheet over my head and traipsing about as a ghost."

"You might have used the sheet as a toga," Macie suggested.

"Clever." Aylesworth said with an appealing grin.

Given the look on Finn's face, he did not agree with Macie's suggestion. "I, for one, commend ye for yer decision not to subject us to the sight of yer bony arms," he said.

Aylesworth smirked. "I might've forgone the costume entirely. As you did."

"I'll have ye know I *am* in costume." Finn tugged at his lapels. "A tragic villain if ever there was one."

Aylesworth turned to Macie. "He's serious?"

"Indeed," she said. "You might say he's quite mad."

"A mad scientist?" Aylesworth plopped the hat back onto his head. "Victor Frankenstein, I presume. Or perhaps the sinister professor who predicted I would never succeed in the field?"

Macie shook her head. "Do you give up, Mr. Aylesworth?"

"I surrender," he said. "But only to you, Miss Mason."

She bit back a grin. "Finn, if you would be so kind as to end the suspense."

"Henry Jekyll," he said, his tone gruff. "Or, if ye prefer, bloody Mr. Hyde."

"He *is* the more interesting of the two, isn't he?" Aylesworth replied dryly.

Finn nodded. "The dangerous half of a man always is."

Aylesworth glanced past them as a female voice called his name. "Blast it, she's here."

"She?" Macie repeated curiously.

"Lady Fenwick's aunt. She's been after me to appraise her collection." He sighed. "I'd hoped she'd was still on the Continent."

"Ye could always hide behind that blasted hat."

"It's too late for that." Peter Aylesworth turned back to Macie. "I meant what I said, Miss Mason. Do give it some thought. I trust you know how to reach me."

"I do," she said. "I expect I'll soon be in touch."

"Believe me, I will be waiting," he said. "Try to keep out of trouble, Caldwell." Tipping his hat again, he took his leave, heading to meet the bird-thin woman whose calling of his name seemed a summons.

When Aylesworth was well out of earshot, Finn leaned closer, lowering his voice to a conspiratorial whisper.

"Am I to assume ye've changed yer mind about chasing off every man between the ages of twenty and eighty?"

"Not at all." She shot him a little scowl. "Why would you even consider the thought?"

"Ye didn't look like a woman who wanted me to chase off the intrepid professor."

"I presume you are referring to Mr. Aylesworth."

"The one and only."

"As a matter of fact, I was enjoying our discussion. He is a fascinating man."

Finn took a drink from a passing server and regarded Macie with a look she couldn't read. "Fascinating, eh?"

"He's brilliant, you know. My grandfather held him in high regard." Macie took a sip of her champagne. "He is a true scholar and quite an explorer."

"A man who knows how to embark on the adventure of a lifetime, eh?"

"Ah, you were paying attention."

He nodded. "So, what did the man want ye to think about?"

"If you must know, he suggested I might join his research team on a future expedition."

"Ye'd tote yer camera around some old ruins?"

"There'd be a bit more to it than that," she said. "I expect I would relish the experience."

"If it's adventure ye seek, ye should pursue it." Finn rubbed his jaw, seeming to mull over the thought. "Ye would do a fine job."

Macie had been prepared for a flippant response, but she detected nothing of the sort in his tone. Nor on his expressive features. She couldn't quite explain why, but suddenly, she felt a bit off-kilter. She pulled in a calming breath. "You mean that, don't you?"

"I wouldn't say it if it were not the truth," he said. "Ye have a true talent, Macie. Now, back to my question. Are ye ready for this charade of yers to be over?"

"It's rather early in the game, don't you think?"

"I've reason to think it's a game we should not be playing."

"Perhaps that explains why you haven't even been trying. Other than glowering at Mr. Aylesworth and a few nervous nobles, you haven't given anyone a reason to believe you were not merely watching over me."

"Ye didn't need me shadowing yer every move."

"It's not just that. You know what I mean." Macie met his eyes. "You know the terms of our agreement."

"Terms of our agreement?" Again, he rubbed his jaw. "Ye sound like one of the solicitors who pens the documents for our company."

She hiked her chin. "I have no doubt you understand what I mean. I am tired of having to suffer the attentions of boors and fools and cads."

"I see that, lass. But ye shouldn't be willing to shut out every man because of these foolish blokes."

I'm not. Macie drank in the slightly gruff sound of his voice. *I don't want to shut you out.*

Oh, dear. The thought jarred her. She couldn't possibly be falling for Phineas Caldwell. That was the last thing—the very last thing—she needed.

"At the moment, that's a chance I'm willing to take." She forced a thin smile.

"Ye're sure of that?" Finn's eyes narrowed as he seemed to study her. "Ye wouldn't want to give the intrepid explorer Aylesworth the wrong idea, now. Would ye?"

"That will not be a problem. Mr. Aylesworth is interested in my skill behind a camera. Nothing more."

"I would not wager my last dollar on that, lass. He is a man. And he has eyes in his head."

Macie bit back a grin. "Why, Finn Caldwell, if I didn't know better, I'd suspect you were jealous."

"Not a chance."

"Well, now that we've settled that, may we move to another topic of conversation?"

The notes of a waltz filled the room. He glanced toward the ballroom floor. His eyes lit with a low fire as he turned back to her. "If ye're set on playing this game, it's high time we make our move."

A whisper of warning played in her thoughts. *I've reason to think it's a game we should not be playing.* Perhaps he was right. Was this scheme mere folly? Or was there a risk to this charade, if only to her heart?

Banishing her doubts to the recesses of her mind, she squared her shoulders. "Shall we give them something to talk about?"

He flashed a sly grin. "If that is what ye want, who am I to deny a lady?"

Chapter Twenty

A S THE STRAINS of a waltz droned on, Finn gazed into the narrowed eyes of the woman he awkwardly led through the motions of the waltz. He smothered a chuckle at the irony of her words. *Shall we give them something to talk about?*

Macie had certainly gotten her wish, hadn't she? Though not in the manner she'd anticipated.

As if she'd read his thoughts, her mouth dipped down at the corner, not quite a frown. *Bloody hell.* He winced as Macie's not-so-dainty slipper mashed his toes. Again. Was she deliberately stepping on his feet? No, he doubted that. She'd nibbled her lower lip, as she tended to do when she was embarrassed or worried.

By thunder, between the two of them, they could do nothing right. While weaving through the dancers in the ballroom, they'd clumsily collided with another couple, nearly toppling the bejeweled crown perched upon a scowling socialite's upswept hair. Moments later, Macie had nearly detached the preposterous tail from a dandified lion. Not that she was completely at fault. The scrawny noble within the costume had seemed nearly overwhelmed by his bulky, ridiculous mane. Even so, her cheeks had turned scarlet while she apologized for the single errant step that left the appendage dangling by mere threads.

For his part, Finn had not felt so bloody awkward since he'd been a green lad squiring about his first debutante. Each step was uneasy, as though he wore weights on his legs, each movement overly stiff as he held her as far from his body as the dance would allow. As for his own aching toes, he'd lost count of how many times Macie had managed to tread lightly—and not so lightly—upon his feet. With each wayward press of her shoe against his, he gave silent thanks for the decision to wear sturdy boots with his half-hearted attempt at a costume.

By the time they'd suffered through a few dances, Macie's mortified reaction to trampling upon the bloke's costume had eased, though her features were still a bit pinched. Through her terse, plastered-on smile, she appeared as ill at ease as he was. Perhaps even more so. Had she sensed the truth he was unwilling to speak?

You haven't given anyone a reason to believe you were not merely watching over me.

As her words had tumbled out, he'd seen the disappointment in her eyes. Blast it, he had not intended to let her down. If she were some other woman, he could mimic an infatuation. He could make a show of holding her close and brushing his mouth over hers and whispering in her ear words the others could not hear, but would assume were spoken with desire and heat and passion.

She'd wanted him to pretend to be lovestruck, to put on a bloody charade. And all to drive off the *noble nobs* she detested. With another woman, he might've been able to pull it off.

But not with Macie.

The act she wanted him to perform was too blasted close to the truth.

He gazed down at her. She'd dressed as Maid Marian. Her fitted gown hugged her curves and flared softly over her rounded hips, while the light green silk intensified the emerald hue of her eyes. With her long, chestnut brown hair swept back in a simple braid, her high cheekbones and full mouth were framed to perfection. She was beautiful.

So bloody beautiful.

If Robin Hood's lady had been as striking as Macie in that

gown, the notorious archer would've spent far less time gallivanting around Sherwood Forest and more tending home and hearth.

His chest tightened. In all his life, he'd never known such a longing to simply caress a woman's cheek, to brush his fingers over her lips and smile to himself as her lips curved in response to his touch. Blast it, this need was unfamiliar. So bloody unlike any hunger for a woman he'd ever experienced.

If he didn't hold himself in tight check, there wouldn't be a damned thing he could do to stop himself from admitting the truth. Even to himself.

He wanted her.

He hungered to taste the sweetness of her lips. Longed to feel the softness of her curves beneath his hands. Needed to see a subtle, sensuous smile for his eyes only. But she was not meant for a rake like him.

Macie was off limits.

Forbidden.

It shouldn't matter that he wanted to touch her. To kiss her. To whisper words of love.

Finn pulled in a low breath. He had a job to do. The deal with Mason Enterprises would ensure that his family's business could thrive for years to come. He'd do well to keep that in mind. He'd promised to watch over Macie, to protect her from the jackals. If he gave in to the hunger he could scarcely deny, he would betray her brother's faith in him. And the faith his family had entrusted in him.

He had to think of Macie as well. She was determined to chase away the fortune hunters. But he'd no doubt she would someday encounter a man who was a good match for her. A man of who didn't give a damn about her fortune. A man who shared her passions. Perhaps, even, a man who could offer her the adventure of a lifetime, as she'd put it. He could not stand in the way of a man who might be the one for her.

Finn set his attention on her delicate features, if only to distract himself from the temptation of her body. Meeting his gaze, a bit of confusion dipped her brows lower. She pressed her lips together, more of a pout now than a frown.

Had she sensed the truth?

He stiffened his elbows, increasing the distance between them. Not that he had a choice. It wouldn't do for her to feel the undeniable evidence of his body's response to her. Blasted good thing he'd worn a sack coat and not the ridiculous hose her friend had wanted to inflict upon him. Now wouldn't that have been quite the blasted scene?

The musicians slowed their tempo, and the strains of the waltz faded. The notes of a more vigorous dance filled the room. Macie slowly shook her head and gently pulled away from his light hold.

"I believe I've had quite enough." Her voice was low and husky, and an emotion he could not read played on her features. Was that anger? Or sadness in her eyes?

With that, she turned and left him standing on the dance floor.

Bloody hell.

HURRYING AWAY FROM Finn and the smiling dancers who'd managed to move to the rhythm of the music without creating chaos, Macie wanted nothing more than to escape her humiliation. She should have known better than to think her plan would work. But she'd never imagined it could go awry in such dreadful fashion.

Her hopeful scheme should've created the illusion of a fairy tale romance that might finally throw the heiress hunters off her track. But utterly nothing had gone as planned. The quarter-hour or so she'd spent on the dance floor with Finn had seemed an eternity. Goodness, it was bad enough when she and Finn collided with a dagger-eyed dollar princess and her scowling prince. But her awkward steps that had nearly stripped a foppish lion of his tail created a humiliation worthy of the name *Calamity Macie.*

But that was not the worst of it.

No, that moment had come with Macie's dawning awareness that as they danced—if that was what one could truly call their awkward *one-two-three, one-two-three* movements across the floor—Finn had rigidly extended his arms. Why, he'd held her as far from himself as humanly possible. And even that distance did not seem to suit him. When they were together, he'd been ill at ease, his expression pinched, as if he were counting the moments until the night was over. A block of cold marble might have conveyed more warmth than the tense set of Finn's features.

He'd cautioned her against her scheme. More than once, actually. Had he known all along that he could not bring himself to convincingly feign an attraction?

Well, that was it. So much for her little game. Perhaps it was for the best. She had no true flair for deceit. And evidently, neither did Finn.

She spotted Nell tucked away in a shadowy corner of the ballroom, once again smiling and flirting with her handsome buccaneer. *Good for her.* At least one of them was enjoying the evening.

Macie glanced about, hoping to catch the attention of a passing server. A sip or two—or more—of champagne would be just the thing. She located a crisply dressed server, crossed the room to select a flute from his silver tray, and went in search of a retreat from the music and chatter and sounds she would ordinarily find quite pleasant. For the moment, all she wanted was to be alone with her thoughts.

She navigated past a gaggle of costumed socialites who murmured something they found rather humorous as she went past. Had they witnessed the awkward show she'd put on with Finn?

Let them have their laughter. She'd brought it on herself, now, hadn't she?

Exiting the ballroom, she found herself in a gas-lit corridor.

She tried to adjust to the sudden quiet. Odd, how it seemed so peculiar to be away from the noise of the party. Taking a small sip from her glass, she made her way down the hall. She spotted a door. Was that an entry to the gardens? A stroll in the fresh air might be just the tonic she needed.

Suddenly, a hand caught her elbow from behind. *Definitely not Finn.* He would not have pressed his fingers into her skin with punishing force.

Jerking free of the brutal hold, she whipped around. The ruff-wearing sot who'd suffered an undignified encounter with Finn stared at her. An ugly leer twisted his mouth. "You're not enjoying yourself." Reeking spirits on his breath assailed her. "I could change that."

Blast the infernal luck.

"Do not ever put your hands on me again." She gritted the words between her teeth.

"You don't know who you're talking to, do you?" He bit off the words with clear contempt.

"I do." She hiked her chin. "And that, sir, is why I'm leaving."

He reached for her again, but she slapped his hand away.

"Who do you think you are?" His mouth twisted into a scowl. "You're nothing but a bloody merchant's daughter."

She turned to walk away. "You've said quite enough."

He clamped rough fingers over her upper arm and yanked her around to face him. "Don't you dare turn your back to me."

Macie stared down at the glass in her hand. "Release me, you drunken cad." With that, she tossed the champagne in his face.

His hold on her tightened like a vice as rage contorted his angular features into an ugly mask.

Fear trickled along her nape, but she would not show it. Macie met and matched his icy stare.

"Unhand me. Now." She kept her voice under rigid control. "Or you will regret it."

His grip eased. Had her words given him pause? His rough hold loosened, freeing her arm, but his fingers curled around the puffed sleeve of her gown.

"You've put yourself on a bloody shelf, so high and mighty. All you have to recommend you is your father's—" His last word choked into a gasp as his hand fell away.

Macie looked up into Finn's angry eyes. He'd seized the Shakespearean-attired boor by the edges of his collarless shirt. With a deliberate lack of speed, he hauled the rotter onto his toes.

Her pulse raced. She'd been prepared to put the tactics Jon had taught her to use. But the sight of Finn as he glared at the belligerent sot who now squirmed against his hold was something to behold. Most impressive, indeed.

"If ye value yer teeth, ye will not utter another word." The quietness of Finn's voice accentuated the danger in his tone.

The viscount's eyes went wide. He nodded frantically.

"Evidently, I did not make myself clear the first time we spoke. If ye harass Miss Mason again, ye *will* answer to me. Do ye take my meaning?"

Again, the boor nodded.

"Fortunately for ye, Miss Mason would prefer that I not resort to physical violence. Ye owe her a debt for her kind restraint." Finn's gaze hardened. "Personally, I would enjoy teaching ye a lesson, man to man."

The man's Adam's apple bobbed in his throat. "That will not be necessary. I will not trouble her again."

"Ye know what will happen if ye do, don't ye?" The edge to Finn's voice was hard as flint.

"I do."

"Good enough." Finn released the man. "Now get out of her sight. Before I change my mind."

Darting from Finn's reach, the viscount looked as if he might actually break into a sprint as he rushed back to the ballroom.

Finn gently took her hand. "The rotter didn't hurt ye, did he?"

"No." She met his questioning gaze. "Sadly, he did cause me to waste a glass of perfectly fine champagne."

"That can be easily rectified." His brow furrowed as he studied her face. "Ye should not have come out here by yerself."

"All I wanted was a bit of peace." She sighed. "A few moments to myself after the fiasco of this evening."

"If the bastard had gotten ye alone . . ." Rubbing the back of his neck as if it suddenly ached, Finn broke off the thought.

"I do believe I could have handled the likes of him."

"Do ye now?" Finn sent her a little scowl. "Surely ye know what the likes of a cur like that is capable of."

"I would not have let it go much further. My brother has shown me certain ways to defend myself if the need should arise."

With a gentle touch, he cupped her face in his hands. "Ye may have been able to keep the bastard at bay. But given time, he may have hurt ye." Macie's breath caught as he traced his thumb along the curve of her chin. "Ye must trust me to protect ye."

"I have no doubt that you will." She hiked her chin, unwilling to show the surge of emotions swirling between her heart and her mind. "You have a task—protect the heiress, even from herself. And you're ever so dedicated to seeing that task through."

He set his jaw. "Ye don't make it easy, lass."

"Should I?" She folded her arms and regarded him for a long, silent moment. "I'd think a man like you would relish a challenge."

"I am beginning to think challenges are overrated."

She narrowed her eyes, flashing a brief scowl. "Such as the Herculean challenge of pretending to see me as something more than an heiress in need of a bodyguard?"

"Ah, yer blasted game." His expression went cold. "If ye wanted a performance, ye should have found a bloody thespian."

A performance.

His words stung, but she squared her shoulders and forced a cool tone. "I simply do not understand why you must be so very distant. No one would believe you were anything other than a brawny chaperone."

"Ye think not?"

"I'm quite positive. You've mastered the art of playing the vigilant protector. But tonight—even more than most nights—you've been so cold. It seems all you could do to even touch my hand." She pulled in a breath. "Can you deny it?"

He raked a hand though his hair. Meeting her gaze, his eyes gleamed with an unfamiliar intensity, even as a slight, wry smile played on his mouth. "Cold?" Slowly he shook his head. "I'm a blasted better actor than I thought. God above, lass, can ye really tell me ye haven't felt it?"

She nibbled her lip. "Finn, what are you saying?"

"What I'm saying, Macie, is this." Finn's voice was low and edged with gravel. "Ye're beautiful, lass. So blasted beautiful, a man like me doesn't even have the words to tell ye . . . all night, I've wanted to do this." He caught her hands in his. His smile broadening, he pulled her close. "I want to kiss ye, Macie."

She met the fire in his eyes. A flame of her own kindled deep within her as she ran her fingers through the silky strands of his hair. "Do you, now?"

He held her to his long, lean body. His warmth was a potent elixir, a delicious heat that seemed a caress. Brushing his lips along the sensitive curve of her cheek, he whispered against her ear. "More than ye could ever know, my sweet lass."

She looked into his eyes, drinking in the passion in their amber depths. Raising up on her toes, she coiled her arms around his neck. "I believe I would like that . . . I want you to kiss me."

That. And more.

"I want to make ye wild for me, darling Macie." He pressed a fleeting caress to her lips. Light and sweet and tender. "Believe when I say this, lass," The light in his eyes kindled a delicious heat as he took her hand and led her to the gardens. "Tonight is only the beginning."

✳

Chapter Twenty-One

MACIE HAD THOUGHT herself daring—at least, far more daring than the socialites and dollar princesses who would content themselves with a life that was little more than an existence. Settling for hearth and home with a man who offered little beyond his name and title was not in the cards. Not if she could help it. In the past, she'd stirred a scandal here and there—some strategic, others, not at all by design. Driving away the nobles who wanted a taste of her father's money, she'd taken chances with her good name. But now, in a dimly lit garden, she took the biggest risk she'd ever dared.

Standing in the garden courtyard, she smiled even as her pulse raced. As Finn pulled her close, she drank in the heat of his long, lean body. The faint scent of bergamot filled her senses, and she savored the feel of his powerful arms holding her tight. She savored every sensation. Every touch. Every delicious moment.

Oh, dear, this was perhaps the greatest chance she'd ever taken. Ever so much was at stake now.

She pulled in a shallow breath as the reality cascaded over her. If she did not proceed with great care, she would risk more than her reputation. More than her precious *good name*.

She might very well lose her heart.

The faint illumination of a single gaslight torch accented Finn's carved features. My, he was handsome man, wasn't he? But there was more to him than the rugged cut of his jaw. More than the keenly intelligent amber eyes that at that very moment looked into hers. More than the sensuous curve of his mouth.

So very much more.

The passion for life that gleamed in Finn's eyes drew her in. He wasn't one to settle for a life that did not suit him. He would not be content with an existence of starched shirts and keeping up appearances. Rather, he was his own man.

For as long as she'd known him, Finn had possessed the ability to drive her to distraction. He'd never flattered her with words he did not mean. Never sought to curry her favor and seize a chance to nab an heiress for his own. Years ago, he'd looked upon her as a girl, his friend's sister who was simply *there*.

But now, all that had changed. The expression in those captivating eyes drew her in. No longer was she merely Jon's sister. In his eyes, she saw the heat and the passion and the truth of his hunger—his hunger for her. And her alone.

The faintest of smiles played on his mouth. "Ah, Macie. I could hold ye all night, here in the moonlight."

She coiled her arms around his broad back. The sleek muscles beneath his jacket flexed beneath her touch. Reaching up, she looped her arms around his neck and stood on tiptoe to press a kiss to his throat.

He lightly framed her face between his hands, gazing down at her as if what he saw was very rare. And so very precious.

"Ah, Macie, ye're perfection."

His thumb traced a path over the curve of her mouth, gliding gently over her lower lip. Dipping his head lower, he brushed his mouth over hers. Softly at first, as if merely tasting the flavor of her lips. So tender. Yet sensual. And bold.

She pulled in a low breath as he deepened the caress. Coiling her arms around his neck, she relaxed against him, drinking in the heat of his lean male body.

Holding her with a light touch, he kissed her deeply.

Taking. Giving. Seducing. The caress kindled the intangible heat that flowed between them to a roaring flame.

A low sound like a groan in the back of his throat rippled through her senses, betraying his need. Good heavens, his kiss was oh, so very delicious. Each moment stirred passion and sweetness and an intense joy in her heart.

It all felt so very new. So very right.

His tenderness blended with a desire more intense than she'd dreamed possible. She melted against him, craving the closeness of his body. He was the one she wanted. Body and soul, she wanted this man.

And no other.

Macie felt his body tense, and he eased back, putting a hand's breadth of space between them. His voice was raw, his breath ragged.

"Macie, we must . . . we must . . . stop."

"And if I don't want to?" she teased.

"We must." He gazed down at her, passion darkening his eyes. "This . . . this isn't how it should be, lass. Ye deserve so much more. More than I can give ye."

"Your kiss is all I want." Hands around his neck, she tugged him closer. "All I need."

"Ah, my sweet lass, don't ye know . . . how bloody much I want ye." His gravel-roughened words held an edge of pure need. "But this . . . this is not the time. Not the place."

In her heart, she knew he was right. She delighted in his touch. But a few stolen moments could not be enough.

"One more kiss," she whispered against his lips. "That's all I ask."

"Aye." His sensuous half-smile warmed her heart. "One more. For now."

And then, he claimed her lips. Teasing. Caressing. Tempting her with what was yet to come. Leaving her ever so slightly weak in the knees.

She closed her eyes and drank in every sensation as if it were a true delicacy. Ah, how utterly sweet life would be in this man's arms.

Tonight is only the beginning. Finn's rough-edged words whispered in her thoughts.

Indeed. This night, these delectable kisses might well be worth the risk. If only her heart was not so very tender. And she were not still a wee bit wary.

He was the one who'd made her yearn to toss away the shields she'd erected for so very long.

Macie smiled to herself. *How very unexpected.*

FINN HAD BEEN a cheeky lad scarcely out of short pants when he'd stolen his first kiss. Since that mischievous peck on the lips, he'd believed he knew what it was to kiss a woman. Knew how to kiss her well and leave her breathless. A kiss had seemed a fleeting pleasure, a sensual caress that had no meaning beyond the moment.

But since he'd taken Macie up on her challenge, everything had changed. From the first moment he'd taken the time to look upon her as a woman—not a lass, not the sister of his friend— Finn had known he'd discovered something rare. Something precious.

And now, he'd tasted true pleasure, found in a simple caress.

Now, as he drank in the feel of her in his arms, he held his desire in check. Her eyes were wide with a look that betrayed the innocence she tried to hide. Her chest rose and fell with each shallow inhalation, and she gazed up at him with a look of true trust. Her lips parted, ever so slightly. Pure bloody temptation.

Drawing the pad of his thumb along the curve of her bottom lip, he pulled in a low breath. How he wanted to savor the taste of her lips. That, and so much more.

He wanted her in his arms. And in his bed.

By thunder, he wanted Macie more than he'd ever wanted anything in his life.

But this was not the bloody time. Nor the bloody place. Only a single door separated them from costumed revelers, musicians, servers, and their esteemed hostess. He had to rein in his instincts before anyone came upon their rendezvous.

Her eyes narrowed, silently questioning. "Is someone coming?" she asked.

"It's possible," he said.

"I find the prospect rather exciting." She gave him a fetching little grin. "How very unexpected."

"We need to get back to the ball."

One delicate brow arched. "Before the gossipy hens begin to cluck?"

"If I have my guess, they've already begun."

She shrugged. "Let them say what they will. I'm not afraid of them."

"Ye do like to tempt fate, now don't ye, Macie?"

She pulled in a breath, then met his question with one of her own. "Why did you stop? Tempting fate, that is?"

"I didn't," he said. "Every moment I'm with ye is taking a chance."

Her mouth quirked at one corner. "You don't want to risk my precious *good name*?"

"No, lass. I can't chance losing what little is left of my control." He threaded a silky tendril of her hair around his finger and tucked it behind her ear.

"Is that so?" Her smile was coy and lovely and tempting enough to drive him to madness.

"With every beat of my heart, I want ye more."

Gently, she pressed her hand to his chest, her warmth penetrating the linen of his shirt. Bloody hell, was she bent on driving him mad?

"Your heart is strong, Finn. And true." She raised up on her tiptoes and kissed him again, the caress soft and delicate and sensual. "As is mine."

A familiar voice cut into the quiet moment. Blast it, was that

Nell? Taking a step back, he met Macie's slight, sudden frown. So, she'd heard it, too.

"She's signaling me. Just as we'd agreed." Macie's voice held a quiet tone of resignation as she quickly eased out the crumples in her skirts with the heels of her hands.

Without another word, Finn smoothed Macie's wayward curls into place. At least, as well as he could. There was nothing to be done about the rosy flush on her cheeks, he thought, smiling to himself.

"Let's go." He caught her hand in his. "Before the queen's guard itself comes searching for ye."

"That would be best," she said, sounding like she was trying to convince herself.

He opened the door and scanned the corridor. *No one in sight.* He motioned to Macie to follow him.

They'd made it to the end of the corridor before Nell encountered them. "Oh, thank heaven," she said breathlessly. "I was hoping to warn you."

"Warn me?" Macie's forehead furrowed.

"That dolt of a baron is carrying tales that you were accosted . . . by Finn."

"Oh, that lying sot," Macie said between her teeth.

"You need to return to the ballroom," Nell went on. "Lady Fenwick has dispatched the fellow who watches over the security of the house to look for you."

He resisted the urge to utter an epithet. "That bloke is not going to be content until he's had an encounter with my fists."

"That will not help matters. You'll need a suitable explanation for where you'd gone." Nell's gaze swept over Macie. She smiled. "Beyond what one might assume."

"You mean beyond what is obvious," Macie said with a sly little grin.

"I suppose I do." Nell motioned to them to follow her along a different hallway that led to the back of the ballroom. "Jason showed me this route."

"Jason?" Macie asked as they hurried down the corridor.

"One of the musicians. He's the violinist . . . I think."

"Thank goodness you've spent the evening getting to know everyone," Macie said.

Nell's dark curls bobbed as she shook her head. "Not everyone. I could give a fig about those pinched-face debutantes. So, do you know what you're going tell them?"

"If the question arises, I'll simply speak the truth. At least, the first part of it."

They entered the ballroom through a door behind the musicians' stands. Shadowed as it was, it was possible that few noticed or cared about their obviously covert reappearance.

Within moments, Finn felt a penetrating gaze directed his way. *Bloody hell.* Lady Fenwick stood on a balcony, appearing to survey the crowd through opera glasses. Lady Drayton stood to her right, her pinched features growing even more tight as she stared down at him.

"Yer favorite hostess has spotted us," he said to Macie.

"It would have to be her, wouldn't it?" Macie sighed in resignation.

"Oh, dear," Nell said. "On the bright side, perhaps she'll cool her attempts to make a match."

"Not likely," Macie said. "A little tarnish on my name won't dull the shine on my father's shillings."

Suddenly, an ox of a man who wore an ill-fitting suit rather than a costume stepped into their path. He stared down at Macie. "You're Miss Mason, are you not?"

"I am." She affected a prim tone. "Might I ask what concern it is of yours?"

He didn't answer her, but shifted his attention to Nell. "And who might you be?"

"My name is Miss Blake. This gentleman is our escort, Mr. Caldwell. Might I ask why you are inquiring?"

"Lady Fenwick asked me to look into an incident." He glared at Finn as if he'd absconded with the queen's jewels. "There was a report that Miss Mason had been maltreated by a guest."

"I don't know what you're talking about," Macie said. "Unless you are referring to the drunken boor who spoke to us in the rudest manner."

"I am not." He eyed Finn with a look of clear distrust. "As a matter of fact, your escort fits the description of the man who'd been observed accosting you."

"Do not make accusations ye cannot back up." Finn controlled his voice, infusing a steady calm into his words.

The bodyguard kept his eyes on Finn. "My job is to determine what happened to Miss Mason while she was nowhere to be found. A rather peculiar situation, I'd say."

Macie hiked her chin. "I'll ask you not to speak of me as if I am not standing directly before you. I can speak for myself."

The bodyguard nodded. "I will be direct, Miss Mason. Do you have reason to fear this man?"

"How utterly absurd," she replied.

As the hulking bloke continued to eye him with suspicion, Finn squared his shoulders. Bugger it, he'd rather not have to use his fists tonight, much less against a man who stood half a head taller. But if matters took an ugly turn, he'd be ready. Bloody shame he had not carried his walking stick that night. If Lady Fenwick's bodyguard raised a hand in violence, the silver gargoyle would make quite a point.

With Lady Drayton following close at her heels, Lady Fenwick marched up to them. Intrigue brimmed in her narrow-eyed gaze.

"Oh, Miss Mason, you gave us a bit of a worry," Lady Fenwick said, keeping her voice low.

"A bit of worry, is it?" Macie's eyes sparkled with a touch of defiance. "I am at a loss as to what has caused your concern. It would seem that someone has stirred intrigue where none exists."

Lady Drayton flashed a thin-lipped glare. "The viscount was quite clear about what he'd witnessed."

Finn could no longer hold his tongue. "Considering the manner in which the gangly fop spoke to Miss Mason, he should count himself fortunate—"

"Miss Mason, there ye are." A familiar voice cut into his words. Glancing over his shoulder, he saw her—the Dragon had finally decided to make her appearance. As usual, her timing was perfect.

Wearing a gown of shiny red silk and an elaborate bejeweled crown, Mrs. Elsie Johnstone—the aunt Logan had dubbed *the Dragon* in their youth—strode up to them with the commanding manner of the queen she portrayed.

Mrs. Johnstone sent Macie a speaking glance. "My dear, it would seem I lost track of ye after lingering in the garden."

Though she had no idea of the Red Queen's identity, Macie played along. "Oh, my, we should have waited. But I longed for a sip of something cold and bubbly."

"Mrs. Johnstone, what a pleasant surprise." Lady Fenwick's smile was as sincere as her tone. "I'd feared you would not be able to join us this evening."

"I would not have missed this for the world." Mrs. Johnstone said. "I arrived a bit late and quickly found myself dashing off to the garden to take in the brilliant night sky. The Comet Sagittarian was quite spectacular."

"Indeed," Macie agreed, throwing Nell a wink.

"I do not believe I shall ever forget the sight," Nell added.

"I do wish you had let me know of this event." Lady Fenwick's disappointment sounded genuine. "Is it possible I might still observe it?"

Lady Drayton frowned. "I don't recall my son mentioning anything about a comet."

"Sadly, it was a fleeting phenomenon." Mrs. Johnstone paid Lady Drayton's comment no heed. "I looked for you, but I believe you were entertaining some very important noble or other at the moment we decided to go to the garden."

"Pity," Lady Fenwick said. "Next time, please do keep me informed. I am counting on you, my friend."

"Of course." Mrs. Johnstone smiled. "We were fortunate that Mr. Caldwell was free at the moment to escort us."

"So, the mystery is solved," Lady Fenwick said brightly. Dismissing the bodyguard, she expressed her intention to cross the boorish viscount from her guest list, invited Mrs. Johnstone to tea, and hurried off with a still-frowning Lady Drayton to mingle with her guests.

Waiting until the ladies were out of earshot, Mrs. Johnstone took charge of the introductions in typical fashion.

"Miss Mason, it is my pleasure to meet ye. I am Mrs. Elsie Johnstone. Logan MacLain is my nephew."

"I'm pleased to make your acquaintance. Please, do call me Macie."

"Macie, is it?" Mrs. Johnstone's gaze seemed to settle on Macie's tousled hair and slightly swollen mouth. The quirk of her brows told Finn the woman had already pieced together what they'd been up to during the time Macie had supposedly been observing the night sky.

"Since I was a girl," Macie replied.

A thin smile played on Mrs. Johnston's features. "I suppose Mary Catherine is a bit of a mouthful."

"Quite so," Macie said, then proceeded to introduce Nell.

"That was quick thinking, Mrs. Johnstone," Finn said. "Well-timed, as always."

"Indeed, it was," Macie agreed. "You solved what might have been an exceedingly awkward situation."

"There was no comet tonight, was there?" Nell said. "I suspect Harold . . . Lord Drayton, that is . . . would've mentioned it."

"Ye're correct, Miss Blake. I simply made it up."

Nell flashed a brief grin. "The name *did* sound highly scientific."

"Did it now?" Mrs. Johnstone cocked a brow. "On the day I was born, the sun was in the constellation Sagittarius. It seemed a fitting name for a comet. Hardly a stroke of brilliance."

"You were entirely convincing," Macie said.

"She's a clever one, she is," Finn said. "And she knows it."

Mrs. Johnstone reached up to adjust her crown atop her chestnut and silver hair. "One would have to be clever to tidy up the fixes Logan and ye have gotten into over the years." She sent him a speaking glance. "Between the two of ye, I've become an expert."

Finn smiled. "Ye'll get no argument from me."

"If that is not a rare event, I don't know what is." Mrs. Johnstone smiled. "Ye've never been one to back down from a fight. In the days ahead, I suspect that quality will serve ye well."

Chapter Twenty-Two

*T*ONIGHT IS ONLY *the beginning.*

The notes of Finn's husky voice whispered in Macie's thoughts, stirring her to restlessness. With a sigh, she fluffed her pillow, then stared aimlessly at the darkened ceiling. Finn's kiss had ignited a spark in her, a simmering heat she did not want to extinguish. Even her sweet fantasies of Mr. Darcy and Mr. Rochester could not quench this yearning.

She pictured Finn alone in his room in the downstairs quarters. Alone . . . in his bed. With the image of his unclothed body, his bedcovers arranged just so to reveal his powerful chest to her gaze, a fresh current of need rippled through her body. Her cheeks heated at the thought.

Could he be thinking of her at that very moment? Did he long for her touch? For her kiss?

Just as she longed for him?

With a sigh, Macie lit the lamp on the chest and flopped back onto the mattress. Curled by her feet, Cleo lifted her sleepy head. Her green eyes glowed with the reflected light. Was the cat actually frowning at her? Well, the indulged feline would simply have to get over her little snit.

An idea Macie might have dismissed as near madness tempted her. *No.* She immediately swatted away the notion, banishing the tempting mental image of Finn not quite asleep in his room. Alone. In who knew what state of undress.

She simply could not consider joining him in his plain yet sturdy bed.

Could she?

No man before him had stirred this tender desire within her. She hungered for Finn's touch. Longed to caress his skin. To learn what brought him pleasure. But above all, she thirsted for the connection of their hearts. Their minds. Their souls.

Whenever she was with Finn, he saw her for the woman she was. Not the woman society deemed she should be. In his eyes, she was a beauty. Not because she wore the most fashionable clothing. Not because her hair was coiffed just so. Not even because he found her face to be pretty and appealing. No, it went far deeper.

When she was with Finn, she could see the truth in his eyes. They were connected in a way she'd never experienced. Never expected. Two kindred spirits who'd finally, maddeningly, stumbled upon each other.

Earlier that night, standing with Finn in the garden of Lady Fenwick's elegant home, she'd taken the risk of being found alone with him. In his arms. Savoring his kiss. She'd thought herself quite daring then.

But now, she contemplated taking a risk which might well make her heart soar.

Or leave it in tatters.

Macie slipped her dressing gown over her shoulders, donned her slippers, and tugged the ribbon tie of the dressing gown tighter around her waist.

Would Finn be shocked to discover her in his room? She smiled at the thought. Would he take her to his bed? Or send her away? She simply had to find out.

She had to take this chance.

Macie quietly navigated the stairs to the downstairs quarters. Steps from Finn's room, she hesitated. The sound of Mrs. Tuttle's voice drifted through the sturdy door to her room. Macie's breath caught. She listened more closely. Rumbles of loud snoring reached her ears, with a few mumbled words thrown in for good measure. The tension eased from her shoulders. The housekeeper was deep in her slumber.

Macie bit back a giggle at the noise. Poor Finn, trying to sleep through this racket each night.

Shoring up her courage, she went to Finn's door. She pulled in a breath, as if that might ease the sudden surge of her pulse. Could she do this? Had she truly gone mad with her hunger for this man?

It wasn't too late. If she tiptoed back to her room, he'd be none the wiser. He wouldn't even know she'd stood inches beyond his door.

She could simply come to her senses and return to the quiet of her own bedchamber . . . to her own bed.

The door opened with a mild creak of protest. The faint illumination of her lamp cast light and shadows over Finn's long, lean form. The bedclothes had slid low, resting over his legs and lean hips. His powerful upper body was bared to her sight.

Macie's gaze trailed over his broad shoulders to his chest, sleek-muscled and firm. Curly light-brown hair feathered over the taut muscles. Then lower, tapering over the contours of his chiseled abdomen she instinctively yearned to explore with her fingertips.

Her mouth went dry. *Oh, dear.*

Finn blinked against the lamplight, his eyes adjusting from what had been near-complete darkness. "Macie, is something wrong?"

She pressed a finger to her lip, signaling him not to speak. "We mustn't wake Mrs. Tuttle," she whispered. "May I come in?"

Tossing aside the quilt, he wore only a pair of loose-fitting trousers. His expression was still drowsy when he came to her.

"Did ye hear a noise?" he asked, motioning her into the chamber. "Did something frighten ye?"

She shook her head and set the lamp on the table. "Nothing is amiss," she said, closing the door behind her.

His brow furrowed with confusion. "What's this about?"

"This."

Summoning every whit of daring she possessed, Macie curved her fingers over his bare shoulders, rose up on her toes, and pressed a kiss to his tempting mouth.

A soft sound of pleasure escaped him, and his arms coiled around her. Pulling her to his muscular body, he held her close and threaded his fingers through her hair. "So bloody beautiful," he whispered in a husky rasp.

And then, he deepened the kiss. Searching. Seeking. Seducing. All melded into this delicious caress.

Her knees suddenly went weak. She melted against him, the heat of his body blending with hers as he held her in a possessive yet deliciously tender embrace.

"Ye drive me mad, Macie," he whispered against her lips.

His hands glided down her back, the heat of his touch penetrating the thin cotton of her clothing. Boldly, he cupped his hands over her bottom and held her nearer still. The undeniable evidence of his desire pressed against her softness. Utterly male. Unyielding. Demanding.

"Ye see what ye do to me, lass?" His voice was low, edged with gravel.

Ah, she did. And she liked it. So very, very much.

She answered his passionate query without words. Canting her hips to draw him even closer, she kissed him again. Parting her lips, she drank him in. The taste of his caress. The feel of the crisp, dark curls on his chest beneath her eager fingers. The sound of his low moans of need.

A hunger more powerful than physical desire kindled deep within her. Her pulse raced as a wave of anticipation crashed over her. For so very long, she'd lived without passion. Without tenderness. Without love. But now, she could not deny the yearnings of her heart.

Without warning, he broke away and raked his fingers through his hair.

She could only gaze at him, stunned. Suddenly, it felt as though the air had been squeezed from her lungs. "What is it?" she murmured after the span of several heartbeats.

"Macie . . . lass . . . this isn't right." His words seemed a raw confession.

"You're wrong," she whispered. "Everything about this is right."

"Ye don't know what ye're saying." Finn caught her hands in his. "What ye're doing."

She gulped against a sudden rush of emotion. "Tell me you don't think this is merely a game."

Slowly, he shook his head. "To the contrary, this is all too real." He brushed a butterfly kiss over her cheek. "But that doesn't change the fact . . . this is not the way it should be."

"And if I disagree?"

His lips slid over hers, tender and undemanding. "Ye deserve so much more than this."

She pulled in a breath, inhaling the crisp, masculine scent of bergamot and man.

"I want you, Finn. Can't you see that?"

His hands framed her face. For several beats of her pulse, he simply looked at her, as if to memorize every nuance of her expression.

His lips brushed a light kiss over her temple. "I do, lass. And bloody hell, I want ye more than ye can imagine."

"And if I want to spend this night with you?"

"Macie, I can see the truth. Ye're more innocent of the ways of men and women than ye like to let on. I'm not wrong, am I?"

Pressing her lips together to steady her emotions, she shook her head. "Why does it matter to you?"

"Because ye deserve better than this." A soft smile curved his mouth as he studied her. "Tell me the truth, lass." His lips brushed a feather-soft caress over hers. "Are ye a virgin?"

"Is it so very obvious?" she whispered.

"Only to a man who has seen the wonder in yer beautiful

emerald eyes."

She cocked her chin, summoning a bit of boldness. "And if . . . if I think it's time."

"That moment will come." His voice was a husky rasp as he lightly stroked the curve of her cheek. "But not tonight."

She turned away. Suddenly, the delight she'd felt in his arms had transformed to something far different. Her heart felt as if it had been caught in a vise, and there was only one choice. She had to get away. Now.

Macie rushed to the door, but he caught her wrist. "Don't go, lass. Not yet."

She gulped against the sudden burning pain in the back of her throat. "I must return to my own room . . . to my own bed."

Where my heart is safe.

"Turn around, Macie." Each syllable seemed a husky plea. "I need . . . I need to tell ye more . . . I need to tell ye what I'm thinking."

She choked back tears she could not bear to shed. Not in front of him. "You made yourself quite clear."

He moved to stand in front of her. Not quite blocking her from the door, yet making it clear he wanted her to stay.

"Ye came here tonight of yer own free will. And ye'll leave of yer own free will." He stepped to the side. "But I am asking ye to give me time . . . time to explain."

"Very well." She forced out the words.

He took her hand within his and led her to the bed. "Shall we sit?"

"Aren't you afraid of the scandal? A virgin sitting with a half-clothed man on his bed?"

"I don't give a damn about scandal." He studied her with hooded eyes as his thumb caressed her palm. "Ye're all I give a damn about, Macie."

She met his eyes, even as she struggled against a fresh wave of feeling. "Is that so?"

The fine lines around his eyes crinkled in what seemed genuine confusion. "Why do ye doubt it, lass?"

"Isn't it obvious? I came to you." She dropped her gaze to the braided rug beneath their feet. "But you rejected me."

"Ye're wrong, my sweet lass." He swept his lips over the back of her hand. "I want ye . . . more than ye can imagine. But yer first time with a man should be special."

Macie's heart raced. She turned to him and caressed his cheek. The dark-brown stubble on his jaw was rough and crisp against her fingertips. With a little sigh, she relaxed.

"It will be special, Finn," she said. "Just being with you . . . being held by you . . . is special."

"Ye deserve fine sheets and luxury. Ye deserve to awaken in my arms in the morning without fear of stirring a scandal." The faintest of grins tugged on his mouth. "Ye deserve to be kissed to distraction. Not stolen moments with the sound of Mildred Tuttle's snores and gasps in our ears."

"Oh, dear, that is a valid point, now isn't it?" Macie said, just as Mrs. Tuttle cried out for someone named Phil.

"I told ye, lass, and I meant every word—tonight is only the beginning." He drew the pad of his finger over her bottom lip. "Someday, when the time is right, I will teach ye how good making love can be." His small grin broadened. "For now, I'll teach ye a bit about pleasure. If ye still want my touch." He hesitated for a heartbeat. "If ye still want me."

Macie's breath caught in her throat. *Oh, my.*

"I do like what you are up to."

"Do ye now?" he teased.

She nibbled her lower lip. "Indeed."

"First things first." He untied the ribbon on her dressing gown and opened the robe, revealing the nightdress that hid little from his heated gaze. "May I?"

She nodded, and he slid the dressing gown over her shoulders. It pooled behind her on the mattress.

"And now, shall we free yer hair from this braid? It's lovely when it flows free and loose down yer back."

"Yes," she murmured.

With great care, he freed the strands in the carefully woven plait that reached past her nape. Her unbound hair fell free to her back.

"Beautiful," he murmured. "So blasted beautiful." He touched the lace at the collar of her nightdress, then released the tiny mother-of-pearl button at her neck. "I'd like to see ye, love. May I?"

"I'd like that," she whispered as his fingers skimmed along the sensitive column of her throat.

Taking his time, he freed the column of buttons, parting the lacy cotton fabric a bit more with each until he reached the fastener at her waist. And then, he eased the dress from her shoulders, baring her to his gaze.

As she met his eyes, a shiver of awareness ran through her body. No shame. No fear. Simply awareness of his intense male gaze taking her in. She saw the passion in his eyes. Saw the way his amber-brown irises had darkened with the force of his desire for her. Suddenly, she felt a power unlike any other she'd ever felt.

"My God, ye're lovely." His husky rasp unleashed a current of pure yearning through her—heart and soul. And in that moment, she felt truly, utterly beautiful.

He drew her close, kissing her with a burning heat. "I want to feel ye, my sweet."

"Oh, yes," she whispered.

She wanted his touch. She wanted his kiss. She wanted *him*.

As she reached to touch him, he stilled her hand. "Not yet, love."

His slightly roughened hand traced a slow path along her collarbones. He pressed tender kisses along the path. And then, he moved lower, trailing feather-soft touches from her throat to her breasts.

She tingled with pure sensation as he teased her delicate skin with tiny kisses. Dipping his head, he caressed her, each touch and press of his mouth more delicious than the last.

Kindling the heat within her, his hand found the hem of her gown. "Tell me what ye want, love?"

"You," she murmured.

He slid his left hand under her nightdress, brushing lightly against her calf. "Ye want my touch . . . here?"

"Yes," she murmured.

His hand glanced over the back of her knee, and she realized she'd sighed.

"And here?" His fingers skimmed along her thigh, stirring a delicious tingling.

"Yes," she whispered against his mouth.

"Ah, love, I want to drive ye wild."

"You already have." She kissed him then, weaving her fingers through his hair and savoring the pure masculine scent of the man she adored. His low groan of pleasure unleashed a fresh little thrill through her body.

"Ye do know how to test a man's restraint, don't ye, love?" He eased her down against the bed, one arm curved around her back, while the other rested upon her hip.

Macie nestled into the crook of his shoulder. Her fingers glided along his collarbones, mimicking the path he'd taken over her body, before skimming over the contours of his powerful chest. Dark, crisp hair feathered over muscles well developed by his athletic pursuits. Her fingertips danced over the satin-smooth skin, even as she drank in the subtle scent of shaving soap on his skin.

Growing more adventurous, she trailed her fingers along the tapering hair that led to the dark line over his belly, he caught her hand again. "Is this yer idea of torture, lass?"

"Well, that is rather peculiar," she teased coyly, knowing full well what he meant. "Judging from the sounds you're making deep in your throat, I'd say you rather enjoy it."

"I do, lass. Too bloody much," he said in a voice edged with gravel.

"I rather like that. It's so deliciously wicked." She brushed a kiss against his stubble-roughened jaw. "The very thought of tempting you *too bloody much* makes me weak."

"This night, I want only to make ye mad for me." His voice was delightfully confident. "And me alone."

He propped himself on one elbow, gazing down at her. "I'm going to touch ye now. Tell me . . . tell me if ye want me to stop."

The very thought of his skin teasing hers spurred all manner of heady thoughts. Wicked. Delicious. Stirring her desire to a fever pitch.

With a delicious blend of tenderness and hunger and sweet delight, he claimed her mouth. His barely leashed passion stirred the fire within her to a blaze. Whispering sweet words of adoration against her mouth, his words were a sensuous rasp. And when he dipped his head lower, anointing her body with kisses, she curled her fingers over his muscular arms, pressing her fingers into his skin, savoring the feel of his powerful male body.

She heard herself moan, sounds like little gasps from her parted lips. And then, his warm touch glided over her thighs. Each moment of contact was a tender melding of sweet pleasure and torment. How she needed him. His touch. His kiss. And more.

Instinctively, she canted her hips, a silent plea. His eyes flashed, and she knew in her heart he'd understood. He knew what she needed. He knew how to ease the bone-deep need that had overtaken her senses.

His fingers lightly brushed the triangle of curls between her thighs. His clever fingers stirred her wanting, seeking and finding the core of her pleasure. Gently, he teased her with his touch, stirring the flames within her body. Within her heart.

"Do ye want this, love?" His words were quiet and raw and heated.

"Please," she whispered as he kissed her again. "So very much."

"Yer wish is my command." A subtle smile played on his

mouth. "Ye'll like this, my sweet. I promise."

His clever fingers worked their magic. Touch upon touch. The pleasure grew from tiny ripples of delight to waves of pleasure so very intense, she was in danger of being swept away.

A rogue wave of sensation washed over her, seeming to carry her away. The rush of feeling carried her out of reality, so intense she felt a bit mad. Sheer pleasure swirled around her like a whirlpool from which she had no desire to free herself, wave upon wave upon wave of pure joy.

A sense of utter contentment filled her heart. She felt as if she drifted back to shore, into the safe haven of his embrace.

When she met his gaze, the heady blend of primal desire and tenderness in his eyes melted her heart. God above, did he have any idea how she longed to look into his eyes every night? Every morning. Every day.

"Do ye have any idea how beautiful ye are, lass?" He skimmed over her bottom lip with his thumb. "If I live to be a very old man, nothing could ever compare to those beautiful green eyes, radiant with pleasure and desire." His mouth curved, the most subtle of smiles. "Desire for me, my love."

She nestled against his lean, strong body. For a long moment, she watched the rise and fall of his chest, delighting in the sight. He was vital and strong and, hopefully, he was hers. Just as she was his.

"Ah, Finn, I'd say you've succeeded in your quest. I am wild for you." She kissed him again and smiled to herself. How delightful that she could lie with him and kiss him simply because she wanted to. "Truly and deeply and utterly mad for you, Mr. Caldwell."

THE SUN'S FIRST rays shined through the curtains, rousing Macie from a thoroughly delightful sleep in Finn's bed. In Finn's arms.

Ah, she could easily become used to mornings like this.

Macie scooted to the edge of the bed and pressed her feet to the cool wooden floorboards. She turned back, and for a long moment, her gaze lingered on Finn.

Goodness, he was such a handsome man. He lay on his back, the hazy light dancing over the contours of his muscular chest. One arm stretched out against the mattress, as if he dreamed of holding her to his body.

A little sigh escaped her. She'd delighted in those moments of pleasure in Finn's arms. Were they simply stolen moments of joy? Or had she found a man she could love for the rest of her days?

Time would tell the tale. Donning her dressing gown and slippers, she tiptoed back to the bed just long enough to press a soft kiss to Finn's mouth.

It wouldn't do for anyone—especially Mrs. Tuttle—to encounter her leaving his room.

So of course, as luck would have it, Mrs. Tuttle peeked out of her chamber at the precise moment Macie closed the door to Finn's room behind her.

Their eyes met. An awkward silence followed, broken when Mrs. Tuttle smiled even as she gave her head a regretful shake.

"Miss Macie, are you waiting for me to say something?"

"Honestly, I was hoping you were walking in your sleep," she said with a brief grin.

"Not a chance." The older woman regarded her with care-worn features. "I can only hope you know what you're doing."

"I believe I do," Macie said, sounding perhaps more confident than she felt.

"I do hope so." Mrs. Tuttle shuffled out of the room, clutching her flannel dressing gown around her. "Promise me you will do this one thing for me, Miss Macie."

"And what might that be?" Macie asked gently.

"Take your time, dear." The housekeeper reached out and tucked a wayward curl behind Macie's ear. "Promise me you will guard your heart."

✦

Chapter Twenty-Three

"RISE AND SHINE, Mr. Caldwell," Mrs. Tuttle said. "You have a visitor."

"A visitor?" Finn's voice sounded like a cross between a croak and a groan even to his own ears. He pulled the blanket over his chest and raised up on his elbows.

Macie's housekeeper frowned. "He says his name's Tim. Mr. MacLain sent him."

Her words jarred him from his drowsy, sleep-deprived state. What in blazes was going on? Had something happened to Amelia or her babe?

"Where is he?"

"I'll send him in." The housekeeper beat a quick path to the door, pausing to throw him a scowl over her bony shoulder. "I do think I shall be having a few words with Miss Mason. First, a rogue for a bodyguard taking up residence, and now a messenger from a tavern, of all the unexpected things, knocking on the door before I've even had my morning tea."

Finn donned his clothing and retrieved his shoes before Logan's gangly assistant walked through the doorway.

"My apologies for disturbing ye." The soft-spoken young man fiddled with the driver's cap in his hands. "I'd gone to yer home, but when ye were not there, Logan figured ye might be here."

"Did he, now?" Finn pulled on his second boot. "Has something happened to Amelia?"

Tim shook his head. "Mrs. MacLain is well. It's nothing like that."

Bloody hell, why was Tim so ill at ease? "Then why in Hades are ye here?"

"We were at the Rogue's Lair awaiting the arrival of a shipment. While we were there, a constable came by to tell Logan something he thought ye should know."

Finn could feel his impatience rising. "What is it?"

"It's about Miss Mason."

A strategically timed little cough caught their attention. Tim shuffled on his feet as they both glanced to the doorway. Macie stood in the doorway, questions dancing in her gaze. She strolled into the room, dressed in an unadorned walking suit in a shade of pale green that accentuated the color of her eyes. For a change, she had not pinned back her chestnut brown curls. They tumbled in loose waves over her shoulders.

By thunder, she was beautiful. Finn pulled in a breath, pushing the thoughts away. This was neither the time, nor the place, to think about running his fingers through her silky dark hair. And it sure as hell wasn't the time to consider how bloody much he wanted to once again savor the sweetness of her mouth, which was now set in an intrigued semblance of a smile.

"News about me? How very curious," she said in a husky voice that betrayed she had not been awake for very long.

"Not about ye, Miss Mason." Tim seemed to be considering his words carefully. "My name is Tim. I'm Mr. MacLain's assistant. He asked me to deliver a message."

Macie's complexion paled, even as her expression betrayed little emotion. She stood quite still, as if she braced herself against what he was going to say. Whatever the news was, Finn knew damned well they weren't going to like it. Tim's apprehension only served to fray his patience.

"What is it, Tim?" Macie asked gently.

"It's a bit harsh for a lady's ears, Miss." Again, the messenger shuffled his feet. "Mr. MacLain instructed me to tell Finn."

Macie hiked a brow. "But the message does pertain to me, does it not?"

"I suppose it does," the young man admitted reluctantly.

"You will not offend me." Her mouth thinned. "I promise you that."

Finn shoved his fingers through his hair. Bugger it, Logan would not have dispatched a messenger at the crack of dawn if the news were good. He suspected he already knew what Tim had to tell him. Unpleasant or not, Macie needed to hear it.

"Out with it. Now," he said.

"Mr. MacLain's acquaintance got word about the intruder in the old house of yers." Tim's gaze dropped to the rug beneath their feet. "The man . . . he died during the night."

Died.

The word echoed in Macie's ears. Her pulse raced as the news triggered an instinctive alarm. This should not have rattled her so. After all, this turn of events was not entirely unexpected. The elderly professor had seemed to be in desperate straits. Perhaps he had not been poisoned after all. Could it be possible that his heart had given out? He'd been quite agitated and filled with fear.

Leave. Before he comes . . . for you.

The old man had uttered the warning moments before he collapsed. Now, any hope of an explanation was gone. She might never know his reasons for his desperate words. Nor why a man of learning would sneak inside the library her grandfather had so treasured and wildly toss books about the floor.

"Well, then, lad, have you told Miss Mason all you need to say?" Mrs. Tuttle asked pointedly as she marched over to the window and threw open the curtains with a dramatic flair.

The young man's throat bobbed nervously. "Yes, ma'am. That's all of it."

Mrs. Tuttle turned to him and planted her hands on her hips

in that imperious way of hers. "In that case, it would be best if you ran along. There's work to be done, and as you can see, Miss Mason has not yet had a chance to take a sip of tea, let alone enjoy a bite of her morning meal. Any further unpleasantness can wait until later."

"Yes, ma'am," Tim's gaze shot to Finn, who nodded his agreement that the young man's presence was no longer needed.

"Why don't you come along with me, Miss Macie?" Mrs. Tuttle said, her tone more motherly than usual. "I'll put on a pot of tea while I ready the morning meal."

"Thank you," Macie said.

Mrs. Tuttle sent Finn a speaking glance. "I trust you'll be joining her, Mr. Caldwell," she said. "I presume the two of you have a bit to discuss."

MACIE NIBBLED HALF-HEARTEDLY at her toast and marmalade. Given the news the young messenger had delivered, it was all she could do to take a few bites. Finn sat within arm's reach, his appetite heartier than hers, though the furrows on his forehead betrayed his tense thoughts.

My, the morning had certainly taken a turn, hadn't it? She'd awakened shortly after dawn, gloriously contented following a delicious interlude in Finn's bed. Pity she had not been able to spend every moment of the night in his arms. In the all-too-brief moments they'd shared together, he'd caressed her so tenderly, she had marveled at the wonder of it all. She'd never dreamt a man's touch could be so very gentle, yet so commanding and sensual. Finn had stirred her body and soul to heights of pleasure unlike any she'd ever experienced. And then, later, in her own chamber, she'd drifted to sleep, luxuriating in dreams of his warm, strong body. When she'd opened her eyes as the early rays of sunlight drifted through the windows, even though she was alone, she'd been utterly content. Even Mrs. Tuttle's stern look when she spotted Macie roaming about at all hours of the night had not diminished her happiness.

Pity the bliss had been regrettably short-lived. The sound of the messenger at the door had stirred Macie to full alertness. Something was wrong. She knew that, even before the reluctant young man had conveyed the upsetting news.

"It's quite sad that the old professor didn't recover," she said, taking a sip of tea. "But I see little reason to worry. Poison is a highly personal means to commit a murder, or so I've read. If he was indeed killed by a toxin, he had to have been targeted . . . most likely by someone he knew."

Finn stirred a cube of sugar into his tea. "We know there is a common thread that links the two of ye."

"My grandfather."

He nodded. "The connection is too close to dismiss."

Mrs. Tuttle bustled through the door to the dining room. "Miss Macie, you have another visitor. She says she's here for teatime."

"Teatime? Surely Mrs. Johnstone did not misunderstand—"

"No, Macie, I did not mistake yer meaning," Mrs. Johnstone said as she strolled through the doorway. *The Red Queen from the masquerade.* In her beautifully tailored tweed walking suit, the tall, strikingly beautiful woman whose abundance of dark hair was threaded with silver cut an imperious figure even without her faux crown. In her right hand, she held a large yellow parasol, while a small black reticule dangled from her left wrist.

"I asked her to wait in the parlor," Mrs. Tuttle said, displaying her exasperation as Mrs. Johnstone leaned her brolly against a side chair, appearing to make herself at home.

"I do apologize for the intrusion, but time is of the essence." Mrs. Johnstone's mouth thinned, taut with tension. "I understand ye've received the unpleasant news."

Macie sent her housekeeper a speaking glance. "Might I trouble you to put on another pot of tea?"

"'Tis no trouble," Mrs. Tuttle said, making a quick exit.

Macie met Mrs. Johnstone's solemn gaze. "You are referring to the man who died last night?"

She offered a matter-of-fact nod, then turned to Finn. "Ye haven't told her, have ye?"

Finn shook his head. "I'd intended to explain it all before ye arrived for tea."

She nodded her understanding. "Sadly, certain aspects of this situation are quite troubling. Amelia did not think I should delay my arrival, not even until later in the day."

A sudden tension filled Macie. "Would you be so kind as to tell me what is happening?"

"Shall we cut to the heart of the matter?" Mrs. Johnstone adjusted her skirts and seated herself in a wingchair. "My dear friend, Amelia MacLain, has requested a favor of me. She believes ye may be in need of my services."

Macie's brow furrowed. "Your services?"

"In view of recent developments, there's reason to suspect ye may be in danger."

"In danger?" Macie shot Finn a pointed glance. "Should I expect that everyone you've ever known will greet me with that warning?"

Finn rubbed the back of his neck as if it suddenly ached. "It's tempting to believe the threat ended with old man's passing, but we cannot take any chances."

Mrs. Johnstone nodded her agreement. "The situation with the intruder at Bennington Manor is quite troubling."

"The old man did not pose a threat. He seemed frightened. Perhaps even distraught."

"He had good reason to be," Mrs. Johnstone nodded. "I understand he spoke to ye."

"He appeared to be out of his senses. His words were quite peculiar," Macie said. "We understand that he might have been poisoned. That could explain his mental state."

"That is possible. Or perhaps he was desperate because knew

his time was short." Mrs. Johnstone's mouth went taut, and she seemed to hesitate. "Do ye have any idea what the man was searching for?"

Macie swallowed against a sudden tightness in her throat. Mrs. Johnstone's tone bore a distinct urgency. Had something else happened? Something dreadful?

"I've no idea. He was rummaging through all sorts of books. There seemed to be no reason to it."

"Until we determine what Professor Smythson was searching for, we won't know the true nature of the threat," Mrs. Johnstone said. "If there *is* something in the house that someone was willing to kill for, we cannot assume they will stop at the professor."

Chapter Twenty-Four

ILLING TO KILL for.

Mrs. Johnstone's grim warning unleashed a chill along the length of Macie's spine. As she laced her fingers into a loose knot, Finn came to stand behind her chair. His touch upon her shoulders was firm, so gently reassuring.

"I am sorry to be the bearer of a distressing truth," Mrs. Johnstone went on. "Rest assured we will take whatever precautions are needed to protect ye."

The professor's murmured word echoed in her memory. *Murder*. His voice had been weak. Yet filled with desperation.

"After I came upon the old man, he tried to warn me. At the time, I thought he was delirious. He told me to leave." She pulled in a calming breath. "He said someone would come after me."

"He may have wanted to protect ye," Mrs. Johnstone said. "Well, then, it's a very good thing I'm here."

Macie pulled in a low breath, calming herself as Mrs. Johnstone's words triggered a fresh warning. Before she could utter the question that sprang to mind, Mrs. Tuttle bustled in with a tea service on a silver tray.

"A good thing, eh?" the housekeeper scoffed, crinkling her nose as she placed a delicate cup before their guest and filled it with piping hot tea. "Are you thinking to bash the villain in the noggin with that enormous brolly of yours?"

"That *is* one of its uses," Mrs. Johnstone said with an enigmatic smile.

"Mrs. Tuttle, please," Macie implored her tart-tongued housekeeper to be civil, then turned back to Mrs. Johnstone. "You mentioned that Amelia asked you to come here. Precisely what do you have in mind?"

"Quite simply, I am here to assist in yer defense until the danger has passed."

Macie's attention wandered to the oversized parasol propped against the chair. She didn't want to admit it, but she was inclined to agree with Mrs. Tuttle's skepticism. "I'm sorry, but I don't entirely understand."

"Ye will. In time." Mrs. Johnstone added a splash of milk to her tea. "First, ye need time to quiet yer thoughts after this morning's unpleasant news."

Mrs. Tuttle frowned. "If there's a maniac running about the city with his eyes on our Macie, she needs to be heading home to the country, far from this place."

"There is no maniac running about," Macie said. "I have no intention of leaving London."

"Your mum and your papa would think otherwise," the housekeeper said. "They'd want you to come home."

Macie gave her head a little shake. "I shall be cautious."

Mrs. Tuttle frowned. "I'm not sure you know the meaning of the word."

"I shall be exceedingly vigilant." Macie flashed a little smile at the protective woman who'd helped bandage her scrapes and bruises when she was a girl in braids. "I give you my word. Now, will you stop your worrying?"

"I'm not sure I know how to do that." Mrs. Tuttle folded her arms and regarded Finn for a long moment. "You will watch over her, won't you?"

"I will protect her." Finn's amber-brown gaze locked with Macie's, solemn and determined. "With every fiber of my being."

SETTLING INTO A cozy nook of her study, Macie allowed herself time to simply drink in the quiet. Cleo curled up near her feet, her contented purring like a soothing tonic. She reached to pet her, then selected the pencils she would use for her sketches.

Oh, how she relished the calmness. Macie leaned back against the plush cushions of her window seat and put pencil to paper. Sketching out ideas for her next photographic endeavor at the old theater in the West End, she felt the tension drain from her body. The concert hall had not been used in more than a year, but rumors swirled about the spirits of performers of days long past who still treaded the boards of the grand stage. Very soon, she'd venture inside with her camera, ghosts or not. Somehow, it felt as if she were on borrowed time.

There was no telling how long she'd be in London before she'd be forced to return to her family's country home. Jon would soon return from Scotland. Upon learning of the professor's murder, would he insist that she leave the city?

As she mapped out her plan for the exhibit, she drew heavy lines against the paper, if only to release some of the tension welled within her. Jon would be very displeased to know she'd stumbled upon a murdered man. Her ever-practical brother would do whatever it took to avoid any risk. After all, it would certainly create a nasty scandal if she fell prey to a villain, now wouldn't it? Heaven only knew Papa and Mum would never let him hear the end of it.

Macie's thoughts turned back to her planning. Moments later, Nell peeked in the door. "Might Mrs. Johnstone and I have a word with you?"

"Of course," she said, even as her delightful peace flitted away. "I'll join you in the parlor."

As soon as Macie entered the room, she read the concern on their features. Nell handed her a cup of tea and sat by her side on the sofa. Cleo leapt up onto the cushioned back, her imperious expression making it seem as if she actually took in their discussion.

"I am aware that Finn is seeing to yer protection." Mrs. Johnstone regarded her with a warm gaze. "Amelia asked me to assist. If a threat does indeed exist, think of me as another line of defense."

Her unexpected words cut through Macie's apprehension. *Not another bodyguard. Not another chaperone.*

Much less a woman who carried herself like a stern Scottish nanny.

"Good heavens, no." The words tumbled from Macie's mouth before she could hold them back.

Mrs. Johnstone's brows quirked. "No?"

"No." Macie held her voice steady. "I have no need of a chaperone."

Mrs. Johnstone softly shook her head. "I have no intention of serving as such, though I would enjoy accompanying ye about the city from time to time."

Macie let out the breath she'd been holding. "What do you have in mind?" She slanted Nell a glance. "It would appear I am the only one who does not know."

"In my life, I've enjoyed occupations which many might consider unconventional. That has always worked to my advantage," Mrs. Johnstone explained. "I have acquired specialized skills in the area of personal defense. Specifically, techniques and resources a woman might readily put to use."

"My brother has shown me ways to deter an assault," Macie said, her memory conjuring an image of a drink-addled lord, a codpiece, and her well-placed knee.

"Excellent. That is a good start," Mrs. Johnstone said. "Perhaps enough to fend off an overly amorous scoundrel. But sadly not enough to stop a determined criminal."

"That is where Finn comes in."

Mrs. Johnstone's forehead crinkled. "Ye wish to be tethered

to a protector's side every moment of the day?"

"Of course not."

"Very good." Mrs. Johnstone's words were met with Cleo's luxurious yawn. The woman's serious expression brightened. "Would ye like to see what I have to offer by way of instruction?"

"See?" Macie sat up a bit straighter.

"At times, words simply will not do." Mrs. Johnstone offered a cagey smile, then went to the door. "Finn, would ye please join us?"

He seemed to hesitate as he entered the room, but smiled as he met Macie's gaze. "So, what do ye think?"

"If nothing else, I am intrigued."

Mrs. Johnstone turned to him. "I do believe a demonstration is in order."

Finn regarded her with the look of a man heading to the Tower. "Ye don't mean—"

She nodded and threw a glance toward Macie. "Consider it a sacrifice for the greater good."

He cocked a brow. "A sacrifice, eh?"

"Oh, I do like the sound of this," Nell spoke up with an unusual glee. Goodness, this was a side to her friend Macie had seldom seen.

"I will not hurt ye," Mrs. Johnstone assured Finn, her tone not quite sincere.

"We both know better," he countered.

She flashed a half-smile. "A brawny man like ye could not possibly fear a woman old enough to be your mum."

"I should've stayed in Scotland," Finn uttered under his breath.

Mrs. Johnstone flashed a look of challenge. "Ye know what to do."

"Blast it." Finn muttered, as if for his own ears only. And then, louder. "This is for ye, Macie."

With that, he charged headlong toward Mrs. Johnstone.

Macie gasped. Surely Finn—all six lean-muscled feet of him—

would not attack a woman. "Stop, Finn!"

Her plea was unnecessary.

Mrs. Johnstone's arm whipped forward, blocking his advance. With sure, confident motions, she seized his arm. And twisted it. Hard. Another quick, sure movement, and she slammed him to the floor.

Ooof. Finn landed with a thud. Lying flat on his back on the rug, he stared up at the ceiling. "Blast it, I'd forgotten how much that hurt."

Mrs. Johnstone brushed her hands together as if wiping away dust. "All part of the training. Ye know that, Finn."

For a moment, Macie took in the display without a word. For her part, Nell could not hide her delight at the spectacle.

"Most impressive," Nell gushed. "Might I have a go?"

Finn shot her a glare. "Not on yer life."

Mrs. Johnstone extended a hand to Finn, but he waved it away as if anticipating a double-cross. "I am capable of getting up on my own," he said gruffly, even as he continued to face the ceiling.

"Is that so?" Macie could not resist teasing him. "It does appear she got the better of you."

Coming to his feet, he flashed a grin. "Would ye believe me if I told you I was acting?"

"Not for a moment."

"Ye're a shrewd lass, I'll give you that." His grin broadened. "'Tis only my pride that's wounded."

"As I mentioned, whatever indignity ye've suffered is for the greater good." Mrs. Johnstone turned to Macie. "I am not here to act as a chaperone; I am here as a teacher."

Curiosity washed over Macie. "In the art of manual combat?"

"Not precisely." A thin smile played on the older woman's lips. "I am here to teach ye to withstand a threat."

"To drop a man to his knees?" Nell added with bloodthirsty enthusiasm.

Mrs. Johnstone's brow furrowed. "If need be."

Nell's eyes gleamed. "When shall we begin?"

"I'd no inkling you had a taste for such . . ." Macie struggled for the right word. "Violence."

Finn slanted her a glance. "It's always the quiet ones, ye know."

"Indeed," Nell replied with a grin.

"I've brought each of ye a gift," Mrs. Johnstone said, retrieving the creamy yellow parasols she'd propped up behind the sofa.

Nell ran a fingertip over the weights sewn into the ribs. "Wielded with a degree of force, this could make quite an impression."

"I must admit, it is a clever design," Macie said. "But I have no reason to carry a sunshade after dark."

"A valid point, indeed." Mrs. Johnstone displayed an elegant handkerchief she'd stashed in her reticule. The embellished linen square sparkled with tiny bits of stone that had been polished to a shine. "One must properly prepare for any eventuality. Take this bit of lacy fluff. Carried in a purse, ye might access it at any time." She touched a fingertip to the gleaming weights. "Employed with a flick of the wrist against an attacker's face, I'd wager he—or she—would think twice before continuing their assault."

Nell took the cloth in hand. "Genius."

"Now that we've seen a bit of what an ordinary woman can—" Mrs. Johnstone began.

"*Ordinary?*" Finn disagreed.

Mrs. Johnstone paused. "Should I consider that a compliment, Mr. Caldwell?"

Finn shrugged. "No one could ever view ye as ordinary, Mrs. Johnstone."

"Indeed," she said coolly, though a smile lit her eyes. "I do believe in being prepared.

"Now, Macie, as I was saying, I am here to instruct ye in the art of self-defense. That is, if ye're ready and willing to learn."

Finn leaned against the sofa table, stretching out his long legs. "God help the badly behaved lord who crosses yer path, Macie.

The gent will have more to worry about than a port stain on his cravat."

Macie met his gaze. "Perhaps his fellow boors will think twice before they vex me."

"I suspect they already do," he said. "They simply cannot resist the challenge."

"Challenge?" Macie said. Was Finn speaking for himself as well?

A wry grin played on his mouth, but his expression suddenly shifted. "It's not a mystery." His amber gaze held hers, and for a heartbeat, she nearly forgot they were not alone. "'Tis a universal truth, Macie: men always desire what they cannot possess."

PERCHED ON AN overstuffed chair in her sun-dappled parlor, Macie sipped tea and discreetly studied her guest. Mrs. Johnstone's attire was elegant, yet no-nonsense, and the woman's precise manner of speaking brought to mind the harried governess her father had hired to teach Macie to behave like a fine young lady. Pity Miss Beasley's lessons had offered instruction Macie had little interest in learning.

But Mrs. Johnstone's fiercely independent demeanor was delightfully different from the dour, always-tasting-a-lemon set of Miss Beasley's bland features. Unlike the perpetual weariness in the prim governess's expression, Elsie Johnstone's eyes twinkled with a bit of mischief. She became especially animated while recalling the youthful exploits of her nephew Logan and his cousin Finn. Following her sister's death, Mrs. Johnstone had stepped in to assist Logan's father in raising his two young boys. And there was no denying that the woman's unique skills might well prove more valuable than Miss Beasley's consummate mastery of etiquette. After all, it wasn't as if an attacker would give a fig about impeccable manners.

Mrs. Johnstone had proven her ability to land a vigorous man like Finn on the floor. Why, she'd knocked the breath out of him, and he'd shown reluctance to demonstrate the next phase of her defensive tactics. If she could inspire wariness in a powerful man like Finn, what harm could the woman's tactics unleash on an aggressor bent on mayhem?

"Well, enough of my reminiscences." Mrs. Johnstone peered over the rim of her porcelain cup. "We've more important matters to discuss. While I fully intend to be of service, I will not be a millstone about your neck."

Macie took another sip of oolong tea. Had her initial reaction to Mrs. Johnstone's presence been so very obvious? She decided upon a diplomatic response. "I cannot imagine anyone would ever see you as such."

"Excellent." A thin smile brightened Mrs. Johnstone's eyes. "I recently had the pleasure of attending your Edinburgh exhibit. I understand ye're now capturing the charm of the Bennington estate."

"Charm?" Macie considered the word. "If only my father shared your opinion of our grandfather's home. He sees it only in terms of shillings and pence."

Mrs. Johnstone lifted a brow. "Andrew Bennington was yer grandfather?"

"Indeed." Macie pictured the old man she'd adored. "He liked to say we were two of a kind."

"I can see that," Mrs. Johnstone said. "I was fortunate to make Andrew's acquaintance some years ago. My dear husband, Franklin, and I attended a number of dinner parties where yer grandfather was a welcome guest. I am a great admirer of his early work with Greco-Roman antiquities. Andrew's treatise on the goddess Athena was particularly fascinating."

"You've read my grandfather's essays?"

"Franklin and I shared an interest in mythology. We greatly enjoyed yer grandfather's examination of the subject. Many years ago, we traveled to the Mediterranean on our honeymoon to explore. We'd always longed to return." The light in Mrs. Johnstone's blue eyes dimmed. "But we waited too long. One night, my husband was taken unexpectedly. And that was that." She let out a sigh. "But enough about me. Are ye planning a return to the manor in the near future?"

"I'd planned to set up my camera later today," Macie explained. "When the exterior lighting is just right."

"Finn will accompany ye?"

"I don't believe so," Macie said. "Nell often acts as my assistant."

"I would very much like to join ye."

"You truly do not need to trouble yourself on my behalf," Macie said gently.

"It would be no trouble. I'm quite intrigued by this medium. The artistic possibilities are without limit."

"Indeed," Macie agreed. "In that case, I'd be delighted if you would accompany us."

"It will be my pleasure." Rising, Mrs. Johnstone retrieved her lemon-yellow brolly, pointing out the tiny weights fastened to its ribs. "Just so ye know, I will be prepared."

Chapter Twenty-Five

"MRS. JOHNSTONE, YOU really must see the interior of the house," Macie said as she adjusted her tripod, setting it level on the uneven pavers near the house's massive front steps. "You're welcome to explore as much as you'd like."

"Especially the library." Nell's eyes lit with interest. "The scene of the crime."

"How very dramatic." Macie frowned for effect. "I don't find that at all humorous."

"But unfortunately, it is indeed accurate," Mrs. Johnstone said.

A hint of a smile tugged at Nell's mouth. "Once you've looked about, you may develop some insight into what occurred."

"I have some experience in these matters," Mrs. Johnstone said with a serious air. "I am particularly interested in the volumes Professor Smythson had been searching."

"I do hope you can find some clue as to what he was seeking." Macie fiddled with the angle of her camera. With any luck, she'd have precious minutes without interruption once Nell and Mrs. Johnstone immersed themselves in their investigation.

"Give me time, my dear." Mrs. Johnstone's flicker of a smile told her she'd read her expression. "Give me time."

"Come with me." Nell flashed a little grin. "And do watch for the spirits who roam this place."

"Ah, a spectral encounter. One can only hope." Brimming with excitement, Mrs. Johnstone followed Nell inside.

Macie positioned her camera to capture the large stone lions who stood silent guard over the place. Gazing into the lens, a ripple of awareness crept over her nape. She turned to face the unpleasant man who'd claimed an acquaintance with her grandfather.

"Mr. Neville," she uttered as a terse greeting. "What brings you here today?"

He regarded her for a long moment without speaking. Appearing on edge, he tugged the brim of his hat lower. Odd, given the clouds and lack of glare. "Might we speak privately, Miss Mason?"

She squared her shoulders. "I see no need. My position on your interest in my grandfather's books and papers has not changed."

Mr. Neville shook his head. "Miss Mason, this is a matter of dire consequence. It requires . . . discretion."

"Discretion, is it?" She cocked a brow. "I'm afraid you're wasting your time. I have no intention of selling so much as a scrap of old newspaper from my grandfather's collection."

"You must hear me out." He lowered his voice to scarcely more than a whisper. "You must listen. Your grandfather—"

"Please, do not tarnish my grandfather's memory by bringing him into this conversation."

"I had to come." His breath came in sputters. "Andrew would've trusted me to help you."

To help me. Goodness, was the man ill? Or suffering delusions? She detected a faint odor of spirits on his breath. But the drawn expression on Mr. Neville's face was not the result of too much liquor. The lines of concern seemed all too genuine. As was the fear in his eyes.

She moved closer. "Mr. Neville, you don't look well."

"No. Not unwell. But not . . . not much time." He bit the words between his teeth. "Your grandfather trusted me . . . with his research. I must have his papers."

She squared her shoulders. "I will not part with so much as a single document."

"Miss Mason, I need that research." Reaching for her, he caught her hands between his leather-gloved palms. "You don't know what you have."

She pulled away from his hold. "I've heard quite enough."

He glanced about, seeming to search the street. As he turned back to her, he pressed a hand to his chest. To his heart. "You must listen to me."

"Mr. Neville, you look unwell."

Pulling in a labored breath, he dabbed his brow with his pocket square. "You must heed what I say."

His hands were trembling. He needed help. "You are not well," Macie said firmly. "I must find—"

The rattle of carriage wheels over the cobbles startled her. Macie's words caught in her throat. Moving swiftly, the elegant black coach appeared as though it might actually bound over the curb.

As the carriage slowed to a stop, the door at the top of the stairs creaked open. Her brows knitted with questions, Mrs. Johnstone called down to her. "Is there a problem?"

The old man caught her hands again, his hold startlingly firm. "It may be too late for me," he said with a lack of emotion, as if he'd resolved to face whatever it was he feared. Turning away, he headed to the carriage. Pausing before the coach, he cast her a lingering glance. "If you will not listen to me, Miss Mason, I can no longer protect you."

MACIE RETREATED TO the small garden terrace behind her townhouse. The sun was low in the sky, its rays warm and refreshing. Cleo sashayed close behind, the cat's tail at a jaunty angle as she surveyed the garden with a bright-eyed excitement.

Inhaling the aroma of fresh lavender and fragrant roses, Macie smiled to herself as a bee flitted energetically from one blossom to the next, not a care in the world. She crossed the small courtyard to her favorite plant, a beautiful tea rose with coral pink buds nearly ready to bloom.

The cat sauntered about, then took a spot on a garden bench. Stretching out her body, she nearly covered the surface.

"Cleo, you do know how to stake your claim, don't you?" Swishing her skirts to the side, Macie made herself comfortable on the cement bench across from where her pet luxuriously basked in the sun.

Determined to clear her thoughts, Macie drank in the sights and smells that served as tonic for her weary mind. Usually, a few moments with her flowers and greenery and sunlight were all it took for her to relax and push away her worries, if only for a time. But after a few minutes alone with her thoughts, she could not deny, especially to herself, that her encounter with Mr. Neville had rattled her. In fact, she suspected an entire hothouse full of roses would not have done the trick.

"Do ye mind if I join ye?" Mrs. Johnstone strolled from the house, carrying a silver tray with cups and a pitcher of iced tea.

"Please, do," Macie said.

Mrs. Johnstone set the tray down beside Macie and poured each of them a drink. She turned to the bench Cleo had claimed and gently nudged the none-too-happy cat just enough to clear a space for herself. If a cat could scowl, Cleo was certainly doing just that.

"Ye were a bit quiet in the carriage," Mrs. Johnstone began. "I could not help but hear a bit of what the old man said. Did he upset ye?"

"He was not well. I am concerned about him." Macie took a sip of cool tea. "Honestly, I suspect he was in his cups, but there was something else . . . something that left me uneasy."

"He implied he'd been protecting ye," Mrs. Johnstone said.

"Why would he think such a thing?"

"I truly don't know. Mr. Neville has made it clear that he wishes to obtain my grandfather's collection, including his research. This afternoon, he said something rather peculiar." Macie set her teacup on the bench. "He told me I don't know what I have."

Mrs. Johnstone's forehead crinkled. "I've heard that yer grandfather donated many of the most valuable artifacts before his death. There wasn't much left, was there?"

"Most of what remained after he passed away was bequeathed to museums from Wales to the Highlands. I told Mr. Neville as much upon our first meeting. Perhaps he was not convinced."

"Ye should seek a full appraisal of the remaining artifacts."

"An excellent suggestion." Gathering her thoughts, Macie stared down at the precise pattern of bricks beneath their feet. "The old gent has not inquired about the sculptures and vases and such. He's far more interested in Grandpapa's library. Especially his research. And there is something else—something the man said that seemed rather odd."

"What was it, Macie?"

"He said it might be too late for him." Picturing the look on his face, she pulled in a breath. "At first, I thought he was referring to getting his hands on whatever it was he wanted. But when I looked into Mr. Neville's eyes, I saw fear."

"How very troubling," Mrs. Johnstone said in a no-nonsense tone. "I shall have to ask about town and ferret out what the man's story truly is."

The door to the garden opened, and Mrs. Tuttle came onto the terrace. "I do hope I'm not interrupting, but you have a guest. He says his name's Aylesworth, and he's of the opinion you will wish to speak with him."

"Indeed," Macie perked up at the news. "Please, do show him in."

Moments later, Macie greeted the professor as he joined them in the garden. "Good afternoon. What a pleasant surprise."

As he offered greetings in turn, Cleo fixed him with a curious gaze. Stretched out to her full length on a chaise, the cat regarded him with a look of feline annoyance.

"I know my visit here was unexpected, but I needed to speak with you," Professor Aylesworth said. "There was no time for formalities and protocol."

"Think nothing of it," Macie replied. "Formalities and protocol are highly overrated."

"I thought you might see it that way," he said. "I wanted to discuss my upcoming journey to Athens. There is a strong possibility that I may be able to bring you along to document the expedition."

"How very exciting." Macie's pulse beat a bit faster. "Of course, I do have my work here in the city."

"I'm willing to arrange the timing in such a way that you may finish preparing for your planned exhibition."

Mrs. Johnstone gave a strategic little cough. "Am I to understand ye're suggesting that Miss Mason—an unmarried woman—travel with a contingent of researchers to another country?"

"It goes without saying that she would be accompanied by a companion. A woman of experience and maturity." The grin he flashed could melt the sternest of hearts. "Perhaps a woman like you, Mrs. Johnstone."

"Oh, dear. How I would treasure another opportunity to see Athens," she said, her tone surprisingly wistful.

"Very good," he said. "We shall see what arrangements can be made."

"Professor, this all so very unexpected," Macie said. "Before our conversation, the possibility had never entered my mind."

"Your expertise would be a true asset to our research, Miss Mason."

She met his warm gaze. Peter Aylesworth was an accomplished scholar, a man her grandfather had held in high regard. And now, he'd proposed a golden opportunity.

By all rights, she should be giddy with excitement. Yet the thought of leaving London twisted Macie's emotions into knots. This was all so very sudden. She'd come to thrive in the bustling city. There was so much for her to see. So many fascinating locations and intriguing people to portray with her camera. Could she leave it all behind, even for a few months?

Oh, you can tell yourself that's why you don't want to leave.

As Finn's oh-so-appealing grin flashed in her thoughts, she had to admit the truth. At least to herself. The prospect of parting from him—especially now, when she was coming to know the real man behind the tempting smile—well, that was another story, entirely. How could she put aside the longings of her heart?

"I understand my proposal is rather audacious," Professor Aylesworth went on. "But I'm confident you will find the experience rewarding."

"It is audacious, isn't it?" Macie agreed. "But also quite exciting. I shall give the matter serious consideration."

"Excellent, Miss Mason." He raked his fingers through his straight dark hair. "I do not wish to hurry your decision, but the plan has changed. Time is of the essence."

"Is it, now?"

He gave a solemn nod. "I am expected to leave for Athens within a fortnight. I should be able to delay my departure for a few additional days if that would allow you to make arrangements to accompany the team."

"My, that is rather soon." Macie took it all in. "I will inform you of my decision without delay."

"I do hold hope the answer will be 'yes.'" The professor frowned as Cleo leapt from her perch. The cat crept up to him, her expression both wary and exceedingly curious.

Macie grinned. "I think she likes you."

As Cleo brushed against the professor's trousers, he quirked a brow. "Do you, now?"

"Professor Aylesworth, I have perused yer latest research," Mrs. Johnstone said. "We share an interest in ancient cultures. I find the history of the Nile Valley particularly fascinating. Have ye considered an expedition to Egypt?"

"I must confess, I've never developed a keen interest in the civilization," he explained.

Mrs. Johnstone lifted a brow. "My, I do find that surprising."

A slight smile played on his lips as he threw Cleo a glance. "Too many cats."

"Oh, dear," Macie said lightly. "Not an aficionado?"

He shrugged. "When I was a lad, my family owned hounds. I understand their motivations far better than those of felines. Cats display a certain aloofness, wouldn't you say?"

"Most definitely," she agreed.

"This cat is a fitting pet for you. Intelligent. Observant. And fiercely independent."

"I consider that a high compliment."

"Indeed." He moved to the door. "Miss Mason, I do have another request. Before I depart for Greece, I would like to review your grandfather's journals. His research has served as an inspiration for my own endeavors."

"Of course. Grandpapa would be pleased to know you continue to value his work."

"*Value* is putting it mildly," he said. "I have no doubt I will find precisely what I need within those pages."

BEFORE FINN HAD a chance to ring the bell to announce his arrival at Macie's townhouse, the door opened with a groan of its hinges. The housekeeper, a woman whose expression seemed fixed in an ever-present frown whenever he was in her presence, looked even more sour than usual.

"You might've used the servant's entrance, as we agreed," Mrs. Tuttle said, tersely, as if the words pained her to speak.

"And miss the sight of yer smiling face?"

"Ye must be confusing me with someone else," she said in a flat voice, though a touch of cheek brightened her eyes.

"Never," he said with a shake of his head. "Ye're an original, Mrs. Tuttle."

"That I am." Her expression softened. "Miss Macie's in the garden. With the she-devil and the bird wit who fancies herself a coquette."

"She-devil, eh?" He scratched his chin, debating whether to suggest *dragon* in its place. "Ye've had prior experience with Mrs. Johnstone, haven't ye?"

"Experience?" Mrs. Tuttle waved away the word. "Misfortune is more like it. Quite some time ago, my dear sister was employed by the she-devil and her husband. Bess suffered an injury to her foot, so I came to assist. Worst five weeks of my life, I tell you." She scowled. "The woman runs a household like a captain commands a ship. So precise and perfect."

"I do understand," he said with a little grin.

"Will you be dining with Miss Macie tonight?"

"Ye know I would not pass up a chance to eat yer cooking," he said.

"Flattery comes natural to rogues, doesn't it?" Mrs. Tuttle flashed a wry grin.

"Actually, it's a required course of study," he said with a quick smile, then headed to the garden.

"Oh, it's you," Nell said casually, glancing his way as he stepped through the French doors.

He folded his arms and leaned against a sturdy column. "An enthusiastic greeting if ever I've heard one."

"I was hoping Professor Aylesworth had returned," Nell said. "Sadly, I missed my chance to speak with him."

Finn hitched a brow. "Returned?"

"He paid a visit to follow up on an idea he'd mentioned at the ball." Macie's tone sounded deliberately bland.

"The professor will soon embark on another research trip to Athens," Mrs. Johnstone spoke up. "It's rather exciting."

"Athens, is it?" He plastered on a thin smile as he turned to Macie. "The destination for the adventure of a lifetime?"

"That might be a bit of an overstatement, but I don't doubt the trip would prove exciting."

Finn rubbed the back of his neck, as if that might ease a sudden ache. "It might be just the thing to inspire another exhibit."

"I imagine it would," she said a bit too primly.

"I'd be delighted to accompany you," Nell said. "And perhaps, to become better acquainted with the professor."

Macie regarded her friend with a weary expression. "With any luck, you will not be napping if he pays another visit."

"I had no way of knowing he would pop in," Nell said.

"Indeed," Finn said. "It's not as if it was an ordinary occurrence."

"Quite true, Mr. Caldwell," Nell agreed. "Actually, very little that has occurred in recent days has been ordinary."

"Speaking of ordinary occurrences—we were not expecting you so soon," Macie said in an obvious effort to change the subject. "Has anything happened?"

"I have uncovered new information on the other professor—the dead one."

Macie's eyes widened. "Have you now?"

"My inquiries have turned up some curious facts." Finn took a seat on a concrete bench and stretched out his legs. "As it turns out, Professor Smythson had been in London for some time now. He was well-known in the city. But not for his scholarly pursuits."

"What are you saying?" Macie asked.

"He left Scotland nearly three years ago. The man had resigned his position at the university following some sort of scandal."

"A scandal?" Mrs. Johnstone's interest seemed to perk up. "Of what nature?"

"He was accused of falsifying certain documents in his research."

"Do you know what type of documents?" Mrs. Johnstone pressed.

He shook his head. "After he left Scotland, he forged a connection with London's antiquities dealers. Until his past caught up to him."

"Oh, dear, how dreadful," Nell said sympathetically.

"After that, he was known to frequent taverns, bemoaning the bitter turn his life had taken to anyone with a listening ear," Finn went on. "Murray at the Rogue's Lair recalled the man being deep in his cups, railing against the injustices he'd suffered."

Macie looked skeptical. "So, am I to understand you've gleaned this information from barkeeps about town?

"That was a starting point," he explained. "From there, I called in some favors. Ye'd be surprised how much ye can learn about a man in pubs and gambling dens."

Mrs. Johnstone sat up straighter. "Gambling dens, you say?"

"My sources tell me Professor Smythson had a fondness for wagering. Unfortunately, his luck did not match his enthusiasm."

Mrs. Johnstone nodded her agreement. "His gambling might have been the root of the scandal. At least in part."

Macie's brow creased with fine lines of concern. "None of explains his connection with my grandfather."

Finn plowed his hand through his hair. Bloody hell, he wished he had the answers she needed. "I found nothing that linked him with yer grandfather. But I'm still searching."

Her mouth thinned. "Thank you."

"We will puzzle this out, Macie." As Cleo jumped onto the bench and stretched into a leisurely sprawl beside him, he rubbed the cat behind her ears, receiving a bliss-filled purr in response. "That much, I can promise ye."

Chapter Twenty-Six

A S A GIRL, Macie marched to the rhythm of her own drum, or so her mother had said. Heaven knew she'd given her governesses more than their fair share of aggravation when she rebelled against the tutelage meant to prepare her to be a fine lady. She'd much preferred to traipse along with her brother and his boyhood friends through the wooded lands surrounding their country home. Her imagination had run wild as she peered into dark hollows, climbed trees, and navigated slippery stones by gentle streams. At times, she'd felt a fright, but all in all, the experiences had been exhilarating. Far more so than mastering an embroidered stitch or knitting a perfect cable. Her father had sternly disapproved of the way she gallivanted about with the lads, as he'd put it. But Mum, a free-spirited redhead whose complexion was dotted with freckles, had encouraged Macie to explore her world to her heart's content.

A month earlier, she would have been utterly thrilled by the prospect of a research trip to Athens, accompanied by a dashing professor, no less. Documenting the expedition would allow her to develop her craft at a new level entirely. She could envision the excitement her photographic portrayal might garner, while the journey itself would be something unlike anything she'd experienced.

So why was she sitting alone in her garden, gazing up at the crescent moon, holding back emotions she didn't want to feel?

Very little that has occurred in recent days has been ordinary. In one rather flippant sentence, Nell had neatly described Macie's life since the moment she'd slipped on a puddle of some awful burgundy wine and fallen directly into the hands of Finn Caldwell. Ever since she'd looked into his eyes that night, nothing had seemed quite the same.

If the opportunity to travel to Athens with Professor Aylesworth and his team was indeed offered, she'd be a fool to turn it down. Wouldn't she? Weeks earlier, the answer would've come easily. But now, so much had changed.

For so very long, she'd quieted the longings of her heart. She'd felt so certain that she would have to somehow become someone else in order to marry. The kind of love her mum and papa had cherished for so many years seemed unattainable, a mere fantasy for a woman like her.

Until she'd kissed Finn.

Until she'd delighted in the sound of his husky voice when he told her she was beautiful. Savored the feel of his skin against hers. Reveled in the pleasure of his touch.

Until she'd opened her heart to him. And him alone.

Could she bear to leave Finn for weeks, perhaps even months? There was so much to learn about him. So much to learn about each other. And the bond they were forging.

And there was another concern, wasn't there? If Finn's worries were justified—if she had somehow become mired in some criminal's vile scheme, she could not risk putting Professor Aylesworth and his fellow researchers in danger. If the situation were not resolved before his departure, she could not even consider accompanying the group.

She wandered over to her tea rose. Beneath the dim gaslight of the sconce, it seemed to glow with golden tones as its subtle aroma surrounded her.

"Are ye well, my sweet?" Finn's gravel-edged tones warmed her. Throughout the night, he'd been cool to her. Distant. Perhaps even aloof.

"My sweet, is it?" She turned to him. "Given that you'd scarcely said two words to me since dinner, I find that a bit surprising."

He crossed the patio, joining her by the roses. "I'd defy any man to get a word in when Nell and Mrs. Johnstone are in a spirited conversation." He threaded his fingers through a rogue tendril of her hair and swept it behind her ear, a tempting smile playing on his lips.

"That doesn't entirely explain your reticence. It's rather out of character, you must admit."

"Is it now?" He caught her fingers in his, making tiny circles with his thumb over the back of her hand. "At times, a wise man knows the less he says, the better."

"And tonight was one of those times?"

His shoulders lifted and fell, a casual shrug that contradicted the primal heat in his gaze. "It was." He grazed his fingertips along the curve of her jaw. "A complicated situation has become even more tangled. We both know ye'll soon have a decision to make. Aylesworth won't wait forever."

"So, it's his visit that's troubling you."

"In a word, yes." Finn didn't dance around the subject.

She bit back a little grin. "Why, Finn, am I to believe you're jealous?"

"Of that pompous arse?" His eyes flashed with emotion, contradicting his flippant words.

"That *pompous arse* is a scholar, and by all accounts, a gentleman."

"Gentleman?" he scoffed. "The bloke fights dirty. That's a bad sign, in my book."

"As I don't anticipate engaging the man in a bout of fisticuffs, I can say that does *not* signify as a problem in *my* book. Besides, Nell is rather taken with him."

"*Nell* is not the subject of his interest." Finn's voice was low and gruff and so very appealing. "That honor belongs to ye, Macie."

The raw emotion in his voice touched her at a primitive level. She met his intent gaze. Finn truly was jealous, wasn't he?

How very appealing.

She pulled in a low breath, steadying the slight racing of her pulse. "Professor Aylesworth's interest in me, for lack of a better word, is tied to my skill behind the camera. He wishes to document the expedition. There's nothing more to it."

"Do ye really believe that?" Finn raked his fingers through his hair.

"So, you think it's all a lie?" She took a step back, folded her arms, and shot him a glare. "A mere ploy to flatter me?"

Finn gave his head a brisk shake. "I don't question that he respects the artistry in yer work. He'd be a fool not to see yer talent." His gaze locked with hers. "But Macie, he's still a man."

"Am I to believe that a man cannot embark on an endeavor with a woman present without there being some . . . complication?"

The line of his jaw hardened as he considered her question. "I cannot say it is not possible. But in the case of Peter Aylesworth, I have my doubts," he said. "Macie, I saw how the man looked at ye."

"And precisely what did you see?"

"He looked at ye like he'd come upon some rare treasure."

She pulled in a low breath. "Really, Finn, it's not like you to be so . . . poetic."

"Ye think I'm exaggerating, do ye?" He slowly shook his head. "The man looked at ye like a bloody goddess had come to life." Finn reached for her again, caressing her cheek with a feather-light touch. "He looked at ye the way I did at the moment ye fell into my arms."

Macie swallowed hard against a sudden rush of emotion. "As I recall, you were none too taken with me that night."

"And that's where ye're wrong, Macie. I was looking upon a beautiful lass, a diamond far out of my reach. I knew that truth all too well."

Her pulse beat a steady rhythm against her ears. "And now?"

"Now, I know that I want ye. In my arms. So close, I can feel the beats of yer heart." His smile warmed every inch of her body. "Whatever the risk I might have to take, Macie—ye're worth it."

Reaching up, she drew her fingertips over his stubble-roughened jaw. A subtle aroma of bergamot and soap filled her senses. "I rather like this side of you, Finn Caldwell."

"Do ye, now?" He brushed a kiss over her lips. Soft. Gentle. Yet searing with unspoken need.

She smiled beneath the heat of his gaze. "As a matter of fact, I might say I adore it."

A sensuous smile played on his mouth. "Ah, ye're a true temptation, lass. If ye were mine . . . if we were truly alone, I'd prove it to ye. Right here beneath the moonlight."

Macie's heart raced. At this moment, she didn't care about anything else. Or anyone else. Only this man. And the decadent heat of his kiss.

"And if I want that as well?"

"Someday, lass." He framed her face between his hands. His mouth brushed hers, a gentle caress. And then deeper. Stronger. Claiming her kiss, leaving no doubt of his hunger. He kissed her again, a light touch of his lips to hers, seeming to savor every precious moment.

"And if that someday . . . could be tonight?" she whispered against his mouth.

"Ye're so bloody beautiful," he said, his voice raw with need. His hands fell away, even as his gaze locked with hers. "I've never wanted anything in my life more than I want ye."

Macie sighed. She ached for his touch. For his kiss. For the sound of her name on his gravel-edged voice.

She pressed a kiss to his lips. "When you look at me like that, the world melts away."

His arms slipped around her again, drawing her close. Her cheek pressed to his broad, hard chest, to the white linen shirt that came between her and the heat of his skin. Oh, how she wanted it gone. Her hands went to tug the ends of his shirt loose. Boldly, she inched the fabric higher, but he stilled her hands.

"Ah, Macie, I want ye, lass. But bloody hell, ye deserve more than a hurried passion." He traced the curve of her face with his fingertips, infinitely gently. "Ye deserve more. Ye deserve everything that I can give ye."

"Oh, Finn," she breathed his name in a sigh. Her fingers threaded through the silky strands of his hair. "In this moment, I am yours."

"There's no need to rush in, lass." A smile played on his lips, deliciously wicked. "I want to savor every inch of yer beautiful body. I want to hold ye in my arms all bloody night." He kissed her again, a caress filled with heat and longing and tenderness. "A proper seduction takes time. Someday, Macie, ye'll know how much I need ye. And then, ye will be well and truly mine."

"My, Macie, you are distracted, aren't you?"

Nell's gentle nudge pulled Macie from her thoughts. Gazing down at the hustle and bustle of the street below her grandfather's parlor, Macie had drifted into a comfortable daydream. It seemed fitting, really, that her thoughts on this gloomy afternoon would be filled with images and all-too-recent memories of Finn. He'd been the subject of her dreams the night before, in those long hours after he'd crept up the stairs with her to her room, but left her safe and sound and thoroughly sated. In those delicious moments, he'd kissed her until she was wild for him. He'd brought her to a peak so intense, it had left her nearly mindless with the sheer pleasure of it. And utterly besotted with the man she adored.

But he'd held back. Teaching her the ways of pleasure with his gentle hands and delicious mouth. Bringing her delight beyond anything she'd ever imagined. But he would not claim her as his own.

Not yet. Not until the moment was utterly right.

A proper seduction takes time.

Finn had become so very protective of her. He'd vowed he would never go beyond what she wanted him to do. He would not hurry their seduction. *How very delicious.* The very thought of it made her want him all the more.

"Are you well, Macie?" Nell pressed. "You're not yourself today."

Macie tucked her thoughts of Finn in the back of her mind. Sweet memories of his tenderness were just the thing to fill a long, lonely night. But for now, she had to form a coherent thought in response to Nell's question.

"I suppose I am a bit distracted," she said, turning to meet Nell's curious gaze.

Nell looked to be fighting back a grin. "Mr. Caldwell?"

"Is it so obvious?"

"The truth is in your eyes," Nell said. "You cannot hide it. I know you too well."

"That you do, my friend," she said.

"Personally, I think it's grand," Nell said.

"So do I," Macie said. "For now, I suppose I should ready my equipment. If I'm to photograph that creepy old theater in time for my exhibition, I need to get to it."

"That place gives me a chill. I do think the rumors are true."

"You believe there are ghosts?"

Nell grinned. "It would be exciting if there were, wouldn't it?"

"I'm not quite sure I'd wish for that kind of excitement right now."

"To each her own," Nell said with a brief grin. "Mrs. Johnstone is still in the library reviewing some of your grandfather's papers. It's all quite fascinating."

"I'd no idea you were interested in antiquities."

"Your grandfather's perspectives are intriguing, even to someone who has not studied ancient myths."

"He was a brilliant man," Macie said. "At heart, he was a teacher. He wanted to share his passion for the ancient world."

"Indeed," Nell agreed. "I'm going to spend a bit more time with his papers until you're ready to depart for the theater."

As Nell left the room, Macie took up her sketchbook and settled into a comfortable chair by the window. She needed to give some thought to the images she wished to capture. Now, with her thoughts more settled and surrounded by quiet, she could focus on the gloomy old theater.

She'd put pencil to paper for a pair of rough sketches and had begun a third when Nell and Mrs. Johnstone bustled through the door.

"Macie, you need to see this," Nell said, joining her by the window.

"What have you found?" A blend of excitement and puzzlement swept over Macie as Mrs. Johnstone entered, a small rosewood cabinet in her hands. "You have my grandfather's writing box?"

"Its contents were quite an interesting find," Mrs. Johnstone said.

"How did you open it? The key is tucked away in grandfather's safe. I simply haven't had the heart to search through it yet."

Her friend sported a cheeky expression. "That lock was no match for the talents of Nell Blake."

"A woman of many talents," Mrs. Johnstone commented, sounding genuinely impressed. "I've found the ability to best a lock to be a valuable skill."

"Why does that not surprise me?" Macie said.

"Honestly, this one was a bit of a bugger. Very cantankerous." Nell tapped the front of the box with one finger. "It took me a bit of longer than usual, but it could not defeat me."

Macie hiked a brow. Her friend had secrets, indeed. "Longer than usual?"

"You might have said I was a snoop as a girl. Let's just say that my older sister, the oh-so-perfect Cecily, never possessed a diary I could not read."

"You're horrible," Macie teased.

"Ceci thought so," Nell said.

Mrs. Johnstone chuckled, then gently nudged the discussion back on course. "Shall we turn back to the matter at hand?"

"Of course." Nell lifted the lid and retrieved a page that seemed to have been torn from a journal. "Is this your grandfather's handwriting?"

Glancing down at the notes, Macie recognized her grandfather's brash scrawl. "Most definitely."

Nell took a few neatly folded sheets from the box. "There's more. Pages of research."

"I cannot say that surprises me. Grandpapa wrote prolific notes on his collection. He filled many journals."

"There is something else, though—a rather exciting find." Enthusiasm colored Nell's voice. "Take a look, Macie."

"Do be careful, Nell," Mrs. Johnstone advised as Nell lifted a yellowed document from within the box. "You would not wish to damage the parchment."

Holding it gingerly by the corners, Nell displayed a letter penned with dark slashes of ink. As Macie leaned forward to take a better look, Mrs. Johnstone pointed out the notation in the upper corner of the page.

"This date places it in the sixteenth century," she said. "Over time, the script within the body of the letter has faded. But I can make out references to Michelangelo and Titian. This document may be quite valuable."

"My grandfather collected the papers of many Renaissance scholars," Macie said.

"Is it possible he'd hidden more away?" Nell said.

"I suppose he might have."

"That bothersome Mr. Neville might have good reason to want to get his hands on your grandfather's papers." Excitement brightened Nell's gaze. "This library might contain many more old letters—a trove of hidden treasure."

Chapter Twenty–Seven

THE THEATRE ROYALE had once been a grand theater, a jewel where many an esteemed thespian had walked across the stage. Now, years after audiences had filled the upholstered seats and applauded as the performers took their final bows, the plush burgundy curtains had faded over time, the boards were dulled from age and lack of care, and the once-dazzling crystal chandelier in the aging yet still elegant lobby now bore massive cobwebs. As Macie positioned her camera to capture the barren feel of the stage, she pulled in a low breath and released it on a sigh. The quiet seemed almost oppressive. She might actually welcome the sight of a specter or two, if only to liven up the place.

A dull ache pounded against her temples. She pressed her fingertips to her forehead, as if that might ease the low throb and drown out the chaos of her own thoughts.

Both Nell and Finn had wandered off to explore various parts of the theater. Since the three of them had arrived, Nell had seemed unusually quiet. That had certainly not been the case as they'd traveled in Finn's carriage to the theater. While Finn took the reins, Nell had excitedly discussed the letter in the rosewood box, interrupted only by the lurch of the coach over a few particularly large bumps in the road. She saw the discovery as an exciting revelation, a vital clue that could explain Professor Smythson's motives for his frantic search in the library.

A sudden jolt stirred her, and she looked down to see that one foot of the tripod had slipped into a crevice on the marble floor. *Drat the luck.* She crouched low to reposition the leg. As she adjusted the camera, she spotted Finn as he entered through the side door. His brisk steps closed the distance between them.

"You look weary, Macie. Ye might consider putting this off to another day."

"I'll be fine," Macie replied. "Working with my camera ener-gizes me."

"Ye're headstrong, lass." He flashed a little grin. "Like me."

The warmth in his smile was just the elixir she needed. "You like that, do you?"

"More that ye know, Macie." He traced the curve of her face with his fingertip, looking as if he might kiss her. "Ye're just—"

Displaying utterly atrocious timing, Nell strolled the door, interrupting Finn's gravel-edged words. She cut a direct path to the stage. "I do hate to be the bearer of bad news, but I suspect that unpleasant Mr. Neville is in the vicinity."

Macie felt the dull throb in her temples begin anew. "He's here?"

"A coach bearing a monogram on the door is outside the theater, waiting at the curb," Nell said. "I believe I saw that carriage at Bennington Manor when the old man approached you."

"Bloody hell," Finn said, his voice turning gruff. "I'll have a word with the gent."

Macie shook her head. "Not quite yet," she said. "I'll speak to him. After all, I can't have him think he can intimidate me."

As they headed to the lobby, Finn stayed close by. Seeing no sign of Mr. Neville, they stepped outside.

The coach was nowhere to be seen. Macie's shoulders relaxed as tension eased from her body.

"The weasel must've thought better of it," Finn said.

Macie rubbed the back of her neck, easing out a sudden ten-sion. "If he did follow us, I simply cannot understand what the man could possibly think to accomplish."

"It's possible I was mistaken," Nell said.

"I find that unlikely," Macie said. "You have a keen memory for details."

"Perhaps not as keen as I'd thought. In any case, now I can take a peek at the dressing rooms. I have an idea for a photograph that might prove interesting."

"An excellent idea," Macie said as they reentered the building. As Nell headed toward the massive spiral staircase, Macie headed to the stage with Finn.

She'd scarcely had time to adjust her camera lens when a scream rang out. The terror in the piercing cry sent a chill along her spine.

"Nell!"

They darted from the theater, coming upon Nell by the stairs. She stood motionless as if frozen by fear.

"Thank heaven," Macie rushed to her side. "We heard you scream."

"I didn't mean to frighten you," Nell murmured. "It's . . . it is awful."

"What's happened?" Finn said, his tone firm yet gentle. "Tell us what you've seen."

Nell pointed to the lobby where patrons had once obtained refreshments. "He's there."

"Stay here." Finn cut a path to the bar. His gaze fixed on the floor behind the counter. "Good God."

Macie rushed to see what had left Finn stunned. "Oh, no." The horror of the sight slammed into her. "This cannot be happening."

A man lay in the shadows, an ebony cane topped with brass at his side.

Mr. Neville.

A bitter taste rose in the back of her throat. Macie pressed a hand to her mouth. She struggled against the instinct to flee.

Finn dropped to the floor and examined the man for signs of

life. He slowly shook his head.

"I'm sorry, Macie. He's gone."

Dear Lord.

Macie's pulse thundered in her ears. Emotion welled in her throat. "Perhaps his heart gave out."

"That is a possibility," Finn said, doubt clear in his tone. "Macie, Nell, look away. This is not a fit sight for yer eyes."

"I need to see this," Macie said, holding her voice calm despite the quivering of her hands. "I need to know what has happened."

Finn came to his feet. "I will summon the authorities. But not until after we've left this place. Not until ye're home behind a heavy door with a solid bolt."

"Do you think . . . someone did this to him?" Nell asked, her voice quaking.

Finn's expression was grim. "There's blood on the cane. Most likely his."

"It's happened," Macie murmured. "Again."

Finn caught her hand in his. Warm and strong and reassuring. "I need to get the two of ye away from here."

"Wait. Do you see it? There's something there," Nell said. "Something near his right hand."

Crouching down, Finn retrieved a small, torn piece of stationery that lay behind the counter. "This scrap?"

"Yes," Nell said as he brought it to her. As she examined the ragged paper, she appeared to steel herself. "How very peculiar."

"What is it?" Macie asked. "What have you found?"

"I'm not entirely certain." Nell stared down at the scrap, her eyes widening. When she spoke, she kept her voice to a near whisper. "Mr. Caldwell, we must leave this place. Now."

"MY DEAR, ARE ye feeling unwell?" Mrs. Johnstone's eyes betrayed her concern as she strolled into the parlor of Macie's townhouse.

Macie straightened her spine and forced a small smile. "I'm a bit weary. Nothing more serious than that."

Mrs. Johnstone went to the sideboard and poured two cups of tea. "Ah, my dear, I know how upset ye must be."

"I'm not destined for a career on the stage, now am I?"

"This is all so very troubling. I'm more than a bit shaken myself. I was not even there to witness the horrible sight." Mrs. Johnstone placed the cup on the table beside Macie. "This may help to calm yer nerves."

Macie inhaled the rich aroma of the oolong as she pulled in low breaths. She had to compose herself. She'd be of no use to anyone, not even herself, if she could not calm her own fear.

"It does seem rather like a bad dream, doesn't it?"

"Indeed," Mrs. Johnstone perched upon a wing chair. "So, what has the inspector determined about Mr. Neville's death?"

"They have assumed natural causes." Macie sighed. "While Inspector Bradley took meticulous notes on what we'd all witnessed, he seemed to have already reached the conclusion that Mr. Neville had suffered a spasm of the heart."

"A rather convenient deduction," Mrs. Johnstone said with a frown. "Less possibility for scandal, I'd say."

"Indeed. At this time, the detectives have established no connection between his death and Professor Smythson's murder." Macie pressed her fingertips to her temples. "It's baffling to me that they cannot see the similarity. When Professor Smythson collapsed, the physicians believed he had suffered a heart attack. But later, they noticed the signs of poison."

Mrs. Johnstone's brow furrowed. "I understand that Finn spotted a tear in Mr. Neville's coat."

Macie nodded. "Someone might have rummaged through his pockets. Finn also noticed blood on the man's walking stick. It simply doesn't make sense." Macie stared down at the painted flowers on the teacup, gathering her thoughts. "And then, there is the matter of the scrap of paper Nell spotted near Mr. Neville's hand. It's quite small and rather ragged, but I do recognize my grandfather's handwriting."

Mrs. Johnstone nodded with interest. "Might I have a look?"

"Of course." Macie went to her desk, retrieving the scrap of paper she'd carefully stored in the drawer.

Mrs. Johnstone took her spectacles from her pocket and examined the ragged-edged remains of what might have been a letter. "This does look rather like the writing in yer grandfather's journals. Pity all that is left is this snippet."

"I believe Mr. Neville had been clutching a letter and someone tore it from his hand," Macie explained.

"Indeed. This scrap might have been left behind." Mrs. Johnstone held the paper up to the window. "I can make out the name of a Grecian goddess. *Aphrodite.* And another word." She hesitated. "*Deceived.*"

"The inspector did not find that word nearly as troubling as I did. As the paper was not discovered on Mr. Neville's person, he dismissed the find as coincidental." Macie pulled in a breath. "Why, he didn't even collect it as evidence."

"How very frustrating," Mrs. Johnstone returned the paper to Macie.

Macie placed the scrap back into the drawer. "Even if Inspector Bradley's theory is correct—even if Mr. Neville's heart gave out—the detectives have not yet deduced a motive for Professor Smythson's murder."

"With any luck, Finn and Logan will find some answers as they make their own inquiries. Logan has a way of tracking down the sources he needs."

"I do hope so," Macie let out a long slow breath.

I can no longer protect you.

Mr. Neville's anguished statement played in her thoughts. A chill trickled along her nape. Why had the man followed them to the theater?

Andrew would've trusted me to help you.

Mr. Neville had referred to Grandpapa by his given name. At the time, she'd thought the elderly man had been using that familiar name to convince her that her grandfather would have wanted her to sell his papers and books to him. Had she been dreadfully mistaken?

"At this point, we have far more questions than answers," Mrs. Johnstone said. "Only one thing is certain now. The threat is quite real. We must be especially vigilant."

You don't know what you have. As the memory of Mr. Neville's low voice whispered in her thoughts, another faint chill danced over the back of Macie's neck.

His words had been a warning.

"He said my grandfather would have wanted him to help me," she said, staring down at her porcelain cup. "I thought he was trying to convince me to do what he wanted."

Mrs. Johnstone offered a grim nod. "Perhaps he was telling the truth. If he knew your grandfather possessed the Renaissance letter, he might have feared someone would covet such a valuable document."

Nell walked slowly into the room, carrying the rosewood writing box. She placed the container on a marble-topped table. "Mr. Neville might have had another reason to come after you."

A sudden apprehension washed over Macie. "What do you mean?"

Nell pursed her lips, as though she carefully considered her words. "While taking another look at your grandfather's research, I noticed something peculiar about this box—the bottom of the container is more shallow than the walls are deep."

Mrs. Johnstone sat up straighter. "Ye suspected a false bottom?"

"At times, those gothic tales I've read have proven instructive." Nell pointed to the corner of the lining, then tugged it toward her. "This contains a hidden compartment."

"How very odd," Macie said. "Grandpapa never mentioned anything of the sort to me."

"It's possible he modified it to construct the concealed space. In the excitement of discovering the Renaissance letter, I overlooked small flaws which hinted that the box had been altered." Nell pursed her lips, looking as though she was considering her words carefully. "The two of you need to see this."

She handed Macie ragged-edged pages that appeared to have been torn from one of her grandfather's journals. "Each notation refers to a different artifact or letter," Nell said. "I don't understand precisely what it all means. But I have a sinking suspicion."

"A suspicion?" Mrs. Johnstone questioned as she rose from her chair and leaned in to glance at the page. "Might I have a better look?"

"Of course," Macie said.

While Mrs. Johnstone read over the notes, Nell placed a partially faded letter in Macie's hand. "This was also in the false bottom," she said. "It's not nearly as old as the Renaissance letter. But it is rather curious that your grandfather made notations on the document."

"How very peculiar." Macie's gaze swept over the letter. "That's quite unlike his usual working methods."

She studied the document, a missive penned in French during the time of Napoleon. Her command of the language was fair at best, but she could decipher that it had been written by someone on an expedition near Rome. As she took in each of her grandfather's jottings, the significance of the letter grew clearer.

"Macie, my dear," Mrs. Johnstone said, looking up from the journal pages. "It would appear yer grandfather had grave doubts about a number of his acquisitions."

A dull ache settled into the pit of Macie's stomach. "Doubts?"

"If I am interpreting his notes correctly, it would seem he questioned their authenticity." Mrs. Johnstone's mouth settled into a terse line. "If I may be blunt, he believed they were frauds."

Macie swallowed hard against a sudden, bitter lump in her throat. She handed the century-old letter to Mrs. Johnstone. "And he'd found the proof."

Chapter Twenty-Eight

"COUNTERFEITS, EH?" LOGAN poured two fingers of whisky from his personal stock at the Rogue's Lair into a glass and handed it to Finn.

"Her grandfather's documents spell out his concerns. It's all rather technical, over my head. We need to find out if his suspicions were justified." Finn reached for Macie's hand and gave it a reassuring squeeze.

"There's money to be made in the antiquities market. Every bloke with a shilling to spare wants some old vase or another in his home." Logan gave Macie a glass of sherry, then settled into the leather wing chair behind his desk. "I noticed Amelia admiring a Roman amphora at an exhibit, so now I'm on the hunt."

"An amphora?" Finn asked. "What in blazes is that?"

Logan looked as smug as any dandy. "A two-handled vase."

"Bloody hell, ye're a refined sophisticate now." Finn chuckled under his breath. "That's all Amelia's doing, no doubt."

"My bride has attempted to broaden my interests." Logan looked pleased with himself and his all-too-recent appreciation for culture. Finn resisted the urge to frown at his cousin, though it would've been justified.

"What's next? A blasted fresco on the wall?"

"Not bloody likely."

"The amphora would be such a thoughtful gift," Macie spoke

up. "Amelia will be delighted."

"Only if it doesn't cost a blasted fortune," Logan replied. "My bride is eminently practical. The vessel must also be small enough to fit on a high shelf to keep it out of the wee beast's reach."

Macie smiled. "The wee beast?"

"My wife's pet."

"So, how is good old Heathy doing these days?" Finn asked. "Chewed up any boots lately?"

Logan looked weary. "Not in the last month."

"The hound is nothing but fur and teeth," Finn said, picturing the high-strung terrier in his mind. "But I'd have to say he's a fine judge of character. He warmed to me immediately."

"I try not to hold that against him," Logan said with a low laugh.

"I'll have you know Cleo is also an excellent judge of character," Macie added. "You know she likes you, Finn."

"I've spent an entire night with yer cat breathing down my neck," Finn said, chuckling at Logan's puzzled expression.

"Ah, there's a story there," Logan said.

"Someday, I'll tell ye over a pint," Finn said as Macie flashed a knowing smile.

"Good enough. For now, tell me what I can do for ye tonight."

Macie took a sip from her glass, as if to fortify herself. "My grandfather found reason to believe certain antiquities he had acquired were not, in fact, genuine."

Logan leaned back, taking in her words. "Ye have evidence?"

"Not yet. But I'm convinced the proof is hidden somewhere in his library." She laced her fingers together, as she tended to do when she was worried. "In time, I will find it."

"We suspect someone else knew about the evidence," Finn added.

Logan turned to Macie. "The old gent ye encountered?"

"The professor," Macie replied. "And there was another man who wished to buy my grandfather's books and papers—Hiram

Neville. It appears he'd trailed us to the theater before his heart gave out."

"Bloody peculiar." Logan drummed his fingers on his desk. "These cheats are blasted clever. Counterfeit antiquities. Forged art. There's no sense of honor among these thieves." He sent Finn a speaking glance. "Ye must be especially vigilant with the lasses' safety. As we learned from Amelia's experience with art forgers, the curs are a ruthless lot."

Seeing the way the color drained from Macie's face, Finn reached for her, placing his hand on hers. "I will not let down my guard. Ye can rest assured of that."

"Of that, I have no doubt," Logan said with a look of solemn confidence.

Finn took a drink, his thoughts racing. "If these deaths are connected with fraudulent antiquities, the thieves must be on edge, wondering who will be next," he said. "Someone may be nervous and running his mouth."

Logan nodded. "I'll make some inquiries. If there's chatter, Murray and his assistants will pick up on it."

"Thank you," Macie said. "I greatly appreciate any assistance you might offer."

"Anything for ye, Macie." Logan's dark eyes flashed with a smile. "I hear that the Dragon has taken a liking to ye."

She blinked. "The Dragon?"

"My aunt, Elsie Johnstone," Logan explained coolly. "Finn and I gave her that nickname when we were lads."

"It's not a secret," Finn said.

"The woman is bloody proud of it." Logan grinned. "She still thinks we're incorrigible."

"Because we are," Finn said.

"Well, I think she's a charming woman," Macie said. "So clever with an abundance of interests."

Logan cocked a brow. "Charming?"

"But clever is fair enough," Finn said. "Ye'll get no argument from me."

Their conversation took a lighter turn while they enjoyed their drinks. As they prepared to take their leave, Macie paused to admire a silver-framed portrait on the sideboard. Amelia had smiled serenely for the photographer, while her *wee beast* bore what seemed a mischievous grin.

"So, this is Heathy," she said with a genuine warmth in her voice. "I see the mischief in his eyes."

"Amelia is devoted to that pup. She'd taken him in some time before we met. I do believe that chewing machine on four legs knows how good he's got it since she found him." Logan's smile was genuine. "Ye won't find a kinder heart in a woman."

Finn nodded his agreement. "Ye're a lucky man."

"Indeed." Logan turned to him, his expression speaking louder than his words. "The road was not always smooth, but it led me to her. Sometimes the wisest thing a man can do . . . and the hardest . . . is to open his eyes and see what's been right in front of him the whole bloody time."

THE CRESCENT MOON was low in the sky as Finn escorted Macie from the tavern. Finn caught her hand in his, drawing her near. The soft light from a gas lamp gleamed over her face, accenting the shape of her mouth, the soft curves of her cheek. By God, she was a beauty.

Right in front of him the whole bloody time. Logan's words played in his thoughts.

Finn smiled to himself. Was it so very obvious that he'd fallen for her?

Fallen for her.

Bloody hell, he had. Hadn't he?

For so long, he hadn't ever fathomed the possibility that he might feel this way, this intense longing simply to be near a woman. Any woman.

But Macie had changed all that.

He wanted to be near her. Every day. Every night.

Someday, with any luck, she would be his. In his arms. In his bed. At his side, until he took his last breath.

They would forge an unbreakable bond, just as Logan and Amelia had.

Someday, very soon.

He led her to his carriage, held the door for her to enter, and instructed Reggie to take the long route back to her townhouse. His driver smiled a sly smile and tipped his cap.

He joined Macie in the coach. Sitting by her side, he held her hand in his, taking in the gentle, wistful expression on her face.

"Logan is certainly a wonderful husband, isn't he?" she said as his driver cracked the reins and the carriage started its steady rumble over the pavement.

"As devoted as they come," Finn agreed. "When we were younger, far more foolish men, if ye'd told me Logan MacLain would settle into a contented life of hearth and home, I would've scoffed. But now, I see what a lucky man he is."

"Amelia is fortunate to have entered into marriage with a man who supports her endeavors. That is such a rare quality."

"He respects Amelia for the woman she is. Logan would not want to change her. Not in any way."

"Again, a rare quality," she said. "Amelia's ladies' lending library is a vibrant haven for learning and discussion. And her charitable pursuits are thriving. With all of it, Logan has offered his full-bodied support."

"If need be, he'd move the moon and stars for her." Finn considered his own words. He'd described his own feelings for Macie.

Why was it so hard to convey what was in his heart? Blast it, why hadn't he told her?

The adventure of a lifetime. She'd deemed her description of the research trip to Athens as a bit of an exaggeration. But still, there'd been truth to her words. Seldom would she be offered such an opportunity to utilize her talents and display her artistry.

Bugger it, the very thought of her gallivanting off to Athens with the bloody arrogant professor dug into his gut. With him, or any other man under ninety. But he couldn't stand in her way. He'd have to let her make up her mind. Only then could he tell her what was in his thoughts. And in his heart.

Leaning closer, Finn brushed a kiss against her lips. "I've been wanting to do that all night," he said, threading his fingers through her hair.

"Oh, you have, have you?" She flashed a teasing little grin. "Funny thing . . . I've been thinking the same thing."

He turned. Gently, he framed her face in his hands.

"I never want ye to change, Macie." He drew in a breath, inhaling the subtle aroma of lavender on her skin.

"That is a very good thing. I don't think I'd even know how."

"A very good thing, indeed." He leaned in to kiss her again. "Ye're bloody perfect . . . just the way ye are."

IN ALL HIS years, Finn had seldom suffered a sleepless night. To the contrary, he'd generally dozed off within moments of his head hitting the pillow. That was, until lovely Macie came into his life.

Between a too-short settee serving as a torturous, make-shift bed, a cat with fish breath breathing against his ear, and the assortment of peculiar snores, cries, and words that broke through the wall between his room and Mrs. Tuttle's, he'd endured a variety of disturbances. But none of those annoyances compared with the insistent workings of his own mind and body.

He pounded the pillow with his fist and tossed about on the bed for good measure. As Mrs. Tuttle blurted out something about a gent named Arnie, he buried his head under the blankets.

Bloody hell, there was no rest for the weary.

His thoughts raced. Staring up at the ceiling in a pitch-dark room, he hungered for the touch of a woman who was—at least for now—off limits. His sweet fantasies of Macie had eased the need of his body, but he was by no means content. His wanting for her was intense, a deep-seated craving only she could entirely sate.

In the carriage, he'd loved her tenderly. The quiet, shy sounds of her pleasure were like a delicious elixir for his soul. But now, the mere memory of her muffled cry of bliss against his mouth had him hard again. If she were his, she'd be in his arms at the very moment, nestled against his chest as he drank in the satin feel of her skin.

If she were his . . .

He folded his arms behind his head and stared into the darkness. By thunder, he would not go another day without telling her what lay in his heart. He would not go another day without confessing the truth.

He loved her.

God above, he'd never loved anyone like he loved Macie. She was a beauty. Brilliant. Witty. Headstrong. She was bloody perfect. And by some bloody magnificent stroke of luck, she cared for him. That much was certain. Did she crave his nearness just as he craved her? Did she feel a longing for him, just as he longed for her?

He was right for her. In his heart, he knew that elemental truth. He'd love her until his last breath. And above all, he did not want to change her, not one whit.

But would she be content with a life with a man like him? Could she? He'd been born to a merchant's family. He was neither a noble nor a tycoon. He would do whatever it took to offer her a good life filled with passion. Filled with love.

But would that be enough? For Macie? For her title-hungry father?

Damnation, why was he giving so much as a thought to what her father wanted? Macie was a woman—a gorgeous, headstrong woman. She'd make her own decisions. And she'd made it clear she had little regard for the noble nobs who chased after her.

Rolling over, he gave the pillow an extra thump. He'd told her she was beautiful. He'd told her he wanted her. But like a fool, he'd hesitated to tell her the one truth that truly mattered.

He was in love with her.

Would his love for Macie hold her back from her dreams? He hadn't wanted to take that chance. But now, lying here, he knew he couldn't go another day without telling her how much he loved her.

From there, they'd figure out the rest.

If she loved him.

Chapter Twenty-Nine

F INN'S RESTLESS NIGHT was followed by an even more tension-filled morning. After eking out some sleep, he'd awoken with an edgy energy. Blast it, he didn't want to go one more day without telling Macie the truth. But the time had to be right. It wasn't as if he could simply blurt out his feelings over the meal Mrs. Tuttle had prepared, much less with the women clinging to every word.

"Did you sleep well?" Macie asked as she dabbed a bit of jam onto her toast.

He reached for his tea, needing the fortification. "Is it so obvious?"

Seated by her side, Nell fixed him with a narrow-eyed look, no doubt taking in the dark circles and small cuts on his chin from his rushed, haphazard attempt at shaving. Bollocks, he must look like a man who'd spent the night carousing rather than lying alone in a bedchamber, unable to quiet his own thoughts.

"Actually, it is," Macie said. "I do hope Cleo did not disturb you. She possesses a surprising ability to open doors and creep inside."

He shook his head. "The cat did not decide to pay me a visit. Actually, it might've been better if she had. The purring tends to put me to sleep."

"Cleo has taken a shine to you. A rare thing, indeed. She's rather finicky about the humans in her life." Macie's soft smile reached her eyes. "Nell and I will be leaving shortly to pay Amelia a visit. Mrs. Johnstone is coming with us. She'll be arriving with her phaeton shortly."

"Ye're going to chance riding with her in that little carriage?"

"I'm eager to give it a try," Nell said. "I may just purchase one myself. Another thing to give my illustrious papa gray hairs."

"She drives like she's rushing to a fire." Finn pretended to shudder. "Ye're braver than I."

Macie flashed a brief grin. "I imagine you'll welcome a bit of peace and quiet, away from the female of the species for a bit of time."

Truth be told, his reaction was entirely the opposite. But he didn't need to tell her that. She'd enjoy the moments she spent in Amelia's company, free from her *bodyguard*. He'd waited this long to tell her what was in his heart. That evening, he would take her to a fine establishment and tell her he wanted no other woman. He needed her. And her alone. For the rest of his days.

"MR. CALDWELL, YOU have a visitor." Clutching her feather duster, Mrs. Tuttle eyed him with undisguised annoyance. "It seems I spend more time acting as your butler than attending to my own duties."

"My butler?" Looking up from the architectural plans he'd been reviewing, he considered the notion. "To tell the truth, I've never had one. So, I must admit, this is a novel experience."

"That lad from the tavern is here to see ye. Says his name's Tim."

Finn jolted from his relaxed solitude. "Send him in."

"I'm sorry to interrupt ye, Mr. Caldwell," Tim said, shuffling his feet a bit. "But Mr. MacLain says it's important."

"Thank ye, Mrs. Tuttle," Finn said, turning back to Tim as she took her leave. "Ye've brought a message."

"Mr. MacLain's come upon some information ye may find useful."

"He's at the Lair?"

The young man shook his head. "He'll be at the café until midday."

"Good enough," Finn said. "I'll meet him there shortly."

As Finn set aside the drawings he'd been looking over, he paused, eyeing the layout of the entry hall of Bennington Manor. The grand staircase was showing its age, but it was still sturdy. Renovating the lower floor of the place would not be an easy task, but he could certainly oversee skilled craftsmen capable of the task. He smiled to himself. If Macie accepted his proposal, he'd see to it that her beloved grandfather's home was preserved in style. He had the funds to start, and his share of the profits from the contracts with Mason Enterprises would provide most of the remaining cost.

Cleo hopped up on the desk, eyeing the drawings with her golden-amber eyes. She met his gaze, seemed to nod her approval for his plans, and sauntered over to the window to bask in the midday sun.

Calling over his shoulder to Mrs. Tuttle to let her know he'd be leaving her in peace for a bit, he walked onto the pavement, blinking against the sunny sky. A rare thing, that. Perhaps, just perhaps, it was a good sign of what was to come.

When he arrived at the Rogue's Respite, he spotted a familiar conveyance—Jon Mason's brougham. Now that was a bloody surprise. Why in blazes was he back in London, days before his expected return? Evidently, he'd attended to matters in Scotland with his typical take-charge efficiency. He would not have left Inverness had operations not been running smoothly. Likely, he'd be in good spirits. All in all, it was an excellent development, another good sign of things to come.

You will *bear in mind that she is* my *sister . . . at all times.*

Considering his friend's words before he'd entrusted him to watch over Macie, it would be a show of good faith to let Jon know of his desire to marry her. Not that he needed her brother's permission—or her title-hungry father's say, for that matter, but it would be good form to declare his intentions before popping the question to Macie.

Yes, this was definitely working in his favor. He would inform Jon straightaway of his intentions to wed Macie.

It sounded easy enough in his thoughts. So why did he feel like he had a fist digging into his gut?

As he made his way up the stairs to Logan's office, he heard the men's voices. When Finn entered the room, Jon's face betrayed his surprise.

"Now this is a welcome I had not expected." Seated in a leather Chippendale chair, Jon smiled broadly. "Finn, it's good to see you."

"I presume everything in Scotland is under control," Finn said.

"Operations came together more swiftly than I expected. As my father would say, the train is back on the tracks." Jon scratched his chin, as though he pondered a thought. "You look no worse for wear. I see you survived your time with Macie."

"Indeed," Finn said. "She and I got on . . . well."

Bloody hell, that was an understatement, if ever he'd uttered one.

"And not one scandal to speak of," Jon said casually.

"Ye could say that. If ye don't count stumbling upon a dead man in a reputedly haunted theater."

"I did get word about that when I arrived last night." Jon's expression dimmed. "At least no one thinks she's responsible. I understand the gent expired of natural causes."

"That's the detective's conclusion," Logan spoke up. "At least for now."

"For now?" Jon's brow furrowed. "Should I ask?"

Finn shook his head. "'Tis a long story. I will brief ye on the details."

Jon shrugged. "I suppose something of that nature was bound to happen, sooner or later. Macie traipses about with that camera of hers in the most dismal places. But you kept her out of trouble. That's all that matters."

Finn's thoughts flashed to the costume ball, precisely to the moment when he'd been sorely tempted to toss the ruffle-necked viscount who'd dared to touch Macie out on his noble arse. "There were some close calls."

"I don't doubt it was a challenge," Jon said.

"At times." God knew he'd faced a challenge reining in his own instincts when he was with her. He set his mind to the task at hand. He'd waste no more time before telling Jon his intentions. "There's something ye need to know."

"You can start by telling me this, Finn—what's your bloody secret?"

"There is no secret," he replied with a shrug.

"Ah, there has to be. We both know Macie rebels at any attempt to rein her in."

Rein her in. Why in blazes would anyone want to hold a brilliant woman like Macie back from following her own heart?

"The lass has a mind of her own."

"Now that, my friend, is putting it mildly. She's a force of nature." Jon pointed to his hair. "You see these gray hairs? Each one should have my sister's name on it. But enough of that. I know what you want to discuss." He smiled broadly. "Consider the contracts yours, my friend."

By hellfire, the deal was done.

He'd secured the contracts for his family's distillery. He had justified his family's trust.

"That is tremendous news. You won't regret this."

Not until I tell you the truth about Macie. And me.

"I've seen no mention of her name in the scandal sheets. For that alone, I owe you, Finn. A blasted miracle, I'd say."

Jon's tone was like a burr beneath Finn's heel. His view of Macie as a crisis to be managed was so blasted far from the truth.

"Ye trusted me to watch over her." Finn kept his tone deliberately bland.

"You earned every one of those contracts. And then some," Jon said. "I suppose Macie's charade kept her out of trouble while it held the heiress hunters at bay."

Jon's attitude rubbed against the grain. Suddenly, Finn understood why Macie chafed against the restrictions of her life. But he held back the first words that came to mind. For now, he had to speak his intentions.

"Jon, there's something ye need to know."

"We'll work out the details of the contracts. My assistant handles all the business with numbers and calculations and such," Jon went on. "I must admit, I had my doubts. But there is a code of honor among rogues like you and me."

Logan coughed against the fist he held to his mouth.

"Wouldn't you say so, Finn? Some things are simply off limits." Jon studied him over his steepled fingers. "Simply not done."

As Logan made another deliberate cough against his balled hand, Finn followed his gaze to the open door.

Bollocks.

Amelia strolled through the doorway with Macie by her side. Nell and Mrs. Johnstone lingered in the corridor outside the room.

"Hello, Logan. Please pardon the intrusion," Amelia said with a soft smile. "We did not wish to interrupt."

"Yer presence could never be considered an intrusion," Logan said. The look in his eyes made it clear he was as besotted with his wife as he had been on the day they exchanged their vows.

"I wanted to share our latest acquisition with the ladies. I so adore the watercolor piece." Scanning the room, she frowned. "I thought it was hanging behind your desk."

"I asked Murray to display it in the front dining room."

"A delightful placement," Amelia said. Her eyes narrowing, she offered Finn a perfunctory greeting, then turned to Jon. "It's good to see you've returned safely from your journey."

"All is well at the Inverness store. We shall soon be open for business."

"How wonderful." She slanted Macie a speaking glance. "Ladies, shall we proceed to view the painting?"

"Of course," Macie said. "I do require a moment, if you don't mind."

Amelia sent Finn a speaking glance. A warning. "Of course."

Macie flashed her brother a soft smile. "A code of honor among rogues, you say? I had no idea such a thing could exist."

"If honor can exist among thieves, then why not rogues like your brother?" Jon questioned in a wry tone.

"Indeed." Macie's gaze was colored by an emotion Finn could not entirely read. How much had she heard?

"Aren't you going to welcome me back?" Jon asked.

"Of course." Macie graced her brother with a faint smile. "I'm delighted to see you've made it back to London, and without so much as an additional gray hair. I shall have to see to that matter immediately."

"I do wish you wouldn't." Jon appeared oblivious to the not-quite-teasing tone of her voice.

As she spoke, Macie seemed to deliberately avoid meeting Finn's eyes. "I shall endeavor to remain scandal-free. If one does not hold stumbling upon dead men everywhere I turn against me."

"I'm told the man who collapsed at the theater was old enough to be our grandfather." Jon sounded quite rational. "I hear the unfortunate fellow perished from natural causes."

"We can hope that is true," Macie said blandly. "I presume all is well in Scotland, or you would not be here."

"Operations are running smoothly. Until the next crisis, that is."

"Excellent. Papa will be pleased, I'm sure," Macie said. "I suppose congratulations are in order, Mr. Caldwell."

Seldom had Finn felt as tongue-tied as he had at that moment. Seeing his hesitation, Macie added, "For the contracts. How nice that your family's business will now have a tie to mine."

He felt as if he were walking into a trap. "The arrangement will provide benefits for both family enterprises."

"Indeed. I do know how vigilant you are about fulfilling the terms of an agreement." Her smile was radiant, even as daggers flashed in her emerald eyes. "You certainly met all the terms of our bargain, though I do understand it was a challenge. But you persevered, did you not?"

Bloody hell, she was magnificent. Especially when her eyes gleamed like that.

"Persevered?" Finn shook his head as he met her gaze. "*That* is not the word I would use."

She blinked and pressed her lips together, appearing to swallow against an emotion she didn't want him to see. "In any case, this is truly an excellent time to inform my brother of my exciting news."

Jon sat up straighter, his interest perked. "You've finally found a man capable of convincing you to walk down the aisle?"

"No, silly, it's nothing so banal as that. Not to mention, convenient for you." A subtle half-smile played on her lips. "This recent development might prove a wee bit scandalous, but I do hope you'll understand why this adventure is so important to me. Grandpapa would be so very proud of me."

Adventure.

Bollocks. Finn braced for a bare-knuckled fist to the gut while Jon studied her, looking as if he was preparing for a very large boot to drop.

"Macie, what are you talking about?" Jon asked.

"It is truly the most exciting news," she said, dropping her voice as if she were sharing a scandalous secret. "You see, Jon, I've been offered the opportunity to participate in a research expedition to Athens. I shall be their documentarian. And I've decided to accept."

Chapter Thirty

A CODE OF *honor among rogues . . .*

My, her brother had certainly made the nature of his bargain with Finn clear, hadn't he? As Macie wandered through her garden, the words tumbled about in her thoughts. Again. And again. The words had cut her deeply, though Jon had no way of knowing what he'd done. Evidently, Finn had no desire to reveal the turn their relationship had taken.

He had no reason to, now did he? Even as the pain went bone-deep, she had to face the truth. He had not lied to her. Not really. Finn had made her no promises. He'd uttered no declarations of *forever*. The word *love* had never passed his lips.

Despite her heart's dull ache, she knew the truth. Finn had fulfilled the terms of their bargain—the very terms she'd set. She had expected him to play the part of the besotted bodyguard. *The heiress and her rake.* Those had been her own blasted words. She'd thought herself clever then.

Now, she knew what a foolish game she'd played.

What's your bloody secret? Macie rebels at any attempt to rein her in. Her brother's words burned in her mind. How dare he speak of her as if she were an unsolvable problem to be contained.

Her cheeks heated with anger at the very thought. Macie pulled in a long, slow breath to calm herself. Dipping her head low, she drank in the lush aroma of her roses. She closed her eyes, savoring the scent. Such a true pleasure.

Pleasure.

She opened her eyes and moved to the ornate wrought iron bench. She'd allowed herself to be swept away by the pure bliss she'd found in his Finn's arms. My goodness, she'd never experienced anything like the delight of his touch when he held her. When he kissed her. When he explored her body. So gentle and tender and deliciously sensuous.

Finn had never pressed her to do anything she hadn't wanted to do. In truth, he'd refused to take all she'd wanted to give. No wonder, that. Now, it all seemed so very clear. As it was, each of them could go their separate ways with no complications. Nothing to cause a scandal. Nothing to permanently bind him to her, nor her to him. Nothing that would compromise her value on the marriage mart. And above all, nothing that might endanger the business deal he'd negotiated—a deal which involved reining in Jon's wild, wayward sister as if she were a beast to be tamed.

Finn had played it smart, hadn't he?

Perhaps Jon was right—there truly was honor among rogues.

Pity she had not heeded his warning. *I've reason to think it's a game we should not be playing.* She hadn't taken his true meaning then.

But now, she understood all too well.

Cleo strolled up to her and meowed, then jumped onto a high-backed chair. Seated as she was, regarding Macie with a pensive gaze, the cat looked rather like the pet of some long-dead Egyptian ruler.

Smiling to herself, she took the folded letter from her pocket and reread the neatly penned missive. Professor Aylesworth's script was as measured and controlled as he was.

> *I have secured a place for you and a traveling companion of*
> *your choosing on our research expedition. We shall depart in a*
> *fortnight. Please advise as to your decision.*
> *Yours, P.N. Aylesworth*

The journey would be an adventure she'd carry with her for the rest of her life. At first, she could not truly contemplate accepting the position. The thought of leaving Finn behind had filled her with doubt, especially when their future seemed to be in the process of unfolding.

But now, that was no longer a consideration, was it?

The sound of heavy bootsteps and Mrs. Tuttle scolding someone drifted to her ears, alerting her even before the French doors opened that her peace was to be short-lived.

Finn strode onto the terrace with an exasperated Mrs. Tuttle on his heels.

"I tried to tell him not to come in, Miss Macie," she said. "But he's a hard-headed man."

"That I am," he said, his tone low and gruff. "I require a few moments of Miss Mason's time." He narrowed his eyes. "Without yer presence."

Macie met the older woman's anxious eyes. "It's all right, Mrs. Tuttle. You may go."

"You're quite certain?"

"Yes." Macie nodded as she refolded the letter and tucked it inside her skirt pocket. "Thank you."

After the housekeeper had departed, Macie met Finn's direct gaze. "So, you've come to collect whatever items you've left behind?" She gave a little shrug. "You did not need to trouble yourself. I would have asked Mrs. Tuttle to gather them up and have them delivered to you."

He came to her, motioning to the bench. "Might I join ye?"

Emotion welled within her, but she was determined to maintain a calm demeanor, even as her pulse sped up. She would not allow him to see how he'd affected her. "Please, do make yourself comfortable."

He glanced at Cleo, who seemed to be actually scowling at him. "If that were a hound, I'd be worried she was giving thought to sinking her teeth into me."

"I'd say it's still a possibility." She forced a little smile. "If I were you, I would not let down my guard."

"Point taken." He reached for her hand, but she primly laced her fingers together and folded them in her lap. He nodded his understanding. "Macie, I don't know what ye heard, but I can explain."

"I find no explanation is needed. Perhaps we should have announced our presence . . . but you must see how your conversation with my brother was quite informative," she said, keeping her tone even by sheer will. "Once again, allow me to congratulate you on closing the deal with my brother for those all-important contracts. You fulfilled the terms of your agreement." She willed herself to speak the words that were so very bitter. "Just as you fulfilled the terms of our bargain. Quite brilliantly, I'd say."

He raked a hand through his hair. "Macie, it's not what ye think."

"Isn't it?" Tears she refused to shed scalded the back of her throat. "My brother has long treated me as a problem to be dealt with, just as he managed the so-called minor catastrophes that arise within my family's businesses. This time, my brother recruited you, of all people, to rein me in. And you did so, and in fine form. How did he put it?" She pinned him with her gaze. "The charade kept her out of trouble, or some other drivel."

"Yer ridiculous scheme was not my idea, Macie. I told ye what I thought of it."

"But yet, you went along with it. And you took it a step further. You led me to think you were different." She dragged in a breath. "You weren't like Jon and my father and all the others. You weren't a man who wanted to control me. You made me feel as though you valued me. And my dreams. And I believed you." She swallowed hard, determined to say what needed to be said. "Which part was real, Finn? And which was simply a convenient means of managing Jon's *rebellious* sister in order to close your deal?"

She dropped her gaze to the stones on the terrace, fighting

the urge to weep. To cry out. To plead with him to convince her she had it all wrong.

"Macie, look at me, lass." His voice was low and rough and edged with gravel.

She forced back the tears and faced him with her chin held high. "I suppose Jon was right. You did keep me out of trouble, so to speak. I was too busy hanging on your every sweet whisper."

He stood silent for a long moment, his expression unreadable. "So that's it, Macie? Ye think everything I said, everything I did . . . ye think it was all a lie?"

"Not a lie." Her heart softened as emotion flared in his amber gaze. "It's possible we were caught up in the moment. After all, you are a man. And I am a woman." She drew in a low breath as the memory of their passion washed over her like a stormy wave. "Circumstances neither of us could have predicted compelled you to stay near, day and night. Danger heightens emotions, does it not?"

Gently, he cupped his hand against her cheek. "Macie, what occurred between us was more than the heat of the moment."

"In my heart, I wanted to believe you're better than the rest . . . better than the heiress hunters." Blinking back tears, she met his gaze. "Jon wanted to know your secret . . . wanted to know how you kept me in line, as if I were an errant child."

He plowed his fingers through his hair again. "He is wrong to think of ye in that way."

"I would have to say I agree."

"I do agree with him on one point. Ye're a force of nature, Macie." He drew the tip of his finger along the curve of her cheek, seeming to study her. "Believe me when I say I did not lie to ye." His voice grew rough with emotion.

"I do believe you. Hearing the words from your lips, I at least feel comforted that you did not deceive me." She came to her feet and went to the wrought-iron fence, peering out into the street just beyond the garden gate. "You told me you wanted me."

"I meant every word," he said, following her. "Ye should

know that."

"I believe I do," she said. "And I wanted you. Quite desperately, really. But you would not take what I so willingly offered. I wanted to feel that I was yours, body and soul." She swallowed hard against the burning lump in her throat. "But you could not allow yourself to take my oh-so-precious virginity. I suppose there is, indeed, honor among rogues."

A muscle in his jaw worked with tension. "It was not the time. Nor the place. Ye deserve better than a clandestine tumble in the dead of night."

"Shouldn't I have had a say in that decision?" She pulled in a long breath and held his gaze. "I knew my own mind, Finn. And I knew I wanted you, more than I've ever wanted anything in my life. But you held back. You would not *ruin* me." She sighed. "God, how I detest that word. But absurdly, it's how my worth is judged. And you ... you would not risk going against your equally absurd rogues' code."

Heat flared in his gaze. "What happened between us had nothing to do with any blasted code."

"As I recall, you did not correct my brother on that notion. And you did not inform him that you played a far more intimate role in my life than brawny chaperone." She felt a tear slide down her cheek. She swiped it away and searched his eyes for the truth. "Finn, I've no reason to believe those moments we spent together were more than a fleeting passion for you. And most likely, one of many."

He regarded her for the span of several heartbeats, his jaw hardened as he studied her. "That's where you're wrong, Macie," he said, his voice a gritty rasp. "I've never known a woman like ye. And I doubt I ever will again."

"Ah, we've well established that I'm a blasted *original*. I suspect any woman with a mind of her own who dares to show it might be described as such." She swiped away another rebellious tear. "Tell me, Finn, how am I to believe what went between us was more than a flare of passion between a man and a woman? It isn't as if you've said you love me."

"And if I did speak those words?" He scrubbed a hand against his jaw. "Would that make this right?"

"Make it right? Ever the problem solver, eh?" She slowly shook her head. "Finn, I don't know what's left to be said. Why did you come here?"

His jaw hardened, even as he caught her hand in his. "I needed to talk to ye. Ye've already made yer decision about Athens. But ye should reconsider."

"Should I now?" Unable to stop herself, she reached out and touched his face, drawing her fingertip over the bristles of new beard on his unshaven jaw. "I've decided it's best if I leave London for a time. And you must admit, it is a grand opportunity."

"Ye shouldn't leave, Macie. Not now."

"If not now—when? After all, there's no point in delaying it. Your time as my *besotted bodyguard* has come to an end. Jon certainly won't approve of you sleeping in the servants' quarters now that he's back, will he?"

"Macie, ye have to listen to me."

She turned to her roses, pinching off a spent bud, then another. "Don't worry, I won't say anything to Jon that might endanger the deal you wanted so badly."

"And if I told ye I did not give a damn about the contracts?"

Much more of this, and she'd entirely lose control. The very last thing she wanted was to weep before him.

"You would be lying if you said those contracts didn't matter. I can only imagine how lucrative the deal must be for your family's business." She snapped off another withered bud. "As for our arrangement, you've certainly fulfilled your part." She moved to the doors. "I will leave for Athens in a fortnight. Until then, I need to clear my head. I'd prefer that we stay apart."

Finn came after her, but he did not reach for her. Did not touch her. Did not kiss her. Rather, he stood very still, as if stunned by what had gone between them.

"Regardless of what happens between us, ye should not go to Greece. Not now. Not with that arrogant bag of wind."

"Arrogant, is he? My, isn't that ironic, coming from Phineas Caldwell." She squared her shoulders and hiked her chin. "I see no reason not to seize this opportunity. Why, even Jon did not voice an objection. I will have a companion, after all. There will no question of harm to my precious *good name*."

"Ye're not a naïve lass. The man might respect yer talent. But ye should not trust his motives."

Ah, the gall of this man.

"I am growing weary of men telling me what I am and am not allowed to do." A defiance filled her, and she hiked her chin. "At the end of my life, I do not wish to regret missed opportunities."

"Macie, listen to me." He spoke the words in a raw voice.

She gulped against another surge of emotion. "I think you should leave now."

"As ye wish." He'd made his way from the terrace into the sitting room when he turned back. "This isn't about us, Macie. Do not underestimate that man. He's not a noble fop ye can easily best."

She hiked her brows, throwing him a glare. "And what would make you think I would want to *best* him?"

"Macie, that's the game ye've learned to play."

Chapter Thirty-One

IN THE WEEK since Finn walked away from the garden and out of her life, Macie had tended her roses, photographed the interior of a grand old hotel reputed to host the ghost of a bride who'd met a tragic fate on her wedding night, and planned an exhibit of her Bennington Manor photography. Mrs. Johnstone had insisted that they continue her instruction in defensive maneuvers, and the two of them had catalogued the contents of her grandfather's safe. Whenever she'd had the opportunity, Macie had plastered a smile on her face, lest anyone think she missed Finn playing the ever-devoted bodyguard. She'd gallivanted about the city without him looking over her shoulder, and she hadn't even encountered another dead man. That, at least, was something to be pleased about. Wasn't it?

Pity her smile was as genuine as the cheap plaster replica of the Venus de Milo her brother had given her as a gift when he was a lad.

The whirl of activity kept her busy and focused on something—anything—other than the sly grin of the man she so desperately missed. Only in the evenings after Nell and Mrs. Tuttle had headed off to bed, and she was alone with Cleo purring at her side, did she allow herself to admit that the dull ache in her chest was very real. And it wasn't going away. Of course, it was too soon to think she'd be over him. If only the pain was not intensifying with each lonely night.

On the afternoon of the eighth day after she'd watched Finn walk away—how absurd that she could give an exact count of the days—Macie settled into a chair in the garden, allowing herself an hour or so away from the hustle-bustle to relax with the gothic novel she'd been itching to devour. With book in hand and a snoring cat at her feet, she began to read. Before long, she caught herself staring at the page without really taking in the words. In those tales, the heroine was always so vulnerable, so very much at the mercy of the men in her life, whether they were villains or heroes. Very much *unlike* herself. No one could say that Mary Catherine Mason was at the mercy of any man, now could they?

If only her own heart would agree.

Nell strolled through the French doors, a silver tray in hand. "I thought you might enjoy a cup of Earl Grey."

"Thank you," Macie said, setting her book aside. She'd lost interest in the story rather quickly, hadn't she?

"I do wish you would have joined me at the ladies' lending library this morning. Amelia served a delightful brunch, and Mrs. Johnstone and I enjoyed the most stimulating discussion. She is truly brilliant."

"Indeed." Macie accepted the cup from Nell's hand and took a sip. "Did she tell you about our discoveries in Grandpapa's vault?"

Nell shook her head. "Most of our discussion centered on books and Amelia's plans to expand her library."

"Pity I missed it. I shall definitely pay a visit before I leave on my journey."

Nell seemed to hesitate. "Macie, I've been meaning to talk to you about the trip."

"It would be marvelous if you wished to accompany me. As you know, I'm meeting with Professor Aylesworth this after-noon. There's still time for you to join us."

"It's not that." Nell perched upon a wing chair, teacup in hand. "I'm not sure this is the best choice for you, Macie."

"How could you possibly doubt it?" Macie said. "Professor Aylesworth is a brilliant voice in his field. And above all, my grandfather trusted him, which speaks well for his character."

Nell's brow furrowed. "But I do think there might be a good reason for you to stay."

Macie blinked. "In London?"

Stirring her tea, Nell seemed to avoid Macie's gaze. "For a while, yes."

"And precisely what might that reason be?"

"I don't know how to say this, so I'll just tell you outright." Nell swished the slender spoon about in the cup. "Finn is leaving before the week is out."

Macie let out a low breath. "Phineas Caldwell's actions do not factor into my decisions."

"I think you're making a mistake."

Macie blinked again. "I am making a mistake?"

"Finn is not the cad you think he is. Good heavens, I saw how he looked at you." Once again, she nervously stirred her tea. "Amelia wanted to pay you a visit, but her physician has advised her to rest. So, she asked me to tell you what she thought you should know."

Macie took a sip of tea, mentally bracing herself to speak the truth. "I don't believe Finn is a cad. If he were, he might have found himself with an heiress for a bride. Such an undertaking might have proven even more lucrative than his precious contracts."

"I do understand," Nell said. "But it doesn't change the truth."

"The truth?" Macie sighed. "And what might that be."

"The man is in love with you."

Macie's heart raced. A cascade of emotions stormed her defenses. "He . . . he said this?"

"Not in so many words." Nell set her cup aside and walked over to the potted lavender. "He's a stubborn man. Perhaps even more stubborn than you."

"Then why does Amelia believe he loves me?"

"Oh, dear, where do I begin?" Nell seemed to brighten up.

"Since the two of you have been apart, he's been an utter wreck. After a time, the barkeep had to cut him off, and since then, he hasn't touched a drop. But he's thrown himself into work. He keeps to himself when he's not at the solicitors' office dealing with *blasted contract negotiations*, as Logan puts it. When he comes into the café, he orders supper, but leaves much of it on the plate."

"None of that means he loves me."

Nell met her gaze. "Logan and Amelia are convinced Finn is in love with you. But, in Logan's words—the *bloody fool* hasn't faced that fact yet."

"Oh, I don't know what to believe." Macie gulped against the sudden burning lump in the back of her throat. "I don't know what to do."

"I suppose what comes next depends on you." Nell's tone was gentle. "The two of you deserve to give this a chance. And that, my dear friend, might well take some time."

"Oh, Nell, I simply don't know." Macie's voice sounded raw to her own ears.

"As I see it, it's not complicated. Not truly. It all comes down to one very important question." A faint smile played on her friend's mouth. "Do you love him?"

MACIE STARED AT the empty trunk sitting in a corner of her bedchamber. She'd had her brother bring it down from the attic in preparation for her journey, but she had not been inclined to pack so much as a crinoline. Tears welled in her throat, but she choked them back. Blast it, she would not give in. She would not weep over Finn Caldwell. He'd gotten what he wanted. The contracts with Mason Enterprises had been what he'd needed all along.

Stretching out on the bed, she closed her eyes and pictured

his face. In the moments before she'd asked him to leave her, she'd seen no sense of triumph in his eyes. To the contrary, a deep sadness had blended with indignation. My, she'd accused him of being a true cad, hadn't she? She'll called his motives into question. He'd been wounded by her words, but he had not lashed out. He had not retaliated. Rather, he'd given her what she asked for. He'd left her standing there, watching as each step took him farther from her.

Do you love him? Nell's question tormented her. In her heart, she knew the answer. Just as she had when he'd walked away.

She loved him.

She loved Phineas Caldwell.

This was not a passing fancy. Not an infatuation. No, this was far deeper. Far more profound. The man exasperated her. Drove her to distraction. Challenged her to break down the barriers she'd erected around herself.

And God, how she loved him.

Opening her eyes, she stared up at the ceiling. Could they make a go of it? Heaven knew it wouldn't always be easy. But somehow, he'd always seen through the ice she used as a shield.

Her heart was more tender than she wanted to admit, even to herself. More vulnerable. For so very long, she hadn't wanted to take the chance it might shatter.

Only Finn had made her feel she could take that risk.

Sitting up, her attention fixed on her trunk. When her heart was aching for Finn, a journey far from London had seemed to be the cure she needed.

Now, she knew she'd been mistaken. What she needed most was time. Time to consider that perhaps, just perhaps, Nell was right. Time to fully realize the yearnings of her own heart. Time to hear the truth from Finn's own lips.

In that moment, she knew precisely what to do.

With each bump of the hansom cab against the cobbles, Macie clutched the edge of the seat with one hand while holding tight to the braided handle of her satchel with the other. With any luck, her teeth would not rattle out of her head before her meeting with Professor Aylesworth. Thankfully, the route to the café where they were to meet was mercifully brief and the extraordinary find she'd stashed in the handbag was not fragile.

She arrived with time to spare. A rare feat, she smiled to herself. Well, she certainly did not want to keep Professor Aylesworth waiting.

"Miss Mason, I'm pleased you could come." The professor stood to greet her as she walked through the door. With his dark hair combed neatly back, the fashionable tweed jacket that emphasized the breadth of his shoulders, and the silver tie at his neck accenting the hues of his gray-blue eyes, he cut quite a handsome figure.

Waving off the maître d', he escorted her to a table in the shadows of a back corner. They made pleasant, meaningless conversation as the waiter brought a pot of oolong tea and cold finger sandwiches. After the server took his leave, Aylesworth's expression turned more serious.

"You've made your decision, Miss Mason?"

"I have," she said. "I must remain in London. For the time being, at least."

"You're quite certain?"

She nodded. "Perhaps at another time."

"I'd be lying if I said I was surprised," he said. "You have distinct ties to this city. I understand you have plans to renovate Bennington Manor."

"The planning is underway." She met his intent gaze. "With the success of his recent ventures, my father is more amenable to funding the project."

"Excellent." He tapped a finger against the rim of his cup. "As you know, I worked with your grandfather for nearly five years. His library deserves to be preserved."

"I quite agree," she said.

"If it were not for this expedition to Greece, I would be willing to assist you in assessing the collection. No doubt some of the texts are antiquated, but much of it should not be cast aside."

"I see no reason why we cannot keep the collection intact until you return. Your expertise would be quite valuable."

"Very good. I will rest easier now."

Macie reached for her cup and took a sip. "He spoke well of you, Professor."

"It's good to know. Even though we did not always see eye to eye, I held Andrew Bennington in the highest regard."

"The most brilliant minds will often see things through a different perspective."

"Indeed," he agreed. "I attempted to convince him of that very fact. But he could be quite a stubborn man."

"Oh, Grandpapa had his moments," Macie agreed with a smile. "Professor, before you leave, I do have a favor to ask of you."

His brows lifted. "How might I be of service?"

She pulled in a breath, steadying her nerves. A sudden doubt crept into her mind. Perhaps she should not impose upon Professor Aylesworth, especially with such a troubling matter.

"Is something wrong, Miss Mason?"

"I'm tempted to deny it, but I have reason to fear something had happened before my grandfather died . . . something that was most definitely *wrong*." She took another sip. "I found something in my grandfather's library. I don't quite know what to make of it." Opening her bag, she removed neatly folded journal pages. "Perhaps you might analyze these notes. Hopefully, you will allay my fears. Or at the worst, confirm them."

He removed his spectacles from his jacket pocket, then carefully took the paper from her hand. His brow furrowed as he examined the handwritten notes.

"Good God," he said, more to himself than to Macie.

"What do you make of it?" she asked.

"I suspect my conclusion is the same as yours," he said, keeping his voice low and measured. "These notations refer to museum pieces he'd acquired."

"He feared they were forgeries."

"Where did you find this?"

She let out a slow breath, as if she could calm her accelerated pulse. "My grandfather had hidden them in his study."

"The letter he refers to might be authentic. Of course, I would require a more detailed examination before making the determination." He looked over each document again, then handed them back to her. "This page from your grandfather's journal lays out his suspicions."

"I should take these to the police." Macie stared down at the intricate pattern in the lace tablecloth, focusing her thoughts. "I had not wanted to tarnish my grandfather's repute as a scholar, but it seems I have no choice."

"Miss Mason, I see his concerns. But no compelling evidence."

Tension coursed through her body. "There *is* evidence."

"What have you found?"

"There is proof."

"You're quite certain?"

"At least, I think it is evidence. I don't know entirely what to make of it." She tucked the documents inside her bag. "I shall notify the authorities in the morning."

"Before you do, I should take a look at what you've uncovered. There may be no need to involve the police."

Macie's stomach tightened. Professor Aylesworth would know far better than she how to interpret the letter Nell had discovered. With any luck, she could avoid sullying her grandfather's legacy.

"I do hope you're right."

"Where is it?" He met her gaze. "Where is this proof?"

"Locked safely away in Bennington Manor. I didn't dare bring it tonight." She reached for her cup, taking a sip of tea to soothe her raw voice "Perhaps you might meet me there in the morning?"

As he shook his head, she read the concern in his eyes. "Miss Mason, this matter cannot wait."

Oh, dear. "You think there may be a connection with Professor Smythson's death?"

"There may be a common thread. If there is, you may be in danger." He held her gaze. "Once I've examined the document you've discovered, we can determine if it is, indeed, proof. At that point, we will involve the authorities." He reached out. With a gentle touch, he brushed an errant tendril of hair behind her ear. "I need you to take me to it."

SITTING ALONE AT a table by the fireplace at the Rogue's Lair, Finn downed an ale as he waited for Logan to join him. His cousin was behind closed doors in his office, attending to some business or other regarding the tavern accounts. *Better him than me.* Logan had far more of a head for business than he did. Not to mention the fact that at that moment, he couldn't even pretend to care about profits and losses and blasted expenses.

Staring down at his drink, he drummed his fingers against the tabletop, as if that might occupy his nervous energy and his thoughts. Despite his best efforts, an image of Macie flashed through his thoughts. Her emerald eyes flashed, seeming to tease him with a promise he knew was most likely lost to him forever.

A foul epithet bellowed by a towering bloke in a dandy's clothes tore him from his thoughts. The sot hurled darts at a bullseye he had no hope of hitting, becoming louder with each errant throw. More belligerent. Until finally, the man gave up and wound his way to the bar. The Lair's newest employee, a good-natured barmaid Finn knew only as Carrie, attempted to serve the sot, only to become the target of his angry outburst.

Damn and blast. Finn had had enough. It was bad enough listening to the drunk when he was merely being obnoxious. But now, he was threatening an employee. A lass, no less.

Finn marched up to the sot. "Ye've said quite enough. Ye're not to speak to a lady in such a manner in this pub." *Or any place, for that matter.*

The man met his gaze. "And who says?"

"Ye just heard me say it, mate. It's not a valid question now, is it?"

"Bugger off." The sot turned back to Carrie. "Now, are you going to do what I told you, you little witch?"

"It's always the big ones, isn't it?" Finn muttered under his breath, though loud enough for the man to hear—a final warning of sorts.

"I need another drink, you little shrew."

"Ah, that's it," Finn said, more to himself than to the sot. He clamped his hands down hard on the man's forearm. And twisted. Hard. "Now I have yer attention—apologize to the lady."

"Bugger—" the big man ground out, even as he grimaced in pain.

"Wrong answer." Finn drove his fist into the sot's solar plexus.

Ooof. The big man doubled over in pain just as Logan came out of his office and descended the stairs to the bar.

"He gave ye some trouble, did he?" Logan motioned between Carrie and the drunk.

"Mr. Caldwell showed him what's what," Carrie said with a faint smile.

"He should think twice next time," Finn said. "If I see the angry bloke again, I will not be so patient."

Logan called upon his barkeepers to show the sot to the door. He then grabbed a drink for himself and joined Finn at the table.

"It's good to see ye looking fit again, my friend," Logan said, surveying Finn's appearance over his stein.

"'Tis amazing the difference a razor and a bar of soap can

make, eh?" Finn smiled despite the gnawing feeling Logan had not invited him here merely to sample his latest brew.

"Ye'll get no argument from me."

"Logan, cut to the chase. Why did ye ask me to meet ye here?"

"Cut to the chase, eh? Ye sure ye're ready for that?" Logan studied him for a long moment. "Finn, have ye spoken to Macie?"

"Not since she asked me to leave."

"Fair enough," Logan said. "The lass was angry. Can ye blame her?"

Finn shrugged. "She should've trusted me."

"We both know how Jon speaks of her, as though she is a problem to be solved. You saw her expression when Macie overheard what he was saying, but ye said little to counter his view."

Finn rubbed his neck, fighting a sudden tension. "She knows I do not share his opinion."

"Worse yet was his blasted talk of some bloody rogues' code. Amelia is not one to use profanity, but later, when we were alone, she expressed her opinion of this so-called code in terms that surprised even me."

"I was a dolt to play along," Finn admitted. "But Macie should've known how I feel about her."

Logan cocked a brow. "She should've, eh?"

It isn't as if you've said you love me. Macie's words taunted him. God above, he'd been a blasted fool.

"It's too bloody late now. She has her mind set on traveling to Greece." Finn kneaded the tense muscles in his neck. "It's what's best for her."

"Best for her?" Logan challenged him. "That fop of a professor might well have an ulterior motive. Ye know that as well as I do. Yet ye're returning to Scotland while she embarks on a journey with that bag of wind?"

Finn stared down at his empty glass. "It's what she wants."

"Ye're quite sure of that, are ye?" Logan prodded. "I recall a man—matter of fact, I'm looking at him—who called me a dunderheaded mule when I nearly let Amelia leave me behind."

Finn resisted the urge to chuckle. "I had a flair for language in those days."

"Ye still do. And ye're still full of hot air."

"Bloody hell, Logan, this is hard enough." He shoved his fingers through his hair. "I won't stand in her blasted way."

"When Amelia was planning to leave for America, ye didn't think I was being noble. Ye thought I was a fool. I might say the same of ye."

"I have to face facts." Finn drummed his fingers in an even rhythm. "This is what she wants."

"Tell me this, and then I'll leave ye be," Logan said. "Do ye love her, Finn?"

Love.

The word seemed so simple. One blasted syllable. Yet it was the most complex, complicated, difficult word in the world to utter.

"Yes," he said, facing the truth. "Yes, I do."

"Then ye know what the answer is, my friend," Logan said. "Ye bloody well know what to do."

Suddenly, a familiar female voice drifted over the casual sounds of the pub. Finn turned to the sound. Mrs. Johnstone strode toward them with Nell at her side. Why in blazes were they here?

"Amelia thought ye might be here," Mrs. Johnstone said. "Have you seen Macie this afternoon?"

"Here?" Finn didn't try to hide his confusion. "Ye know the lass would rather spend a night in the Tower."

"Oh, dear," Nell said. "She had planned to meet Professor Aylesworth for tea, but when Mrs. Johnstone and I went to the café, she had already left."

Logan nodded his understanding. "With Aylesworth?"

"That would appear to be the case," Mrs. Johnstone said.

Tension gripped Finn's chest, but he affected a cool demeanor. "Macie is an independent woman. She comes and goes as she pleases."

"It is not her independence that concerns me." Mrs. Johnstone shook her head. "It would appear Professor Aylesworth is not the man she thinks he is."

Finn read the concern on her features. "What are ye saying?"

"I've been making inquiries about the man," she explained. "I presume you are aware he served as Macie's grandfather's research assistant for some time."

"It's no secret," Finn replied. "Macie first met the man when she was a young lass."

"This is where it gets interesting. And rather troubling," Mrs. Johnstone said. "Aylesworth has ties to both of the men Macie encountered."

"Both of the men who died," Nell added grimly.

"Some years ago, Aylesworth studied under Professor Smythson," Mrs. Johnstone went on.

"And Neville?" Logan asked.

"Hiram Neville was kin to Aylesworth—his uncle, to be precise." Mrs. Johnstone appeared to choose her words carefully. "Yesterday, I was taking tea with friends who are devotees of a ripping good mystery, when one brought up the unfortunate experience at the theater. Between bites of watercress sandwich and sips of tea, Lady Vivian casually revealed her husband and Neville had belonged to the same club. Evidently, Neville had not been himself in recent weeks. He'd begun to imbibe quite heavily, and one night, the man revealed an ugly secret. He was deeply concerned for someone he did not name—someone who had been like a son to him. Mr. Neville feared the man had committed a crime and was growing desperate to avoid imprisonment. Or worse."

Finn saw the concern on her face she could not hide. *Bloody hell.* "He was referring to Aylesworth."

"At this point, we cannot be certain. I did not make the connection until I learned the family ties between the two men."

Mrs. Johnstone's tone was taut with tension. "But if I'm right, if Neville was distraught over his nephew's desperate path, he might have been killed to silence him. And Macie—"

"Good God." Finn's blood ran cold. "I've got to find her."

Chapter Thirty-Two

"MY GRANDFATHER MUST have been devastated to think he'd been deceived by a counterfeiter. The very thought of it . . . of how he must have felt . . . it's heartbreaking."

A sudden sadness washed over Macie as she watched Professor Aylesworth at her grandfather's mahogany desk, silently studying the century-old letter Nell had discovered. Grandpapa had been so meticulous in his research. So scrupulous in his dealings. How could he have been deceived?

With any luck, Aylesworth would be able to correctly interpret her grandfather's cryptic notes. Her grandfather had regarded him as a calm, cool-headed researcher. Ever analytical, the man possessed a keen-eyed ability to detect the tiny flaws which distinguished a true relic from a clever fraud.

As the pendulum on the clock ticked off each passing moment, nervous tension crept through her body. Her fingers tightened around the handle of her parasol to keep them from trembling.

Holding it up to the light, the professor closely examined the aged sheet of vellum. His brow furrowed, he placed the letter beside the journal pages on the desk and met Macie's gaze.

"I suspect his notes have been misinterpreted," he said. "I see nothing of concern."

"Are you quite sure?" His dismissal of her grandfather's suspicions seemed premature.

Aylesworth offered a solemn nod. "He has rigorously documented his observations, but it appears he was out of his depth."

Macie took the missive in hand. "He believed this letter proved the antiquities in question could not be genuine."

"It would appear he was mistaken," Aylesworth softened his tone. "Your grandfather often called upon me to interpret documents as well as to offer a rational counterpoint to his conclusions."

"But he didn't turn to you. Not this time." Macie let out a low breath. "Why would he have kept this to himself?"

The professor shrugged. "Andrew Bennington was a proud man. If he thought he'd been duped, he may have wanted to keep the matter quiet."

"So, you don't believe his suspicions were justified?"

"At this point, I'd say there's no reason for concern, Miss Mason."

"I do wish I could say I was relieved." She gazed down at her grandfather's notations—notations which corresponded with the document the professor had so summarily dismissed. "But my grandfather was not one to reach any conclusion without clear evidence."

"And you believe this is it?" Aylesworth shrugged. "I have to say, I am not convinced. Not yet. But I'd be willing to give the letter a more thorough examination, if only to set your mind at ease."

"Thank you, but I would not want to impose, much less when you're preparing to embark on your journey."

"It will not pose a problem" he said, removing his spectacles. "Once I'm at my laboratory, I will be able to do what needs to be done."

She shook her head. "For now, I prefer to secure the documents. As I understand it, Professor Hedges is not traveling with your team."

"He is not," Aylesworth replied quickly. "What does Hedges have to do with any of this?"

"My grandfather spoke highly of him, just as he did of you. I may seek a consultation."

"With all due respect to Professor Hedges, he does not possess the necessary expertise. You may trust me to conduct a thorough analysis." He rose to his full height and came around the desk. "I owe it to Andrew."

As he spoke, a muscle ticked in his jaw. Macie met his eyes. She saw it then. Saw it so very clearly.

He was lying.

An alarm screamed deep within her. Why had this man—this man her grandfather had long trusted—lied to her?

She reached for the documents on the desk, but he blocked her. Gesturing to the letter, Professor Aylesworth's mouth set in a grim line.

"Ah, Miss Mason . . . I wish you had not seen this."

She took a step back, then another. "Professor, is something wrong?" Macie already knew the answer, even as she managed to speak the words without trembling.

"Yes, as a matter of fact there is." He plowed one hand through his hair, raking his fingers through the dark strands. "You've created this situation, you know. Just as your grandfather did. I never wanted any of this to happen."

"What . . . are you talking about?" Slowly, she continued edging toward the door.

With swift movements, he closed the distance between them. His broad back blocked the doorway.

"You're as stubborn as that old mule was, aren't you?" he said, nearly under his breath. "I'll tell you when we're done."

"I don't much care for your tone," she said, unwilling to betray the sudden fear coursing through her veins. She tightened her grip on her parasol.

"This is all your fault." His eyes narrowed. "If you'd packed up your camera and come along with me, I would've have had this place reduced to ashes before you returned . . . an accident waiting to happen." He shoved a pile of her grandfather's old books to the floor. "So much old, dry paper. So much fuel for a fire."

"Why are you saying this?" she asked, deciding on the optimal spot on his body to aim her blow.

"You are a beautiful woman." A tone akin to regret filled his voice. "If I'd had my way, you and I might have soon been warming a bed in Italy. But now, you've destroyed everything."

"I don't know what you're saying. You must tell me what this is about." She tried to keep his attention on her words and not on the subtle movements of her hands as she gripped the parasol.

"Miss Mason, you are a poor liar." He raked his fingers through his hair again, as if he were agonizing over his thoughts. "If your grandfather had simply let sleeping dogs lie, none of this would have happened."

"My grandfather trusted you." Macie gulped against a sudden bitterness in her throat.

"Not enough." Aylesworth stared at her, contempt in his eyes. "The old fool came to me with his conclusions, and I dismissed his suspicions. But like you, he wasn't convinced."

Old fool. The words seemed like a slap to the face. Macie swallowed her anger. She had to know the truth. "What happened then?"

"By the time I went after the evidence, he'd hidden the documents. No one knew where his blasted safe was concealed in this monstrosity of a house."

"What did you do to my grandfather?"

He slowly shook his head. "Not a blasted thing. My efforts to convince him to entrust the documents to me did not work. Before I could convince him to cooperate, his heart gave out."

Macie let out a breath she'd been holding. At least her grandfather had not suffered at this cad's hands.

"So, you are not a cold-hearted murderer."

"Blasted shame I cannot confirm your theory." A slight smirk played on his mouth. "If only your grandfather had not shared his suspicions with Professor Smythson."

The room seemed to tilt beneath Macie's feet. "You . . . you killed him."

"He left me no choice."

"But why?"

"The day before your grandfather died, he went to Smythson with a document that confirmed the antiquities were not authentic. Trusting fool that he was, Smythson sought my expertise on the matter. After the professor gave me the letter, I destroyed it. For months, I thought my problem had been solved with the strike of a match. But when Smythson got word that a major piece sold to a collector was believed to be a fraud, he remembered what your grandfather had told him. There were more letters, he told me. More evidence. And he intended to find them." Aylesworth gave his head a dramatically rueful shake. "A bit of poison in his tea did the job. If I'd had more experience, I would have better estimated the proper dose."

"Dear God." Macie gripped the parasol tightly. "Why are telling me this?"

"I intend to offer you a choice, Miss Mason. Together, we will take this pile of rubbish your grandfather so carefully assembled, place it in the fireplace, and watch it burn down to the last ash. And then, you will take me to his safe and prove nothing else remains. Then, and only then, will you walk out of this house."

She struggled against the fear surging through her. "I don't believe you."

His eyes gleamed with venom. "I won't even try to stop you from leaving this room. Unless you're afraid of what will happen when you reach the stairs. A nasty tumble in all those bulky skirts . . . I doubt your dainty neck would withstand the fall." His mouth curved into a serpentine smile. "Shall I prove it to you?"

She dragged in a calming breath. "You don't have all the documents." Macie forced herself to meet his contemptuous gaze. "There is another safe. I will take you to it." Her voice trembled, but she kept her voice strong.

"You wouldn't be lying to me, would you now?" He cocked

his head, studying her. "We both know what happens when people betray me, don't we?"

Macie gripped the handle of her parasol. A strike in the face might disable him. But she couldn't chance it. Not yet.

"My uncle knew," he went on. "The surly old bastard figured it out. He knew what I'd done. And what I was going to do to you. He thought he could persuade you to sell your grandfather's papers, as if that would solve this problem. Fool that he was." His hands went to his throat, nervously toying with his necktie. "I let him meddle in my affairs. Until he went to warn you."

A fresh wave of horror washed over her. "At the theater?"

Vile amusement played on his mouth. "I'll never forget the look on his face when it dawned on him . . . when he realized I'd poisoned him. He didn't know I'd followed him to the theater. By then, he'd begun to feel the effects. He actually dared to strike me." Aylesworth swept a lock of hair off his temple, revealing the cut the old man had inflicted. "I could have throttled him with his own cane, but it was more satisfying to simply watch the life ebb from his body."

My God, such an evil man.

Macie's pulse thundered in her ears. If she cried out, no one would hear her scream.

There was no one to help her. No more time. She had to get away.

She had to save herself.

Her mind raced. If she struck him with the parasol, he would see the blow coming. Standing so close, she could not muster much force. He could easily block the strike.

And then, she would have no chance to escape.

If she had to use the umbrella as a weapon, the element of surprise would work in her favor. She had to put distance between them. That was her only chance.

"You knew my grandfather, better than most. Surely you, of all people, understand he would not have relied on a single vault to secure such crucial documents."

He regarded her for a long moment. "Where is it?"

"It's hidden behind a bookshelf."

"Take me to it."

She nodded her agreement as she turned toward her grandfather's desk. "It's here," she said. "Behind the barrister bookcase."

Aylesworth followed her as she crossed the room. Standing before the shelves, she turned to him and affected a look of helplessness. "I cannot move this on my own. I do not possess the strength."

He put his hands on a shelf and pushed on the heavy shelves. "If you are lying to me—"

Now.

Macie lifted her parasol, holding it rather much like she'd held her brother's cricket bat when they were children. Mustering as much force as she could, she whipped around.

Crack.

The umbrella connected with the side of his head. Hard. Bellowing in pain, he spun on his heel.

Again. Macie swung the parasol, aiming directly for his face. Its weighted ribs smashed into the bridge of his nose. He cried out.

Run. Still clutching the parasol, Macie darted from the room.

Spewing epithets, he chased her. Closing the distance between them. On her heels.

His hands clamped over her shoulders. She whirled around, freeing herself. With all her might, she plowed the umbrella into his midsection.

"You little shrew," he murmured, still fighting to control her.

One hand pinned her upper arm. His free hand wrenched the parasol from her grip.

He dragged her to his body, holding her to his chest. "How very foolish."

"Go to Hades."

Instep. Mrs. Johnstone's firm voice echoed in her thoughts. Macie slammed her heel upon his foot. He grunted in pain. *Ribs.*

She drove a sharp elbow into his side. Murmuring foul words in a voice raw with misery.

Bolting down the corridor as if a phantom were on her heels, she ran into a chamber. Before she could secure the door, he blocked it with his arm. Crashing into the heavy panel, he forced his way into the room.

Blood streamed from his nose. Rage flared in his eyes as he ripped his tie from his throat.

"You made me do this," he said, each quietly spoken word raw with malice. "It didn't have to end this way."

She took a step away from him. And then another and another. Until there was nowhere else to go. Backed against the far wall, she searched for a means to escape. She had only one weapon left. God help her.

She fished the embellished handkerchief from her skirt pocket. Towering over her, he smiled as he curled each end of the tie around his hands.

"They'll find you at the bottom of the stairs," he said with an eerie calm. "A broken neck suffered during a tragic fall."

Macie screamed. Pure instinctive fear wrenched the cry from her lungs.

As he smiled in triumph, she seized the moment.

Macie whipped the cloth across his face. The studded fabric cut into his jaw and nose and mouth.

"Bugger it," he muttered as he tried to tear the cloth from her hands.

Macie held tight to the cloth, even as she bolted away.

She careened through the door. And straight into the man she loved.

FINN STARED DOWN at Macie. He'd found her in time. *Thank God.*

The raw fear in her eyes was like a blow to the gut. "Finn," she murmured. "Oh, God, Finn."

He caught her hands in his. "Aylesworth?" She nodded, and he choked out the words that pained him to speak. "Did he hurt ye?"

"No. Not yet," she said.

Aylesworth stalked out of the room. His face bore the bloody marks of Macie's efforts to protect herself. *Brave lass.* By God, he was proud of her.

And filled with rage at the man who'd forced her to fight.

He couldn't let it get to him. He could not let it make him reckless. Or foolish.

"Ah, the touching reunion." Aylesworth brandished a stiletto in his right hand. "Pity it will be short-lived."

"Macie, I want you to leave," Finn said.

"Yes, do run along," Aylesworth said with a smirk. "Wherever you go, I'll be there soon enough . . . after I settle things with your *bodyguard.*"

"Go, Macie." Finn uttered the words as a command. "Now."

Reluctantly, she went to the stairs. He saw her begin to descend the steps.

Aylesworth lunged. Finn jumped back, avoiding the blade. Another strike of the knife came, and then another. Finn dodged each thrust. The rage in Aylesworth's eyes betrayed the truth. The man was frantic. Desperate. More careless with each wild attempt at drawing first blood.

Through it all, Finn worked out his strategy. Calculated where he'd land his blows.

Aylesworth lashed out. Finn edged to the side, not quite far enough. The tip of the blade sliced into his arm. The pain scarcely registered in his preoccupied brain, but he heard Macie cry out. The terrified sound tore at his heart. She should not have to see such sights.

He would end this. And quickly.

"I was going to break yer nose again. For old time's sake," Finn taunted. "Looks like the lady already took care of that."

"Bugger off."

"She gave ye a beating, didn't she?" Finn jeered.

"I *will* gut you." Aylesworth ground out the words between his teeth.

Finn eyed the man's jerky movements. The angrier Aylesworth was, the more he took the bait. Each thrust of knife was wilder. More imprecise.

"You're a dead man."

Finn shook his head. "Not bloody likely."

With that, he lunged, quick as a whip. Catching Aylesworth's wrist, he gave a hard twist. Then another. Aylesworth groaned.

Finn wrenched the man's arm. Aylesworth groaned, but kept his fingers stubbornly clenched around the knife.

"Drop it." Finn added more force to his hold. "Or I'll snap yer bloody arm."

"Go to hell."

"Not tonight, ye rotter."

Finn gave the bastard's captive limb another vicious twist. Aylesworth's raw cry filled the room.

The blade clattered to the floor.

Finn pinned him in an agonizing hold. "Ye should not have touched her."

"Bugger off."

A sudden, piercing pain radiated from Finn's thigh. Gritting his teeth, he stared down at the ivory handle protruding from his leg.

A switchblade.

Bollocks.

He should've known the bastard would have a hidden knife. The cur had always fought dirty.

Shock filled Aylesworth's eyes. Finn cocked a brow. Had the rotter truly believed a bit of pain would get the better of him?

He tightened his grip, blocking the man's attempt to take hold of the pocket-sized knife he'd thrust into Finn.

"Ye're mad if ye think I'm letting ye go after her."

Aylesworth glared at him, defiant despite Finn's unwavering hold. "Crude brawler . . . nothing more." Blood dripped down the bastard's face as his mouth twisted into something resembling a grotesque grin. "Finish this, Caldwell."

"Ye think I should kill ye, eh?" Finn gulped a breath, tamping down his anger and his pain. "The thought is bloody tempting."

Fear glazed Aylesworth's eyes. "I will not endure prison."

"Don't worry, mate. Yer stay there won't be long. The hangman will not be cheated out of his due."

Aylesworth struggled against his hold. "Go to hell."

"Ye'll get there first."

Suddenly, Aylesworth's leg kicked out, catching Finn below the knee. Another kick landed within a hand's breadth of the knife.

Bloody hell.

Finn ground his teeth and held the dirty cur in an iron-clad grip. He eyed the bastard, seeing the bloodlust in Aylesworth's gaze. If he gave in to the throbbing pain, the bastard would win. He'd go after Macie.

By hellfire, this was one fight he couldn't lose.

Aylesworth was right. It was high time he ended it.

Finn jerked the cur up by the collar and slammed a fist into his jaw. The *crack* of bone against bone sounded in his senses.

Aylesworth's groaned. But still, he stood.

Finn aimed his next blow directly to the chin. His knuckles connected with such force he heard the bastard's teeth rattle.

Aylesworth's head slumped forward.

He collapsed.

Finn shook out his hand, easing the stinging throb in his split knuckles. He glanced down at the rug, confirming to himself the bastard was out cold. Aylesworth would never hurt Macie. Not as long as Finn had breath in his body.

He heard her cry as she ran from the spot where she'd waited on the stairs. "Finn!" she called. "Dear God, Finn!"

She stood before him, her eyes wide with shock as her attention fell to the knife still lodged in his leg.

"Good God," she murmured.

"I've had worse."

She looked like she gulped. "You have?"

"Ah, ye always can spot a lie, can't ye, lass?" He pulled in a breath. Was the room beginning a slow spin? "Macie, I need ye to get something . . . anything . . . we can use to restrain this bastard." He had to work harder for each word.

She rushed to the window and untied the braided cord holding back the drapes. "Will this do?"

"Aye."

She gathered several of the ties and rushed to Aylesworth to secure his wrists. Finn stopped her.

"Give them to me. I won't have ye within the bastard's reach."

Fighting the dizziness in his head, he crouched at the bastard's side and bound him hand and foot. Blast it to Hades, his leg throbbed like a thousand banshees prodded him. But he knew better than to remove the blade. It was all that stood between him and a dangerous loss of blood.

Finn heard Logan's voice before he saw him. "Finn, what the hell happened?" he called as he mounted the stairs.

"Go, Macie. Tell Logan we're in here." His voice was getting weak. Too weak to bellow a reply.

As she nodded her response, her mouth pulled tight with concern. "Finn, we've got to summon a physician."

"In due time. Get Logan."

She hurried away. Moments later, the pounding of Logan's boots and a woman's shoes on the wooden floor drifted to Finn's ears.

Logan rushed in with Mrs. Johnstone close behind. Their gazes landed first on the unconscious man on the floor before pivoting to Finn's upper leg.

Logan's brow furrowed. "Well, ye don't see that every day, do ye?"

Finn threw him a scowl. "Watch over Macie, will ye?"

"I don't believe that will be necessary." Mrs. Johnstone crouched to examine the wound. "This doesn't look like anything that's going to be the end of ye."

"Blasted reassurance, if ever I heard it." Finn forced out the words. There seemed to be two of her, each watching him with a clear look of concern. *Bloody peculiar.*

Finn felt the room sinking beneath him.

Bollocks. It wasn't the room.

The strength ebbed from his legs. Suddenly, the walls tilted around him, and he could no longer keep his balance.

Suddenly, he felt Macie's arms around him. Holding him to her body, she eased his descent. As he slid slowly to the floor, she stayed with him, her skirts flaring out around her as she knelt on the rug beneath them. Pillowing his head on her lap, she gazed down at him. Her emerald eyes brimmed with concern as she murmured his name.

By God, he hoped Mrs. Johnstone was right. He wanted more time. More time with Macie.

Finn drank in her features. He wanted to memorize the sweet tilt of her lips. The soft curve of her face. The caring in her green eyes.

Until the room faded to black.

Chapter Thirty-Three

"ARE YOU GOING to tell me what in blazes happened?"

Her brother's heated tone chafed Macie's already ragged nerves. For what had seemed like ages, she'd paced outside the bedchamber where the physician was examining Finn's injury. Much more of this, and she might actually wear a path in the rug.

She stopped her pacing and shot him a glare. "It's quite a long story, Jon. As I cannot bear to bring on a megrim at this moment, it shall have to wait until morning."

"I do understand you've suffered an unpleasant experience." Jon rubbed the back of his neck as if it ached.

"Unpleasant?" She met his words with a wide-eyed glare. "Quite the understatement."

"Point taken," Jon said. "But a man was rendered unconscious in this house . . . by the man who was supposed to be protecting you, no less. And now I am hearing the blighter Finn knocked out was a murderer. An explanation is in order."

She flashed a scowl. "The man who was supposed to be protecting me, as you put it, saved my life."

Jon met her gaze. "If you were in grave danger, Finn should have thought to get you out of London. Staying in the city was a significant error in judgment."

"Really, Jon? He fought to protect me. He might have died." She pulled in a breath and released it slowly to calm herself. "And might I say, he was magnificent."

Turning away, Macie went to the stained glass window at the end of the corridor and gazed down at the comings and goings beyond the mansion. The sun was low in the sky. *Thank God.* Soon, this horrid day would be over.

And then, another chapter would begin. But would the story play out as she hoped?

Jon followed her. "Magnificent, eh?" He drummed his fingers against the windowsill. "It seems you've had quite a change of heart where Finn is concerned."

"He saved my life." She gazed down at the street below. "I'd say his doing so was rather impressive, wouldn't you?"

"I've heard rumblings, Macie. At first, I attributed them to your romantic charade." He cleared his throat. "The two of you set more than a few tongues to wagging."

"Am I truly supposed to give a fig about gossip?"

"Give a fig? Really, Macie. All the money spent on fine tutors might've been better spent at Epsom Downs."

"Oh, don't be insufferable." Macie refused to look at him. "Trust me when I tell you this is not the time."

Her brother regarded her thoughtfully. "When were you going to tell me there was something between you and Finn?"

"I had not planned to," she said truthfully. "There is nothing between us."

"You expect me to believe that?"

"Jon, I truly do not give a whit about what you believe. Or do not believe."

"Macie, you are my sister. I feel a duty to—"

"Duty?" The word set her teeth on edge. "I am not a child. I would think you would know better by now."

"We shall discuss this later," Jon said, his voice flinty with tension.

She cocked her chin in defiance. "Indeed."

As her brother walked away, Macie relaxed a bit. She didn't want to argue with Jon, nor offer vague excuses for the hints of scandal he'd evidently heard.

Her thoughts were on Finn. And Finn alone.

He had been so very brave. So very protective. From her position near the top of the stairs, she'd been on tenterhooks as she watched Finn disarm Aylesworth, only to discover the cur carried a well-concealed blade. Even after Aylesworth had plunged the knife into Finn, he'd given no ground. He had fought through the pain, yet he'd restrained himself at the moment when he could have ended the professor's life in a rush of anger. He'd ensured Aylesworth would face justice for his heartless crimes.

Logan had summoned a physician while Mrs. Johnstone remained with Macie and Finn. Now, behind the closed bedchamber door, the physician dealt with a cantankerous patient who wanted the blade out with no fuss. Despite the physician's initial reassurances, Macie knew she could not quiet the worry in her heart until she saw with her own eyes that Finn had suffered no lasting harm.

How she wanted to see him. And then, perhaps—if the moment was right—she would kiss him. She would bare her heart.

She would tell him the truth—she loved him. Quite desperately, in fact. But would he welcome that truth?

Only time would tell.

Gazing from the window to the street below, Macie spotted Logan's single-seat carriage arriving at the house. His assistant, Tim, hopped down from the driver's bench and hurried up the front steps.

Mrs. Johnstone had anticipated his arrival and had gone down to greet him. After they joined Macie in the corridor, Tim removed his cap, uttered a polite greeting, then knocked on the door to Finn's chamber, a small garment bag in hand.

"It's about time." Finn's voice was strong, a bit surly, and the most delightful sound she'd heard in days.

Mrs. Johnstone motioned her to join her on a settee in the hall. The velvet bench sat beneath a portrait of Macie's grandfather and grandmother when they were young and so very much in love.

"Yer grandmother was beautiful," Mrs. Johnstone said. "Ye look very much like her."

"I've always been told I most resemble my mum." She smiled. "I never realized how much she had in common with her mother."

"She's a spirited woman, isn't she?"

Macie considered the question. "Yes, she certainly is." She looked at Mrs. Johnstone. "How did you know?"

"Because her daughter is one of the most spirited women I've had the pleasure to meet."

"Your words mean a great deal to me," Macie said as warmth washed over her.

"I've been wanting to say this for a while now, but I did not wish to meddle. Ye and Finn must make your own choices." A smile played on her mouth. "But I cannot help but feel he's met his match."

The words had scarcely left her lips when the heavy door creaked open and Finn limped into the hallway.

He wore the clothing Tim had brought in the bag, a plain white linen shirt that hung untucked and dark brown trousers. His hair looked like he'd run his fingers through it in lieu of a proper comb, and a cut on his cheek looked as if it had been cleaned and stitched.

Macie heart raced. Good heavens, the image of him—on his feet, bold and vigorous, a look of true spirit in his eyes—was a sight she'd remember to her last breath.

"Thank ye for yer assistance, Mrs. Johnstone." His voice was surprisingly strong. Finn's gaze fell on Macie. "If I may have a private moment . . . a moment of Macie's time."

"Indeed," Mrs. Johnstone agreed with a smile. "I was just on my way downstairs."

Macie met Finn's eyes. "Tell me this, lass . . . tell me the cur did not hurt ye."

"I am well." She reached up to touch his cheek. "And you?"

"I'll live. Ye can count on that." A hint of a smile curved his mouth. "Macie, there's something—"

Heavy footsteps on the stairs cut into his words. Jon marched toward them, even as Mrs. Johnstone called after him to allow Macie and Finn this moment of peace.

Her brother eyed Finn with blend of anger and confusion. "Macie claimed a megrim would get the better of her if she told me the truth. But now we know you won't be heading to meet your maker anytime soon, so I'll ask you the same question. What in blazes happened here?"

Finn cocked his head. "I'm sensing ye have a bone to pick with me."

"As a matter of fact, I do." Jon pinned Finn with a glare. "I trusted you to watch over my sister."

"Aye, I did." Finn's tone was measured.

"For that, you have my gratitude," Jon said. "But she should not have been gallivanting around London with dead men in her path and scandal brewing. You were supposed be protecting her."

"Scandal brewing, eh, my friend?" Finn's eyes narrowed. "It's not the *dead men* that worry you, is it, Jon?"

"You should have sent her home, to the country." Jon seemed to evade his question. "She would've been safer there."

"I wished to stay in London," Macie spoke up. "If I'd expressed any desire to leave, Finn would have seen me safely home."

Jon's mouth pulled tight as he considered her words. "It was blasted poor judgement."

"Macie is not a child," Finn's tone was hard as flint. "Ye've no right to treat her as one."

Jon gave his head a rueful shake. "You had your own reasons to keep her here in London. Didn't you, Finn?"

Finn regarded him coolly. "As a matter of fact, I did."

"Your job was to protect Macie from her own schemes." Jon rubbed the back of his neck, seeming to knead out a sudden tension. "I should not have trusted you to watch over her."

"I've no intention of playing by yer blasted rules." A muscle in Finn's jaw tensed. "Macie is a woman . . . a beautiful woman who deserves a man who would move heaven and earth to have her." He slanted her a glance that sent a little thrill coursing through her body.

Macie curled her fingers over her brother's forearm, hoping to calm the storm in his expression. "Jon, there is no need for you to be upset."

"You think not?" Jon slowly shook his head. "There is a sense of honor among men, Macie. Even among rogues. An unspoken code."

"How very preposterous," she scoffed, stepping back to glare at him.

He frowned. "Are you truly set on turning my hair gray?"

"Your hair is none of my concern, dear brother. And frankly, whatever happened between Finn and me is none of *your* concern. I am *not* a problem you need to solve. I am not a crisis you need to manage." Macie gulped against the sudden burning emotion in her throat. "And above all, I am not a possession to be bartered to the dullard with the most impressive title."

"Surely you understand I'm looking out for you." Jon's expression softened. "For your future."

She pinned her brother with a cool stare. "I'll ask you to leave. I've heard all I wish to hear."

"I will. Soon enough." Jon rubbed his neck again. "But first, a matter of consequence remains to be discussed. If talk of your relationship, for lack of a better word, with Finn reaches Father, I can guarantee he will see little reason to do business with the Caldwell distillery."

"The blasted contracts, eh?" Finn was calm, but anger flickered in his eyes.

"If you think the deal is set in stone, you're wrong. Those contracts can be terminated."

Finn's expression revealed little of his thoughts. "So, that's the way it's to be, eh?"

"But cancelling the contracts will create a storm of its own," Jon said, ever pragmatic. "People will ask questions."

Macie held back the first ugly words that came to mind. She pinned him with a cold gaze. "And Father wouldn't want that now, would he?"

"There is no way to predict the full repercussions," Jon said, his tone infuriatingly even. "Therefore, I am suggesting a solution."

"What in hellfire are ye talking about?" Finn demanded.

"It's not complicated." Jon drummed his fingers against the console table, his rhythm infuriatingly precise. "You'd intended to return to Scotland within the week. Stick to your plan. Go home to the Highlands." Jon slanted Macie a glance. "And stay away from my sister."

"How dare you interfere in my life!" Macie shot him a scowl. "I am so utterly disappointed in you."

"I am looking at this realistically, Macie. A little discretion about whatever went on between the two of you will blunt the impact of any random tales that make their way back to Father." He turned to Finn. "If you follow what I've suggested, I will do everything in my power to preserve the deal. Do we have an understanding?"

Finn scrubbed a hand over his jaw. He met Jon's hardened expression, and then, his gaze drifted to Macie. A sly half-smile played on his mouth as his attention lingered on her face. When his focus shot back to Jon, he stood taller, even as he winced while putting more weight on his injured leg.

He calmly met Jon's question with one of his own. "Have ye gone daft, mate?"

Macie pulled in a breath. She certainly had not expected such a response.

"What in blazes are you talking about?" Jon snapped back.

With a shrug of his shoulders, Finn met Jon's scowl. "I'll ask ye again, Jon. Have ye gone daft? Only a man who is as addled as they come would think I'd put a blasted contract ahead of Macie."

"You do realize what you're saying?" Jon sounded incredulous. "You'd be a fool to put this deal at risk."

"I can't say as I give a damn." He pinned her brother with a look of steel. "Understand this, Jon—I will *not* stay away from yer sister. Not unless the request comes from her mouth. And hers alone."

Jon studied him for a long moment. "You would walk away from a deal that will enrich your family's business for years?"

"It that's what it takes." Finn spoke each word as if it were a vow. "I'll walk away from London. I'll walk away from every last shilling in these blasted contracts. But I will *not* walk away from her. Now, do *we* have an understanding?"

Macie's pulse sped. The determination in Finn's eyes melted away every doubt she'd ever had.

For his part, her brother regarded him as if he'd gone quite mad. "And if I won't stand for it?"

Finn's eyes narrowed, his expression that of a man only a fool would dare to cross. "As I see it, you do not have a say in this matter. This is between Macie and me."

Jon's face betrayed his shock. "Think of what you're saying, Finn."

Finn's gaze softened as he turned to her. "When I return to Scotland, I intend to have the woman I love by my side. I *will* make her my bride." He reached for her hand. "If ye will have me, Macie."

Oh, dear. A rush of pure joy left her a bit dizzy.

"Do you mean it, Finn?" She drew her fingers over the stubble-roughened curve of his face. "Please, tell me this isn't a dream."

His mouth curved in a deliciously tempting half-smile, and he gave his head a little shake. "Macie, my darling, if this were a dream, there'd be a bloke on a violin and a few romantic verses penned by some poet who fancies himself the next Byron."

"Quite so," she said, a little smile tugging at her lips. "And my blasted brother would not be standing there, scowling at me."

"Ah, lass, this is all very real." Pulling her close, Finn framed her face between his hands and looked into her eyes. "And this is the truth . . . the truth I've carried in my heart." He brushed his lips tenderly over hers. "I love ye, Mary Catherine Mason. If ye'll have me, if ye'll speak vows of love and commitment with me, if ye'll marry me, I will kiss ye every night until I take my last breath."

Macie's heartbeat raced. How she'd longed for this moment. Longed to hear those precious words. She met his eager gaze.

"I do love you, Finn. So much, my heart is near to bursting from the joy of it. But there is one thing . . . one condition we must settle before I say 'yes.'"

A muscle ticked in his jaw. Oh, he was nervous. *How delightful.*

"What is it, Macie? I'll do whatever it takes to give ye whatever yer heart desires."

For a very long moment, she simply drank in the love and affection and heat in his eyes. And then, she smiled. "You said you will kiss me every night, did you not?"

"Aye, I did, love."

"That won't be quite enough. Not at all."

His sly smile told her he'd read the truth in her eyes. "Is that so?"

Her heart swelled with pure love for this man she so adored. "I shall expect you to kiss me every night. And every morning."

"Consider it done, lass." His cheeky grin warmed her all over. "And as frequently as possible at all hours in between."

"I do like those terms," she said, raising up on her toes to kiss him again.

The sound of her brother's purposeful cough pulled her from the moment. Finn gave a slight nod as she eased from his embrace.

Macie regarded her brother with a slight frown. "I'd nearly forgotten you were there."

"I gathered as much." Jon raked a hand through his hair. "Tell me this, Finn. Is there any chance you're a long-lost duke?"

He shook his head. "Highly doubtful."

"An errant earl?" Jon went on. "Or perhaps, a long-missing marquess?"

Finn's eyes narrowed as he studied her brother. "Not a chance."

Macie eyed her brother with a touch of annoyance. "What in heaven is this all about?"

He regarded them with an impassive expression. "By thunder, if this isn't the last bloody discussion I'd ever expected to have with you, Finn. But truth be told, I do believe I will enjoy informing father of this new development. One final question," Jon said, a broad grin marking his features. "Will you be inviting this daft dolt to the wedding?"

Macie rushed to her brother and threw her arms around him. "Oh, Jon, I wouldn't have it any other way."

Jon's eyes lit with affection. "You deserve this, Macie. You deserve this happiness. Now, don't spend this time with me. I'd wager your husband-to-be would like to spend these moments with you and not his future brother-in-law."

"Jon, ye know I love her." Finn's expression warmed. "More than life itself."

"I see that, now." Jon shook the hand of the old friend who'd soon become family, then headed to the stairs. When he looked over his shoulder, his smile was genuine. "I'll leave the two of you to . . . begin making plans."

Finn caught Macie's hands in his. "My sweet lass." He pulled her to him. "I'll never get enough of yer kiss. Of your beauty." He looked as if he'd gulped against emotion. "Of ye."

"Oh, Finn. I never dreamed of a moment so very sweet as this." Macie threaded her fingers through his silky, wheat-brown hair. "Of all the men in London, it simply had to be you."

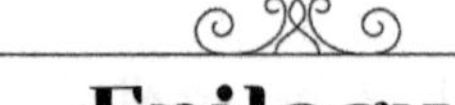

Epilogue

One year later

"IF I HAD not witnessed this transformation with my own eyes, I would not have believed it possible."

Standing by her brother's side in the parlor of Bennington Manor, Macie smiled at Jon's expression of wonder as he watched Finn engaged in a game of peekaboo with his godson. A month shy of his first birthday, Finnegan MacLain giggled boisterously as her husband covered his face again and again. Each time the precious little boy laughed, Finn matched his joy with a broad grin.

"Transformation?" Macie scoffed playfully. "I don't know to what you are referring, dear brother."

"Come now, Macie. Not long ago, if someone had told me Finn Caldwell would be playing with Logan's chubby miniature on a Friday night rather than . . ." Jon broke off his thought as Macie's cat sauntered over and rubbed her fur against his immaculately creased trouser leg.

Lifting a brow, Macie finished his sentence. "The activities of a well-seasoned rogue, perhaps?"

Jon frowned at Cleo as she happily pranced over to her little upholstered bed by the hearth. "In a manner of speaking," he went on. "Then again, I never would've wagered you would be happily wed and settled into what one can only describe as domestic bliss."

She flashed a little smile as his words warmed her heart. "It is rather astonishing, isn't it?"

"Quite so. If I'd known the two of you were meant for each other, I would have concocted some scheme to bring you together years ago." He pointed at the hair on his head. "If I had, I suspect I'd have far less gray to speak of."

"In truth, you should be thanking me. Those strands of silver lend a look of distinction."

"That's one way of putting it." He shrugged. "I suppose a touch of distinction suits me when I'm conducting business."

"Indeed." A grin tugged at her lips. "Especially when you act like your collar is too tight."

Just as Jon shot her a playful scowl, Macie watched as her husband placed a contented babe in Amelia's waiting arms.

Finn strolled toward them. The gaslight cast by the sconces on the wall gleamed like flecks of gold over his wheat-brown hair and emphasized the definition of his carved cheekbones. Suddenly, the warmth from the crackling flames in the fireplace was no match for the inner heat curling in her belly.

Macie's mouth went dry. The very sight of the man she adored with all her heart still held the power to unleash a current of longing through her body, from the tips of her toes to the lips that hungered for his kiss.

Judging from the flickers of heat in her husband's golden-brown eyes, she was not the only one possessed with a sudden hunger. Finn curved a possessive arm around her and brushed a light kiss over her cheek.

As Finn and Jon engaged in conversation, Mrs. Johnstone joined the gathering through the French doors.

"It's good to see ye," she said as they went about the exchange of greetings. "Macie, I want to commend ye on yer newest exhibit. The photographs of Athens are quite striking."

"Thank you. The experience was one of the most rewarding of my life." Macie glanced toward her husband. "With Finn by my side, the journey was all the more exhilarating."

By my side. In his arms. Beneath the sheets of our bed. Deliciously wicked images popped unbidden into her thoughts. *My,* she hoped her cheeks had not flushed.

Mrs. Johnstone strategically cleared her throat. "Shall we make a date to take tea? There is a marvelous new café near the gallery. Ye must tell me all about yer stay in Athens."

"I would enjoy that very much," Macie managed as Finn coiled his arm around her waist, a most definite distraction.

"Finn, I understand ye've completed the plans for renovation of this grand old house," Mrs. Johnstone said. "Where do ye plan to start?"

A sly smile played on his full mouth. "The nursery."

Mrs. Johnstone's and Jon's brows hiked, nearly in unison. "Nursery, is it?" Mrs. Johnstone replied.

"Good God." Jon regarded her with a blend of surprise and happiness. "Are you telling me I'm going to an uncle?"

Macie grinned as Finn proudly answered her brother's question. "In about six months' time."

"Uncle?" Jon tested the word, as if it were somehow foreign. "I do like the sound of it." His brow furrowed. "Have you told Mum and Father?"

"Not yet. Mum and Papa decided to travel by train. They will arrive tomorrow afternoon, and we're expecting Finn's parents the next morning." She hugged her brother and gave him a quick kiss on the cheek. "Please don't tell anyone. We trusted Logan and Amelia with the news, and of course, the two of you. Oh, and I had to tell Mrs. Tuttle. She promised to keep the secret so we might surprise our parents with the news."

"And Nell?" Mrs. Johnstone inquired?

"She's visiting her aunt in Paris until the end of the month. I'm waiting to tell her in person."

"Well, I must say, this is certainly grand news." Mrs. Johnstone enfolded Macie in a hug. "After yer parents arrive, we shall need to have a celebration."

"Indeed," Jon agreed with hearty warmth. "I cannot wait to see the look on Mum's face. She'll be over the moon. Of course, Father will be overjoyed. But I would not wager he'll show it.

Stiff-upper lip, and all that rot."

"Over the moon," Macie repeated. "My, dear brother, you have perfectly described my feelings at this time."

Many hours later, following an evening filled with laughter and warmth and genuine affection, their guests departed for their respective residences.

Finn watched as Mrs. Johnstone's carriage rattled over the cobblestones in the distance. When he turned to Macie, the look of desire in his eyes left no doubt as to his intentions.

"Mrs. Caldwell—bloody hell, I love the sound of that—do ye remember the promise I made to ye?" He pulled her close and gazed down into her eyes. "The night I asked ye to marry me?"

Yearning filled Macie, a delicious longing that went bone deep. "I believe I do, Mr. Caldwell."

"Do ye, now?" Hunger darkened his gaze. "I promised to kiss ye every night, and every morn, until I take my last breath. I aim to keep that promise, sweet Macie." He drew the pad of his thumb over her lips. Teasing and tempting and stirring her desire. "And more."

Her heart beat a brisk tattoo as he held her to his body, the demanding length of him against the softness of her belly making clear his intense need. Oh, how she loved this man.

"I love ye, Mary Catherine Caldwell." His clever fingers released the pins holding her tresses in place, weaving through her curls as they flowed unbound around her shoulders. "I love ye more than the air I breathe. More than life itself."

He kissed her then, the sheer need in his caress leaving her knees weak and wobbly.

"Oh, Finn, I have no words to convey how very much I love you."

His seductive smile kindled the heat in her body to a blaze. "Words are overrated, my love."

With that, he swept her into his arms and carried her to their bedchamber.

"I've been waiting to get ye behind closed doors all night."

Gently, he placed her on the bed, pressing a softer, sweeter kiss to her lips. "Macie, I will adore ye to my last breath. And beyond. To the end of eternity." His words were as desperate against her mouth as his touch was tender. "I will love ye and our babe forever, my darling Macie."

THE END

About the Author

Award-winning author Tara Kingston writes historical romance laced with suspense and intrigue. She lives her own happily-ever-after in a cozy Victorian with her real-life hero and a pair of deceptively innocent-looking cats. When she's not writing, reading, or burning dinner, Tara enjoys movie nights, cycling, hiking, DIY projects, and cheering on her favorite football team.

Visit Tara at her webpage, www.tarakingston.com. If you'd like updates on new releases, historical romance news, excerpts, and more, please sign-up for Tara's newsletter at www.tarakingston.com/newsletter-signup.